PRAISE FOR
THE ROSE OF YORK NOVELS

"A deftly written, reader-engaging, thoroughly entertaining and enthusiastically recommended historical novel that documents its author as a gifted literary talent."　　　　*—Midwest Book Review*

"This admirable historical novel belongs on the shelf of all true Ricardians next to *Daughter of Time*."　　　*—Historical Society Review*

"A perfect ten!"　　　　　　　　　　*—Romance Reviews Today*

"[E]xtraordinary . . . will breathe glorious life into an era of history that's dark [and] tumultuous."　　　　*—Heartstrings Reviews*

"Not to be missed."　　　　　　　　　*—Romantic Times*

THE

King's
Daughter

SANDRA WORTH

BERKLEY BOOKS, NEW YORK

THE BERKLEY PUBLISHING GROUP
Published by the Penguin Group
Penguin Group (USA) Inc.
375 Hudson Street, New York, New York 10014, USA
Penguin Group (Canada), 90 Eglinton Avenue East, Suite 700, Toronto, Ontario M4P 2Y3, Canada
(a division of Pearson Penguin Canada Inc.)
Penguin Books Ltd., 80 Strand, London WC2R 0RL, England
Penguin Group Ireland, 25 St. Stephen's Green, Dublin 2, Ireland (a division of Penguin Books Ltd.)
Penguin Group (Australia), 250 Camberwell Road, Camberwell, Victoria 3124, Australia
(a division of Pearson Australia Group Pty. Ltd.)
Penguin Books India Pvt. Ltd., 11 Community Centre, Panchsheel Park, New Delhi—110 017, India
Penguin Group (NZ), 67 Apollo Drive, Rosedale, North Shore 0632, New Zealand
(a division of Pearson New Zealand Ltd.)
Penguin Books (South Africa) (Pty.) Ltd., 24 Sturdee Avenue, Rosebank, Johannesburg 2196, South Africa

Penguin Books Ltd., Registered Offices: 80 Strand, London WC2R 0RL, England

This is a work of fiction. Names, characters, places, and incidents either are the product of the author's imagination or are used fictitiously, and any resemblance to actual persons, living or dead, business establishments, events, or locales is entirely coincidental. The publisher does not have any control over and does not assume any responsibility for author or third-party websites or their content.

Copyright © 2008 by Sandra Worth
Cover design by Erika Fusari
Cover illustration: *Eleonora da Toledo (1519-74)* (oil on panel) by Agnolo Bronzino (1503-72) © Narodni Galerie, Prague, Czech Republic/Giraudon/The Bridgeman Art Library
Book design by Kristin del Rosario

First edition: December 2008

Library of Congress Cataloging-in-Publication Data

Worth, Sandra.
  The king's daughter / Sandra Worth.—Berkley trade pbk. ed.
    p. cm.—(Rose of York)
  Includes bibliographical references.
  ISBN 978-0-425-22144-0
  1. Elizabeth, Queen, consort of Henry VII, King of England, 1465–1503—Fiction. 2. Queens—Great Britain—Fiction. 3. Great Britain—History—Wars of the Roses, 1455–1485—Fiction. I. Title.
  PS3623.O775K56 2008
  813'.6—dc22   2008033889

PRINTED IN THE UNITED STATES OF AMERICA

10 9 8 7 6 5 4 3 2

This book is dedicated to my daughter Emily

ACKNOWLEDGMENTS

I owe a debt of gratitude to Jean Truax, Ph.D. in medieval history, who assisted me with my research over a period of many months, and who read the final manuscript. Her insightful comments have been incorporated into this book.

"Four things come not back:
The spoken word,
The sped arrow,
The neglected opportunity,
The past."

—OLD SAYING, CIRCA 750 A.D.

YORK AND LANCASTER

EDWARD III

Edward the Black Prince

Lionel D. of Clarence

John of Gaunt D. of Lancaster — m. (1) Blanche of Lancaster — **HENRY IV** — **HENRY V** — **HENRY VI** — Prince Edward d. 1471

John of Gaunt — m. (3) Katherine Swynford
issue born out of wedlock
legitimized 1397
banned from succession
by Henry IV

John Beaufort E. of Somerset — Margaret Beaufort

RICHARD II

Richard, Duke of York

Meredydd Ap Tudor*

Owen Tudor** (2) m. **KATHERINE OF VALOIS** m. (1)

Edmund Tudor E. of Richmond

Jasper Tudor D. of Bedford

Margaret D. of Burgundy m. Charles the Bold

Margaret *Ex. by Henry VIII*

George D. of Clarence m. Isabelle Neville

Edward, E. of Warwick *Ex. by Henry VII*

RICHARD III m. **ANNE NEVILLE**

Prince Edward d. 1484

HENRY VII

EDWARD IV m. **ELIZABETH WOODVILLE GREY**

Mary d. 1482

Cecily
m. (1) Ralph Scrope
m. (2) John Welles
m. (3) Thomas Kyme

EDWARD V 1470–d.?

Margaret d. 1472

Richard D. of York 1473–d.?

Anne m. Thomas Howard

Katherine m. William Courtenay *Ex. by Henry VIII*

Bridget

ELIZABETH OF YORK

Prince Arthur d. 1502 m. Catherine of Aragon

HENRY VIII m. (1) Catherine of Aragon

Margaret m. James IV of Scotland

Mary m. Louis XII, King of France

Broken lines denote missing generations.

*Wanted in England for theft and murder, escaped to his native Wales (see Simons, Eric N.; HENRY VII; Frederick Muller, Great Britain, 1968, p. 1)

**A Groom of the Wardrobe. It is unknown if a marriage took place.

CHAPTER 1

Daughter of the King, 1470

HOODMAN'S BLUFF WAS SO MUCH FUN WITH MY FA-
ther! I hid behind a pillar and peeked out. He was heading toward
me, fumbling like a blind man. "Elizabeth, Elizabeth!" he called.
"Where are you? I can't see you." I laughed. Of course, he couldn't
see me! He was blindfolded with the black silk scarf I had tied
tightly around his eyes. I ran through the chamber, shrieking with
delight as I evaded his outstretched hands.

As he headed in my direction, I abandoned the pillar and fled
around the big table in the center of the room, across to the window seat. I waited there and tried to be silent, but I burst into a
fit of giggling when he bumped into a wall and knocked over a
candelabra. There was no one else I'd rather play with, not even
my sisters Mary and Cecily, who were younger than I, for they
cried too much. But my father was always laughing. He was nearly
as big as the dragon he had told me about in one of his tales, yet
he was beautiful, not scary. He looked nothing like a dragon with
his blond hair tumbling around his blindfold. Though I couldn't
see the twinkling blue light in his eyes behind his scarf, his love

enfolded me as warmly as my favorite blanket as he chased me about the room.

Papa was close now, as if he knew I stood on the window seat. I looked around the room to see where I should go next. *In the corner, behind the coat of armor!* I scrambled down from the window seat and ran there, shrieking. Smiling servants stepped aside to make way for me. The nobles who had been gathering for the past hour gave me smiles, too.

My father turned around as if he could see from the back of his head, and made for my direction again. I squealed with fear and ran toward the silver cabinet against the opposite wall. I crouched beside the chest, not making a sound, not even daring to breathe. The man-at-arms by the door turned to give me an encouraging look.

More nobles entered the hall. This was a bad sign. My father would soon have to stop our game and meet with them around a table behind closed doors. But for now they dropped their gloomy looks to give me kindly smiles as I ran past them into my father's privy chamber. In spite of his blindfold, my father seemed to know exactly where I was, for he moved to follow. He nearly caught me several times as I fled, but I ducked, and he grabbed the arm of a chair instead and bumped the corner of a table. I was glad to be alone with him. Away from his lords, Papa might forget about them and we could play a while longer.

There was nothing in the bedchamber but a four-poster bed, a tall chest, and some large chairs and cushions by the hearth. Papa would never catch me on the bed, for it was huge and I could easily elude him there. I caught at one of the bedposts and hopped up.

"Edward!"

My mother's sharp voice stopped me in my tracks. I ceased my giggling and stood very still on the bed, trying to keep my balance on the soft feather mattress that was covered with a shiny silk bedspread of golden suns and white roses, my father's emblem. I didn't smile anymore, and neither did my father. He took off his blindfold and looked at my mother. She stood in the doorway, her face stern, her gold hair like a halo under her cone-shaped velvet headdress and gauzy veil. But then, unlike my father, my mother seldom smiled. When she entered the chamber, I knew she was angry about something.

"Edward, sometimes I do wonder about you! Playing Hoodman's Bluff with Elizabeth as if you had no care in the world. When your council awaits to discuss urgent matters with you."

"My dear Bess, what cares do I have? What urgent matters await?" Papa laughed. "Is there not peace in my kingdom? Do my nobles not love me, every last one?" He went to my mother and bent down to kiss her cheek, for though she was tall, he was taller than any man I had ever seen.

"Edward, you do try my patience, you know," she sighed.

He knelt at her feet and took her hand as if he were Sir Lancelot before Queen Guinevere. "Dear love, tell me how I can get you to smile?"

Her lips curled up a little. "There is a way, Edward."

"I knew there would be, Bess," he said, rising to his feet. "There always is."

The joy had gone out of him, and he was different. I couldn't tell why, but I knew something was wrong.

"Leave us, Elizabeth," said my mother.

I jumped down from the bed. My mother and father watched me leave the room. I shut the chamber door. The happiness had gone out of me, too.

Outside, the nobles around the table watched me, and they no longer smiled either.

❁

MY FATHER CAME TO ME LATER THAT NIGHT. I WAS in my shift and Nurse was brushing my hair and getting me ready for bed. "Papa!" I cried, running to him in my happiness. He swept me up in his strong arms. I always felt safe there. He gave me a kiss. His breath smelled of wine. Then he looked over at Nurse and threw her a nod of dismissal. She curtsied and shut the door quietly as she left.

"My sweetheart, we had fun today, didn't we?"

I nodded happily. "Wagons and wagons of fun, Papa!" I gave him a tight embrace and kissed him on the cheek.

"Sometimes we amuse ourselves, and sometimes we must tend to weighty matters."

He sat down with me in a chair by my bed. I snuggled in his lap, my arm around his neck. I waited for him to speak again, for he had fallen silent.

"Your mother wished me not to inform you," he said at last. "But I have decided you should know."

"Know what, Papa?"

"I have betrothed you to George Neville, nephew to the Earl of Warwick."

"Warwick the Kingmaker?"

"Warwick," my father corrected. " 'Tis a mistake to call him Kingmaker. I owe my crown to no man."

Papa must have known how bad I felt, for he kissed my brow, and said in a different voice, "George is a nice boy about your age. I feel sure you will like him, and if you don't, you will forgive me, Elizabeth? I had to do it."

"Why, Papa?"

" 'Tis hard to explain, but let me try. The Earl of Warwick has a brother who is a great general. He is loyal to me, though Warwick leads the rebellion against me."

"His brother, the Earl of N-North-amber-land?" I got a bit tongue-tied on the long word, and Papa laughed.

"Northumberland. You are bright for your age, Elizabeth. Your mother said you wouldn't understand, but you do understand, don't you?"

I nodded vigorously. My mother didn't like me because I was a girl, not a boy, and thought me stupid. I wasn't stupid. I just didn't say much because I liked to listen. I reached out and drew my favorite blanket to me from the bed. It was wine and blue velvet, and stroking it between my fingers always helped soothe me.

"Warwick has broken faith with me," my father said and fell silent again.

Because of Mama, I thought. But I didn't say it.

My father spoke. "And his brother, Northumberland, leads my forces. He will have to fight for me against his own kin. I cannot trust him to do that, so I have taken his earldom away from him. In return I have betrothed his son to you, so he can feel he received something precious in return for the loss of his power."

I drew my blanket closer to me as I considered this. I am ashamed to admit I still cuddle my blanket when I sleep, for a maiden of nearly five years should have no need of it. But one thing I surely know. Though I shall give up my blanket one day, I shall have need of my father always. Happiness is being in his presence; happiness is sitting on his knee for a story and balancing on his shoulders as he carries me around the castle halls. Even when I think I'm going to slip off, I'm not frightened, for I know he would not let me fall. How could I ever live without him?

"Will I have to leave you, Papa?" I held my breath as I waited for his answer.

"Not for a long time, my sweet."

The warmth returned to me. "That's good. I don't want to leave you, Papa. I want us to be together forever, and ever."

My father laughed. Then he gazed at me solemnly. "I love you, my beautiful Elizabeth. May God in His mercy grant thee happiness all the years of thy life, my sweet little girl."

It was a blessing, but the way he said it made me feel very sad.

ALL AT ONCE, LIFE CHANGED. MY FATHER LEFT TO fight a battle, and in his absence my mother wept and cried, "Woe, woe!" Grandmother Jacquetta kept telling her, "All will be well, my child. I know it will——" but Mother didn't seem to hear, for she would wail even louder. All around me, panicked servants rushed hither and thither as if the devil were chasing them, and crossed themselves in fear and cried to the Holy Virgin to save them. But no one would tell me what was wrong. "When is my father coming back?" I'd ask them. They'd burst into tears again, cover their faces and run away. These same people had laughed and made merry for my birthday in February, and I didn't understand how everything could be so different now. I felt very lonely and afraid.

One day my mother burst into the chamber where I was taking a music lesson and told me to hurry, we had to flee.

"Where are we going, Mama?" I called out as I ran after her, clutching my lute. But "Hurry, hurry!" was all she would say. We rushed along the castle halls with my half-brothers Tom and Dick Grey leading the way and servants carrying my sisters Mary and Cecily, and fled down the tower stairs, across the windy garth and into the cloisters of Westminster Abbey. A gathering of monks met us and threw open the door of the chapter house and we hurried inside.

"You shall be safe here in sanctuary," they said, "no matter what happens," and lit some tapers, for dusk was falling.

The octagonal room was large, cold, and empty. My mother sank down into the straw on the floor, and sobbed. Grandmother Jacquetta knelt beside her. "Have faith, Bess. Be strong. Remember the babe you carry in your belly. Edward will return. You shall deliver him a son, God willing."

"Mama, I'm hungry," I said.

"O woe, woe!" my mother cried.

"We have nothing to eat, Elizabeth," Grandmother Jacquetta explained. "Maybe, if you're good, the monks will bring us some bread in the morning. Now go to sleep."

I did as she bid and curled up on the straw. I dreamt of my father that night, and for many nights afterwards.

As the weeks passed, my brothers, Tom and Dick Grey, who had always resented me because my father was a king and theirs had been merely a knight, grew meaner in their teasing. They were born of my mother's first marriage to Sir John Grey, killed in battle before Mother married Papa. From their behavior it was hard to guess Tom was nearly a man at thirteen, and Dick only two years younger, for they were more like rowdy boys than well-mannered courtly youths.

"This is all your father's fault!" they cried. "He has lost his throne and run away!"

"He has not, he has not!" I cried back, bursting into tears. But I learned that they were right. The Kingmaker's brother, whose son, George Neville, was my betrothed, had turned against Papa and forced him to flee England. Now Papa was in Burgundy, trying to gather an army so he could fight for his throne.

The days bore down heavily on us. We were always cold and

hungry, and we had few visitors. One who came was a butcher named John Gould. He wore a bloody apron but the meat he brought us of his own charity gladdened my heart and much eased the growl in my belly. In gratitude, I included his name in my daily prayers. Another frequent visitor was Friar Bungey, whom I didn't like as well, for there was something odd about him. My mother and grandmother scarcely felt the same way, though, and they welcomed him heartily, for he brought them news. In a corner of the chamber, they would huddle together, whispering and sharing secrets.

On All Hallows Eve, when my mother was close to giving birth, my brothers invited me to play with them. Then they locked me in the wine cellar. It was dark and damp, and I was frightened alone. I banged on the door and screamed for help as long as I could, but it did no good, and no one came. I finally grew tired and fell asleep on the stone floor among the kegs of wine.

Strange sounds woke me, and I sat up, rubbing my eyes.

It was a chant, and it came from behind the wine casks near the far wall. Torchlight threw shadows all around, but I made out three dark, hooded figures.

Anu, Enlik, Enk . . . Anu, Enlik, Enk—
la Nergal-ya! La zi annga kampa—

I wanted to run away, but I was too afraid to move. Gathering courage, I crept closer and peered around a barrel of wine into the shadows ahead. Though the walkway between the kegs was narrow, I could see straight through to the small torch-lit area between the stone arches and the stairs that led up to the chapter house. A black-draped altar stood against the wall, set with a metal offering bowl and a brazier. A few candles flickered on the floor around the figures, making it hard to see their faces as they moved in the uneven light, but I made out a chalk drawing of a gate on the stone floor at their feet. Four candles burned on the floor, one at each corner of the gate picture.

I stared hard at the three black figures in hooded cloaks. The fat one could be Friar Bungey. The other two had no shape beneath their hooded cloaks, but they looked familiar. They stood against the light, in deepest shadow, their backs to me, their faces hidden.

"In the name of the Covenant sworn between Thee and the Race of Man, I call to thee! Harken and Remember! From the Gates of Hell I call Thee!"

I shivered at the hooded man's harsh voice. He threw a handful of something into the brazier and flames gushed out, then a puff of smoke went up into the air. A moment later the air grew fragrant with incense.

"Nergal, Lord of the Offering of Battle, Ravager of the Enemy's towns, Devourer of the flesh of Man, remember!" He flattened himself on the floor. "For what comes on the wind can only be slain by he who knows the wind; and what comes on the seas can only be slain by he who knows water. Thus it is written in the ancient covenant."

He rose again, took the offering bowl, set it on the floor and removed something from behind the curtained altar. A white rabbit squealed as he held it by the scruff of its neck. The man knelt and raised the knife. The animal cried and struggled for freedom. The blade flashed in the torchlight. He plunged it down hard.

"Nergal, God of Sacrifice, remember!" He lifted the offering bowl high in the air before setting it down again, and poured white flour around the circle twice. He turned back to the altar and raised his arms up over his head. I scooted forward to the cask in front of me and squinted into the shadows, my heart pounding hard, for I knew I wasn't supposed to be here.

"Know that evil spirits are seven, for the seven maskins that tear away the heart of a man and mock his gods."

I shrank back behind the cask and covered my mouth to smother my gasp. The man had donned the hide of a donkey! For a moment I was frightened they'd heard me. He placed the metal pot on the brazier, worked it for a while and took it off. He removed a waxen image from the bowl and held it up. I strained to see what it was through the smoke. *A bear?* He threw it into the pot.

"Boil! Boil! Burn! Burn! I invoke you, Gods of the Night! The Bear is plagued with pain. He cannot stand upright or lie down, neither during the day, nor during the day. His mouth is stuffed with cords! His joy is sorrow, and his merriment is grief!" He took a knotted cord and threw it into the flames. "The word of his doom is spoken. His knot is broken. His work destroyed—"

My teeth began to chatter. *Who was the Bear? Why did they want to break his knot? What did that mean?* I didn't understand any of this, but I knew enough to will myself to be still. For if they discovered me, they might throw me into the boiling pot, too. I crunched myself into a tighter ball and hugged my knees so I could keep myself stiff and motionless.

The three figures were moving in a circle now, chanting. Their heads were bowed, and they seemed to be looking at the picture they had drawn on the floor. Their song gathered speed and they danced faster and faster. They screamed their words:

> *My images have thrown you to the ground of the dead*
> *My images have buried you in a coffin with the dead*
> *My images have given you over to destruction!*

The hoods fell off two cloaked figures. They were women: one, grey-haired; the other, fair. They followed the donkey-man, black cloaks whirling, arms thrashing in a wild frenzy. I was terrified now. I couldn't breathe. These were witches, and everyone knew witches cut people's hearts out and ate them.

"God of the Night, issue a spell to cause consternation to the enemy and infuse his thoughts! A spell to cause ultimate destruction! Spirit of the Graves, remember! His is the dark times!" The donkey-man held a book in one hand and sprinkled water with the other. One of the fearful figures moved out of the shadows. The smoke cleared. Her face was painted white and she was grinning like a madwoman. She kept whirling, kept moving out of the shadows into the circle of light. All at once she stood framed by an arch. The torches flared on her face. I stared. My mouth opened for a scream that reached my throat and trembled there, but no sound came. The witch-woman with the white face—

She was my mother.

❖

NO ONE KNEW WHAT I HAD SEEN, FOR TOM AND DICK had told my mother I was in the privy when she'd asked about me. Soon afterwards, on the second of November, my mother grabbed her pregnant belly, gave a cry of pain, and almost fell down. My grandmother rushed to her side.

"Come, Bess—" my grandmother said. She led my mother behind the white silk curtain that divided the room.

"O woe is me!" my mother sobbed behind the curtain. "Woe, woe! A pallet on the straw instead of my beautiful room at the Tower for the birth of my child—how can this be? How, Mother?"

"Hush, daughter. If Edward wins the battle, you will soon be back at the Tower."

" 'Tis the fault . . . of the . . . Nevilles," my mother panted. "I shan't forget it."

"No, we won't forget."

"If Warwick's brother . . . hadn't gone back . . . to his side, none of this would have happened . . . Edward would still . . . be king."

"I know, daughter. I know."

"A curse on that beast . . . that bear, Warwick . . . *Kingmaker* he calls . . . himself! When I am back in the Tower . . . and queen again, Warwick will . . . wish he were dead!"

"*Sssh!*" said my grandmother. "It will be so. Did not the friar assure us? Now concentrate on giving birth to this child. And make it a son."

"A son!" my mother cried. "O God, give me a son!" Her voice went very loud and was filled with a terrible pleading that frightened me. Then she fell silent, except for her whimpers of pain.

There was a knock at the door of the chapter house. I rushed to open it. An old woman with big yellow teeth curtsied to me. "Marjory Cobb, midwife, m'little lady," she said.

I threw the door wide open. With quick curtsies to me and my sisters, she hurried to my mother and grandmother behind the curtain.

"Me Graces," she said. "I come at Dr. Sergio's call. His horse went lame and had to be reshod. He's a-comin' soon as he can get another, m'ladies."

I heard whispering and knew my grandmother was telling the midwife about my mother. "Good, good," the midwife kept murmuring. After a short silence, broken only by my mother's moans, she said, "All's well enough. Should be soon now."

I sat on the straw in the corner of the room, near the door, hugging my knees and rocking to and fro as my mother wailed behind the curtained partition. Within the hour, there was another knock at the door. I jumped up and sprang the latch. Dr. Sergio rushed in. His cloak was wet, for it was raining outside. He didn't greet me but went directly behind the curtain. The grown-ups murmured together while my mother screamed and sobbed.

"Push!" the midwife called. "Push, now, hard!"

"Hard!" said Dr. Sergio. "One more time!"

My mother screamed again, much louder this time. I hated that she was hurting so badly. My sisters did, too. They hollered and cried, and there was no consoling them, so I gave up and covered my ears, but it didn't help. My sister Cecily pulled my sister Mary's hair, and then screamed for my mother, and tried to run to her behind the curtain, but I stopped her. She struggled in my arms and cried louder. If my grandmother hadn't forbidden me to leave the chapter house, I would have fled to the cloisters to be with my brothers, Tom and Dick. Their joyful shouts as they played ball came to me through the window that was cranked open for air. I envied them. I gave Cecily a comb to play with and set her down. Bowing my head in my lap, I tried to remember the song my father used to sing me at bedtime.

"God be thanked!" cried the midwife. " 'Tis a boy!"

"A son," my grandmother said with wonder in her voice. "An heir!"

"A son and heir!" my mother cried. Her voice was strong again, and there was such pride in it. *"A king!"*

The next few weeks were filled with much ado about the babe. My mother fed him at her own breast, since we had no wet nurse and little food except the meat brought us by John Gould, the butcher. He gave it to us of his own charity, for we had no money or gold. Dr. Sergio came often to check the babe's health, and pronounced it good. He also brought us news of Papa.

"King Edward is still in Bruges, Your Grace, and his brother-in-law, Charles of Burgundy, refuses to see him. But in time King Edward will prevail. He always does."

As Dr. Sergio was leaving, he passed me in my corner by the

door and took my hand in his. "Child, why are you so cold? Why do you sit at the door as if to flee your family? Here, draw near to the brazier so you can get warm."

I shook my head and recoiled. The brazier reminded me of the wine cellar.

"She has been acting strangely of late," my grandmother said. "We can do nothing with her. She refuses even to eat the meat that the butcher brings us, and keeps her distance from us all."

Dr. Sergio returned to her side and bent his head. He murmured something and I caught the word *jealous*.

Let them think what they wanted.

✸

ONE SNOWY DAY, JUST BEFORE YULETIDE, I OPENED the door to a heavy knock. "Abbot Milling!" my mother called out before I could exchange greetings with him.

I stepped aside and he rushed past me. Abbot Thomas Milling was a familiar face, and my mother always asked him the same question the moment she saw him.

"What news?" she demanded breathlessly.

I knew she was more anxious for the tidings he carried than for the food he said he brought for our souls, and on this occasion Abbot Milling was bursting to tell her.

"God be praised, Charles the Rash—I mean, the Bold—has seen fit to look with favor on King Edward's cause. He's outfitting a fleet for him as we speak." He lowered his voice to a whisper and glanced over his shoulder. "Come, my daughters, let us gather round and pray for the success of King Edward against Warwick . . ."

I screwed my eyes shut. No one would pray harder for my father's victory against Warwick than I. To have my father near me again, to run with him around the castle halls again! All this seemed a dream to me, as if it had never happened, for it was so long ago . . .

Abbot Milling took confession from my mother and grandmother, and left.

On my fifth birthday, the eleventh of February, 1471, three days before the Feast of St. Valentine, Abbot Milling brought me a small slice of cake. I divided it into eight slivers: two for my sisters, two for my brothers, two for my mother and grandmother, one for the abbot, and one for me. That meant no one got much more than a few crumbs, but oh, how sweet they tasted! He poured us wine and then he gave us the news.

"King Edward has left Burgundy for England. He is expected to return soon to give battle. But Henry VI's fiery French queen, Marguerite d'Anjou, has not departed France yet. 'Tis said she doesn't trust Warwick, though he has kept his word and restored her mad husband to the throne. 'Tis said she would rather dally in France than fight at his side for her husband."

This news cheered my mother and grandmother. They clinked their battered iron cups and laughed merrily as they drank, ignoring the babe's cries for the first time since he was born.

"Now let us gather round and pray. Prayer is food for the soul, and food for the soul is as important as food for the body, is that not so?" Abbot Milling said, as was his wont.

Dr. Sergio and Abbot Milling came many more times, bringing us small gifts and whispering their news. Then on a blustery day in March, Friar Bungey came. I opened the door at his knock and shrank back when I saw who it was. Leaving the door to slam in the wind, I fled to the back of the room and hid my head in my arms.

"Elizabeth! How rude of you," my grandmother said angrily while my mother opened the door to him again. Grandmother came and stared down at me. "Whatever is the matter with you, child? Come and apologize immediately!"

I didn't move. I didn't even lift my head to look at her. Then I felt my mother's shadow fall over me. Slowly, I peeked up from between my arms.

She pulled my head back by the roots of my hair and slapped me hard across the cheek. "Come this instant, Elizabeth," my mother hissed through the ringing in my ear, "or you shall receive a beating you will never forget." She took my hand and pulled me to my knees. I was so afraid that I wet myself. Ashamed and miserable, I made a curtsy to Friar Bungey, hoping no one noticed. Friar Bungey nodded and made the sign of the cross over my head, but he didn't appear to see me. His eyes held a strange glitter, and he turned his attention to my mother right away.

"The battle will be fought very soon, Your Grace. Warwick has refused to lay down his arms for a royal pardon if he submits. But not all the tidings are ill. The king's brother, George, Duke of Clarence, has abandoned Warwick's side and joined King Edward's— where he belonged from the first, God be praised!"

"Amen!" my mother and grandmother cried together.

"Both sides are marching to join battle. You must pray."

It was very silent in sanctuary after he left. My mother and grandmother didn't say a word and went about their tasks without talking to one another. My sisters and the babe cried, but I tended them as best as I could. I, too, dwelled on my thoughts, which were of my father, and I didn't speak unless spoken to. When the abbey monks began to chant their hymns for Vespers, we all knelt and prayed. Even my little sisters placed their palms together and murmured along with us.

The days passed, but no news arrived until after Easter. One night as we were dining, seated on straw in our bare room, there was a commotion of men outside. The door burst open, and soldiers stumbled in. We leapt to our feet and stared at them. We all knew they brought news of battle.

"York has lost!" cried one of the men, collapsing against the wall. "York has lost . . ."

I looked at my mother and grandmother. Both had gone as white as the sheets we used to sleep on. Slowly, my grandmother let herself down on the floor and sat there, not saying a word. My mother stood in the middle of the room. She looked bewildered, as if she had not understood. Her mouth moved to speak, but no words came.

Then she fell wailing to the floor.

I LAY AWAKE IN MY CORNER ON THE STRAW ALL NIGHT, curled up with my sisters. My mother cried, and my grandmother comforted her, and the church bells struck the hour, and the monks chanted their hymns.

"We are undone!" my mother kept sobbing. "Warwick will slay us."

"Hush, daughter. Warwick would never do such a thing. He is a knight, and takes his knightly oath most seriously."

"He can't let us go!"

"He may keep us confined, but he wouldn't kill us. We are no threat to him—" She broke off. A silence hung in the air.

"We are not," my mother said, "but the babe is." She burst into a fresh fit of sobbing.

"Daughter, we know not for sure what happened at Barnet. First reports of battle are often wrong. Edward may still live. Edward may have even won. I remember at Agincourt—"

My mother sobbed louder.

All through the night it went like this: my mother thinking dire thoughts, and my grandmother telling about her life. She had been a princess of Luxembourg, and had seen much in her time. She had wed the Duke of Bedford, and since King Henry had no queen then, she'd been first lady of the land before she'd ever wed my grandfather, Sir Richard Woodville.

As dawn broke, our chamber filled with light. My sisters awakened and the babe stirred and cried for his food. My mother gave him the breast. When a group of monks came to our door with a few eggs, some cheese, and some bread, we said our prayers and gathered round to break fast. We had just finished the eggs and taken a sip of wine when a great noise came from the abbey court yard. Horses snorted and men shouted, and there was the clank of armor.

"Can we go see what's happening?" Tom asked.

"Can we go see what's happening?" Dick asked. He always repeated what his brother said, for he was only ten and wanted to appear as grown as his older brother.

"Go," my mother whispered, "but be very careful, and keep away from them. They might be Lancastrians and take you captive."

The boys ran to the door.

"Don't forget to come back and tell us what you learn," Grandmother said.

My mother and grandmother took one another's hand as they

waited and bowed their heads in prayer: *Ave maria gracia plena dominus tecum* . . .

As the voices of men and clanging of armor grew louder, and the footsteps drew nearer, I looked at my mother. She had gone very pale, and her voice was a low murmur. Suddenly the chamber door burst open and my magnificent father stood there, laughing. He shone like a king from an illuminated manuscript, his plumed helmet with the golden emblem of sun and roses under his arm, his fair hair falling around his face. He was beaming from ear to ear, and he lit up our drab chamber like a torch.

"Papa, Papa!" I cried, tears blinding me. I ran to him and he swept me up into his arms. Oh, how wonderful it felt to be in his arms again! I hugged him tight. He was the sun, and the moon, and the stars in the sky! He was the rainbow, and laughter and light. I didn't dare blink in case he disappeared. I heard my mother's cry of joy and my sisters' giggles as they threw themselves against his legs.

"Fortune has turned her wheel and smiled on us again," my grandmother marveled. "Welcome, King Edward!"

My mother held up my brother. "Behold thy son!" she said. "I have named him Edward!"

I shall never forget the look of joy on my father's face as he saw my brother for the first time.

✸

WE MOVED INTO THE PALACE THAT NIGHT. HOW good it felt to have sweets, and soft sheets, and to be surrounded by velvet again instead of straw! Gathered around the fire, seated in my father's lap, my brothers and sisters at his knees, we learned what happened at the Battle of Barnet.

"We were outnumbered, as usual," my father laughed. "But we were victorious—as usual!"

"How, Papa? Tell us how!" I insisted, bobbing up and down in his lap, and then all my sisters and brothers chimed in to demand the same.

"You will not believe it. 'Twas almost supernatural!" my father said, a look of wonder in his eyes. "On Easter Sunday, just before we gave battle, a great mist came down from the sky. It descended over the field of Barnet and confounded my enemies, so they did not know who was their foe and who their friend. And they slew one another, not knowing who they slew. That's how we won!"

A strange chill stole over me.

"And Warwick?" my mother asked quietly.

"Warwick is dead."

My mother smiled. "And his brother, John Neville?"

"Dead."

My father put me down and rose abruptly, the smile gone from his face.

He left before dawn the next morning. There was another battle he had to fight.

CHAPTER 2

King Edward's Court, 1471

WE WATCHED OUR FATHER'S VICTORY MARCH INTO London from the window of our chamber in Westminster Palace. The people were beside themselves with joy. They cheered and threw white roses, danced and sang, and drank wine poured from kegs that stood at each street corner. My grandmother watched, smiling, seated at my side by the open window.

"Are my father's enemies all dead now?" I asked.

"Aye," she said. "King Henry's son, Prince Edward, died in battle." She exchanged a look with my mother.

"I wouldn't be surprised if the news of his son's death kills Henry," my mother replied with an odd smile.

My father appeared. He was riding his shining black horse, surrounded on either side by his brothers, my uncles George of Clarence and Richard of Gloucester, and a host of nobles. Behind them a column of soldiers trailed into the distance.

"Papa! Papa!" I called, waving wildly. But he couldn't hear me over the tumult of the crowd. He was dressed in armor, without his helmet. A broad smile lit his face as he waved to the people. He caught a white rose from the shower that rained down on him and threw it to someone in the crowd. "Who's that girl?" I asked Grandmama Jacquetta.

"Nobody," my mother answered.

"She's pretty," I said.

Suddenly the mood of the crowd changed and beneath the cheering I caught boos and an ugly hissing. "What's happening?" I cried.

"The people have caught sight of Henry's queen, Marguerite d'Anjou," my grandmother said. "See, she rides at the back of the procession, in the wooden cart." She pointed into the distance.

"Why are they throwing things at her?" I demanded.

"Because they hate her. She did bad things to England."

"What bad things?" I asked. I was fascinated now, but my grandmother just said, "It's too hard to explain. You'll know when you grow up."

The jeering of the crowds grew so loud, it hurt my ears. I left the window seat. My father was arriving in the palace courtyard, and I couldn't wait to greet him.

❀

LIFE WENT BACK TO NORMAL. MY FATHER GAVE ME a terrier pup that I named Blossom, and she followed me everywhere I went. Music, feasting, and laughter filled all our days, except when my uncles came to court, for there was fighting between them. One day after my uncle George of Clarence had left, I found my father standing alone by the window in a chamber full of people. Everyone was silent and the minstrels had stopped their music. He was clutching a book. I went to him. Papa swung me up and sat me down on the window seat, but he didn't smile.

"Why are you sad, my dear lord father?" I asked.

"This prophecy, sweet child," Papa whispered, his voice cracking in a way I had never heard before. He showed me the book. "Can you read?"

I shook my head. "I am only six, my lord father." I didn't remind him that I'd had no schooling in sanctuary.

My father looked like he was going to smile, and then the sad look came back. "It says, my dear child, that no son of mine shall be crowned king, but that you shall be queen and wear the crown in their stead."

The warm feeling wrapped around my heart again. My father loved me so much that he even worried about my happiness when I was grown! "My lady mother likes being queen," I said, wanting to put his mind at ease, "so maybe I shall like it, too, Papa."

Papa smiled. Gently, he stroked my hair.

But my uncles kept coming back. That made my father sad again, and my mother angry. Nurse said my uncles were mad at one another because my uncle Richard of Gloucester wanted to marry Anne Neville, the sister of Uncle George's wife, Bella, and George didn't want him to.

"Why not?" I asked my nurse, as I stroked Blossom in my arms.

"If your uncle Richard of Gloucester marries Anne, your uncle George of Clarence will have to share Bella's inheritance with him, and he doesn't want that. He wants to keep all his wife's money. Your Uncle George loves money."

"So does Mama," I said.

Nurse smiled, but she didn't say anything more.

"I like my Uncle Richard better than Uncle George," I said.

"So does your father, my sweet," Nurse replied. "Now, put down your dog so I can plait your hair."

I did as I was told. "I like Uncle Richard because he brings me gifts and plays with me when he's here," I went on.

"He loves children," Nurse said as she combed my hair.

"You like him, too, don't you?" I said, suddenly aware of the different note in her voice.

"Your uncle Richard of Gloucester is a generous prince," she said with a smile. "Always gives me a gold piece when he comes."

My mother grew big with another child and we moved to Shrewsbury for the birth. She kept to her chamber and we didn't see her much. While she was confined, my father's mother, Cecily, Duchess of York, made an unexpected visit to us from her castle of Berkhamsted. I was playing with my new puppy. There was a huge commotion outside in the courtyard and I heard my father calling out from down the hall. I ran out of my chamber. A maiden was fleeing my father's privy suite and my father came out after her, hopping on one leg as he tried to get his boots on. His shirt hung out over his hose.

"God's balls, don't just stand there!" he called out to his Knights and Squires of the Body, who had panicked looks on their faces. "Get this place in shape—you know how she is! Elizabeth—" he cried, catching sight of me. I went to him and he grabbed me by the shoulders. "Be a sweetheart and do your papa a favor?"

I nodded firmly.

"Go and forestall your grandmother—talk to her, do something, anything, stand on your head—whatever it takes to delay her getting here!"

He returned to his chamber and I scrambled toward the tower stairs without further ado, Blossom at my heels, barking wildly. My father needed my help, and I'd do anything for him.

"Grandmama! Grandmama!" I cried, seizing her hand as she emerged from the tower staircase. I curtsied before her. "Oh, Grandmama, 'tis so good to see you!"

"Elizabeth," she said. "As disheveled as always. Does your mother ever bother to order a new gown for you?"

"Grandmama, I just got this last month," I said, looking down in disbelief at my beautiful blue silk dress trimmed in beaver.

"Then you're growing too fast. Stop eating so much."

I curtsied. "Aye, Grandmama."

Unable to think of anything else to delay her with, I stepped aside. She swept past me down the hall. "And have your dog groomed once in a while," she called out, without turning to look at me again. "He's scruffy."

Mary and Cecily appeared at the threshold of the nursery, hand in hand with their nurses, who fell into deep curtsies before Grandmama.

"Do you not have a comb in the entire castle?" Grandmama demanded, addressing Mary's nurse.

"Indeed we do, Your Grace," she replied from the folds of her curtsy.

"Then use it. The children look like urchins." Cecily began to cry. Grandmama ignored her and turned her attention to the men who had fallen to their knees before my father's chambers as if they would guard him from her with their lives.

"My son's royal attendants, I presume?"

There was a murmur. "You smell like a guild of tavern-keepers. You should be ashamed of yourselves." Grandmama pointed at one of the knights with her silver-tipped cane. "You're as scruffy as Elizabeth's hound. Who are you?"

"Sir William Norris, Your Grace."

"Oh, a Lancastrian," she sniffed. "Well, you're not with Henry VI now. Get yourself bathed and properly attired."

"Aye, Your Grace," replied Sir William, coloring as others tittered.

"I shall never fathom why my son insists on surrounding himself with such rabble, Lancastrians and—" She was about to point to someone else with her cane when Papa appeared.

"Ah, Mother," said my father cheerfully. He was clad in a rumpled scarlet velvet doublet and high black boots. He advanced to embrace her. "How pleased I am to receive this gracious and unexpected visit!" he said with a big smile.

"No, you're not," she said. "You've been drinking. Your breath reeks of wine. You always were a lush, Edward. The castle is a disgrace. You should know better. You're far too indulgent." Her eye caught on my fifteen-year-old brother, Tom, trailing Papa. "So you're Earl of Huntingdon, now, Thomas? You and your endless relatives will soon have devoured all the wealth and honors in the land and left nothing for anyone else."

Tom gave her a bow.

"Come along, Edward. I have serious matters to discuss with you. Richard and George are at each other's throats over Anne Neville. Incidentally, what's this I hear about your new harlot?"

My father froze in his steps and exchanged a shocked look with my brother. All the knights and squires stared at Papa with their mouths open.

"What's a harlot?" I asked my nurse.

" 'Tis time to play in the garden," she said, taking my hand and dragging me along. The other nurses followed with my sisters and baby brother, little Edward.

Six weeks later, on the seventeenth of August, 1473, my mother gave birth to another son. We moved back to London and the palace filled with rejoicing. My brother was named Richard for our uncle of Gloucester and our two "Richard" grandfathers, Richard, Duke of York, and Richard Woodville. My father was so pleased with my mother that he gave her something he had refused to grant her till now. He appointed her brother, my uncle Anthony, Lord Rivers, guardian to my little brother, Edward, Prince of Wales, and they left for Ludlow.

✿

THE SEASONS PASSED. I FROLICKED ON THE FROZEN Thames in the winter with my sisters, Mary and Cecily, and picnicked on the castle lawns in summer with the court, and rode my palfrey through the woods of Windsor in the autumn. Life was sweet. Laughter was everywhere, and wherever we went, the loud cheering of the people followed us. But today, as I stood in the summer sunshine at the castle gates with my sister Mary, and my sister Cecily, and my two-year-old brother, Dickon, everyone was silent and my heart was heavy as a lead ball in my breast. Papa was leaving for war. He was going to fight King Louis of France.

His armor glittered in the sun and his crimson plumes nodded in the breeze as he led his men down the hillside, Uncle Anthony at his side. Papa sparkled like a god as he moved, but with every stride of his horse, the tears at the back of my eyes stung more sharply. Dickon bawled, but Mary and I did not dare weep. Mary was eight years old now, and I was nine, and we had to behave like princesses and not show emotion or my brothers Tom and Dick Grey would tease us mercilessly. So would Cecily, who watched me quietly and did not cry.

It seemed odd to me that my mother stood alone to wave Papa off, but Grandmother Jacquetta had passed away soon after Papa's victory against the Kingmaker.

"Is Papa going to die?" Cecily demanded, directing her question to me. "Will the French slay him?"

I didn't understand my sister Cecily. She had such an uncanny knack of giving voice to my worst fears that sometimes it seemed to me that she said and did things just to spite me. Had she seen the tears in my eyes and wanted to make them roll down my cheeks? I turned my back on her and headed toward the chapel without a reply. My sister Mary's voice floated to me on the summer breeze. "Papa is the greatest warrior in the world and has never lost a battle. The French can't hurt him. No one can." She was my good friend, as well as my sister.

Mary was proven right. Papa returned in September, sooner than anyone ever expected, and he bore wonderful news.

"My ladies," he said, laughing as he flourished me and my sisters and my mother a grand bow, "I return to you a rich king, having won the war against France!"

"Rich?" my mother repeated, her face breaking into a rare smile. "What do you mean, Edward?"

"You, madame—you and I shall dance away the days of our lives in ease and comfort, for Louis was so afraid of me that he paid me a king's ransom to leave France in peace, and return to England! *A king's ransom*—" He laughed with abandon at his own jest. "And he shall keep paying for another twenty years!"

"How much, how much?" demanded my mother, her eyes sparkling.

"Fifty thousand gold crowns a year!"

A disbelieving look took hold of my mother's features, and she put out both hands to my father in stunned surprise, words failing her. Laughing, they swung around together as I had done with Mary as a child. Giddy and happy, my mother fell into a chair, holding her sides with laughter. It was a strange sight to see her like that. As if she were a girl.

"As for you, my princess," Papa said, bending a knee before me and taking my hands into his own, "I have brought you a most splendid gift."

My heart went fluttering in my breast and my lips broke into the widest of smiles. "What, Papa? What could you bring me that is better than having you back?"

"Ah, my beloved daughter, 'tis a jeweled crown of your own that I bring you!"

My mother gasped, pushed out of her chair. "A crown of her own? What do you mean, Edward?"

"To seal my treaty with Louis, I promised Louis's son the hand of our daughter, Elizabeth." He rose to his feet and beamed at me like the sun that was his emblem. "I have betrothed you to Charles the Dauphin. You will be Queen of France one day."

My mother's hand went to her heart. "Queen of France? I shall be the mother of the Queen of France?" She turned her glittering eyes on me. "Then she must learn French! And from now on, she must be addressed as Madame la Dauphiness!" I looked at both of them in bewilderment.

"But don't you remember? I am betrothed to George Neville, Duke of Bedford."

My mother gave a snort of laughter. "Did no one tell you? That betrothal should never have been. The young Neville has no means. We even had to take his dukedom of Bedford from him because he couldn't sustain it. We can't have you marrying a nobody."

"Come, Blossom," I said, scooping up my dog in my arms.

"Her name is Jolie."

"What?"

"I just renamed her. It's French for 'pretty.' "

Mother gave birth to another babe, named Anne, in November 1475, bringing us more to celebrate, but my betrothal to the dauphin did nothing to endear me to Cecily. She stepped on the hem of my gowns more frequently than usual as she walked behind me.

Each time Mother caught Cecily failing to address me as "my dauphiness," she gave her a scolding. To repay me, Cecily would hide behind my chair and pat my dog as I studied my French lessons, hissing softly to herself, *"Ma dauphin-ess; notre dauphin-ess; votre dauphin-ess . . ."*

"Hush, Cecily! I can't concentrate."

"I wasn't doing anything," she'd say, "except practicing my French on your dog."

One day, I finally objected when my mother gave Cecily a

tongue-lashing. "Mother, leave her alone, I pray you! I don't mind her not addressing me as dauphiness."

My mother slapped me hard across my cheek. "You may not mind, but I do. Let this be a lesson to you. We must demand respect from everyone, or we shan't get it. And while it's on my mind, 'tis time you addressed your brother Tom by his new title, Marquess of Dorset. Is that understood?"

I curtsied mutely, nursing my cheek, which smarted. It was no use. Mother loved titles too much, for her father had never had one until he'd married my grandmother, Jacquetta, Duchess of Bedford. I decided to lodge a complaint against her with Papa.

"Papa, I pray you to stop Mother from insisting that even Mary and Cecily address me as dauphiness. They don't like it, and Cecily is making my life miserable because of it."

"Dear child," Papa said with a sigh, "you must learn to humor your mother, as I do. She's so strong-willed that she will have her way, come wind or high water. Fighting her is useless."

He looked so sad again that I went to him as he sat at his desk over his papers, and gave him a tight hug.

THE YEAR OF 1477 WAS USHERED IN WITH MUCH RE-joicing. In February, I celebrated my eleventh birthday, and soon afterward in March, another brother was born. We feasted and held a masked banquet. I danced with Papa, and laughed a great deal.

My parents named my new brother George for Uncle George, and gave him the title of Duke of Bedford, which Papa had taken away from my former betrothed, George Neville. Uncle George of Clarence, who had been deeply offended when my second brother was named for my uncle Richard of Gloucester, didn't even seem to notice the honor that my parents did him now. Each time he came to court, he brought his own cook and food tasters and raised a terrible fuss, yelling and shouting at my father and mother. He claimed my mother had tried to poison him on a previous visit.

"Why is Uncle George so angry?" I asked Nurse as she laced up my gown one morning.

"His wife died in childbirth, and his babe died a few days later. He's grieving, and he blames your mother for their deaths."

"Why?"

She didn't reply right away. Then she said, "I suppose he must blame someone, poor man."

Though I had many good times with Mary and my three-year-old brother Dickon, I was only too aware that all was not well in my father's kingdom. In good weather and bad, somber-faced messengers hurried across the lawns and pathways of the Tower, Westminster Palace, and Windsor, delivering their missives to my father. This time it was not the Kingmaker but my uncle George of Clarence who was making trouble for Papa. When my father forbade him from putting himself forward as a suitor to Mary of Burgundy, but allowed my Uncle Anthony to do so, Uncle George was roused to fury. I comforted my father in his chamber, sometimes playing my lyre, and at other times, my lute. Often, I sang to him, for he said I had a voice like an angel, but to see him droop in his chair made me ache with sadness. One day, I massaged his broad shoulders. When I was done, he reached up and took my hand.

"Why is Uncle George always so angry with you, Papa?" I asked gently.

He drew me to his lap. "George has always believed himself to be the rightful King of England, Elizabeth. He calls me a bastard."

I gave a gasp of horror. "Papa, everyone knows you are rightful king. Why does he say such dreadful things?"

"We don't know. We think there's something wrong with him. He saw some terrible things when he was a little boy. Henry's queen, Marguerite d'Anjou, captured the town of Ludlow and made him watch what her soldiers did to the townspeople. That may have unhinged his mind, we just don't know . . ."

My father drifted into his thoughts. Finally he spoke again, "Now he has accused your mother of sorcery."

I tensed, swallowed hard. The image of my mother and grandmother and the old friar in the wine cellar at the abbey conjuring up the fog at Barnet rose before me.

My father's voice came again, soft and distant. " 'Tis a deadly charge, witchcraft . . . Punishable by banishment or death."

I forced my dismal thoughts away. Now I understood the full urgency of my mother's pleading with my father to silence Uncle George. The night before last, I'd come upon them arguing in Papa's privy chamber. Mother had been down on her knees, wringing her hands, sobbing. She had never seemed so anxious about anything since the dreadful days of sanctuary. "Send him to the Tower!" she'd cried. "You can't let him spread the tale! You can't let him live! He'll destroy us—destroy our children—Edward, for the love of God, do it—"

Some things were still unclear to me. How would the charge of sorcery against my mother destroy us, his children? I shrugged inwardly. Some matters would probably never be explained, but one thing I knew for certain: I didn't want my mother banished. Though sometimes I thought I hated her, I loved her too. Not as I loved my father, but I didn't want anything ill to happen to her.

The news was not long reaching us. Uncle George had been taken to the Tower. Papa received a visit from my Uncle Richard soon afterward, and I listened at the chamber door as they argued.

"Release him, Edward!" Uncle Richard cried.

"I cannot. Nor will I. He doesn't deserve it."

"He is our brother."

"He is a traitor, and a dangerous one at that. I would be a fool to release him."

"You'll have God's scourge on you if you don't! Remember Cain and Abel."

That made me shudder.

I had seen little of my uncle Richard of Gloucester over the years. After Barnet and the war with France, he'd changed and no longer smiled much. He'd returned to the north and rarely came to court anymore. I was unsure what to make of him. With his dark looks, he didn't resemble the rest of our family, since we were all golden-haired and fair complexioned. And unlike my uncle George of Clarence, who always had plenty to say, my uncle Richard of Gloucester never said much. He kept his thoughts to himself, like me. In that, he was also unlike Uncle Anthony, my mother's brother, who talked a great a deal about poetry and literature and his travels to faraway places. I found myself very curious about this strange and brooding uncle who was so different from anyone else I'd ever known.

I went down to the palace kitchens, where I always picked up information. I loved sitting by the fire listening to the scullery maids chatter as they worked. The head cook never failed to make me welcome with sweets and other delights, and was more prone to answer my questions than Nurse, who said little to satisfy my curiosity.

"See who's a-come visitin'!" exclaimed the head cook with great excitement. She was a round old woman with a round face, and round apple cheeks, and a wide smile. She came out from behind the long table, wiping her hands on her apron, and dropped me a curtsy. " 'Tis a fair day when such a golden princess a-comes to see us, is it not? Ye are joy to look upon, my beautiful little princess. All that bright yellow hair and those big blue eyes, I vow 'tis like lookin' on a fair summer's day."

Everyone smiled at me, and I felt as if I were wrapped in a cozy cocoon of love on this cold and windy November afternoon.

"I wish I could come and see you more often," I said, "but I am kept at my harp and lute lessons, and my French lessons, and embroidery and tapestry lessons, and Latin, and I am scolded when I slip away."

"O my poor sweet princess, who could be sharp with ye? Here, have a seat on the stool and I'll fetch ye some marchpane. We just finished preparing it."

The marchpane was delicious, but I was careful not to gobble it up the way I wished to do, for I also had to mind my manners, being a princess. When they had feted me, they returned to their work, and forgot I was there. That was when I learned about Uncle George.

"Poor child," someone whispered. "To think there's such doings around her, and she'll soon be mourning an uncle."

"Surely the king will pardon his brother in the end?" came another whisper.

"Nay. They say the queen is determined to have Clarence's blood for accusing her of murdering—"

"Shush, man! Ye'll have us all in the Tower, if ye's not careful!"

No one I questioned liked to talk much about my uncles, and it was during a kitchen visit that I'd learned about Anne Neville laboring as a scullery maid. Now I knew my Uncle George lay under sentence of death at the Tower, but I still didn't know why my Uncle George blamed my mother for the deaths of his wife and child when all she'd done was send her own doctor and midwife to tend my Aunt Bella. Though his shadow hung over us during the Yule celebrations, the palace was soon merry again, for there was to be a royal wedding at Westminster. My four-year-old brother Dickon was marrying the richest heiress in the kingdom, eight-year-old Anne Mowbray, Duchess of Norfolk.

In January, as soon as Yule was behind us and church bells had struck the arrival of the new year of 1478, preparations for Dickon's wedding moved forward with full force, though my Uncle George remained in the Tower.

Court glittered with candles, torches, fresh silk draperies, new tapestries, much gilt, and boughs of greenery and fir. Hundreds of nobles had braved the harsh winter journey to London from the far corners of the kingdom to attend Dickon's wedding, and my parents were determined to make it a grand and unforgettable occasion, perhaps to take everyone's mind off the troubles with Uncle George. But during the feast, I noticed the anxious glances cast at my father and mother.

As I danced with Papa, it seemed to me that the laughter that the court jesters elicited from groups of wedding guests was not as gleeful as usual. Between drumrolls, varlets rushed about offering a succession of courses of swan, roasted boar, and jellied partridge. Other servers poured well-spiced sauces and soup over the dishes at a nod. Still others distributed pies, tarts, and fine white bread, as well as fritters, pancakes, fruits, and vegetable dishes, but though everyone smiled as they conversed and drank, I had the feeling their merriment was forced. My father and I made our way back to the high table, back to my glum uncle, Richard of Gloucester.

He sat with his wife, Anne Neville, the Kingmaker's daughter, barely touching his cup or his food. They both watched us take our places at the table solemnly. They seemed very uncomfortable, as if they'd rather be somewhere else. Then my uncle Richard of Gloucester seized my father's arm, leaned close, and whispered something to him in an urgent tone. I didn't catch what it was. All at once, without a word of acknowledgment—at least, none that I heard—my mother and father both pushed out of their chairs and went to dance. Whatever Uncle Richard had said, I knew it had to do with Uncle George, for neither my father nor my mother smiled.

Though my Grandmama Cecily didn't attend Dickon's wedding, she came to court as soon as all the other guests had left. She stayed only one night and no one saw her but my father. Then she returned to her castle of Berkhamsted, where she lived the life of a nun. I heard from the kitchen help that she had vowed never to come to court again so long as she lived. My uncle Richard of Gloucester and his wife left for the north at the same time, but not before I heard one of their household whisper something that disturbed me greatly. "Thus is the queen avenged on yet another of her most bitter enemies."

I had little time to ponder this. On the heels of their departure came the news that my uncle George of Clarence was executed in the Tower. Strangely, no one knew how he died. Listening to the palace whispers, I learned that my Uncle George chose his own death and drowned in a butt of the sweet malmsey that was always his favorite wine. My father fell into a terrible depression and did not emerge from his chamber for a week. Though he had left orders not to be disturbed, I sneaked in to see him.

He was sitting at a table drinking alone, empty wine bottles lolling about at his feet. It broke my heart to find him this way, my loving, laughing father. I stood for a moment, taken aback at the sight.

He glanced up at me and looked away again, but he put out one hand to me as he covered his face with the other. I took it and sat on his knee as I used to do when I was little. I placed my arm around his neck and gave him a tender kiss.

"Papa, Papa . . . if you didn't wish Uncle George to die, why did you have him executed?" I asked. "You are king, after all, Papa, and can do anything you wish."

He didn't answer for a long time, and I thought he hadn't heard me. Then he said, very softly, "Sometimes a king must do what he knows is wrong, what is hateful to him. For the peace of the land."

I had the strange feeling I would never forget my father's words.

CHAPTER 3

Sister of the King, 1483

I MUST ADMIT I DIDN'T MISS MY UNCLE GEORGE. IT seemed to me that another cloud was banished from the realm, and with his death revelry and joy returned to court. My father soon recovered his spirits since my uncles were not there to stir argument. Neither did my mother trouble my father with her demands, for she went to work deciding which of her many relatives should receive what from Uncle George's rich estates. She was also occupied arranging advantageous marriages for her more distant family members now that her twelve brothers and sisters had secured the land's dukedoms and earldoms. Then, like a tempest out of calm skies, sorrow struck again.

Uncle George's namesake, my baby brother George, died within months of my uncle's execution. It was a dreadful thing, and it brought sadness and weeping back to court. My mother feared that his death was an omen, but my father, who didn't believe in such things, dismissed it.

"Pull yourself together, Bess. It was an infection that took him. Children die of infections every day," he told her. Then he went back to his mistress, Jane Shore.

I wondered if Mother knew about Papa's mistress. It was said he loved her dearly, though she was only a mercer's daughter. Gossip held that she was not only very beautiful, but also kind and gracious. Although she refused my father's gifts for herself, those who encountered misfortune in life could rely on her to set matters right for them. Grants of money would be given them; justice would be dispensed, if that was what they sought; their relatives would be released from prison or the Tower, and the charges against them dropped. My father would do anything for her.

Marked by the birth of two more sisters, Katherine in 1479 and Bridget in 1480, and attended by christenings and other blessed occasions, the next few years passed in serenity and celebration. My father's sister, Margaret of York, Duchess of Burgundy, paid us a visit in 1480 amid great rejoicing. My father had not seen her for twelve years after she left for Burgundy to wed her husband, whom Papa liked to deride as Charles "the Rash," instead of "the Bold," for Charles liked to attack other countries for no apparent reason, and was killed besieging Nancy, a town of no consequence.

It was such a happy time that I forgot she had come on a most serious matter. My Aunt Margaret wished to wage war against Louis of France, who was threatening Burgundy, and she sought England's help. Though Papa did not grant her request, he went to great lengths to make her visit a memorable and happy one, with much pomp and circumstance and the giving of gifts, banqueting, and celebration.

Life was full for me in these days, and time passed too quickly. I practiced my Latin and my French, in both of which I had grown fluent, and I taught my younger sisters the art of embroidery and music, in which I excelled, though this did not please Cecily. I also received petitioners in my mother's stead, for dispensing patronage was part of the duties of a queen and my mother did not care to do it. Then, every evening, we gathered as a family to play chess and backgammon in the solar, to listen to music, to sing, to dance.

My fifteenth birthday occasioned much festivity, for it meant I had reached a mature and marriageable age and King Louis of France would surely send for me soon to wed his son, Charles the Dauphin. It pleased me to see my father happy. He laughed heart-

ily, and ate and drank with more gusto than ever, for he had few
worries, and no more challenges to his rule since all his Lancastrian
rivals were dead. The only claimant was someone named Henry
Tudor, who lived in exile in Brittany, but Tudor represented no
serious threat, for his lineage was tainted with bastardy on both his
maternal and paternal sides. He was put forward simply because all
the legitimate Lancastrian claimants were dead in the Wars of the
Roses, and he was the only one left.

With King Louis's gold pouring into our coffers, Papa took
his ease and was no longer obliged to beg Parliament for money.
Nor did he have to work so hard at the business of governing, for
he had many capable men around him after nearly twenty years
of rule. One of these was his Master of the Rolls, a bishop named
John Morton.

"I don't care for him, Papa," I told my father one day when I
passed the bishop leaving my father's chamber. Short and corpu-
lent, with small dark eyes that reminded me of a dead fish, I had
observed him berating his servants in a sneering manner.

My father roared with laughter. "Neither does your uncle
Richard of Gloucester, but he is a great favorite of your mother's,
for he was a Lancastrian, and like her own family, he fought against
me at Towton. If I didn't favor him, she'd make my life miserable!
When you are Queen of France, my dauphiness, you can advise
your royal husband about who shall have his ear, and make his life
hell if he doesn't do your bidding! Just like your mother." He burst
into another round of laughter and took a long sip of wine from
his jewel-studded goblet.

"I shall never do that, Papa."

He interrupted his drink to regard me solemnly. "No, I dare
say you will not. You are not your mother. You are too sweet and
gentle by nature, and more than likely your husband will always
have his way." Then my father drew me to him and cupped my
face in his broad hands. "But, my child, don't let him make *your*
life bitter."

A knock at the door announced Bishop Morton. I gave my
father a kiss on his cheek and quitted the room. At the threshold, I
paused to listen for a moment.

"Your Grace, France continues to threaten Burgundy, and the matter grows ever more dire," said Bishop Morton. "Your royal sister, the Duchess of Burgundy, urgently requests your assistance for her stepdaughter, Mary of Burgundy, against Louis of France. She has sent another missive reminding Your Grace that our own commercial interests are at stake." He offered my father the letter.

"Never," Papa replied, waving the missive away. "We cannot risk losing our pension from Louis. And what about the princess Elizabeth's betrothal? We cannot put that at risk. When she is Queen of France, all will be set right. My sister Meg merely needs to wait. Tell her that—to wait."

I shut the door quietly.

We celebrated another wonderful Yuletide, but the new year of 1482 rode in on a hailstorm, and few were celebrating, for it seemed the Four Horsemen of the Apocalypse rode loose across the land. The harvest had been the worst in many years, and starvation exacted a heavy toll with the onset of winter. The news from Burgundy was not good, either, and this troubled my father, who wanted neither to lose Burgundy's trade, nor Louis's pension. In March, my terrier, Jolie, died, and I was inconsolable for the rest of the month.

Another urgent missive soon came from Aunt Margaret in Burgundy. In March, Mary of Burgundy was killed in a fall from her horse. Her husband, Maximilian of Austria, desperately needed England's help against King Louis of France, who claimed that in the absence of a male heir, the duchy of Burgundy had reverted to France with the death of Aunt Margaret's husband, Charles the Rash. But more troubling to my father than Burgundy was France. I had reached my sixteenth year and was well past marriageable age, and King Louis still did not send for me. To my father's inquiries, he returned vague excuses.

Soon after Easter, as April crocuses and narcissus peeked out from the blanket of snow that covered the palace gardens, my father celebrated his fortieth birthday. My mother arranged for lavish entertainment, and nobles from all over the kingdom attended. There were parades, and the streets of London were lined with tapestries and bright silk cloths that hung from houses and balconies; there was feasting, masques, and plays, and bonfires were lit in the streets. I knew that my father's mistress, Jane Shore, was among those who came to court for the celebration, but I couldn't tell her apart from the noble ladies, neither by her dress nor by her carriage.

Our joy proved brief. On the twenty-third day of May, my fourteen-year-old sister, Mary, in the full bloom of beauty and youth, died of an infection of the ear. I had never felt such pain and shed so many tears. One night, I couldn't sleep. I slipped out of the palace and went down to the river. It had rained heavily and it was dark, almost black, for there was no moon at all, no light, not even any torches, for they had been extinguished by the deluge. I was sitting by the water, clutching the silver crucifix Mary had given me, and weeping, when suddenly there was a flash of blue light and I heard Mary's voice call *"Elizabeth!"* I leapt up and looked around, but there was no one. "Mary?" I cried. "Where are you? O Mary, Mary—"

Only the lapping of the water broke the silence. Yet I knew it was Mary, and that she was safe in Heaven, and I was struck with awe to be singled out this way. I fell to my knees and tearfully thanked God for the comfort He had seen fit to send me.

But the joy of that beautiful moment dulled in the shadow of my grief. For weeks I had no heart for food or merriment. I had lost my best friend. The year of 1482 seemed shrouded in black.

❁

IN AUGUST, SOME GOOD NEWS FINALLY ARRIVED TO break the gloom wrapped around our hearts. This came from Uncle Richard of Gloucester, fighting the Scots on the border. Berwick Castle, the great fortress on the sea that Marguerite d'Anjou had surrendered to the Scots twenty years before, fell back into English hands. Papa was jubilant. As far as Calais, Uncle Richard's victory was celebrated with bonfires, and Papa ordered him to appear before him at Yuletide in order to receive his thanks. Uncle Richard came in late December, as the year of 1482 drew to a close. A few days later, Aunt Margaret's embassy arrived.

Uncle Richard had just returned to the Great Hall where the Twelfth Night festivities were in progress, and had taken his seat at the High Table beside my father, who was merry with drink.

Everyone was so happy, especially my mother and her relatives, who danced to lutes and viols and clapped for the actors who performed the pageant "The Agony of Mankind Besieged by World, Flesh, and Devil." My brothers and sisters and I had dressed in the most lavishly splendid brocaded gowns we had ever worn. But, for some reason I couldn't fathom, Uncle Richard didn't partake in our merriment. He sat at the table, deep in thought, a gloomy expression on his handsome face.

"Louis . . ." Papa was saying to no one in particular, "has had two attacks of apoplexy; he will soon die! That shall put an end to our worries about Burgundy, indeed it shall." He set the jeweled goblet he had been waving around to his lips, but wine splashed on his face. He coughed. Servants rushed to him with gilt-edged towels.

"Sire!" said one of my father's most trusted retainers, Edward Brampton, striding up. He made a bow. "Messengers from Burgundy, my liege!"

"Burgundy . . . Burgundy . . ." Papa burped. "I cannot give up fifty thousand crowns . . . Would you give up fifty thousand crowns, Dickon?"

Brampton seemed embarrassed. "My Lord, they are not here to ask for aid. They bear urgent tidings."

I turned my gaze back on my father. He had sunk into his chair and was muttering to himself, for he'd had too much to drink. My mother was watching him with a hard expression.

"Have them brought in," Uncle Richard said. "I will see them." He rose and took up a position beside Papa's chair.

Brampton left the hall. He returned with two knights. They knelt at my father's feet. "Sire, your royal sister, the gracious Duchess of Burgundy, sends greetings," one began. My father burped.

I felt so embarrassed for Papa, and the messenger seemed distressed. He looked to Uncle Richard. At his nod the man continued, addressing my uncle instead of my father. "As you know, King Louis of France has swallowed up the Duchy of Burgundy and overrun Artois. Flanders is crumbling before him. Therefore, the Emperor Maximilian, unable to find allies against Louis, has had no choice but to make peace with France."

I watched my uncle turn pale. He glanced at my father. Papa no longer muttered but sat quietly. I didn't know how much my father had understood of this exchange, for he made no reaction.

"By this Treaty of Arras, Maximilian has agreed that his daughter Margaret shall marry the Dauphin of France, her marriage portion to be the counties of Artois and Burgundy."

I froze. There was whispering, and then silence engulfed the room. What did this mean? *Surely there is some mistake—I am to marry the dauphin!* I turned my eyes to my mother. She wore a stunned expression on her face and her mouth hung agape. *It isn't possible that King Louis has reneged on the marriage! It means too much to my parents that I wed the dauphin!*

There was a sudden crash followed by a wailing cry. My father had upturned one banquet table and was staggering down the dais toward the next, yelling like a madman. Uncle Richard rushed after him. He grabbed his arm, but Papa shook him off. My father's friend, Lord Hastings, ran to Uncle Richard's assistance. Together they managed to take Papa from the banquet hall, while my father muttered to himself. I rose and ran after them. I heard my father's words as he staggered into his privy chamber. "So many mistakes, Dickon," he moaned. "Too many mistakes . . . Louis . . . Warwick . . . Bess . . . *Bess* . . ."

I had no chance to ponder my father's words after Twelfth Night and Uncle Richard's return to the north, for it soon became apparent that Papa was ailing. Needless to say, my seventeenth birthday passed almost unnoticed, with little joy and minimal celebration. Not since Uncle George's death had he been so despondent and listless. This time it did not pass away, and nothing I did brought the laughter back to his spirit. Morose and silent, he watched court jesters stand on their heads for him, and mummers pretend to be maidens in distress, calling out for help in silly high-pitched voices, and his mouth didn't lift even with the hint of a smile.

Mother worried about his health. I knew it was serious when she insisted in late March that my father's bosom companion, Hastings, whom she had always loathed as a rival, take Papa fishing for Easter. The enmity between my mother and Hastings—nay, between Hastings and all my Woodville relatives, especially my brother Dorset, who had become Papa's other bosom companion—ran deep. At one point, Mother had managed to get Hastings sent to the Tower. But Papa's love for his boyhood friend trumped her jealousy, and in the end Hastings was released.

"He needs a rest from affairs of state. The fresh air of the country will surely do him good," my mother told Will Hastings, who nodded and gave her a bow.

But Papa returned abruptly just before Easter, unable to stand, leaning heavily on Hastings's shoulder, feverish and ailing. Mother put him to bed and summoned doctors to his side. My heart broke to see my magnificent, invincible father, the victor of so many battles, lying so feeble in his sickbed. I didn't leave his side. I feared this was the end. And so did he.

"Elizabeth," he murmured in the night, as candles flickered in the darkness and I sat dozing by his bedside.

I was instantly awake. "Papa! Dear Papa, what is it?"

"Elizabeth, fetch . . . Rotherham. I must add something to my will . . ."

"Papa, you need your rest! Can it not wait?"

"Cannot . . . wait . . . Elizabeth."

"Oh, Papa," I cried, my fingers tightening around his hands and tears stinging my eyes. I laid his palm against my wet cheek and kissed it tenderly. "I will fetch the archbishop. I will drag him from his bed, if need be. You sleep now."

"Make . . . haste"

My father's lord chancellor, Thomas Rotherham, Archbishop of York, arrived bleary-eyed before the rooster's crow, in the thick of the darkness before dawn, and with him came a delegation of other clerics, including Bishop Morton.

"Sire, I am here," Rotherham said kindly.

"I wish . . . to add a codicil . . . to my will," my father managed, struggling with each word.

"Very well, sire," Archbishop Rotherham said, motioning for the scrivener to bring his pen and ink closer to Papa's bedside. The man did so and seated himself in a wood chair. He raised his pen and nodded to the archbishop that he was ready.

"And what is the codicil you wish to add, sire?"

"I name . . . my brother, Richard of Gloucester . . . Protector of the Realm."

"Aye, sire." Rotherham repeated the words aloud for the benefit of the delegation. "Is that correct, Your Grace?"

"Aye . . . correct," Papa said.

The scrivener dipped his quill into the ink and scratched out the words on the parchment. He dusted it with sand and passed it to Archbishop Rotherham, who took a candle between his bejeweled fingers and held it to a tiny silver pot. The smell of melted wax filled the air as he poured its contents over the document. Papa held out his hand, and Rotherham removed the signet ring from his finger. He set the seal and returned the ring to Papa's hand. He held the document up so Papa could see it. " 'Tis done, sire."

Seized by a hacking cough from deep within his chest, a harsh braying, choking cough that would not cease, Papa managed a nod. My heart twisted in my breast as I watched him. " 'Tis all," my father whispered at length.

Archbishop Rotherham made the sign of the cross over my father, and with a bow to me, he departed the chamber, for Papa had already confessed his sins and received extreme unction. The delegation of clergy turned and filed out after him.

As soon as he had shut the door, Papa stretched out his hand to me. "Elizabeth . . ." I drew close and held my ear close to his lips, for his voice was a bare breath.

"Summon . . . Hastings . . . Dorset . . . I must speak to them. Before I die."

I swallowed hard on the wrenching anguish his words unleashed in my heart. "What about Mother?" I asked. He hadn't mentioned Mother.

"Not your mother—" he panted. He clutched my arm urgently, with surprising strength. I pulled my gaze from his hand to his face, and saw fear in his eyes. Thus was I made aware that my father knew—and had always known—the ineradicable enmities my mother's nature had created for us all the years of her life.

I fled the room fighting my sobs, knowing this was the last errand I'd ever run for my father. A sense of urgency and desperation hung over the palace as I sent a groom to summon Hastings and my brother Dorset. Monks chanted dirges and thick crowds gathered before the palace. I saw them through the arrow slit of the tower stairs, standing quietly, their caps at their breasts, the women weeping into their handkerchiefs. I crumpled down on the steps. Removing Mary's crucifix from around my neck, I pressed my lips to the cold metal and prayed to the Blessed Virgin for a miracle.

Within the hour, Hastings galloped through the gates of Westminster Palace and leapt from his horse, a frantic expression on his broad-carved features as he dashed to my father's room, my brother Dorset at his heels. I ran with them through the palace hallways and stairways. The man-at-arms opened the door to the bedchamber.

All was silent here. The drapes were drawn and candles flickered. My father's tall frame was stretched out on the bed, his hands at his side, his face white and pinched in the dimness, his breathing labored. He hadn't opened his eyes at the noise of the door clanging open, and I rested my hand on his. "Papa, Lord Hastings and Dorset are here, as you wished."

He opened his eyes, and a faint smile touched his lips at the sight of his good friends. I withdrew, and stood in a corner by my father's prie-dieu.

"Now I see everything clearly, with the eyes of the dying," Papa said, and his voice surprised me, for it was no longer breathy but stronger than I had heard since he had taken to bed. "I sacrificed England to Louis and to your mother, Dorset. I don't want to sacrifice my sons." Tears shone in his eyes, and my heart broke at the sight of my father swept with such remorse.

"All these years, so many mistakes," he went on. "Edward is too young to be king. He cannot survive without your help. Help me, Hastings! Help me, Dorset! Help England. Soon I will be gone, called to account for my sins by Almighty God. I won't be here to patch your quarrels, to keep peace between your factions. Your enmity will tear the land in two. Surely you see that? Surely—"

My father's chest heaved with the exertion of lengthy speech, and a racking cough seized him. A silence fell as he gathered strength to continue. I glanced at Hastings, but his back was to me and I did not see his face. His head was bowed; his shoulders slumped. I felt him fighting a depth of emotion as he stood at my father's deathbed.

"No use pleading with Bess, only ice in her veins . . . and ambition." My father exhaled the words like a sigh. " 'Tis not enough that you love my sons, if you hate one another. Hatred will tear them down—will undo everything we built together. Hatred will rain grief on England. If you love me, put aside your hatred for one another . . . Swear it over my body while I still live."

I looked at Dorset. His thick mouth worked with emotion, and he held a hand over his brow to hide the tears that trickled down his cheeks. Though I did not see Hastings's face, muffled sobs came from him. His shoulders shook violently, and I knew his face was a mask of grief. Of them both he'd loved my father best.

My father witnessed their sorrow quietly, but when they made no move toward one another, he wrenched himself from his bed and, lifting himself up, cried out with great effort, first to one, then to the other, "Swear forgiveness to one another before 'tis too late—I beg you! Put aside your hatred for my sake! For the sake of my children! For the sake of England. Or all shall be undone!"

Over my father's body, the two men finally reached out and grasped one another's hands. They stood, arms locked in friendship, and vowed forgiveness to one another, their voices cracking with emotion as they did so.

"I thank thee, my dear friends," Papa whispered. "Now I can die in peace . . . knowing all can be resolved." He labored for breath, and said, "I commit my soul to God, and my kingdom and my children to the hands of my faithful brother, Richard of Gloucester." He closed his eyes. "*In manus tuas, domine . . .*"

My breath stopped in my chest. I let out a long, shrill scream and ran to his side. Sobbing, I clutched his limp fingers and kissed his face again and again, my tears streaming over his still, lifeless body.

"GLOUCESTER, PROTECTOR OF THE REALM?" MY MOTHER cried with a gasp of horror. "Gloucester must not get such power! He hates us. He will destroy us."

"Mother," Dorset said. "Be reasonable. The king has ordered it so. There is naught that can be done about it now."

She swung on him. "Naught that can be done? You imbecile! Of course it can be undone! We shall undo it."

"Gloucester has done nothing against us," Dorset insisted. "He's proven himself a just and able governor of the north. People there love him. All is well. Why can you not let things be, Mother?"

She moved close. "All is well?" she hissed in his face. "When Gloucester vowed to get his revenge on me for Clarence's death? When he married the daughter of the Kingmaker, the man who told Edward I was a woman so reviled in the land that no son of mine would ever be permitted to mount the throne of England? All is well? Is all truly well, my dear idiot son?"

"Mother—"

"Have done!" she screamed. "Let me think!"

"I vowed friendship to Hastings, Mother. I cannot go back on my oath."

"Silence! You always were a fool. Go to your women. Let me deal with policy. You have not the intellect. Your brains are elsewhere." She looked mockingly at his groin.

I shot poor Dorset a look of sympathy from where I sat silently observing the scene. He gave me a helpless shrug. We watched Mother pace back and forth across the room as she worked out her strategy. There was no point in my rallying to his defense, and he knew it. Mother despised me.

"We must write my brother Anthony in Ludlow and tell him to get himself back here immediately! There is no time to be lost. Fetch me a scrivener!"

I hurried to the antechamber and sent a servant for one.

" 'Tis imperative my Edward be crowned right away."

"You cannot do any of this without the agreement of the council, you know," Dorset said resignedly. "And they may object."

She threw him a withering look. "We would surely be lost if matters were left in your hands. The council will approve whatever I want. For I shall pack it with our supporters."

Dorset rose. He went to the door and gave an audible sigh. "Hastings will never agree to setting Gloucester aside."

"Fool!" Mother screamed. She picked up a wine cup from a small table and hurled it after him. It missed its target, hit the wall, and landed at Dorset's feet. He bent down, retrieved it. He set it on the table by the door and left.

"Fool," Mother said more quietly. She turned to me. "We must make a clear and determined effort to preserve by force the power we have hitherto exercised by our influence over your father. You understand that, don't you?"

I said nothing.

"Then you are a fool, too."

✿

AT A HASTILY SUMMONED COUNCIL MEETING, PACKED with family and supporters, my mother laid out her strategy.

"I claim the regency for myself. As queen dowager, 'tis rightfully mine." She addressed the council from the head of the table, holding her chin high, looking regal in a magnificent gown of rich crimson velvet edged with gold, a circlet of gold on her hair, which she wore braided on either side of her face, in the manner of Marguerite d'Anjou.

I thought it odd that Mother should think of raising that specter, for mad Henry's French queen had ruled the land through Henry, who was as simple and malleable as a child. Eventually her abuse of power brought about widespread revolt against Henry himself, and my father came to the throne. Had my mother forgotten about Marguerite's end? Sick, poor, defeated, abandoned, and alone, she'd died in exile mourning the death of her young son, the child that should have been king. But everything my mother did was calculated for effect. She must have calculated that reminding the nobles of Marguerite's power would work in her favor, at least for now.

A murmur went around the room, but whether aye or nay, I could not tell.

"King Edward was sick and feverish at the end," Mother resumed. "He was not in his right mind when he added that codicil appointing his brother of Gloucester Protector of the Realm. Was he, Bishop Morton?" she asked sweetly.

"I do not believe he was, Your Grace."

"Archbishop Rotherham?"

"I dare say he was not," the archbishop replied, his long narrow face looking even foxier than before.

"Lord Stanley?" My mother turned to one of the wiliest and most slippery of my father's lords. Stanley had served under both a Lancastrian and a Yorkist king. He'd not only survived them both, but been heaped with honors by both. He was married to Henry Tudor's mother, the pious little woman, Lady Margaret Beaufort. It was from her that Tudor inherited what little claim he held to the throne of England, for she was the daughter of John Beaufort, first Duke of Somerset, the grandson of John of Gaunt, Duke of Lancaster.

"The matter deserves weighty consideration. I am reluctant to say aye or nay at this time," Lord Stanley replied.

She smiled at Dorset and her brothers, Sir Edward Woodville and Bishop Lionel, clustered on one side of the table next to the rest of our Woodville relations and allies.

"Then we are agreed. Gloucester is to be set aside," my mother said peremptorily to a murmur of ayes that came mainly from her side of the table. She picked up another sheaf of paper in order to move on to a different subject when a voice broke the silence.

"We are not agreed, madame," Hastings said.

He rose from his seat. "By the king's will, Gloucester was appointed Protector. Not you, madame. Your name wasn't even on the list of executors, doubtless for precisely this very reason. King Edward feared you would attempt to seize power."

"Lord Hastings, you are out of order. And in the minority here." My mother was bristling, her eyes filled with fury and scorn. "Pray be seated." A cold smile hovered on her lips. Ignoring Hastings, she moved on to the next matter of business. "We must send for my son, King Edward, immediately—and give him a strong escort. Ten thousand men."

A dull murmur ran through the chamber.

"Against whom is our young sovereign to be defended?" demanded Hastings, still standing. He looked around. Many of those who supported my mother averted their gaze or bowed their head. "Such extreme measures are unnecessary. We are not at war, Your Grace."

"But Lord Hastings," my mother said haughtily, "I cannot have England's king travel dangerous roads without a suitable escort to protect him."

"The roads are not that hazardous, Your Grace, and if you insist on such a strong escort, you leave me no choice. I shall retire to Calais." Hastings leaned his full weight on his hands and locked his gaze with her.

I could tell that my mother was remembering the decisive part that Calais had played in Warwick the Kingmaker's day. Like Hastings, Warwick had been Captain of Calais. With an entire fleet at his disposal and an impregnable fortress for refuge, he had managed to evict my father from the throne and restore Henry VI. Warwick had kept Papa out for a full year until the battle at Barnet. My mother dared not let Hastings out of her reach, for Hastings was popular where she was hated, and the people would be sure to rally to him.

Hastings and Mother glared at one another for a long moment, and I had the sense that they were playing a game of chess.

"Very well, the king's escort shall not exceed two thousand men. Are you satisfied?" my mother said at last.

The knight has captured the queen, I thought.

"Aye, madame," said Hastings. "You have been prudent." He sat down, leaned back in his chair, and watched her as warily as a mouse watches a cat. I knew that Hastings had better watch his back now; she would be avenged on him for this insult.

In the solar at Westminster later that evening, while Cecily braided her hair and admired her image in the mirror and Dickon built a tower out of wood blocks and arranged toy soldiers on the ramparts, I told my sisters, Anne and Kate, a tale about knights and dragons while two-year-old Bridget played with a rag doll and Mother railed against Hastings and his veiled threat to use Calais against her. Summoning her scrivener again, she dispatched another missive to my Uncle Anthony, commanding him to hurry to bring Edward to London to be crowned.

But the days passed, and then the weeks. Soon it would be May. Still Edward did not come.

CHAPTER 4

Sanctuary, 1483

"GLOUCESTER SENDS YOU HIS CONDOLENCES, MA-dame," Hastings said as he read a letter that had arrived for the council from my uncle Richard of Gloucester.

"I have been loyal to my brother King Edward at home and abroad, in peace and in war. I am loyal to my brother's heir and my brother's issue. I desire only that the kingdom be ruled with justice, according to law. My brother's testament has made me Protector of the Realm. In debating the disposition of authority, I ask you to consider the position rightfully due me according to the law and my brother's order. Nothing which is contrary to my brother's order can be decreed without harm.' "

The council thought it a most gracious letter, and many who had been uncommitted before now voiced support for Uncle Richard. But my mother took it as proof of Richard's ill will toward us. "See—he writes *'nothing which is contrary to my brother's order can be decreed without harm'*—he means to seize power from us!"

I leapt to my feet. "He does not mean that, Mother! He's merely stating he will not stand for *you* to try to seize power from him. Because it is contrary to what Papa wanted."

"How dare you gainsay me?" my mother cried.

I had never challenged her before. For I hated argument and she thrived on it, and once an argument was started, she would not let it end. But I remembered my father's last wish, and it was for him that I stood up now. Before I could reply, she spoke again. "He means to seize power, and I shall not let him! We'll see who wins this battle!"

When we finally received a missive from Uncle Anthony, my mother almost tore it from the messenger's hands. She read frantically.

"He has left Ludlow, thank God, but he waited until after the celebrations of St. George's Day on the twenty-third of April! He says he saw no need to rush—the imbecile—" She waved the missive furiously at the west window. *"No urgency!"* she screamed, as if she were talking to him. "You mad fool! You great and utter fool!" She bent her head down again to read. "Oh Blessed Mother, help us! He writes that he has arranged to meet Gloucester in Northampton on April twenty-ninth! The half-wit! The addle-brained, noodle-headed dullard! Summon your brother Dick Grey—hurry, girl!" she yelled at me. Because Mother had two Richards from her two marriages, she distinguished between them by calling her elder Richard by his full name.

Dorset and I exchanged a helpless look before I left to fetch my brother.

Dick had been playing dice with a friend, and winning. He was somewhat annoyed to find himself dragged away from the game. "What is it now, Mother?" he asked sullenly when he strolled in with me.

"Does no one understand what is at stake here?" my mother snarled, looking around at us. "Am I the only one with the sense to realize that our lives, our very treasure, our futures are in peril?"

So treasures were as valued as lives. I bent my head to hide my smile.

Mother drew an audible breath. "Dick Grey, you must leave for Northampton at once. Tell your uncle this—under no circumstances should he meet with Gloucester! Tell him 'tis urgent he makes haste to London. Explain that, for our own protection, we are setting aside Edward's will and taking power ourselves. Go, now! Take the fastest horse in the stable and as many men as you can gather on short notice, and go!"

"Aye, Mother," he said, turning to hurry from the chamber.

✿

WE RECEIVED NO FURTHER WORD FROM DICK OR from Uncle Anthony. Instead, one dark night, messengers clattered into the courtyard, awakening us all. My mother met them in her chamber robe.

"Richard of Gloucester intercepted the king at Stony Stratford with the help of Henry Stafford, Duke of Buckingham!" the messenger cried. "He has taken Anthony, Lord Rivers, and Sir Richard Grey prisoners."

"*Jesu—*" breathed my mother.

"Gloucester and Buckingham are now escorting him to London," he said.

"Dear God, we are in great danger!" my mother cried. Her worst fears were being realized. Buckingham hated her. At the age of eleven, Mother had forced him to wed my aunt, Catherine Woodville, so Catherine could be a duchess, and he'd never forgiven her for it. "We must flee into sanctuary! Hurry, Elizabeth, help me pack up our treasure—"

"Our treasure?" I asked in disbelief.

"All our precious belongings—my plate, my gowns, my carpets, my jewels—everything!" my mother replied. "We can't go without our things. Remember how uncomfortable we were last time?"

Servants rushed to gather belongings and drag heavy coffers and furniture to the stables, to be hauled onto wagons and borne to the abbey.

"You must get away, Dorset!" my mother cried when my brother walked into the Great Hall, where she was supervising the packing of the silver plate and tapestries that adorned the room. "God knows what Gloucester will do if he gets his hands on you—he's always hated you! Where will you go?"

"I shall go to Jane Shore," he said.

Mother gave a nod. Everyone except Papa knew that Dorset and Jane Shore had loved one another for years.

With Cecily's help, I gathered all our clothes and locked our jewels in caskets after putting on several of the rings. Then they couldn't be lost, and besides, they were pretty, especially a little gold ring wrought in the shape of a rose that Papa had given me. As twilight descended over London, the chambers emptied. Amid the chaos, a messenger rushed into the palace and fell to a knee before my mother.

"Your Grace, Gloucester is but a mere twenty-four hours' journey away!"

My mother gazed around in panic. "But there's so much still to be taken to sanctuary!" she exclaimed to her chamberlain. "Can you not work faster?"

"Your Grace, the treasure has been rolling into the abbey all day. Everyone is working as fast as they can. But some of the larger pieces get stuck in the passageways. They have trouble pushing them through."

"Then break down the walls between the palace and the sanctuary, you fool!" Mother exclaimed. "And work through the night! Gloucester will be here soon, don't you understand? We must have everything safe in sanctuary before he gets here or he'll steal every last cup!"

* * *

WE HAD AT LAST BEEN ESCORTED BY MY UNCLE ED-ward Woodville to the abbey with all of our belongings. As dawn broke, the Thames was drenched in glorious crimson and gold.

I'd slept fitfully, and at first light I climbed up to the high window that looked out on the river. There, with a cushion at my back, I listened to the cry of the river birds, the ringing of the church bells, the chanting of the monks. All seemed so serene. I closed my eyes, drank in the freshness of the air, tasted the tang of the river water. A sudden rap at the door came as a rude reminder that there was no serenity.

Mother stirred on the pallet where she slept, for we'd been too fatigued to set up her featherbed for the night. I climbed down from my window seat and went to see who had awakened us. It was Bishop Edward Story, my mother's old confessor.

"Story!" Mother cried, dusting off the straw from her hair and gown as she rose. " 'Tis good to see you, dear Story!" She gazed up at him with emotion. "We have been through so much! So much. We are in need of the happy sight of your kind face."

"Your Grace, I deeply regret your presence in sanctuary again. 'Tis a terrible reminder of the old days—the days we thought were past. Here is trouble, yet again."

Mother took his arm and drew him inside. "I wish I had something to offer you, but I have naught. No wine, no sweets. Not until the monks break their fast and fetch us some bread."

That wasn't quite true. Our coffers of gold and silver would buy us whatever we wished, once we arranged to purchase them. But Mother loved playing the martyr. My brother Dickon came to her side and hugged her knees. He laid his cheek against her skirts, and looked at Story. He was nine years old now, a beautiful child with an ivory and rose complexion, bright blue eyes, and hair as gold as wheat shimmering in the summer sun.

Story's gaze went from my mother to Dickon, and his expression turned even more somber. "Your Grace," he said, "regretfully, there is a grave purpose to my visit here this day." He hesitated. "If I may be so bold?" At Mother's nod, he continued. "As long as you keep His Grace, Richard of York, with you in sanctuary, the life of young King Edward V is secure."

My mother paled. She turned her gaze on Dickon, who was looking up at her with a puzzled expression. I had the sense that, until this moment, Mother herself hadn't fully comprehended what she had set into motion. Driven by fear and hatred, she had tried to seize power without assessing the risks of failure. Still, I was not concerned. George of Clarence, with his irrational behavior would have posed a clear danger, but not Richard of Gloucester. My Uncle Richard was loyal and prudent, and my father had placed his trust in him with good cause.

Noise and shouts suddenly came from the Thames. I scrambled up to the window, and a gasp escaped my lips when I looked out.

The White Boar emblem was everywhere; the entire river was covered with boats crowded with the Duke of Gloucester's men.

"What is it?" my mother breathed, standing motionless in the
middle of the room, clasping Dickon.

I swallowed. "Uncle Richard's men are guarding the river
entrances."

A commotion in the cloisters drew our attention to the door.
We waited, trying to decipher the meaning of the sounds: men's
voices; clanging armor; the long strides they took. For an instant,
time barreled backward and I was reminded of the precious moments before my father rescued us from sanctuary. We had thought
him dead in battle, and then the door had been thrust wide, and
there he stood, towering, magnificent, a shining golden god, smiling at us.

But the men standing in the open doorway did not smile at us.
Their faces could not have been more grave. I recognized one of
them: a dark-haired young man from the palace who had been a
Knight of the Body to my father. Our gaze locked, and I felt an
instant's warmth. Then his captain stepped forward, and gave my
mother a stiff bow.

"Who are you, and what do you want?" she demanded
haughtily.

"Sir John Nesfield at your service, Your Grace. We are sent by
His Grace, the Duke of Gloucester, to make sure you are comfortable." His gaze touched on our belongings stacked high, coffer on
coffer.

"We shall never be comfortable here. But at least we are safe
from our enemies," she said pointedly.

Sir John Nesfield, one of Richard of Gloucester's most faithful
retainers, raised an eyebrow, and made another stiff bow. "We shall
be outside, if you need us."

The door closed. I began to search the coffers. Moving stuff
aside, I came across a French grammar book. "Cecily, here's something for you, dear sister," I said, passing it to her. Then I picked
up my lute.

LATER THAT EVENING, THE MONKS BROUGHT US A
jug of wine, a pot of leek soup, and some loaves of freshly baked
black bread. I tore into this simple supper, thinking it more delicious than many feasts at the palace. When my mother and sisters
were resting, I quitted the chamber and moved into the cloisters
with my lute. A thin moon hung low in the dark sky, surrounded
by a myriad of twinkling stars, and the air was warm and fragrant
with the scent of roses, lilies, and a blossoming pear tree. The shadows of soldiers and monks flitted across the courtyard, and I knew
they all watched me, but I did not care. Taking a seat on a bench
at the edge of a pond in the herb garden, I strummed the chords of
my lute and raised my voice in song to the heavens:

> *We blow hither and thither,*
> *We know not whence we go,*
> *nor why.*
> *But memories are time's gift to keep*
> *They comfort still,*
> *And thou art there, though we see you not . . .*
> *Though we see you not.*

A vision of my laughing father engulfed me. Blinded by tears, I
lifted my eyes to the stars that sparkled in the night sky. Suddenly a
twig crunched underfoot behind me. I leapt to my feet and swung
around, my heart pounding.

"Forgive me, Your Grace," a man's voice said. He emerged from
the shadows. "I didn't mean to startle you. I followed the beautiful
melody, and it brought me to you."

It was the young man who had been Knight of the Body to
my father.

"Sir Thomas Stafford of Grafton," he said, with a bow. "You
have an exquisite voice, my lady. Like an angel."

I bit my lip to stifle the sob that threatened my composure.
"My father used to tell me that."

"Your father was a splendid king. Nothing is the same without
him."

"I know."

"I miss him sorely."

"Thank you," I said.

"Perhaps you'll sing again out here sometime?"

"Perhaps."

"Allow me to escort you back?"

I looked up at him as I took his arm. He had a finely chiseled profile and a strong jaw that somehow reminded me of Papa. I tore my glance away. *Memories are time's gift to keep; they comfort still.*

But do they? They felt more like something I had lost than a gift to keep. I drew an audible breath and steeled myself to move forward in the darkness of the night.

❁

THE BLARE OF CLARIONS AND THE RINGING OF BELLS erupted amid a sudden roar of cheering. I climbed up on a stack of coffers by the window to see what was happening. The river view was partially obstructed by other buildings and rooftops, and though I was tall, I had to stand on tiptoe to get a look.

" 'Tis my uncle of Gloucester! Our cousin of Buckingham is with him and they have Edward with them!" I said.

"I want to see!" Dickon cried. "Me, too!" four-year-old Kate demanded, as did eight-year-old Anne and even little Bridget.

"But you're all too small," I said. "You can't see even if I pull you up here on the coffers. But I'll tell you everything—I won't leave out a thing!" I turned my attention back to the street. The procession had moved, and I had to crane my neck awkwardly to see them in the distance.

"The three of them are riding in front! Edward is in blue velvet, and Buckingham and Gloucester are in black—"

Ear-shattering cheers nearly drowned my words. I stared at my uncle astride his white charger. How regal he looked! And though he was dark, I realized, with a twinge of my heart, that he reminded me of Papa. But then, why should he not? He was my father's brother. I strained to see him until he was lost in the crowds of the procession.

When my mother burst into tears I clambered down, drew myself to her side, and placed my arm around her shoulders. "Do not weep, dear mother. We know not what lies ahead, but my uncle of

Gloucester is a good man. He loved Father, and must surely love us too. All will be well."

❖

THOUGH WE WERE IN SANCTUARY, PEOPLE CAME AND went all day, delivering our purchases, caring for our needs, bringing us news. One of these was the butcher, John Gould. He had changed a great deal since the last time we'd seen him. I dimly remembered a man who was unkempt and frightening, for he had worn a bloody apron then. But the old man who stood before us bore no resemblance to my childhood memory. He was dressed most elegantly in a black velvet cap set with a jeweled brooch, an attire of rich green silk and camlet, and a black mantle edged with beaver trim over which was hung a massive gold chain.

"Your Grace," he said, flourishing a deep bow, "I am sore distressed to find you in sanctuary once more."

"John Gould," my mother said, offering her hand, which he kissed. "You are kind to visit, and I am pleased to find you have prospered so well since last we saw you."

" 'Tis thanks to your great kindness that I am a rich man now, Your Grace. You showed me much favor in appointing me the chief purveyor of meat to the royal castles."

"Had we prospered ourselves, no doubt I could have procured for you the office of mayor of London one day."

He gave my mother another deep bow. "God willing, you shall be back in the palace soon, Your Grace. In the meanwhile, I remain your faithful servant and shall provide your meats, whether or not you pay, Your Grace."

"Thank you, John Gould. Praise be to the Lord, we are not penniless this time and have no need of such charity as we did before Barnet. However, we would be grateful for your visits bearing us any news you deem we should have."

One piece of news we did receive came from a messenger to Bishop Morton, a Dominican friar.

"Gloucester has sent a request north for men to come to his aid," the man whispered. "He claims 'tis now clear that Your Grace was planning to murder him and his cousin, the Duke of Buckingham, and all the old royal blood of the realm—'by subtle and damnable ways.' His words, Your Grace," the Dominican said. "He has requested the north send him an army to protect him against you with all haste."

I turned my eyes on my mother. How could Gloucester believe her capable of such a monstrous thing, to murder innocent people merely for the royal blood that ran in their veins? What had she done to merit such a reputation?

An emissary newly arrived from the council urged Mother to leave sanctuary and return to court.

"So Gloucester can murder me?" she demanded, along with her haughty refusal.

She strode back and forth in her impatient way along one of the velvet partitions. "If Gloucester crowns Edward, he will have no choice but to receive us at court. Then shall I get my revenge on him!"

Several days hence, after nightfall, a rap came at the door. When I opened it, a cloaked woman stood before me, her face shrouded from view by a hood. She glanced over her shoulder in a way that denoted the urgency of her visit and slipped inside without waiting for an invitation.

When the door was shut, she dropped her hood, and I saw a woman of utter and incredible beauty, perfect in the lineaments of both face and body with golden hair waving around her delicate features. I knew instinctively that this was my father's well-known and exquisitely beautiful mistress, Jane Shore, now the mistress of my brother Dorset.

"I came to tell you that the Marquess of Dorset has fled England, Your Grace," she said with a curtsy to my mother. "You need not worry about him any longer. He is safe now."

"God be praised!" my mother cried.

But Jane Shore didn't return her smile. "That is the good news. I bring other tidings not so pleasant."

My mother's elation vanished. A hush fell over the chamber as we waited.

"These are dangerous days for a woman alone," Jane Shore said.

I realized she was embarrassed about something, and her next words made clear what that was.

"In the absence of the Marquess of Dorset, Lord Hastings has offered me his protection, and I have accepted. I have no children of my own and have always loved King Edward's sons dearly. Lord Hastings has confided to me"—her beautiful eyes filled with a troubled expression—"his fear that Richard of Gloucester plans to set his nephews aside and take the throne himself."

Our gasps of horror echoed through the chamber.

"How does he know this?" my mother asked.

Jane Shore threw a glance over her shoulder before she continued, "He knows they are plotting something, for there have been many secret meetings from which Lord Hastings has been excluded."

"But Gloucester is preparing to crown Edward as we speak. Why should I believe Hastings? He is no friend to us. He shared Gloucester's exile in Burgundy, and fought with him at Barnet and Tewkesbury. He limited the guard I wished to place on my son, and thus enabled Gloucester to seize King Edward at Stony Stratford. Why should he care what happens to my Edward now?" demanded my mother suspiciously.

"His love for your husband runs deep, and Gloucester knows that. He also knows that Lord Hastings took a vow to King Edward to protect his sons. In view of Gloucester's threat to the royal princes, Hastings now regrets his support of Richard of Gloucester and wishes reconciliation with you. He has sent me here to seek your agreement to smuggle your son Richard of York out of England, where he will be safe. My Lord Hastings hopes with the help of several others, among them Lady Margaret Beaufort and her husband Lord Stanley, to find a way to also free young King Edward from his uncle of Gloucester's grasp. Does he have it, Your Grace?"

My mother seized her hand. "He has it, Jane Shore."

We waited for further word. But none came. Until at last, on the thirteenth day of June, a nun arrived at our door.

"There is grievous news! The plot to free the sons of King Edward IV has been discovered," she whispered. "Lord Hastings was beheaded immediately, forced to lay his head on a log. Lord Stanley is in the Tower. Archbishop Rotherham is under arrest. Bishop Morton has been placed in Buckingham's care and sent to his castle of Brecknock in Wales. Mistress Jane Shore is in the Tower."

I looked up at the window where I had last seen my uncle Richard of Gloucester. How could I have been so wrong about him?

So horribly, horribly wrong?

CHAPTER 5

Niece of the King, 1483

EACH DAY WE WAITED FOR NEWS BREATHLESSLY, knowing that the momentum of events, like the torrent of a powerful waterfall, would not slow its current but would rush ahead with gathering force until it plunged over the precipice. Where that precipice lay, how sheer would be its fall, we dared not guess. In the meanwhile, tidings gushed into our ears, carried by all sorts of persons: servants, friars and monks, nuns and tradesmen, and those friends who were able to disguise themselves successfully past the guards.

"Beware, Your Grace!" came a whispered warning. "The Duke of Buckingham is a born orator who means to persuade the council to take Prince Richard of York from you in sanctuary!"

My mother clutched Dickon to her. "They will not get you!" she told him, smoothing his fair hair and kissing his tender cheeks. "I shall slay them with my bare hands, if need be!"

But late one evening, a royal delegation arrived, headed by Thomas Bourchier, the old Archbishop of Canterbury. While the lords waited in the Star Chamber in Westminster Palace, the archbishop and Lord Howard came to my mother.

"As you are well aware, Your Grace, we have made numerous efforts in good faith to induce you to come forth from sanctuary, and you will not," Archbishop Bourchier said, his face dour. Behind him, Lord John Howard stood at the door, his hair shining beneath his black velvet cap like the silver lion of his insignia. Howard had been one of Papa's most trusted lords, a Yorkist from the first, and remained true even after my mother took from him the dukedom of Norfolk that was rightly his, and gave it to Dickon. I could not tell where his sympathies lay, but I doubted we could claim them. "Therefore we have come here to take your son, Richard of York, from you, by force if necessary," Archbishop Bourchier said.

I gasped, and Cecily gave a sharp cry. Dickon ran to Mother and threw his arms around her skirts.

"You, an archbishop, dare make such a threat against your queen, and your God?" Stark fear glittered in her eyes. She tightened her hold on Dickon, who now clasped her skirts with all his strength.

"We go against you, not God. For valid reason."

"Give me one!"

"Your Grace, the council is afraid that if they allow Prince Richard to reside with you, you will send him out of the county under pretense of danger."

" 'Tis no pretense. He is in danger from Gloucester!"

"Madame, the truth is this. You hide your children under the wings of the church for no good purpose except to shame the rightful government of this land. 'Tis your own desire for power that drives you now, as it always has. King Edward—God assoil his soul—for the good of the realm, set you aside from governance, for knowing you, he feared you, Your Grace."

My mother was at a loss for words. She burst into tears.

"Your Grace, King Edward needs his royal brother's company," Archbishop Bourchier said more gently. "King Edward's brother must be present at his crowning. Allow us to take Prince Richard to join him at the bishop's palace. We have no desire to use force, but we are empowered to do so if you refuse."

My mother wiped her eyes and looked at him. She was trembling visibly, and her color had sickened to gray. But she was not yet ready to hand Dickon over. Since tears and defiance had failed to work, she attempted argument. The archbishop finally cut her off.

"Madame, I will not dispute the matter with you any longer. 'Tis the same to me whether you render him to me, or we take him, for the end result does not change. We shall have custody of Richard, Duke of York. There is one difference, however. If you give him up willingly, I pledge on my life and honor that no harm will come to him. If you do not, I shall depart immediately, freed of my trust, and determined never to concern myself with the matter again."

My mother had lost; she had to surrender Dickon. There was no way out. Her expression was one of utter wretchedness.

"You can take this gentleman," she said, her voice shaking. "But before you do, may I be permitted a moment alone with my son?"

Archbishop Bourchier inclined his head in assent.

Mother led Dickon to a far corner of the chapter house. All eyes were upon her as she knelt before him and took both his hands into her own. She spoke to him in hushed tones, every so often pausing to wipe away tears with the back of her hand. To her words, Dickon nodded his head obediently. I overheard her whisper, *Do you remember the password?* to which he nodded again, but what the password was that she gave him, I didn't know. As I watched their brutal farewell, my misery was so acute that it was almost a physical pain. Biting my lip, I looked away.

With a swish of her silk gown, Mother rose. "Farewell, my own sweet son! Almighty God be thy protector, Dickon. Let me kiss thee once more before we part, for God knows when we shall kiss again!"

Composing herself with effort, she took him to the archbishop.

"Into your hands I place my son, and my trust," she said, her voice hoarse with emotion.

As we gathered at the door, Archbishop Bourchier conducted Dickon to a deputy of nobles waiting far down the cloisters. We watched his small retreating figure. He looked back one last time before he disappeared, and even from the distance, I caught the sparkle of tears.

❊

MOTHER WAS DISTRAUGHT. SHE WEPT COPIOUSLY, AND I could do nothing, say nothing, to console her. Eventually she slept, though even in her sleep she cried out.

Unable to find rest, I stole out to the herb garden. Sir Thomas Stafford, the knight who had befriended me in the garden, saw me leave the chamber, as I hoped he might, and followed me across the green to the edge of the pond, behind the cloistered buildings. It was a cold night, and I had a blanket around me for warmth. We took a seat on the bench.

"How is Dickon, do you know, Thomas?" I asked.

"He is fine, princess. The deputy of nobles conducted him to Westminster Hall, and the Duke of Buckingham met him there. Then Buckingham took him by the hand to Richard of Gloucester, who waited at the door of the Star Chamber. Gloucester embraced your brother affectionately and conducted him to the bishop's palace. I'm sure he's fast asleep now, not like his sister." He gave me an arresting smile.

But I couldn't return his smile. I was desperate to ask him a question that I knew I shouldn't dare to ask. "Thomas, should we be afraid?"

Even in the moonlight I could see the astonishment on his handsome face. He took my hand into his own. "Elizabeth, my dear princess," he said. "Do you really think I could serve a cruel and wicked man—someone who is capable of hurting an innocent child?" There was tenderness in his tone and a probing query in his brown eyes as he gazed at me.

For a long moment, I looked back at him, at his open, handsome face that spoke of honor and integrity.

"No," I replied at length. "But sometimes, we make mistakes. We think ourselves a good judge of character when we are not." In my mind's eye, I saw myself in the sanctuary window watching Richard of Gloucester ride past, thinking what an air of nobility he possessed, how much he reminded me of my father, and then I heard Jane Shore's warning in my ear: *Richard of Gloucester plans to set his nephews aside and take the throne himself.*

"I hope I never disappoint you, my princess," Thomas said.

I turned my gaze on him. I took in the strength in his face, the compelling eyes, the carved features.

"You will never disappoint me, Thomas," I said softly. On impulse, I removed Mary's silver crucifix from around my neck and pressed it into his palm. "Take this, Thomas. To protect you from harm."

He lifted my hand to his lips, and my heart seemed to rush to the spot he kissed.

❖

I DIDN'T SEE HIM AGAIN FOR A WEEK. BY THEN, EVERY-thing had changed.

We learned from our laundress that my brother Edward's coronation, scheduled for Sunday, the twenty-second of June, had been postponed. On the very day it was to take place, a preacher named Dr. Ralph Shaw gave a sermon at St. Paul's Cross, implying that we were illegitimate and the crown belonged to Richard of Gloucester. It was an ugly sermon, and we were heartened to learn that no one cheered except a few men at the back of the crowd whom Buckingham had paid.

So it is true, I thought. I hadn't wanted to believe that my uncle of Gloucester, who had loved us and played with us when we were young, had been so utterly corrupted by the lure of a golden crown that he'd proved false to my father. Until this moment, I realized I hadn't truly believed that my mother had anything to fear from him. She'd always had a tendency to turn a sand hill into a tower. "O Bess, let it be," my father used to say. "You make a spectacle out of every small matter. People are not as wicked as you think. Let it be. Let it be."

But this time she was right. My uncle of Gloucester was indeed planning to set aside my two brothers and take the throne himself. Such was the man whom my father had loved above all others, in whom he had placed his full trust with his dying breath.

With the aid of friends like the butcher John Gould, my mother lost no time getting to work hatching a plot to rescue my brothers from the bishop's palace. Dr. Sergio, who had treated us since the first sanctuary days, proved a solid ally again. Many others streamed in and out with news, messages and hope. Then came shocking tidings.

Dr. Sergio regarded us with anguished eyes. "Your Grace, my dear ladies, I regret to be the bearer of vile and distressing news, too abominable to be believed, yet to its truth I attest. On Wednesday, the twenty-fifth day of June, your brother Anthony Woodville, Lord Rivers, was executed at Pontefract, along with your son Sir Richard Grey."

My mother fell to the floor, wailing and screaming, and beating her breasts, "Woe, woe! O dear God, no—"

From that dreadful moment on, the news grew progressively worse.

"Your Grace, Richard of Gloucester has proclaimed King Edward's marriage to you invalid and your offspring illegitimate!" Dr. Sergio reported.

The words he uttered roared in my ears.

"On what grounds?" cried my mother.

"Bigamy, Your Grace." At Baynard's Castle, Buckingham had declared Richard of Gloucester the rightful King of England. He stated that not only had my father's marriage to my mother led to "great misgovernment, tyranny and civil war," but that it was invalid, because King Edward stood troth-plighted to one Lady Eleanor Talbot, daughter of the old Earl of Shrewsbury at the time they were wed.

My stomach clenched tight, my heart pounded erratically in my chest, and I felt my entire body tremble as I listened. It was as if I had fallen into a dark river and its wild currents were sweeping me away to where I had no wish to go.

"Further, 'tis stated that King Edward's marriage was invalid because it was made in secrecy, without the agreement of the lords of the land and—" Dr. Sergio broke off and averted her gaze.

"What else?" demanded my mother. "What else do they claim?"

Dr. Sergio flushed. "They claim it was secured through— through—witchcraft. By you and your mother, Jacquetta, Duchess of Bedford."

My mother gave a gasp and swayed where she stood. The penalty for sorcery was exile or death.

Dr. Sergio gave us a hurried bow and departed, leaving my distraught mother seated in the corner of the chapter house, sobbing. This frightened the babes, two-year-old Bridget and three-year-old Kate, who joined their cries to hers, and refused to sleep.

"Mother, mother, come to bed. Don't let the children see you like this—" I pleaded, but she was deaf to all my entreaties.

We thought these were the worst tidings that could ever befall us until Dr. Sergio returned to attend my mother the next day.

"She has been this way since you left yesterday," I told him as we watched my mother weep.

He gave her a posset. "She will soon sleep," he said gently with pained eyes.

"Is there any further news?" I asked.

"I regret to say there is."

I indicated a pair of velvet chairs set against the wall, beside a niche that held a statue of Mary cradling the babe, Jesus. We took our seats; he leaned close.

"Buckingham offered the throne to Gloucester. He was reluctant to accept but—"

I waited.

"He took the crown. This morning, accompanied by a number of nobles, the Duke of Gloucester went to Westminster Hall and seated himself in the marble chair. From this day, the twenty-sixth of June, King Richard dates his reign."

Until this moment, the trembling that had seized me was a thing invisible to anyone but me, but now it burst into a shaking that convulsed my body. With great effort, I raised a hand to my dizzy head.

"I shall prepare you a posset, like your poor mother." He summoned Cecily to my side to hold my hand and took out his herbs and medicines once again.

My head was giddy, as if I had twirled a thousand times around the room. I felt nauseated; I closed my eyes. And again came that feeling that I was being swept away in a dark, rushing river—to where I did not know and dared not contemplate.

AFTER A WEEK OF NURSING AND SEDATION, MOTHER was back to her old self, pacing to and fro in the room and swearing vengeance on Richard III.

"I shall gut him alive like the traitor he is! I shall gut Buckingham as well. All who have injured us—anyone who took part shall suffer the full penalty of treason. How dare they set aside my sons!"

"All these lies," I said despondently. "Why are people so cruel, how can they make up such tales—" I looked at my mother for affirmation. She slowed her pacing but did not reply.

"They are lies, aren't they? All lies, Mother?"

"Of course," she said, but something in her tone struck a wrong note. Then she went to the door of the chapter house, opened it, and called out instructions to the nurse who played with the little ones outside on the green turf. From along the cloisters, Cecily's laughter floated back to me for an instant as she jested with our guards. I had a moment's longing for Thomas, whom I had not seen for nearly a week now.

Assailed by an inexplicable unease, I turned my attention back to Mother. "They are lies, aren't they?"

"Where is my ruby and diamond brooch, you know, the one in the shape of a peacock—" she replied, searching through one of her jewel caskets. "I know I put it here last week. Did someone take it?"

Sudden realization swept me. Now I knew for certain that my mother was hiding something. A chill gripped me as I rose from the rushes. I grabbed my mother by the arm and turned her toward me.

"Dear God, it's all true, isn't it?" I cried, dropping my hand.

My mother made no answer; she just looked at me.

"My father committed bigamy, didn't he?" I screamed. "You knew all along, didn't you? We are illegitimate—*illegitimate!*" I examined her face with horror. "How did he hide it so long?" Again, she made no reply. "He didn't, did he—Clarence found out, didn't he? Is that why he died? Answer me, Mother. I am entitled to know!"

My mother closed her jewel case with a heavy sigh. "Very well, I suppose you are."

We stood in the center of the chamber, and the dismal light of day seemed to grow dimmer with each word she spoke.

"Bishop Stillington, the man who married your father and that . . . woman, broke his silence. He told Clarence, just as I knew he would, God rot him."

"Why didn't Clarence tell Warwick?" I cried, trying to comprehend the knowledge that we were bastards, as Gloucester had claimed. "Why didn't Warwick use it against us before Barnet?"

"Warwick didn't know. He was dead by then. Stillington didn't tell Clarence until the death of Clarence's wife and child—whom Clarence in his madness claimed I poisoned."

"Did you?" I demanded. I did not know what to believe any longer.

My mother threw me a look of disgust. "No, but I would happily have had Stillington killed and be done with the whole business once and for all. But your father wouldn't hear of it." She quickened her pacing. "He sent Stillington to the Tower for three months, and released him after an interview. Your father always was soft. He fell for the old fool. Said Stillington had promised him never to divulge the secret again—'I never spoke of it before, Your Grace,'" she mimicked, "'and never will again! Believe me, sire, it was a momentary weakness brought about by too much wine and sympathy for *poor Clarence*—'" She spat on the rushes. "'Poor, grieving Clarence, whose misery touched my heart—'twill never happen again, sire. I swear it on my soul, sire.' And your sop of a father fell for his promise! And here we are! Here—" She slammed a silver tray from its perch on a stack of folded Saracen carpets and yanked a tapestry down. "Here we are in this hole! All thanks to your father. He hadn't the guts to be king. I was the real king! And he betrayed me, God damn him!"

Ripped from my shock by the fury that swept through my veins, I seized her arm.

"How dare you curse my father's memory! Papa had his faults, but 'tis to you we owe everything that has happened to us—the hatred of the people, the jealousy of the nobles, the wars, the blood—

we owe it all to you. To you, and your ambition, Mother! You will stop at nothing to get what you think the world owes you."

She slapped me. Without thinking, I slapped her back. She stared at me for an instant, stunned by my action, then struck me again, cutting my face with her ring. I felt a stinging pain and touched my burning cheek; I stared at the blood on my hand. Fury, hatred, and anger at the captivity and deprivation I had known for months in sanctuary blinded my vision. I gave a cry and lunged at her, yanking her hair with all my strength, kicking and punching her. We fell to the floor and tumbled over one another, tearing one another's clothes, scratching one another's faces, screaming our curses.

"How dare you? How dare you—after all Papa did for you, you witch—" I cried.

A gasp of horror sounded at the door. From the corner of my eye as I rolled around on the floor striking and beating my mother, I saw Cecily make the sign of the cross at my words. Then she screamed for help and several soldiers appeared at her side. They rushed in and grabbed me. They pulled me off my mother, and held her, for she attempted to strike me again as they pinned me by the arms.

"How dare you? How dare you—after all Papa did for you! Don't you dare insult my father's name in front of me again. We are here because of you," I screeched, hoarse with anger. "And you alone!"

✿

THE WASHERWOMAN WHO CAME, THE MERCHANTS who delivered us their goods, the soldiers, the servants who ran our errands and obtained small necessities for us still treated us with respect, but there was a subtle change in attitude and no mistaking our fallen rank.

"Dame Grey," said the yeoman farmer, "I have brought you fine plums picked from my own small orchard this day. See—"

My mother took one from him, but her eyes never left his face. No longer was she addressed as "Your Grace," for now she was not queen dowager but merely the widow of Sir John Grey, slain at the Battle of Northampton. As for us, we were bastards, without lands or money, except for what my mother had hauled into sanctuary.

I no longer played my lute, for my heart lay too heavy for music, but I liked to go to the garden after Matins, to be alone, to taste the air that was fragrant with the scent of herbs, to listen to the sound of the rushes sighing in the breeze. Above me the stars sparkled in the night sky, as they had for thousands of centuries. *They have heard all the cries of mankind, both of joy, and of sorrow; there is nothing new for them in mine.*

Sir Thomas Stafford finally returned. He found me one night as I stood at the edge of the pond. His voice came at my shoulder. "My princess."

His dark hair stirred in the breeze, and he looked so handsome, so pure. I smiled to see him again, and then I remembered. "You are aware of all that transpired in your absence?"

He nodded.

"Then you know I am not princess any longer."

"You are your father's daughter, and you will always be my princess."

We stood side by side, silently. In his presence, the furious rage and despair I felt about our circumstances abated. He took my hand and turned me to face him fully.

"Elizabeth—"

I lifted my blue eyes to his brown. 'Twas the first time he had called me by my name. And why not? I had no title; I was neither princess nor queen. And despite his words, I was even unsure if I could call myself "the king's daughter." Only one thing remained certain. I was still Elizabeth.

"Elizabeth . . . Surely you know? No matter what life brings, my heart is yours forever."

He kissed my hand tenderly, oh so tenderly! I moved nearer and before I knew it, his lips were on mine and my arms went around his neck. My heart was racing again, and once more I felt I was in a river. But this time the currents were sweet with promise and they bore me gently along through the glimmering night.

At last we broke apart to look at one another.

"Now that you are no longer princess to anyone but me, all things are possible, my beloved." He removed something from his breast pocket that glittered in the moonlight: a beautiful sapphire brooch in the shape of a star.

"I want you to have this. It was my mother's, God assoil her soul." He pinned it to my bodice and said softly, "It matches the deep blue of your eyes."

I gazed down at the brooch, swept with a wild sweet joy. As he took my hand to his lips, his eyes never left mine. I could not tear my gaze from his; I did not want this moment to end. I wanted to capture it and hold it to me forever.

But I knew I could not.

CHAPTER 6

Of Kings and Princes, 1484

THE SUMMER OF 1483 MOVED PONDEROUSLY. THOMAS departed to join King Richard and Queen Anne on a progress north to their castle of Middleham, leaving a large void in my life, and my mother grew despondent, for she missed Dickon, who had always been at her side to laugh and give her kisses.

"Are my sons well?" she'd ask our cleaning woman each day.

"Aye, well," the cleaning woman would reply each day, "though sure I am they miss you, m'lady. The princes, they're seen shootin' their arrows in the garden at the Tower, God bless 'em."

One evening in late July, in the twilight after Vespers, a knock came at our door. A priest stood before me.

"I am here to see Dame Grey," the man said. He seemed agitated. I stepped back, and he entered. He cast an anxious glance around, and then, with purposeful strides, approached my mother, who was seated at the table, embroidering by candlelight. He gave her a low bow, as if she were still queen.

"Your Grace, my name is Christopher Urswyck. I am in the service of Lady Margaret Beaufort and have come on a most urgent matter—" He lowered his voice to a bare whisper. "There is much dissatisfaction in the realm against the treatment of King Edward's sons. Efforts are underway to free the princes and depose King Richard. Will you grant your blessing?"

My mother set down her embroidery. Excitement brought a blush to her face. "Who leads the rebellion?"

"Lady Margaret Beaufort is the prime mover of the conspiracy, Your Grace. She is joined by her husband Lord Stanley; his brother William; her half-brother John, Lord Welles; and also by Edward Courtenay, and your own relatives and various other lords. She wishes to rescue your sons the princes from the Tower where they have been moved, and send them abroad."

"Lady Margaret has my blessing," my mother said.

SINCE KING RICHARD AND HIS QUEEN HAD LEFT London for their progress north to York and would be gone all summer, my mother and her allies were free to plot. The conspiracy was soon in full bloom with secret letters going back and forth, disguised messengers speeding all over the country, and armed men collecting at designated points. In addition to Christopher Urswyck, one other of Lady Beaufort's most trusted accomplices in her employ was a man named Reginald Bray.

"Matters have been made ready more speedily than we had hoped," Bray said, his furtive eyes darting around the room. "King Richard's absence has proven most helpful." He gave us a smile that I found oddly sinister.

As the days lengthened and then grew short again, the birds hurriedly gathered themselves into flocks and left to fly south. I watched them enviously. *To be free to go where one willed—*

I couldn't remember what freedom felt like anymore. Sometimes it seemed to me I'd been in sanctuary all my life.

One fall night, as rain fell in torrents, a knock came at the door. I opened it to find a Benedictine nun standing before me. "Dr. Argentine sent me," she whispered. I threw the door wide. Dr. Argentine was my brother Edward's beloved physician.

My mother rose from the table, where she was playing dice with Cecily.

The nun made her obeisance. "Your Grace, Dr. Argentine wishes to inform you he has been unable to see your son King Edward. No one seems to know where he is."

"But he is at the Tower," she said uncertainly. "He was moved from the bishop's palace some time ago."

"Aye, Dr. Argentine has been tending him at the Tower until this month. When he went there yesterday, however, he was turned away. The last time anyone saw the princes was in August, when King Edward and his royal brother were shooting arrows in the garden at the Tower."

The nun hesitated, then spoke again. "Dr. Argentine bids me to tell you that King Edward was suffering from an infection of the jaw that caused him pain and mired him in a sadness that sapped his well-being. He was making confession daily. For he expected not to live much longer."

My mother gasped, then leaned both hands on the table to steady herself. Cecily and I rushed to her side and helped her into her chair. "Didn't expect to live?" she repeated.

There was no further news. The waiting reached unbearable, laborious proportions. A sense of doom seemed to shadow us, felt even by the children. Seated at the table alone, my mother played dice morosely, with an absented air, as I stared into space, mulling my thoughts.

Thomas didn't return. My mother gave vent to her anxiety by pacing more feverishly, and I took to the prie-dieu to pray my heart out for my brothers, and for Thomas. Had the plot succeeded, or failed? Were they all safe, or—

Shutting my eyes tightly, I dedicated myself to my devotions. Not knowing what to ask God for, I left it in His hands.

❧

ONE THING THAT DID NOT CHANGE WAS THE STEADY procession of King Richard's emissaries, who came to request my mother to abandon sanctuary for court.

"Why?" demanded my mother haughtily. "King Richard has my sons imprisoned. Why does he need my daughters? Is sanctuary not prison enough for them?"

Sanctuary, I thought, watching her now, *has been especially hard on my mother*. Her mass of glittering jewels couldn't hide the fact that she was no longer beautiful, for in these months of confinement she had lost a front tooth and her figure had run to fat. To hide her pallor, she overrouged her cheeks, and her once famous gilt hair had grayed so heavily that it had to be dyed. Even her lashes had to be blackened with charcoal, for they had grown scanty.

"Dame Grey," the emissary said, "King Richard and Queen Anne are concerned for your daughters, and for your babes. The deprivations of sanctuary are hard on them. If you allow Elizabeth, Cecily, Anne, Katherine, and Bridget to come to court, King Richard vouches for their safety. He promises to grant them each an endowment and to find gentlemen of good repute to marry them."

My heart leapt in my breast. *Find gentlemen to marry them!* Oh, dear God, if Thomas was safe, if he was as willing as I believed him to be, there was chance yet for happiness, for love—

My mother's voice broke in harshly, "Never! King Richard shall have to drag our dead bodies out himself. But that should not prove difficult for a man without conscience, should it?" Clad in blue velvet trimmed with ermine, she stood rigidly erect near the central pillar in the octagonal room.

"I pray you, Mother—" I cried, stepping forward. "May we at least consider King Richard's offer?"

"What? Are you mad? You wish to wed some humble squire you who were betrothed to the dauphin?" She turned back. "Give your master my refusal," she said coldly.

The emissary bowed. I watched him leave, my heart plunging with despair, wishing with my every breath that I could draw him back.

In the days that followed, though I could still walk the cloisters and go to the pond, we didn't even see the merchants who provided our basic necessities. We were required to hand our lists and our silver to the guards, who placed the orders and delivered our purchases to us. We didn't even see our laundress, but would stuff our dirty undergarments in a pillowcase and hand them to the men-at-arms, who would deliver the laundered items back to us.

Our cleaning woman was one of the few persons allowed direct access to us, and it was she who delivered the latest blow.

"What is it?" my mother asked her as she entered with red, swollen lids, as if she'd been weeping.

"Terrible, terrible it is!" she cried, wiping her eyes. "Unnatural in the ways of man and God—m'lady, there's a rumor about the princes—something too terrible to be believed, yet it looks to be true. M'lady, the princes—'tis said the princes, the dear babes, are dead! Murdered."

It was at the altar of the prie-dieu that my mother beseeched her God for vengeance.

"Blessed Mother, Holy Virgin," she cried hoarsely, racked by sobs, "Thou who knowest what it is to lose a child, hear my plea— punish the monster Richard III who has taken from me all whom I loved! Take from him all whom he loves! Leave him bereft and alone! Destroy him with anguish and make him wish for death as I do!" She lowered her voice. "Blessed Mother, if Thou canst not or wilt not do this, then I call on those who can, though they be sinners. O hear my plea, hear my plea—I cry for vengeance on him who murdered my babes—who murdered my babes . . ." Depleted, she hung her head and collapsed against the wooden rail, weeping.

I shuddered at the grief that summoned her words.

❖

"YOUR GRACE, I COME TO YOU WITH HOPE FOR THE spirit that I am certain will soon heal you." The speaker was not Dr. Sergio, but another man, come to attend my ailing mother. I did not trust him and thought him surely one of Lady Margaret's spies.

My mother made a motion with her hand. "What is this hope you bring?"

"I am Lady Margaret's physician, Dr. Lewis," he whispered. "She has sent me with an urgent message for you."

My mother nodded.

"Lady Margaret wishes to inform you of a recent, unexpected and most welcome development. Henry Stafford, Duke of Buckingham, King Richard's cousin and his most trusted ally, has thrown his lot in with us!"

My mother and I both gasped at the same moment; she for joy, and I in distress. Buckingham was cousin to Sir Thomas Stafford. Was Thomas in on the plot? He hadn't said anything to me before he left on the royal progress. Surely that meant he didn't know? Either way, he stood in terrible danger now. Whether or not he took part in Buckingham's treason, he was condemned by his ties of kinship. I knew I'd barely sleep for worry about him.

"Lady Beaufort desires your agreement to smuggle your daughters abroad so they can wed princes who will continue the fight against King Richard."

It was finally arranged that Buckingham would lead the rebellion.

"Now is time for revenge!" my mother cried. "Down on your knees, everyone. Pray until your knees are raw! God willing, we shall soon dispatch this bloody usurper where he belongs!"

Then we waited.

IT WAS THOMAS WHO BROUGHT ME THE NEWS.
I was so elated to see his dear face as he passed me along the cloister in the first week of October that I halted, almost giving myself away. I resumed my steps to the privy and returned to the chapter house.

Thankfully, the heavy rains abated to a sprinkling by Matins. When everyone was asleep, I left to meet Thomas by the pond. The abbey clock struck the hour of midnight as I hurried over the damp turf. I threw myself into his arms and felt the rush of honeyed warmth and the great joy that always came to me with his touch. Then we drew apart and gazed at one another. Much had happened, and we were so anxious that we both spoke at once.

"How—"

"What—"

We fell silent at the same moment.

"You, first, Elizabeth," he said. "How much have you heard of what has happened?"

I seized his collar, drew his head close, and whispered, "My brothers have been murdered, Thomas! By King Richard, whom you thought an honorable prince!"

He caught my wrists. "Nay, 'tis not so."

I stared at him in bewilderment.

"King Richard murdered no one, and your brothers are not both dead."

"How do you know this?" I asked.

"I know it, as I know my own thoughts. Your brother Edward had an infection of the jaw, and may have died from it, for such things are often fatal, but no one knows for certain what has happened to him."

"I don't understand. How can this be?"

"Because he disappeared from the Tower."

"Disappeared?" I gasped.

"Hush, my love!" Thomas whispered, looking around.

I covered my mouth with my hand to stifle any further cries that I might make thoughtlessly. He took my arm and walked me to the bench, where we took our seats and placed our heads close together.

"Your brother Richard has also disappeared. No one knows what has happened to him, but 'tis believed he lives."

I closed my eyes on a breath and sent a prayer to God that it be so. "Now, I must speak—but you must swear never to divulge what I am about to tell you."

Thomas inclined his head solemnly. "I swear it."

"You are in great danger. Your cousin Buckingham has turned traitor and mounted a rebellion against King Richard."

I was stunned to find that this was no news to Thomas, for he smiled and took my hand gently into his own.

"My dear princess, Buckingham's rebellion failed, thanks in main to my brother, Humphrey, who blockaded the exits across the Upper Severn from Wales and destroyed the bridges. Buckingham's forces couldn't unit, so they dispersed. He was forced to flee."

I regarded him with stunned amazement. So King Richard wasn't toppled; my brothers weren't freed. But Thomas was safe. Tears blinded my vision as I regarded him. "I am relieved for you,

Thomas. But not for my brothers. If Dickon still lives, he is still captive, still in danger."

For a long moment, Thomas didn't reply. Then he heaved an audible sigh.

"Aye, 'tis a harsh, and brutal world," he said softly.

Dr. Lewis was the one who officially informed us of the failure of Buckingham's rebellion. "Lady Margaret Beaufort's lands and titles, and even her person, have been given over in trust to her husband, Lord Stanley, as punishment for her involvement. Bishop Morton, the priest Christopher Urswyck, and Lady Margaret's half-brother, Lord Welles, have fled to Brittany to join her son, Henry Tudor, Earl of Richmond. Sir Reginald Bray has been imprisoned, but thankfully, there have been few executions."

Until Buckingham himself, hiding in the north, was betrayed by a servant. He was executed on All Soul's Day, the second of November.

"The second of November," wailed my mother, sitting on the floor and rocking to and fro, "the second of November . . ."

The second of November was my brother Edward's birthday. He would have been thirteen.

I sank down into a chair and bowed my head in my hands. 'Twas a curious coincidence. The second day of November was a feast day as well as a Sunday. Executions were never carried out on such days, so it seemed Edward's birthday had been purposely chosen for Buckingham's execution. If King Richard went against custom to send a message, it had to be that for some reason I could not fathom, he wished Buckingham to die on Edward's birthday.

When Dr. Lewis brought news of Lady Margaret's plans to smuggle me abroad, my mother readily gave her assent. Perhaps I would be wed to a prince who would fight King Richard for the throne.

I was distraught; I could barely wait to see Thomas. But when I went to slip out of the chapter house that night, I found guards at the door. I looked at them in bewilderment.

"Mistress, you cannot venture forth at night. 'Tis no longer permitted."

King Richard must have known of the plans afoot, for the guards stood there both day and night, and I didn't see Thomas again.

✧

WITHOUT MY BELOVED, SANCTUARY FELT LIKE PRISON.
I couldn't even escape to the herb garden and be alone with my
thoughts. I was permitted to roam only as far as the circle of green
between the cloisters.

Lady Margaret Beaufort did not give up, however. Henry Tudor's determined mother, as scheming as my own ever was, sent Dr.
Lewis to Mother with an altered plan. If my mother would agree
to betroth me to her son, Henry would mount a rebellion to rescue
us and topple the usurper.

"I would betroth her to Satan himself, if he could rid us of
Gloucester and restore us to court!" Mother told him.

I bit down on my misery and averted my face to hide my emotion. I had always accepted this as my destiny, but that was before I'd
known love. Thomas had changed my world, and the possibilities.

Dr. Lewis came to us one more time after Christmas. Now I
learned that, days earlier in Brittany, Henry Tudor had promised to
wed me and prepare for invasion.

Dr. Lewis turned to me. I looked away, my heart filled with
aversion, my hands trembling. A smothered sob escaped my lips. I
fled behind the curtain and gave vent to my despair.

Meanwhile, as we sewed new gowns for Kate and Bridget and
repaired the torn hems of our dresses, the cleaning woman kept
us informed of all that was taking place in King Richard's happy
court. He celebrated a joyous Yuletide and held a disguising to welcome in the new year of 1484. In January he opened Parliament
and enacted laws to protect the common man from abuses of the
law.

"King Richard says innocent people should be allowed bail,
and no one should be put in prison unless he's proved guilty of
the crime he's accused of. A good law, I say," she proclaimed as
she scrubbed a section of tiled floor on her hands and knees. She
squeezed the water from her rag and bent back down. "An' he
says no one should have their property seized before they're found
guilty—seems that's in memory of poor old Mayor Cooke who
was persecut—" She broke off in horror, a hand to her mouth, and

looked at my mother, who had lowered her sewing to glare at her. "Oh, the babe—the babe just spilt some milk—there, there, no matter—Oona's here, Oona's a-comin'—" She rushed over to fuss over Bridget.

Oona went about her tasks without another word all day. It was useless to ask her what she meant, for it involved something my mother had done, and Oona wouldn't dare tell me. Our only other visitor was Dr. Lewis, and I knew he didn't approve of me for my protests against marrying Lady Margaret's son. I filed the information away in my mind, determined to know one day just what had transpired with "poor old Mayor Cooke."

But as I went silently about my own tasks, I wondered most about my uncle. How could someone who showed such caring concern for his people be so evil as to murder young children for a throne? He had even restored to John Howard the dukedom of Norfolk that was rightly his, which my father, at the behest of my mother, had given to Dickon. No injustice seemed to escape his notice, yet here we were. Thomas had assured me King Richard had not murdered my brother, Edward, although he may have died of natural causes. But what of Dickon?

Another royal emissary came on my birthday, the eleventh day of February, 1484. I had turned eighteen, and my thoughts were filled with my father and the carefree happiness of my childhood. So despondent was I that I could barely stir myself to open the door. The emissary, dressed in King Richard's colors of gray and crimson and bearing the royal insignia of the boar on his tunic, gave my mother a deep bow.

"King Richard offers greetings, Dame Grey, and states that he is prepared to pardon you and take a public vow to restore you to your dignity if you abandon sanctuary and bring your daughters to court."

"Pardon me for what?" she demanded. "For taking what belonged to us? Never will I accept anything from the man who murdered my sons!"

She turned her back on him.

My eyes met his, and a sense of sorrow and sympathy passed between us as I escorted him out. At the door, he turned and gave

me a gracious bow and kissed my hand with the greatest deference.
I knew from his look, without any words being uttered between us,
that we both wished things could be different.

March blew in on an icy wind that lifted swirls of snow in the
courtyard. Despite the cold, the North Walk was lined with clerics sitting on benches by tables and bookcases, and along the West
Walk others were washing. The sound of splashing water and the
voice of the Master of Novices instructing his charges filled the
cloisters as usual, yet something felt different. I felt it in my bones. I
climbed to the window, and what I saw then made me gasp. From
far down in the cloisters, King Richard, accompanied by a lone
companion, was striding toward us.

Heads turned as he passed the long row of rush-strewn chambers with doors cracked open for air. At the East Walk, which led
to the chapter house, he parted company with the noble. A hush
fell over the cloisters. The last time King Richard had come to
sanctuary was to remove Dickon from my mother's custody. Even
then he had sent as his emissaries Lord Howard and Archbishop
Bourchier.

He was close now—

"What is it, Elizabeth?" my mother demanded from the table,
where she sat stitching a hem, her needle moving swiftly in her
half-mittened hands. Her fingers paused their busy stitches, and she
looked up.

Outside, the captain of his guards snapped to attention. He
turned to unlock the door. I looked back at Mother. Everyone was
staring at me. I could barely find the words. "The king is coming!"
I cried hoarsely, clambering down. "The king is coming!"

We heard the hushed murmur of low voices outside our door,
then the clinking of the key in the lock. The door was thrown
open.

Richard III stood before us.

He looked most royal in a richly embroidered silver and black
doublet of velvet and cloth of gold that he wore beneath a gray
mantle edged with sable. There was a velvet cap on his dark head,
set with a jeweled boar of diamonds and rubies.

King Richard's gaze touched on us in the far corner, where I cowered with my four sisters. Here was the monster that had killed my brothers! Had he come to seize us? Would he slay us? What manner would be our death? Bridget was too young to die—only four, and Kate not much older. I held them tight to me, for they were frozen in terror.

I stared at him as he stood at the threshold, and thought that he flushed. But not with anger; it seemed more like shame. He waited until the door had closed behind him before he spoke.

"Dame Grey, I wish to set matters right between us," he said.

"Indeed? So you intend to take your life?" She hissed the words with the venom of a snake, and I stared at her. Was she brave, or a fool, to bait the boar? I saw King Richard's hand clench into a fist at his side.

"You do me an injustice," said the king, with dignity.

"*You*—" my mother cried, snarling the word, taking a step forward. "You dare to speak to *me* of injustice? You who set aside my marriage to Edward, who imprisoned me here and took the throne from my son!"

"Lady, you knew of my royal brother's bigamy long before the rest of us. You even murdered my brother George to protect your secret. As to your so-called imprisonment—guilt drove you into sanctuary. You disregarded King Edward's will and tried to seize power. That is treason by any definition, and well you know it."

"Are we to be blamed for protecting ourselves?" Mother demanded.

"By pointing a false finger first? That, madame, is how you have always justified your crimes against others. It was the same with Sir Thomas Malory, and Sir Thomas Cooke, whom you persecuted with false charges, and with Warwick, and with his brother, Montagu— and many others I never knew who paid for your ambition and greed and perished in the battles of your creation. You, Dame Grey, have much to answer for before God!"

"And you who dare judge me—'tis by your hand my sons are dead! May God punish you in eternity, you foul babe-killer!"

"Dame Grey, you condemn yourself with your words. For unlike you, who sent your executioner, the Butcher of England, to murder the Earl of Desmond and his two little boys—I have not stained my hands with infants' blood. As you'll soon learn from the lips of your son, Richard of York."

Mother's mouth fell open. So, I realized, had mine.

Was this true?

Had my mother murdered babes?

Was Dickon alive? Even my sisters stared at King Richard with their mouths agape.

"Dickon?" she murmured feebly, shuffling toward King Richard on unsteady legs. She searched his face. "My Dickon lives?"

I saw King Richard retreat as my mother moved forward, as if she were the monster, and he her intended victim. I felt utter confusion and disbelief. At that moment the door was thrust open and a grimy stonemason entered, carrying a pail and tools, his boy helper at his side. The door slammed shut behind them and my mother swayed where she stood. *"Dickon!"* she cried, stumbling toward him, her arms open wide. "Dickon!"

"Mother, Mother!" cried Dickon, running into them.

My mother fell to her knees. Her body racked by sobs, she clasped my brother to her breast and held him tightly to her, kissing his cheeks, wetting his soft face with her tears of joy. In the corner of the room, I dropped my hold of my sisters' hands, and they let go of mine, and we all came forward to gaze on Dickon in frozen, dumbfounded silence.

CHAPTER 7

King Richard's Court, 1484

FOR THE FIRST TIME SINCE MY FATHER'S DEATH, WE slept. O how we slept—so joyously, so peacefully, so hopefully! With this proof that Richard never harmed my brothers, Mother accepted King Richard's pardon and left sanctuary. Before she did, however, she wrote my brother Dorset in France that all was well and he should return to England. More than that, she dared not say. King Richard had given her the full story and a warning that no one must ever know that Dickon was alive—for his own safety.

King Richard, fearful for my brothers, had suspected there might be a plot to harm them soon after he took the throne. Therefore, he decided to move his nephews north, and hide them there, for safety's sake. But Edward could not be moved. He was ailing with an infection of the jaw, and his high fever precluded a long journey. King Richard took Dickon, as planned, and secured Edward a servant companion so he wouldn't be lonely in his brother's absence.

"Mother, where is Edward now?" I whispered after a guarded look around.

She closed her eyes on a breath, and when she looked at me again, they were filled with agony. "No one knows, not even

Richard—at least, not for certain, but he holds Buckingham responsible. While he was away, he received the news of Buckingham's revolt and of Edward's disappearance. Only Richard's good friend, Sir Francis Lovell, knows that Dickon was taken from the Tower and replaced by the servant boy. So the evildoers think they have both your brothers, Elizabeth. You must never breathe a word of this to any living soul. Richard fears Buckingham had accomplices, and that they are still about and would finish their vile work, if given a chance. Do you understand?"

I nodded. The image of Mother giving Dickon the password flew into my mind. One day, when they met again, no matter how many years passed between them, no matter how much he changed, she would know him.

Our belongings were packed up by royal servants and were delivered to my mother's country house in Hertfordshire, which King Richard had given her. We had the choice of moving in with Mother or going to court, if we preferred. 'Twas an easy decision for me and Cecily. But Cecily was overruled by Mother, who wished her presence in the country with our young sisters. As to be expected, Cecily was upset and blamed me.

I marveled as I was escorted to my room at Westminster Palace. It felt to me that I moved in a dream, so luxurious, so spacious were the palace chambers; so richly laden were the tables, so glittering were the gems, the silks, the damasks, and the velvets of the courtiers; so courteous were the servants, and the nobles, all bowing and curtsying in welcome. Court dazzled with color.

I had forgotten.

Queen Anne received me in the anteroom of her privy chamber. She was lovely and petite, with delicate bones and hair that shone a pale gold, but her eyes were her most striking feature; so unusual a shade of blue, they seemed violet. I towered over her as we embraced and I was enfolded in the scent of lavender.

"Child, welcome. It pleases us more than you can know that you are here with us." Taking my hand, she led me to a chair. "Pray sit by the fire, my dear, 'tis a cold day." She gazed at me, a sweet smile on her lips. "You are even lovelier than I remember. Your eyes are as blue as your sapphire brooch, and your hair is spun gold and has a hint of fire, as mine did when I was young. No doubt you shall have your pick of gentlemen to wed." Then her gaze went to my gown and her smile faltered. Though one of my best, it was stained and frayed from heavy wear and the hardships of sanctuary. "But you must have new gowns. Shall three suffice for now?"

"Your Grace, you are too kind. One would please me greatly," I replied shyly, not feeling completely at ease in such opulent surroundings after my confinement. Though I had been born in this very palace and should have been accustomed to riches, I had come to appreciate the value of a shilling. And three gowns cost a fortune, even for a queen.

Queen Anne gave me a glowing smile. "Would you like to be my lady-in-waiting, Elizabeth?"

"Your Grace, I am honored."

At dinner that first evening, she sat me at her side on the dais, next to King Richard's natural daughter, Catherine, who they called Cat. The curvaceous, green-eyed redhead looked older than her thirteen years and was betrothed to the Earl of Huntingdon. She had been conceived before Barnet, when King Richard, then Duke of Gloucester, despondent with grief, sought solace in her mother's arms after Lady Anne Neville was forced to marry Marguerite d'Anjou's son, Prince Edward of Lancaster. He had thought Lady Anne lost to him forever, but when her husband died in battle, he sought her hand. Though the young widow was a traitor's daughter and had no dowry to bring him, yet he begged Papa's permission to marry her. As I had learned from my father's head cook long ago, that was not the end of the story. For my uncle George of Clarence, to spite his brother, hid Anne away in a London kitchen. Months later, Richard found her and they eloped.

Unable to bear the loss of the man she loved, Cat's mother retired to a nunnery and gave over to Richard of Gloucester the keeping of both their children, Cat and her brother, Johnnie of Gloucester. Since then, there had been no hint that King Richard had ever taken up with another woman. I thought of the contrast with my father, who was said to have left bastards over all England and half of Europe.

A servant brought a platter laden with roasted rabbit and various

other meats. As was my custom, I declined. Without my mother
to harp at me, I felt no need to eat meat, and instead, chose from
among the wide array of food a wafer, a slice of pear, and a few
shelled nuts.

"You do not eat flesh?" asked Queen Anne in surprise.

"Sometimes I eat chicken, and sometimes fish, but I care not
much for either," I said shyly. Then I noticed that Queen Anne's
plate was clear of all flesh. "Your Grace, do you not eat meat?"

"I never touch it, Elizabeth. Since childhood I've had an aversion. My mother used to punish me, but she couldn't change me,
and finally gave up trying. Now 'tis my lord husband who frets and
worries that I'm too thin. Perhaps he'll let me alone now that he
has seen you. You are in glowing health." She smiled and patted my
hand beneath the white banquet cloth.

She is so slender she seems as fragile as a bird, I thought. Indeed, one
of King Richard's pet names for her was "my little bird." Perhaps
her disdain of flesh had something to do with her tenderness for
animals. "They are innocent, helpless," the gentle queen had told
me earlier in the day as she stroked a small, emaciated hound on
her lap that she'd rescued from the streets. "We cannot save them
all, but we must do what we can for those that cross our path."

I was the queen's steady companion as she visited the many
charities she had set up for the poor in the city. There were kitchens that ladled out soup to the hungry from dawn to sunset, and
hospices that took in the sick and dying; for those who needed
money, justice, or royal patronage, she stood for hours listening to
their requests and turned no one away. I had not seen anything on
this scale in my father's court, for my mother detested seeing petitioners, and never let the sessions run long.

I watched the exhausting, steady stream of petitioners come
through the state chamber: knights begging relief from taxes; squires
seeking a position in the royal household; nuns requesting funds to
repair a broken well; clerics seeking funds to take in an orphan
without means; illuminators requesting parchment to make a breviary. None were refused, and to all, Queen Anne gave generously
of both her purse and her time. I had never met a woman like her,
so pure, so kind, so totally without rancor, bitterness, or envy. As I

lay in my soft bed, I recalled the faces of the poor, the hungry, and
the sick who had called out blessings to her as she'd passed. "God
reward thee, O gentle queen!" they cried, kissing the hem of her
garment. "God save Good Queen Anne!"

On my third day at court, I learned that we were making a
royal progress north. Though King Richard would dispense justice
along the way, the main reason for the journey was to see their
son, for both king and queen sorely missed their child, Edward,
named for my father, who they called Ned. When a letter arrived
from little Ned's nurse, the king and queen put their heads close
and clucked over the news she sent, delighting in their child's antics and his progress in learning something new. At the end of the
missive came a few misspelled words from the child himself. They
admired his hand, finding joy in the sweetness of his expression as
they worked out what he had written.

"I look forward to meeting Prince Edward," I said, as I sat with
my sewing.

A dreamy look came into the queen's eyes. "I cannot wait to
see my son, Elizabeth. 'Tis as if the sun rises to its zenith when my
eyes rest on his sweet face." She looked at me and added, "You will
understand one day, when you have your own."

Richard entered the chamber with his nephew, Clarence's boy,
Edward, at his side. We rose and dipped into our curtsies, but he
had eyes only for his wife. He went directly to her, bent down, and
gave her a kiss.

"I was just telling my ladies about our progress north, to see
Ned," the queen said.

"Indeed, I thought it would never come!" King Richard replied. "But I am finally done with pressing state business and here
to tell you we can leave London in two days."

Joyous murmurs sounded around the room.

"M-m-may I c-come, too, L-lord Uncle?" stuttered a small
voice at his waist. Richard looked down at his brother's son.

My heart twisted with pity as I gazed at my little cousin. With
his rosy cheeks, bright blue Neville eyes, and wealth of wheat-
colored curls, Edward, Earl of Warwick, was a beautiful child and
exceptionally sweet-tempered, but his mind was weak, and he was

unable to comprehend at nine what most understood at five. When Uncle George of Clarence had died and left him orphaned, my mother prevailed on my father to grant his wardship to my brother Dorset, and Dorset, caring only for the child's wealth, abandoned him on one of his estates. Alone, unloved, untutored, and forgotten, little Edward of Warwick withdrew into an inner world while in the care of strangers, and many blamed my brother's neglect for the boy's condition.

"Of course you may, Edward. You don't think we'd leave you behind, do you?" King Richard tousled his fair hair.

I blushed with shame, but young Edward beamed, and King Richard and Queen Anne shared a smile with one another over his head.

Thus passed my first week at court. The king and queen spent every evening together, singing, reading, sharing laughter, and playing with their hounds. I had never seen such love, such a happy home, such joy in the exchange of a touch of a hand, a glance, a kiss on the cheek, and I thought with longing of Thomas, whom I had not seen since before Yuletide. I had written him but had not heard back. It seems he was sent to the Scottish border and given a high command, for his brother, Humphrey Stafford, was now one of King Richard's favorites and a most trusted ally.

One day, I thought, fingering the sapphire brooch from Thomas that was always pinned to my bodice, *when King Richard broaches the subject of marriage, I shall request Sir Thomas Stafford to be my wedded husband.* Then maybe I, too, would have a home like theirs, glowing with happiness and serenity.

IN THE BLUSTERY COLD OF A MARCH DAY, THE ROYAL entourage set out for their progress north to Yorkshire. King Richard was accompanied by his queen, some of his lords, and a great train of bishops, justices, and officers of his household. The crowds were sparse in the streets, and the procession only drew the curious, but those present remarked on the king's lack of an armed escort. When King Richard heard this remark, he said, "I rest my rule on loyalty, not on force."

What a kind and noble king he makes, I thought.

I saw my mother briefly as we passed through Hertfordshire. Her joy at the knowledge that Dickon was safe and in good hands was now marred by concern for my brother Dorset. He had left Paris secretly as soon as he received her letter, intending to reach England by way of Flanders. But at Compiegne, he was apprehended by Henry Tudor's men and brought back to Paris, where he was placed under guard. I gave my mother a hug, promised her my prayers, and begged her not to worry. As always, Cecily was cold to me. When I tried to embrace her, she stood as still and hard as a frozen leg of mutton.

"What is the matter, Cecily?" I asked.

"Don't feign ignorance!" she retorted.

"Of what?"

"That she has to marry Ralph, Lord Scrope of Masham," replied my sister Anne.

"You've sent me to live deep in the country to wither and waste away," Cecily bawled. "I hate you, Elizabeth!"

"Cecily, I have no influence with the king and queen and had naught to do with this. You shouldn't have flirted with Scrope and made him fall in love with you when he came to court two years ago. 'Tis your own fault."

"I know you're behind it! You shall probably wed a king somewhere and be queen, and live at court and throw disguisings and feasts, and wear jewels and satin gowns. It's not fair!"

Then she burst into tears again, and nothing I said persuaded her that I was not responsible for her misery.

We crossed the River Rhee, climbed atop hills, traversed valleys, and passed through wintry woods where narcissus and snowdrops peeked through half-melted snow to brighten our path. Our progress was slow, for King Richard wished to hear the petitions of the common people and to dispense the king's justice wherever he passed. No matter seemed too small for his attention. In the villages and hamlets along the way, he was welcomed with pageants and processions and offered gifts of money. But each time, he refused.

"I would rather have your hearts than your money," he said. Then he made the people gifts of his own. In Stanstead Abbotts it was a grant of royal forest land that would greatly ease their burden gathering food for their families; in Barwick, it was a charter of liberties. And everywhere, it was justice. Tirelessly, he presided at the local courts and heard the complaints of the poor. Patiently, with probing questions, he arrived at the truth, and punished offenders.

I thought of a line from Malory—

> *He rooted out the slothful officer*
> *Or guilty, who for bribe had winked at wrong . . .*
> *Clear'd the dark places and let in the law.*

Justice, I realized, was King Richard's passion. Why he cared so much that the law be dispensed fairly without regard to one's station in life, I couldn't fathom. Everyone knew that the nobles stood above the law, and always had. The world was a place where the strong did what they wished, and the weak suffered what they must, and never would that change. Yet King Richard seemed determined to make a difference. Many a heart was gladdened by his visit.

We finally reached Cambridge, where we would rest for a few days before progressing north to Nottingham. Though I had noticed that King Richard owned an extensive library of well-worn books, it still surprised me that he, unlike my father, had a scholarly bent to his mind. He indulged himself in two days of lively discourse on moral philosophy and Latin theology with the chancellor and eminent doctors, and before we left, he bestowed generous grants on the university.

I had been at court only ten days, and already I found much to admire in King Richard and Queen Anne. Here, it seemed to me, stood a true knight from the pages of King Arthur's tales, and at his side, his true love fair.

"King Richard knew Sir Thomas Malory, didn't he?" I asked Queen Anne as we rode along in the cold sunshine.

"Aye, he knew him. But Malory was Warwick's man, and in the end they fought on opposite sides at Barnet. But my lord husband didn't fault him for that, for Malory was a good soul, and had suffered much in life. The law that my dear lord enacted in January, giving the right of bail to the innocent, was in Malory's memory." She let out an audible sigh. "Poor Malory, he'd been confined to prison and denied trial for ten years for offending persons in high places. My father had him released when he returned to England with the Lancastrians, but he didn't live long after that . . ." her voice drifted off.

I averted my face. One of those "persons in high places" was my mother. Evidently, the queen didn't think I knew of her involvement in Malory's persecution.

"Let us speak of more pleasant matters," said the gentle queen, more brightly. 'Tis a splendid day, is it not? Listen to the cries of the blackbirds. How loudly they shrill! Truly such melody is God's gift to us."

But that was the last bit of sunshine we saw, and it was a dreary, drizzling morning in late March when we rode up the hills encircling Nottingham, the royal retinue clattering behind us. High above towered the massive fortress of Nottingham Castle, built on a jutting outcrop of rock that glistened black in the rain. Queen Anne reined in her palfrey.

"What's the matter, dear lady?" inquired the king.

"I don't know, Richard . . . It must be the weather," she said. "Nottingham seems gloomier than ever this day."

"Aye, 'tis indeed a dismal place despite all the money Edward and I poured into it. Even my new tower with its spacious royal apartments and oriel window scarcely seems to brighten it up."

" 'Tis not a place that can be brightened, Richard. It has an air about it."

King Richard gave her a rueful smile. "We'll not stay long, my love."

But affairs kept King Richard in Nottingham far longer than he anticipated, and the queen grew restive and ever more anxious to leave the gloomy fortress behind for Middleham Castle and her son's embrace. March gave way to April and still we could not depart. Easter found us at Nottingham.

"I swear to you, my flower-eyes," King Richard told his queen, "once we have celebrated the Feast of St. George we shall leave the very next morning."

At Nottingham, on the fourteenth of April, we observed the anniversary of the death of Queen Anne's father, the Earl of Warwick, and his brother, John Neville, Marquess of Montagu, who died together at Barnet in the Lancastrian cause. But the Feast of St. George that followed that somber day banished gloom, for the twenty-third of April dawned bright with sunshine. Church bells rang over rolling meadows, which glittered with white and gold wildflowers. Kegs of wine were rolled out into the streets, and everyone drank and laughed. The banquet in the Great Hall that evening was wondrously merry, with a troubadour to recount tales of King Arthur's court and a mummer disguised as a sorcerer to conjure feats of amazement.

When the feasting was done and the tables in the center of the chamber cleared away for dancing, the minstrels broke into a pavane. King Richard offered his hand to Queen Anne, and they took their places on the floor. I noted that the head minstrel had slowed the pace for Queen Anne's sake, for she was as delicate as a snowdrop. Even this small exertion soon tired her, however, and by the time the brief melody had ended, she was out of breath. King Richard led her back to the dais and took his seat beside her.

I danced with my cousin, Jack de la Pole, Earl of Lincoln, King Richard's nephew by his older sister, Lisa. Jack was a merry fellow with bright eyes and red cheeks who loved to jest and place wagers and was never still. I was twirling under his raised hand and laughing at a joke he'd made when, from the corner of my eye, I caught sight of something that stilled my gaiety. At the back of the hall, coming toward the dais, a noble lady dragged herself forward, leaning heavily on a retainer's arm.

" 'Tis the Countess of Warwick—" Jack murmured. "She never leaves Middleham . . . never leaves her grandson's side."

I saw that Jack had gone pale. He turned his eyes to the king and queen, and I followed the direction of his gaze. They were frozen in the moment, their eyes riveted on the countess, their faces white as phantoms.

Clad in a black robe and mantle, unadorned by jewelry, the queen's mother, the Countess of Warwick, shuffled forward, her face contorted in anguish. Her dark figure contrasted strangely with the glittering jewel-colored silks and velvets of the other guests. The minstrels ceased their song and a hush fell over the hall. We stared, then opened a path for her. She reached the dais and stood before her daughter and King Richard, her mouth working with emotion. Slowly, so slowly they didn't seem to move, the king and queen rose from their chairs.

"Ned," the countess said, "Ned, our beautiful boy—is dead—"

"*No!*" moaned King Richard through bloodless, trembling lips. He stepped back and his chair crashed to the floor. *"No! O God, God, no—"*

He was covering his ears; he looked as if he would drop to his knees. He staggered to the wall. Reaching out, he caught the cold stone mantelpiece as his knees gave way. Queen Anne let out a long, guttural half-human wail and fled down the dais, a quivering madwoman, running from wall to wall like a cornered animal until there was no breath left in her. With wild eyes she cast about. Putting her trembling hands before her, she fumbled forward. Her legs collapsed beneath her and she swooned to the floor in a heap.

✿

THE COUNTESS MINISTERED TO HER DAUGHTER AS she lay in her bed, tossing wildly and crying out for her son. And her husband sat sleepless in his chair, holding her hand, keeping vigil at her side, grieving silently. I saw them in a tableau each time the chamber door was cracked open to let a servant pass, and the sight shredded my heart.

How hard it is for him, I thought; *to be a king, to lose an heir; to go on with royal duties as though nothing has happened.* He had put them aside for two days now, but soon they would clamor for his attention. Pity tugged at my heart. He looked slovenly, unkempt; not much like a king at all or even the old fastidious King Richard I had met only a month ago. For two days he had not shaved or bathed, and his white shirt, dingy and stained with perspiration, hung open at his neck. The stark pallor of his face heightened the darkness of the growth shadowing his chin as his stricken gray eyes stared mutely at his wife. Sometimes his lips moved, but I couldn't make out the words. Then one day, I heard him gasp for breath, close his eyes, and murmur, "Forgive me, Anne—Forgive me!"

I couldn't imagine what he thought he could have done.

Along with the physician and the servants tending to the king and queen, the countess moved about the gloomy chamber like one risen from the dead, bringing food and drink, which was returned untouched. From time to time, the weary woman would leave the chamber and, shutting the door behind her with utmost care, collapse on a window seat in the anteroom; sometimes she closed her eyes; sometimes she just stared out into the darkness of the night. I regarded her with a depth of sorrow. She had been orphaned, and widowed; she had buried a daughter and lived to see the destruction of the great House of Neville. But perhaps nothing she had endured compared to this shattering grief.

I inhaled a sharp, pained breath. *'Tis not only their child they have lost,* I thought, my eyes touching on the queen asleep in the curtained four-poster bed and moving to the king grieving silently at her bedside. *They have lost their future and their hope.*

We journeyed to Middleham. As the royal procession wound its way mournfully north, the king's lonely figure rode ahead. Every so often, he cast back at his queen's litter anguished looks of torment and sorrow. I longed to go to his side, take his strong sunburned hands into my own, and comfort him.

The townspeople gathered to watch us pass. Some crossed themselves and wiped tears from their eyes, while others looked on with hard faces. For now it was being murmured that this was surely divine retribution. Ned—King Richard's ten-year-old Edward—had died on the anniversary of his namesake, my father King Edward IV, the child being the same age as one of my brothers.

Wild grief ripped through me. *No!* I wanted to scream at them. *King Richard is innocent. My brother Richard lives!* But since I could not, I rode onward silently. Across the fields, near a village, we saw maidens dance around the colorful maypole, but we did not hear their song, and their gaiety touched us not. We journeyed on at our slow pace. On the sixth day of May, Middleham Castle rose up before us. Sunlight filtered through an opening in the clouds like rays sent from heaven, illuminating the black-draped castle in a strange, pearly light.

" 'Tis Ned's birthday today," said King Richard's son, Johnnie of Gloucester.

A ponderous silence fell over all who heard. I couldn't believe the Fates would be so cruel, to send a father to bury his son on his child's birthday.

There was no relief for King Richard and Queen Anne. Ned had died, and neither of them had been with him. Even harder to bear was the knowledge that he had suffered. Queen Anne sat in a carved chair on the dais in the Great Hall at Middleham Castle, clutching Ned's worn velvet blanket, while King Richard stood stiffly at her side, white-knuckled and unmoving, his face ashen. Together they listened to a procession of doctors, clerics, and servants who related the terrible details of Ned's passing.

He had fallen ill with a bellyache in the middle of the night on Easter Monday after a pleasant dinner and evening of music, and the doctors could do nothing for him. He was in great pain to the end and had cried out for his mother. My gaze went to the queen, who closed her lids and swayed in her chair. He had died the next day.

King Richard had to practically carry Queen Anne from the room, for she could barely stand. In their bedchamber where Ned used to play chess with them and read poetry, the king's son, Johnnie, sat with Clarence's son, Edward, by the cold fireplace. Eyes red-rimmed, their cheeks tear-stained, they stroked Ned's dog, Sir Tristan, as the other hounds watched. Even the animals mourned Ned, for they lay silent, chins flat on the cold tiled floor, a knowing, sorrowful expression in their eyes. In the corner where King Richard's suit of armor hung beneath a tapestry of the Siege of Jerusalem, Clarence's daughter, Margaret, and Richard's love child, Cat, knelt at the black-draped prie-dieu together.

When the king and queen reached the threshold of their room, they halted. Directly ahead, in full view of the window, stood the tall elm where Ned's archery target still hung. The boys rose slowly, followed their gaze, saw the tree. Their faces crumpled. Young Edward of Warwick ran to them, threw his arms around Anne's skirts.

"L-Lady a-aunt," he cried in a strangled voice, unable to control his stutter, "w-w-why did N-Ned have to go? D-Did God n-not kn-know I w-would have g-g-gone for him?"

Queen Anne burst into tears and sank to her knees. She clasped her sister's child to her breast and opened her embrace to young Johnnie, who rushed to her. Cat and Margaret ran to her, too, and King Richard knelt and put his strong arms around them all. Together they huddled on the floor, all weeping, except for Richard, who stared over their heads with a blank expression.

To King Richard fell the duty of arranging his child's funeral. He knew, too, that this blow could kill his queen. Borne in the cart beside me, she was feverish, ailing, and she coughed as if her chest would shatter. I exchanged an anxious look with Cat, who rode beside me. Her father had lost his only son and heir and now might lose his wife, the childhood sweetheart he had adored for as long as anyone could remember.

Such love; such grief. Was it always so in life? I wept at their misery, my eyes lingering on the lonely figure of the king riding ahead.

Even at night, I found myself unable to stop thinking of King Richard, whose silent agony was wrenching. I wished to help him, but there was nothing I could do.

CHAPTER 8

Good Queen Anne, 1484

THE NORTH MOURNED WITH KING RICHARD AND Queen Anne, but in the rest of England men murmured that Ned's death was divine retribution. Had he not died on Easter Monday, the anniversary of my father's death? In the taverns, the blacksmith shops, on the farms and in the manor houses, people crossed themselves and muttered that never before was the hand of God seen so clearly. Some who had not believed King Richard had done my brothers to death before were persuaded now. And I could say nothing. *Nothing to anyone.*

King Richard was not told what his people believed, but it was obvious that he knew, and whom he blamed for the rumors: Henry Tudor. Like me, he had heard the whisperings in the castle, read the condemnation in the eyes of the villagers and townsfolk the nearer we rode to London. Even I found it hard to bear the mute pity on the faces of those who believed Ned had been poisoned. Out of nowhere had come this rumor, to be added to the rest. It was clear that the queen believed it, and clear whom she held responsible for the death of her child. In her drugged sleep she kept crying out "Poisoned . . . Tudor . . . Poisoned . . . Ned, O my Ned—my babe—"

Henry Tudor's name had become the hissing of an adder in the privy chamber of King Richard and Queen Anne.

The steady clippity-clop of horses' hooves filled my head as the queen's litter wobbled along beside me. My heart twisted in my breast. It was July, three full months since Ned's passing, and the queen was ailing, unable to ride, with scarcely enough strength to sit up. It was no wonder. She didn't eat, didn't sleep. After Ned's funeral, King Richard had removed her from the oppression of Middleham and taken her to Barnard's Castle, where they had spent the first honeyed weeks of their marriage, but to no avail. From there, he moved her to York, where the townsfolk had surrounded her with an outpouring of love, then to the hills of Pontefract where the air was cool; then to the sea at Scarborough, where it was fresh. But she was a mother who had lost her only child, a woman who could never bear another; nothing helped ease the affliction that ailed her. All laughter was gone; there was no music for her anymore, no joy at all.

Again, my gaze went to King Richard, riding ahead, casting anguished glances back at his queen's litter. The rumors Henry Tudor put out about him plagued him to misery, for they struck at his core, attacking his good name and his honor, for which he had made such sacrifice all his life. All over the land, placards nailed to church doors proclaimed King Richard the murderer of his nephews, a tyrant, a usurper. But the worst rumor of all was that God, in an act of divine retribution, had seized King Richard's own son. *A Prince Edward for a Prince Edward.*

Aye, Tudor was much on King Richard's mind these days. After months of naval warfare with Brittany, he'd managed to force Brittany to sue for peace. As part of the agreement, Tudor was to be returned to England, but Tudor, well served by either friends or fortune, galloped across the border into France, his pursuers hard on his heels, and reached safety barely minutes ahead of them. King Richard had signed the truce with Brittany anyway, and tried to make a treaty of amity with France, as he was doing with Scotland. But France, though weak and divided by the problems of a minority reign, was united against him. They thought him an enemy of the realm, a notion bequeathed them by the Spider King, Louis XI, whom Richard had offended by refusing his bribe during the expedition to France. Now France sheltered Tudor with promises of aid. Richard's spies had sent word that he would invade England in the spring with a French army at his back.

London loomed against the horizon. King Richard drew in his reins and stared ahead. The royal procession came to a silent halt. I knew he was bracing himself. He had always hated London; it was why he had avoided my father's court. He was a man more at home galloping across the moors with the wind in his face, and his friends were men like himself, who spoke bluntly and didn't hide lies behind their smiles. I followed his gaze as he stared mutely at the line of city wall, towers, steep roofs, and bridges that he had always hated. At the winding river crowded with boats, barges, and ships. At the dingy gray skies.

The sun was not shining on London this day.

※

QUEEN ANNE SEEMED TO WITHER AWAY AS I GAZED. Always frail, she was unable to fend off the sickness that ravaged her. As I sat in her bedchamber at Westminster Palace, waiting to be of service to her mother, the countess, I knew beyond doubt that Queen Anne had lost the will to live. She seemed to welcome death, to embrace it as a blessed release. But if the queen died, what would become of her king?

A stir in the antechamber announced the arrival of King Richard. We stood and curtsied, Cat and I, but he didn't notice us. His gaze was riveted on the delicate form on the bed, sleeping now, thankfully. I watched him cross the room to her side. He was dressed in plain black saye, unadorned by a girdle or mantle; the tight-fitting cote and long hose that molded his strong muscular body were unrelieved by any trimming, not even a gold collar. He wore no jewels except the sapphire his queen had given him, and another, shaped in the image of a gold griffin, and his own signet ring. His complexion was ghastly pale, his cheeks were sunken and sharply drawn, and pain was etched mercilessly in the lines around his eyes and mouth.

The countess vacated her chair beside the queen's bed. The king sat down, and took the queen's hand into his own. Bewailing my own helplessness, I almost cried out as I watched him. There was naught to do but pray—and how I had prayed! Amid the tolling of church bells, the flickering of candles, the chanting of monks, I had prayed for the sweet queen—for a posset, a charm, for something that might save her.

I turned my tearful gaze to the dismal sky. A silver flash came and went in the gloom, lighting the dark clouds for a bare instant. Though I knew it was only lightning, it felt to me like a gift from God, for it brought with it a revelation. *I am not helpless; there is something I can do!* If the queen were to recover, then King Richard could endure, could go on, do his great work changing the world. Queen Anne was letting herself die because she was unaware of her husband's agony. If I could make her see that she was taking him away with her, maybe she'd find the will to recover.

I knew I had to speak to the queen, and I found my chance the next day. The countess left to rest and handed me charge of the royal bedchamber. I slipped into her chair and threw a glance around the room, empty but for a tiring maid who moved quietly about, smoothing a cushion here, exchanging a burned-out candle there. I took a wet rag from a bowl of rosewater set on a small table beside the queen's bed and wiped her damp brow. I handed the basin to the tiring maid and asked for fresh water. She nodded, and quitted the room to do my bidding.

Queen Anne stirred and gave the whisper of a moan.

"My lady queen, may I speak?" I asked hesitantly, drawing near and kneeling by the bed. The queen opened her eyes and looked at me. "There is something you—something which—" I paused, rushed on. "I have no right to speak of it but . . . but . . ."

The unfocused look left her eyes, and they took on a puzzled expression. Then she blinked with astonishment. Reaching out a limp hand, she touched my hair, my face, as if marveling. I had no idea what was on her mind.

"I thought . . . I was seeing myself . . . we look alike, Elizabeth. I never . . . noticed before," she explained.

"My lady queen—" I said anxiously, not wishing to be diverted. "There is something I need to tell—" I fell silent, suddenly ashamed, and averted my face. *What am I doing? I have no right to meddle in private royal affairs!*

"Speak, child," the queen whispered, her voice labored, breathy. "What . . . is it . . . you must tell me?"

I regarded her. She was waiting expectantly. I had no choice. I braced myself and continued. "My lady queen, forgive me, 'tis about your lord husband, the king." Again, I lost my courage and dropped my lids.

I felt the queen's eyes on me. Not daring to look at her, I folded and unfolded a pucker of silk sheet. Her hand came to rest on mine, her touch as light and warm as a gentle breeze. Courage found me again.

"My lady, I fear for the king," I blurted. "He is in great pain, but he mourns in silence. He needs you, Your Grace; he is so alone. The entire way from Nottingham, he rode ahead of your litter and cast back looks of such longing and sadness that I—I—" I broke off again, unable to meet the queen's gaze. I couldn't confide in Queen Anne how my heart had contracted to see his lonely figure riding ahead, how I had longed to gallop to his side and comfort him. "You must get better or I fear the king . . . the king . . ." I swallowed and looked away in confusion.

The dainty hand squeezed my own. "Speak," commanded the soft voice. I lifted pained eyes to the wasted, once lovely face. "Without you, I fear the king may not survive." I bit my lip to hold back the tears that threatened.

There was a long silence. The queen stared at me, then nodded and spoke. I bent my head close to catch the words.

"Thank you, dear child," she murmured.

From that moment on, the queen directed all her energies into getting better and forced herself to take nourishment. Though it made her nauseated, she swallowed hot broth, ate honey, and chewed boiled nuts and raisins. Exertion was taxing, almost painful for her, yet she rose from bed and struggled to stand on shaky legs. She even managed to walk with the aid of two canes. King Richard's joy in finding his queen improved moved me deeply.

"My dearest," he said joyfully, taking her hands into his own, "now that you're better, we'll leave for Nottingham! I had no wish to leave earlier—" He broke off.

I knew his thoughts. He should have gone to Nottingham to prepare for Tudor's invasion. From there, he could be anywhere on the coast quickly, for Nottingham lay in the middle of the country. But doubting his queen's recovery, and facing a bleak future without her, he had made no effort to meet the threat of Tudor's invasion.

We spent three days at Windsor, one of the queen's favorite castles. While King Richard was kept busy with state affairs, Queen Anne sat by the window, drawn by the beauty of Windsor's scenery with its rolling hills, emerald woods, and serene river. She held in her hands King Richard's book, *The Vision of Piers Plowman*, about the weary plowman who dreams of a better world, one where injustice is remedied. On our last day there, leaning heavily on my arm, the queen managed a short stroll in the garden, which was rich with summer blooms. We reached the pleasure garden near the Round Tower and paused, looking down at the river and manicured hedgerows. "What is the date today, do you know? I seem to have lost count," the queen asked.

"The twenty-second of August," I replied.

"How fast the summer is passing!" the queen said sadly. She glanced up at the sky and I followed her gaze. Vivid turquoise; no trace of a cloud. "Such a beautiful day," she whispered.

I looked at the sad, childless queen, clad in her black garb of mourning. "You should be in bed, my lady. The wind is chill. The king will not be pleased."

"The wind is chill, but the sun is hot." The queen smiled at me. "Fret not, child. I can't stay in bed on such a day." She halted on the high grassy slope, suddenly winded. "We shall await my lord here."

Trailing servants set a high-backed chair next to a stone bench by a cluster of rose bushes and withdrew a respectable distance. As she settled into her chair, her glance swept the garden, where she herself had directed the planting of flower beds and hedges the previous summer. Now it was alight with roses, lilies, and violets. Birds celebrated the glorious morning, and from the trees and woods came the song of wood pigeons, wagtails, and larks, while from the pastures outside the castle came the bleating of sheep. A yellow butterfly flitted past, and the queen followed it with her eyes until it disappeared around the hedges. Down on the river's edge, two white swans glided in the jade waters. A wistful smile touched the corner of her lips as she gazed at the birds that mated for life.

I stood stiffly, ill at ease about the whole business. The doctors had warned against such exertion, and King Richard would surely be distressed.

"I can manage the king, dear child," the queen said, reading my thoughts, "and in any case I shall be all right. 'Tis warm even for August. The air will do me good. Now sit."

Reluctantly, I bundled Queen Anne's furred velvet cloak around her frail body, smoothed the skirt of my green silk gown, and took a seat on the sunny bench. " 'Tis not what the doctors say, my lady. They say the air is bad for your fever—"

"Fie on the doctors; they would deny me everything. They think me already dead—" the queen broke off. "Nay, anger serves no purpose. They mean well, but they can't help me. Only God can help any of us." She looked up at a flock of blackbirds soaring past overhead, crying shrilly. "And in this lovely place, I feel His presence." The queen moved in her chair, and a white rose caught in her cloak. She took it into her hands, bent her head to inhale its fragrance. It was in full bloom, the heart exposed. She released it with a gentle touch, and the petals spilt to the ground. For some inexplicable reason, I was seized by great sadness as I watched her.

She sank back in her chair wearily and closed her eyes. I caught a tear at the corner of her eye, and knew she was thinking of her lost child.

The queen opened her eyes and gazed at me. Raising her hand, she touched my hair. With a sigh, she closed her lids again and lifted her face back to the sun. We sat peacefully for a time, drinking in its drowsy warmth. Men's voices and the trample of horses' feet shattered the serenity. The queen sat up and squinted into the sun in the direction of the noise.

From where we sat, high in the pleasure garden near the Round Tower, we had an excellent view of the main entrance. A small troop of men-at-arms had appeared through a distant archway in the castle wall and begun a descent to the Norman Gate. In their midst, a lone woman rode pillion. Thin, rigidly erect, wearing a wimple and dressed in black, there was no mistaking Margaret Beaufort. I watched uneasily as she and her escorts descended to the main gate. As if sensing our attention, Henry Tudor's mother turned her head and stared directly at us. I gave a shiver. There was something deeply unsettling about that woman.

"You don't like her, do you?" said the queen, reading my expression.

I averted my eyes hastily. "N—no, my lady, 'tis not so—"

"You needn't pretend with me, Elizabeth. We are friends." She patted my hand. "The reason I ask is because Margaret Beaufort troubles me also."

"Your Grace—"

"*Anne*. Call me Anne."

Thus emboldened, I dared to speak thoughts I had never shared before. "I know we shouldn't judge our betters, and 'tis presumptuous of me—my lady—*Anne*—" My gaze returned to the Norman Gate, and the chill I had felt earlier engulfed me again. "But Lady Margaret has always seemed cold to me and—and—"

"Aye?" the queen prompted.

"And—" I searched for the right word—"dangerous."

"Lady Stanley had the honor of carrying my train at my coronation, yet she's been at the center of two treasonous plots against my lord, the king, for which he has forgiven her both times."

I felt myself color fiercely. My mother had been at the center of those plots alongside Margaret Beaufort. The queen must have read my thoughts, for she reached out and took my hand into her own. "Child, 'twas not your fault; you were not involved. One thing I've learned in life is that we can only be responsible for ourselves."

I smiled gratefully. "On my part, I've learned that for all his sternness, the king is in truth a gentle and forgiving man."

"Too forgiving, and too gentle, and too easily fooled by showy piety." The queen stiffened and returned her gaze to the gate.

"Something about her troubles me," I murmured. "Could Lady

Stanley be false of heart and using her devotion as a ploy to get her way with others?"

"Dear Elizabeth," Queen Anne sighed, "you are wise beyond your years. Her actions speak of her falseness. I know it goes contrary to what we are told, but I have long believed it is by our deeds, not only our words, that we will be judged."

"I don't even trust that she had a—" The words burst from my lips before I could stop myself. I blushed a furious red and looked down at my hands in confusion. "Nay, I speak foolishly."

"I, too, have doubted that Margaret Beaufort had a vision."

I looked up in stunned amazement.

"She is a worldly and ambitious woman, and an exceedingly intelligent one," Queen Anne replied. "At twelve years of age, she was told to wed dull Suffolk, and she wanted dashing Edmund Tudor. What better way to get her wish than to claim St. Nicholas appeared to her in a vision to demand it be Tudor? She is clever enough to have concocted the story. For she is a respected scholar, fond of translating French writings. Nothing is beyond her intellect."

"I believe those who have truly been vouchsafed a vision would keep it close to their hearts, like a cherished treasure. Not boast openly of it to gain the praise of others."

"Yet I yearn to be wrong," the good queen sighed. "It would be better for my lord husband if I were. If she does not deceive us, she must be without sin. Otherwise, God would not have chosen her for such honor."

"Nay, my lady, that need not be! God grants visions even to sinners, for St. Paul had his while persecuting Christians." I hesitated an instant, and then I entrusted yet another of my secrets to the queen in the hope that the knowledge might comfort her. "And I've had one." Feeling embarrassed by my confession, I fell silent.

"Blessed Mary," the queen prompted with a small smile. "Must I always pry the words out of you, Elizabeth?"

I gathered my courage. I had not had a close friend since Mary's death, and it felt good to speak freely. "It was at Westminster, soon after my sister Mary died—" I told her of my experience after Mary's death. "She said my name only once, yet I knew it was her."

I dropped my gaze. My cheeks burned. Now the queen probably thought me mad. "I've never spoken of it before."

"Sometimes, late at night," said the queen softly, "when I pray, the candles flutter and I think I see out of the corner of my eye . . ." Her voice broke slightly. "I don't know what I see. When I look, it's gone." She closed her eyes, and a tear sparkled as it rolled down her cheek.

I touched the queen gently on her sleeve.

"In no other way has God shown me special favor. I'm certain there are many whom He loves better, who have never been granted such comfort."

The queen blinked, and I had the sensation she was again seeing our resemblance to each other. She leaned forward in her chair and seized my hand. "Blessed are they who mourn, for they shall be comforted," she murmured, almost to herself. She closed her eyes and rested her head against the back of the chair. A smile curved her lips, leaving me to wonder what joyous revelation had come to her.

✿

WE SPENT TWO ANXIOUS MONTHS IN NOTTINGHAM waiting for an invasion that never arrived. Finally as November approached, concluding that Tudor no longer posed a problem until the advent of good weather in the spring, we returned to London.

Royal bugles blared and bells rang for Tierce, but the crowds were respectfully quiet when King Richard and Queen Anne, clad in their dark mourning garb, approached Bishopsgate, followed by the royal procession of peers, knights, bishops, servants, and rumbling baggage carts. The city air was thick with the smell of sweat, horse droppings, and butchered animals, and the skies that hung over the city were gray.

On this chilly morning a bitter wind blew, bearing a dank smell from the river and the shops along Fish Street. The king glanced at his queen with concern. Near the city she had transferred from her litter to her chestnut palfrey to make a more dignified entry. Smothered in furs she smiled at him as her palfrey bore her sedately, not like King Richard's white stallion, which held up its elegant head and pranced majestically before the throng as befitted its royal status. King Richard was met by the mayor and the aldermen of London in their ceremonial scarlet. He listened politely to the mayor's welcome and made the appropriate responses.

At Westminster, the fresh bloody remains of a dead traitor greeted King Richard at the gates.

"Who is that?" inquired King Richard.

"The man named Collingbourne, Henry Tudor's agent, sire," one of his men replied. "He was caught nailing a placard to St. Paul's."

King Richard lowered his eyes. "Take it down. Give him decent Christian burial."

Only once before in history had a king made such a demand, and that was King Henry VI, whom some had called mad, and now called a saint, and whose body King Richard had had transferred from shabby Chertsey Abbey, where my father had buried him, to the splendid Chapel of St. George at Windsor.

In the north, where they knew Richard, they had named him "Good King Richard."

Now I understood the reason.

IN HER PRIVY CHAMBER AT WESTMINSTER PALACE, Queen Anne caressed Ned's little hound, Sir Tristan, who had curled up and fallen asleep in her lap.

"We should be foes, yet you're my dearest friend," she said as I bent intently over my embroidery.

I slid the needle through my tapestry and knotted the wine silk thread. I broke it with my teeth and smiled. "It seems another lifetime when I thought of you and King Richard as foes. How strange life is."

"If we loved as easily as we hated, we could change the world. Is there someone close to your heart, Elizabeth?"

I blushed fiercely. Here was my opportunity to speak of my heart's desire. "Aye, my lady queen." I caressed my brooch. "Sir Thomas Stafford." My pulse pounded as I spoke his name.

"Sir Humphrey of Grafton's younger brother?"

I smiled shyly. "The same."

"King Richard is devoted to Humphrey. He is a loyal and trusty knight. Is his brother like him?"

"Aye, my lady."

"When was the last time you saw him?"

"Before we left sanctuary," I replied sadly.

"Ah . . . 'Tis a long time ago. You are much changed since those days."

"Oh, no, my queen. I haven't seen him for months, and he has not written, but I haven't changed. When the king finds time to arrange a marriage for me, as he has done for my sister Cecily, I should like to wed Sir Thomas Stafford . . . if he'll have me." I colored under the queen's intent gaze. She said nothing in reply. I waited awkwardly. The silence lengthened. Nervously, I filled the emptiness with a question. "You and His Grace have loved one another since childhood, so I'm told."

"Aye, since I was seven years old," she said. "I remember the first time Richard came to Middleham. It was soon after your father was crowned. He was so young, so unsure of himself . . . and frightened." She drifted off into her thoughts.

"Sometimes," I said at length, "though I could be mistaken—" I broke off in confusion. How dared I speak of such a thing? "No, 'tis foolishness."

"Tell me what you were going to say, Elizabeth."

I felt myself turn scarlet again. "Truly, it was nothing, my lady."

"I must know."

My fingers slackened around my embroidery and I turned my gaze to the river. " 'Tis just that . . . sometimes . . . I see an odd expression on the king's face, when he thinks no one is looking."

"Aye?"

"Fear, and doubt, madame. Forgive me, but I've seen that in his eyes, and it wounds me to the heart."

The queen gave an audible gasp. She reached out and gently touched my hair, which I'd gathered beneath a silver circlet and gauzy veil. "Aye, child, I know."

"And I fear for him," I whispered under my breath.

"Because you love him," the queen said.

I shrank back. "No, my lady, no—"

"You must not be ashamed of loving," she said gently.

"I'd never do anything to hurt you—I'd give my life before I'd hurt you!"

The queen seemed about to reply when suddenly she pushed herself up from her chair on trembling legs. Sir Tristan jumped off with a start. She clutched her stomach and bent over as if to vomit. I leapt to my feet and seized her by the shoulders. "My lady, what is it?"

"The foul wind from the river . . . reminds me of something in my childhood." She inhaled a sharp breath and said, "The doctors have been baffled by my illness. Now I know what it is. The White Plague. I caught it from a sailor on my father's ship when we were fleeing Marguerite d'Anjou."

I stared at her in horror. The White Plague was always fatal. Attacking the lungs, it slowly choked life out of a person. Worse, it was a painful disease, especially at the end, when the victim had trouble breathing and coughed up blood and black phlegm.

With a nod of her head, Queen Anne indicated a far window that stood open to the garden. "There," she managed. Leaning heavily on my arm, she made her way slowly to the silver cushioned seat. There was no dark river odor here, only the sweet scent of pine. She patted the empty space beside her. Overwhelmed with misery, I sat down.

"Why must you think you've harmed with your love, child?" the queen asked when she felt strong enough to speak again. "All we take with us when we die is the love we leave behind."

I looked at her blankly.

"Love is all there is, dear child," she explained. "All that matters. All that warms the hearts we leave behind when we depart this world. We take their love, and leave them ours . . . until we are finally reunited, and made whole again." She looked out at the garden. I followed her gaze to a distant tree, a majestic elm with wide, sprawling branches like the one I'd seen at Middleham where Ned's archery target had hung.

Her voice sank to a bare whisper. "Ned has my love, and I keep his—here—" She laid a hand to her bosom. "As long as I live, I'll remember his love—" She gave a sudden gasp.

"Madame, madame!" I cried. "Are you all right?" I wrapped my arms around her to steady her. Nausea plagued her of late, and was coming on with increasing frequency. She calmed, though her breathing was still shallow.

" 'Tis nothing . . . merely a passing pain." The queen spoke haltingly. Giving me a strange look, she whispered softly, almost inaudibly, "You have your father's eyes . . . but they darken. With emotion they darken to violet, like mine." She inhaled a deep breath. "Now, I've something to say. Then you must make me a promise."

"Anything, madame."

"Stop . . . calling . . . me 'madame,' " she breathed, "I am Anne."

"Aye, my dear lady Anne."

"We must plan . . . for the future."

"The future?"

"Yours . . . and Richard's."

I stared at her dumbfounded.

" 'Tis not Sir Thomas Stafford you love, child, 'tis Richard. I've seen the way you look at him . . . Daily I lose strength. It'll not be long now, I know." Her voice was a bare tremor. "Some days are . . . difficult. If I could be at ease about my lord king, I could let go. You are right, dear Elizabeth. He is so alone." Her eyes returned to the tree and misted. "Alone with so much hate around him—" She broke off. "The heaviness I feel around Richard cannot be dispelled, except with love." Lifting her violet eyes to my face, she touched my cheek. "He'll not survive, Elizabeth . . . without love. You must stop denying your feelings for him . . . You must comfort him, help him. He'll need you."

As I stared at her, something inside me shifted. I felt as if a shutter had been thrown open, pouring in brilliant light. The sleepless nights, the pounding of my heart each time King Richard drew near; my shyness in his presence; all of these took on clarity. I turned over this new knowledge in my mind, marveling that I had not understood till now.

"But I'm his niece—"

"Eleanor of Aquitaine was niece to Raymond of Antioch when they fell in love. It did not stop them."

"But they didn't marry!"

"Only because Eleanor and Raymond were already married to others. But you are free . . . and soon Richard will be too."

"We cannot wed one another, my lady queen!"

The queen took me gently by the shoulders. "You must wed him. He must have comfort amid all the grief. We are so alike, Elizabeth. With you at his side, he can bear what he must." She panted with the exertion of speech.

"You are right. I care for him. I see that now," I said softly. "But it makes no difference. He is my uncle. It can never be."

"Would you deny me a reason to live?" the queen cried, tears palpable in her voice.

"My lady queen, what do you mean?" I exclaimed. "How can you say that? I would do anything to help you to live!"

"Listen to me, child." She took my hand. "Each time someone you love dies, he takes a piece of you with him. You have to find a way to live. You have to decide what you will stand for, fight for, die for . . . For me, you are my parting gift to my husband, the one who will save him from loneliness and destruction. Do not deny me a chance to save him, or you will take from me my last hope, all that gives my life meaning."

My mind was in tumult; I didn't know to think or say, so I kept silent.

When the queen spoke again, I heard her softly, as if across a far distance. "I give you my blessing, Elizabeth. . . . Now we have work to do. Richard has had much on his mind, but he wishes the Christmas festivities to be especially bright this year—" She hesitated, drew another deep breath. "We shall *make* him notice you. Aye, Elizabeth, you are what Richard needs. What England needs."

"But the pope will never grant a dispensation."

She heaved a deep breath. "He will . . . for a price. In truth, your blood bond matters not. I have come to believe that God sees no sin in love . . . except where that love brings pain to others." She paused to catch her breath. "You shall bear him children and turn his crown of sorrows . . . into a wreath of roses." The queen's chest heaved with the effort of speech, but she lifted her hand to my cheek with a gentle touch. "You shall make a fine queen, Elizabeth."

She laid her head against my shoulder and I cradled her gently, tears blinding my vision. It was thus King Richard found us when he entered his queen's chamber.

CHAPTER 9

Eclipse of the Sun, 1485

IN MID-NOVEMBER MORE GRIEF CAME TO CROUCH at King Richard's shoulder. His daughter, red-haired, green-eyed Cat, died suddenly from the sweating sickness on the eve of her marriage to the Earl of Huntingdon, and instead of the celebratory songs of her wedding, the palace was filled with sobbing and the dirges of her funeral.

Moreover, with descent of winter, the queen's health failed visibly. As if to spite the Fates that seemed allied against him, the king determined to make the Yule season the most festive the court had ever known.

Though weak and bedridden, the queen insisted on presiding over the celebrations, and the royal apartments teemed with as many people and as much business as the king's council chamber. While a favored hound slept beside her, I stood with the Master of the Wardrobe on either side of the queen's bed, surrounded by servants who undraped fabric for her inspection. There were cloths of gold and tissue of silver, and silks and damasks of every hue—purples, crimsons, greens, blues, and apricots. She was nodding assent to a bolt of violet tissue when King Richard strode in. The Master of the Wardrobe gathered up his fabrics and his meinies and withdrew with a bow. I blushed, and my heart took up a fierce pounding in my breast. Avoiding his eyes, I curtsied and rushed past him.

"Stay, Elizabeth—" Queen Anne called out. I was already half-way to the door and pretended not to hear. "She's so shy . . . Not at all like her mother," the queen said. A coughing fit racked her chest and she gasped for air. Servants rushed to attend her. I stole a backward glance at the door. They were holding a silver basin to her mouth. She threw up bile and laid her head back on the silk pillows. A lady-in-waiting gently wiped blood-tinged mucus from her lips. The king sat down on the velvet coverlet and took her hand. "You're not to tax yourself, my little bird. I can appoint others to the task and—"

I closed the door.

By Yuletide, it was evident to all that the queen was dying. Crushed in spirit, always fragile in health, she would soon be ready to let herself depart this world. The doctors advised King Richard not to share her bed any longer, but he did not comply.

On Epiphany, wearing their crowns, the king and queen sat on their thrones, presiding over the Christmas revelry in the Great Hall of Rufus, which had been decorated with candles and branches of evergreens. The air was fragrant with the scent of pine and bayberry, and the hall glittered with color from the tapestries, silk carpets, and the dazzling gowns and jewels of the nobles. Laughter, conversation, and singing resounded through the chamber. King Richard had donned his sumptuous robes of crimson, purple, and ermine studded with diamonds, and Queen Anne a gown of violet and silver. But she was thin and pale, and so weak she had to be propped up in her throne with pillows. The king could no longer fool himself with hope; his queen was doomed.

Jack, Earl of Lincoln, asked me for a dance, and I took his hand. He led me to the dance floor and we took up our positions. He was King Richard's heir to the crown now, but I knew it wasn't the honor of dancing with the heir to the throne that drew all eyes to me. It was the dress I wore.

The queen had replicated her violet and silver gown, and made me wear the copy. Knowing what a stir that would cause, I had tried to protest. But the queen had insisted.

"But why should we wear the same royal gown?" I had asked.

"So King Richard will notice our resemblance."

"But what will people think?"

"They will think the worst, dear child," the queen had said heavily. "People usually do."

On the dais where they sat, a fire crackled in the hearth, but Queen Anne could be seen shivering. The king kissed her fingers and rubbed her delicate hand between his own. As the dance ended, Jack gave me a bow and I curtsied to him. Humphrey Stafford approached and made me a courtly bow.

"My lady, you look very beautiful this evening," he said, offering me his arm and leading me to the dance floor. "Your hair has the glow of sunlight, and your sapphire brooch matches your eyes. 'Tis peculiar, but my mother had one just like it."

I felt myself redden like a poppy. "Thank you, Sir Humphrey." I fingered my brooch, almost covering it from view. "The star is a well-liked design."

"Indeed."

He'd said nothing about my gown, I noted. We took our positions in the middle of the room and the minstrels launched into a lilting melody, but all I could think about was Thomas. He had been my first love. Had we wed, then Humphrey with whom I danced would have been my brother-by-marriage. I glanced at Richard on the dais speaking to one of his knights. Thomas would forever claim a corner of my heart, but all was now changed.

The melody drew to an end.

"Ah—" Humphrey Stafford said. A shadow crossed his face. A messenger was pushing through the throng and heading to the dais. "I see there is news. Shall we?"

I took his arm and we approached within earshot of the dais.

The man knelt before the king. "Sire! I bring an urgent message from France. Our agents beyond the seas report that, notwithstanding the potency and splendor of your royal state, Henry Tudor will, without question, invade the kingdom this summer."

After a pause, King Richard replied, "Nothing more desirable can befall me than to meet Tudor in the field at last."

He bent his head toward Anne, and the queen's expression grew anxious as they spoke. She drew her fur mantle closer to her.

My glance went to the king. Pale, haggard, more careworn than ever before, he looked in no condition to defend his kingdom. If he met Tudor now, there might well be disaster. And Tudor, shrewd, ruthless, and cunning as he was said to be, no doubt knew it. Margaret Beaufort's son would be able to smell his quarry's blood even from across the seas. My eyes sought Tudor's mother among the throng of guests. I found her standing with her husband, Lord Thomas Stanley, and her henchman, Reginald Bray, beside a traceried window, observing the dancers and whispering together. Margaret Beaufort's go-between in her treason with Buckingham, Reginald Bray, had also received the king's pardon after the rebellion. King Richard's clemency troubled me now. Such people didn't quit brewing their mischief.

"Would you care to stroll about?" Sir Humphrey asked. "There is still some marchpane left on the table of sweets, I believe."

I nodded and we moved down the hall. As we approached the Stanleys, my gaze moved to Thomas Stanley's brother, Sir William, emerging from the crowd on the far side of the hall and striding across to join them. William and his brother bore little resemblance to each other. Thomas was tall and thin; William, short and stocky. Stanley's bushy hair was a flaming red; William's wispy hair barely ginger. Stanley and his wife also made an odd couple. Margaret Beaufort was a tiny woman with a disproportionately long face that made her look top-heavy, almost dwarfish. He was jovial, and she was austere in manner and dress.

I inclined my head as we drew near, and Sir Humphrey threw Margaret Beaufort a small bow. She made a striking figure in her usual black velvet gown trimmed with ermine, but there was something sinister about her. Her long, narrow face, sharply pointed at nose and chin, and pale, glittering eyes gave her the look of a hungry wolf. I thought of what Queen Anne had said, that she strove to look a martyr with her wimple and pious ways, carrying her Psalter around with her, but she was too showy for true piety, and her treasons spoke of a heart far too worldly. My eye went to the book the Beaufort woman held in her hands. There was the Psalter.

The Stanleys and the henchman, Bray, fell silent as we passed and watched us with an expression that made me uncomfortable. Their eyes bored into my back. Humphrey Stafford leaned close. "Unpleasant people," he muttered in my ear. Grabbing two goblets from a passing servant with a silver tray, he gave me one. We both drank deeply.

"Better, eh?" he smiled.

I nodded. Despite the gaiety of the court, I felt a dark undercurrent of unease swirling around us. Drawing courage from the wine, I tried to deny my sense of foreboding and turned to him. "How is your brother?" I finally dared to ask.

"God be praised, Thomas is well, my lady. He's recovering from the arrow he took to his chest on the Scots border."

I couldn't believe it! So this was the reason he hadn't written to me. My eyes flew to King Richard on the dais. *And now—*

"Indeed? I didn't know of his injury," I said softly. "I am glad to hear of his recovery, for he was kind to me in sanctuary. I will always be indebted to him. Did he speak to you about those days?"

"He would have, I'm sure. But I haven't seen him, or even been in correspondence. Though I remember now that there was something he wished to tell me when next we saw one another. I have been away in Calais and France on the king's business since St. George's Day."

St. George's Day. *The day the news came of Ned's death.* My gaze returned to the poor doomed queen propped up in her throne. She was leaning close to her husband, and she held his hand, with a worried look on her face as they spoke. Even as I gazed, they turned their eyes on me. My breath caught in my breast. *They are discussing me.* Dimly, I noted that the minstrels had broken into a merry tune.

"Look!" said Sir Humphrey Stafford with a grin. "Someone has had his fill of marchpane—"

I turned in the direction of his gaze to find a hound sleeping by the table of sweets, all four paws up in the air, his jowls relaxed in a smile on his upside-down face. I laughed aloud at the sight, and as

I did so, I became aware that the hubbub of conversation was dying away. I turned around.

The crowd had parted to make way for King Richard, who was coming directly toward me, on his face the expression of a man unaware, in a trance. As he walked past his guests, they stared after him. He drew up to me and inclined his head. I blushed, sank into a deep curtsy, and took the hand he proffered. As he led me to the dance floor, the minstrels broke into a lilting pavane.

For a terrifying minute, we stood alone. Then Lord Howard and his son, Thomas, fell in behind us with their ladies. Others followed: all King Richard's loyal friends: Rob Percy and Lord Francis Lovell, who had known and loved him since childhood; his nephew and heir to the throne, Jack, Earl of Lincoln; the Lords Scrope of Bolton and of Masham, who went all the way back to his father, and Greystoke, another devoted Yorkist lord. His trusted advisors, Sir Richard Ratcliffe, Sir William Conyers, Sir William Catesby, Sir Robert Brackenbury, and the two Harrington brothers who were Knights of the Body. All faithful, all closing ranks behind him.

Music floated to me from the minstrel's gallery, but it seemed very far away in the dreamy haze that engulfed me. The line moved up and down in rhythm to the melody; we turned, twirled, changed partners, and returned again. Straight ahead, Queen Anne smiled encouragement to me, and for the first time I saw our resemblance to each other: violet and silver dress; golden hair and violet eyes; pointed chins and rosebud lips. I turned and smiled at King Richard.

Silver-haired Lord Howard slapped his thigh and gave a roar of merriment behind me, and I grew aware of the people watching us. Some stared; some whispered with their heads close together; others stole hostile glances. Margaret Beaufort stood with her husband, Lord Stanley; Lord Stanley's son, George; and their henchman, Reginald Bray, watching carefully from the side of the room. The Beaufort woman had an eyebrow raised. On the dais I saw the countess approach her daughter. She bent her head to the queen and murmured something. They both looked at me. Then Queen Anne smiled, a smile meant not just for me, but for the entire court. The countess took her daughter's hand, but there was no smile on her trembling face, only the sparkle of tears.

✦

BEFORE TWELFTH NIGHT WAS OVER, KING RICHARD received still more bad news. The Lancastrian lord John de Vere, Earl of Oxford, had escaped Hammes Castle in Calais and taken men to join Tudor in France. But even worse, as January progressed, Queen Anne deteriorated further.

"I have not much longer," she whispered to me. "I've been unable to persuade the king to wed you, Elizabeth. You must write Lord Howard and enlist his support. Richard admires Lord Howard above all others." She paused for breath. "He is a beloved friend, almost a father to Richard. With Howard's help, surely he will . . . no longer regard this marriage as impossible . . . I will write him also."

Queen Anne could say no more. She burst into a fit of coughing, struggling to spit up the bloody flux from her lungs, and then lay back, exhausted. It broke my heart to see her this way. Why did the good Lord not see fit to put an end to her suffering? Why did she have to linger like this, wracked by pain, watching the emotional toll her death took on her beloved husband?

Why, why, why?

I wrote to Lord Howard.

February arrived with gusty winds, and leaden skies oppressed the land as ill tidings flooded King Richard. I did what I could for the poor queen. We had both heard back from Lord Howard. His pledge of support helped to ease the queen's spirits, though she still suffered much physical pain. Nevertheless, there were a few good moments. That afternoon, she was able to join me in a game of chess.

The bed hangings of silver brocade were pulled back and tied with gilded ropes, and the sun, which had broken through the clouds, slanted into the room through windows that stood cracked open for air. The queen lay propped up on white silk pillows, her arms stretched out woodenly at her sides, dressed in a dark chemise and covered by a gray velvet coverlet embroidered with tiny silver roses. I sat with her, playing chess on the bed.

"Green becomes you, Elizabeth . . . You light up the room . . . with your gold hair and beauty . . . like a tapestry on a grey stone wall."

"Hush, now, my queen. 'Tis your move."

"The knight," Queen Anne whispered.

I moved the knight. "Very clever, my lady. Now let me see how I can salvage myself—" Thoughtfully, I cupped my chin in my hand and considered the board.

Behind me there were footsteps, and suddenly the queen's expression changed to one of joy. "My dearest lord!" she cried. She tried to rise but fell back, choked by a fit of coughing. Then she gagged.

I leapt to my feet, grabbed a basin, and held it to her mouth as she retched, and then I smoothed the queen's damp hair and helped her lie back against the pillows. King Richard rushed to his queen's side and snatched a damp towel from an approaching maidservant. "I'll do it," he barked. He dabbed the gilt-edged cloth to the queen's mouth and winced as he wiped away blood. He accepted a clay cup from a monk. The foul-smelling liquid, thick as oil, seemed to offend his nostrils. "What is it?"

"A tincture of bitter aloe, black poppy juice, and betony, sire. Good for bleeding and cough, and to ease pain and procure sleep."

King Richard slid his arm behind the queen's shoulders and supported her while he tilted the cup to her lips. She was so weak, she could barely swallow. Much of the vile liquid slipped out from between her teeth and dribbled down the side of her mouth. She pushed the cup away, seized by another coughing spell. He handed it to the monk and gently wiped her mouth.

"Is it bad today, my love?" he asked, taking a seat on the bed.

The queen laid her head against his shoulder. I curtsied before leaving, though he didn't look my way. The servants followed and the countess, the last to go, shut the oak door behind her, leaving them alone.

Church bells tolled in the abbey and were echoed down river and across town. I winced. They had been tolling with increasing frequency since Christmas, for Queen Anne's recovery. As I passed the table in the antechamber, I picked up the book I had borrowed from King Richard's library. Heading along the hall, I turned into a small alcove off the private chapel where there was no one about and sat down in the window seat. Like all King Richard's books, this one was a plain leather-bound volume, without jewels or ornamentation, for King Richard did not choose his books for display, but to read. I thumbed the pages open to the flyleaf that bore his signature and motto. His hand was clear, elegant and characteristically devoid of flourish. I lingered over the script, caressing it tenderly with the tip of a finger: *Loyaulte me Lie, Richard of Gloucester.* Loyalty Binds Me.

I turned the volume over in my hands. His book; *Tristan and Iseult.* I went to my marker, and bent my head to read:

> Gone was Iseult's hatred, no longer might there be strife between them, for Love, the great reconciler, had purified their hearts from all ill will, and so united them that each was as clear as a mirror to the other. But one heart had they—her grief was his sadness, his sadness her grief. Both were one in love and sorrow, and yet both would hide it in shame and doubt. . . . Heart and eyes strove with each other; Love drew her heart toward him, and shame drove her eyes away.

"Elizabeth—"

I jumped up with a gasp and the book fell to the floor. I made no effort to retrieve it.

"I didn't mean to startle you. I meant only to thank you for what you've done for my lady queen," King Richard said awkwardly, seeming strangely at a loss.

I blushed. "I wish I could do more, sire." Emotion threatened my composure and I dropped my gaze. "I have prayed but—"

I felt his eyes on me, and my color deepened. I finally managed to tear my eyes from the floor and look at him. He was staring at me as if he'd never seen me before, and in his throat I saw a pulse beating with frantic speed.

"You look like my queen," he said at last. "Not like your mother."

A long silence fell.

So that was it. He saw me as a Woodville, not a Plantagenet.

He stood stiffly, as if unable, or unwilling, to leave. "You have Edward's eyes. Blue as the summer sky." He said nothing more and did not avert his gaze from my face.

"You were dear to my father's heart," I whispered.

"And he to mine." I saw his color rise. The pulse at his neck quickened.

I cried out, "If we both loved him, how can we hate one another?"

"I—" King Richard tried to speak, and fell silent, as if he could not find the words. He turned his gaze away to the window.

Outside, I heard a young couple laugh. Assailed by emotions I had never known before, by a desire that I had never felt, I flushed and lowered my trembling lashes. "By your leave, Your Grace," I said, summoning every ounce of my will, "I should see if the queen needs me."

"She is asleep," King Richard said. He looked utterly miserable.

I didn't know what to say, what to do. I stood there, wringing my hands together. "Then, by your leave, I shall see if the countess needs me."

He didn't grant me permission, but merely stared at me. At last, he gave a terse nod.

I almost broke into a run. In my haste, I brushed past him too closely, and my gown caught on the golden spur of his boot. I yanked it loose and fled. But not before I saw him look at the book I had dropped, bend down, and pick it up.

❧

THE NEXT DAY, KING RICHARD INVITED ME TO STROLL with him in the garden. The February landscape was muted with the earth tones of winter: half-melted snow, barren beds, bare trees. Against this dismal backdrop, the king sparkled like the sun in scarlet and gold. Together we crossed the palace cloisters and passed the snowy central garth, where a group of fur-clad nobles and ladies amused themselves tossing a gilded leather ball. Their laughter was subdued and their sober dress reflected respect for the queen's condition, but I saw a muscle twitch in the king's jaw as we passed. Instinctively, I knew it was because these strangers were merry while he was in despair, and their cheeks were rosy, while his queen gasped for breath.

I averted my gaze. We walked along in silence; King Richard seemed lost in thought and barely aware of my presence, but with every step I felt his nearness like the glow of the sun, and it plunged me into a state of unbearable, inexplicable yearning.

" 'Tis a fine morning, my lord," I managed at last, feeling myself blush. Hastily, I dropped my gaze. "The birds sing loud this day."

"It will soon be spring," King Richard replied. He said nothing more, but I felt him tense at my side. Though I had fastened my hair back at the nape of the neck, a gust of wind suddenly blew it loose around me. I drew my cloak tighter around me against the wind and pulled my hood up over my hair. I saw the king's glance go to my hair and linger there. Then he turned behind him to gaze up at the high window in the white stone palace where Queen Anne lay in her chamber.

"I saw the first jonquil this morning; it broke through the snow," I said softly. "I picked it for the queen. The joy on her face was—" My voice cracked and I fell silent.

King Richard nodded, but he said nothing.

We took the path down to the river and continued to walk along in awkward silence, past strolling clerics and knights with their ladies, and others seated on benches among the hedges. I felt their watchful stare bore into my back. Ahead, the great fountain splashed noisily. Swathed in furs, several young damsels sat on a carpet spread around its smooth stone rim, their admirers grouped at their feet, one strumming a lyre, another playing a flute. A love song floated on the wind. King Richard seemed aware of the eyes that followed us, and his expression darkened.

"It seems a long winter this year," I offered, casting about for something to say. "I shall be glad enough of spring." My mind was in such confusion that I could think of nothing else.

This time King Richard did reply. "Aye," he said. He threw another glance up to Queen Anne's chamber, as if he wished to be there, with her, not here, with me. And still he didn't leave; he just kept strolling at my side, deep in thought.

A group of courtiers bowed. He acknowledged them with a taut nod.

"I hear Lady Scrope of Bolton had another girl," I said. "That makes three daughters."

King Richard didn't respond for a long while. But just when I thought he would not answer at all, he said, "Aye, three. I shall have to consider what gift to send." He bit at his lip and clasped his hands behind him as we strolled, and again he fell into silence. Abruptly, he spoke again. "You know her well; do you have a suggestion?"

I stole a glance at him and blushed again. "Perhaps some cloth of gold—" Shrieks of delight interrupted me and I looked toward the Thames, where a group of children played with a dog on the other side of the riverbank. "Or a hound," I said. "My father, God assoil his soul, gave me a terrier on my fifth birthday, and she brought me much joy."

King Richard winced. "I shall send cloth of gold," he said curtly.

I looked at him, not understanding his sudden displeasure, except that it had something to do with my father's memory. Our gaze met and locked. My heart turned over in my breast and my whole being filled with waiting. A line from *Tristan and Iseult* came to me: *Each knew the mind of the other, yet was their speech of other things.*

He was the first to look away. He said, "My lady, I must leave you now. The queen has need of me."

I fell into a deep curtsy.

He was half way down the snowy path when I arose. Swept with a wretchedness of mind I'd not known before, not even in the terrible days of sanctuary, I watched him, his bleak, solitary figure. For some inexplicable reason, all I could think was that my father had loved him, too. Without warning, tears started in my eyes and rolled slowly down my cheeks. Today was my nineteenth birthday, and I couldn't help remembering.

FEBRUARY GAVE WAY TO BITTER MARCH. WEDNESDAY, the sixteenth, dawned cold, but sunny. After Nones, the queen suddenly began a strange gurgling sound in her throat, and the countess, who had seen much of death, turned moist eyes on me. " 'Tis time," she said urgently. "Send for the king—make haste."

I ran to Sir Richard Ratcliffe in the antechamber.

"The queen—she's failing fast!" I cried.

"The king is at prayers in the chapel. I'll have the archbishop summon him," said Ratcliffe.

"Make haste—" I called after him, my voice breaking.

The Benedictine monks in the antechamber rose and filed into the queen's room. They took up their positions at the far end of the room across from the window, their dark cowled figures barely visible in the shadows. The air filled with the mournful chanting of their prayers. King Richard appeared moments later at the threshold of the chamber. His legs seemed to fail him in the last instant, and he halted, grabbing at the pillar for support. His eyes fixed on the bed, he seemed to will himself forward as he approached. On his face I saw an expression of panic, and my heart twisted.

The silver curtains were tied back. The queen lay stretched out on the great bed, eyes closed, a pale, diminished, almost lifeless figure in white. A gleaming crucifix hung on the dark silk-draped wall over the bed, glittering with a sinister light in the flicker of the candles burning around her. He passed a hand over his face and looked back at the bed. I wanted to run to him, to take him into my arms, to comfort him, but I merely stood as still as a statue in the corner of the room, watching his terrible grief.

The countess sat at her daughter's side in a tapestried chair, with her back to the windows. Sunlight illuminated her figure from behind, and her face would have been in darkness but for the light of the candles. She lifted her eyes to the king and vacated her chair to him. As the king moved to the bed, the doctors retreated, and the servants slipped away. In his gold and white robes, the Holy Book in one hand, a jeweled crucifix in the other, Archbishop Rotherham assumed a stance near the wall, until the moment when he should be needed.

At the queen's bedside, King Richard reached over the velvet coverlet and took one cold hand in both of his. Her breath came in short, labored pants. Sensing his presence, the queen opened her eyes. She tried to speak. He bent his ear to her lips.

An expression of excruciating agony came over his face. He took a moment to compose himself. Then he began to sing:

> *Aye, aye, O, aye the winds that bend the brier!*
> *The winds that blow the grass!*
> *For the time was May-time, and blossoms draped the earth . . .*
> *Wine, wine—and I will love thee to the death*
> *And out beyond into the dream to come . . .*

His voice was deep and resonant, and the words, slow at first, gathered force and flowed freely from his soul. He sang of the deer, the twilight, the wind and the water. I knew it was a song from their youth.

She calmed. Her lips curved into a smile. Then, as the king watched her, she gave a moan. "My little bird, what is it?" he said.

I heard the words from where I stood. "I will wait—for you— in heaven," she said.

The king bent his face to hers, brushing her hair and cheeks and brow with his lips. "My love," he whispered, "my dearest love . . ."

As her eyes closed, he knelt at her side. The monks resumed their low chanting.

"Richard . . ." she murmured feebly.

"I am here, flower-eyes," he said, brushing her damp brow with his lips. "I won't leave you, Anne. I'll never leave you."

The queen spoke again, and I heard my name, *Elizabeth.* . . . But no more. She strained for breath.

"Hush, Anne, hush," King Richard said. He took her hand into his own. Through ashen, quivering lips, he whispered to her.

Queen Anne opened her eyes wide and looked at him. Pure violet, those eyes. Lit from within with a golden light.

"No need for tears, my beloved Richard," she said in a strong, clear, steady voice.

The king gaped at her with astonishment, as I did, as everyone did standing within earshot. Hope flooded my breast; as it must have flooded his. A smile broke across his face, and I knew we both had the same thought. *God has heard our prayers! She will be well!*

"Flower-eyes, my Anne—" the king cried joyfully.

She lifted a hand, touched his cheek.

"I shall see Ned," she smiled. Her hand fell limp at her side.

"Anne!" King Richard cried in panic. *"Anne—!"*

Silence.

With his head on her breast, he clung to her with a choked moan.

And as the king grieved, something happened, something so terrible that I took a step forward in disbelief, The archbishop, who had lifted his great jeweled crucifix and made the sign of the cross over the queen's body, broke off in the midst of his prayer for the dead. Looking up at the window, he stared at the sky. The monks lifted their heads, followed the archbishop's gaze, and ended their song with a gasp of horror. The servants who knelt in prayer crossed themselves for fear. Everyone stood immobile, their faces uplifted to the heavens.

In what seemed an instant, the room had darkened into night. There was no light anymore, only a dismal gloom lit by the flickering light of candles and a strange, eerie silence. No birds sang; no church bells pealed; there was no sound from man or beast. For where the sun had shone a moment before, only a shadow remained. The mighty sun had been blackened by the hand of God.

Clinging to the body of his dead queen, who lay as pale and still as a marble effigy, the king moaned. At last he became aware of the silence, of the shadow that had fallen at his shoulder. He lifted his head, turned behind him, then rose and moved to the window.

He stood there with his head in his hands, a solitary figure in an agony of soul, making no sound, no movement. I couldn't bear his torment any longer, and went to his side. "So many angels came down to guide her to heaven," I said softly, "that their wings darkened the sun."

The king dropped his hands from his face. I smiled at him through my tears, though my heart broke to look at him. Pain was carved in merciless lines across his brow, at his mouth, around his eyes. *Jesu*, but he had aged ten years in a day. I touched his sleeve. "She has been rescued from this dark world, my lord. God has one more angel at His side this day."

We looked for a long moment into one other's eyes, and between us lay our love for Queen Anne and all that we had shared across the years. King Richard took a step forward mutely and collapsed against me. My arms went around his head, and I held him to me like a suffering child.

I saw the countess turn away, tears streaming down her cheeks; the servants bowed their heads, sniffling. Only Archbishop Rotherham remained gazing at us dry-eyed, his face hard.

✦

THE RUMORS BEGAN THE NEXT DAY. *KING RICHARD poisoned his wife to wed his niece,* the placards said. The vulgar sniggered that I had bedded my uncle and borne him a child. The king's councilors met with him behind closed doors, urging him to deny the rumors. But first there was the queen's funeral to attend.

Beneath drizzling gray skies, to the chanting of monks, with the Lord Cardinal Archbishop of Canterbury leading the way and lords and ladies following, Queen Anne's funeral procession wound from Westminster Palace to the abbey. Her bier, covered with black and white velvet and drawn by four black horses, rumbled slowly across the cobbled court, escorted by four knights bearing torches. For once the eternal church bells hung silent and there was no sound but the hoofbeats of the horses and the weeping. Queen Anne had much endeared herself to the poor by her acts of charity and goodness, and the common people came in great numbers to pay their last respects. Gathered before the walls and gates, they watched the solemn cortege.

With dragging steps, clothed in plain dark saye without girdle or trimming, bareheaded and unadorned by any jewels save Queen Anne's small sapphire ring, King Richard walked behind her coffin, and I wondered that so much had changed for him in the mere twenty months since he had taken the throne.

Inside the abbey it was dark and cool. The smell of burning incense filled the nave, and curls of smoke wafted to the gold bosses on the soaring vaulted ceiling. Hundreds of candles and tapers flared; the monks' chant rose in volume and their song resonated against the stone floor and soaring arches. Slowly the funeral procession wound along, past the shadowy sanctuary and the high altar, past the tombs of other Plantagenet kings of England: the Henrys, the Edwards, the Richards . . .

King Richard didn't glance at Henry V's tomb and painted wood effigy of silver and gilt, which had been erected to his memory by his widow, Katherine of Valois, Henry Tudor's grandmother. But at the tomb of Richard II, he looked up at the carved marble figure. I followed his gaze to the mild, childlike face with winsome curls. This was the man who had sown the seeds of the Wars of the Roses between York and Lancaster. For nearly a hundred years England had paid in blood for his deposition and murder. The realm had thought the dynastic struggle had ended with Henry's death.

King Richard closed his eyes and inhaled a long, audible breath. When he opened them again, he stared for a long moment at the effigy of Richard II's queen, another Anne. I thought it a strange parallel that King Richard II had buried his Anne in a frenzy of grief.

He resumed his steps. Near the south door leading into the shrine of Edward the Confessor, the procession came to a halt. There, in that place with its carved stone screen and gold feretory, King Richard and Queen Anne had knelt together to be crowned. Now her tomb yawned open, a cavernous marble pit set on a stone bier. The monks raised their voices to chant the solemn masses and dirges of the Requiem. When it was ended, Archbishop Bourchier stepped forward, opened his Psalter, and droned the Pater Noster.

King Richard's eyes fixed on the unyielding stone, and I could only guess the memories that came to him. His gentle queen, his childhood playmate, the grand passion of his life, was gone, her light extinguished; gone, too, the love that had seen him through the batterings of his childhood, through both his exiles and all the wars. Now, into that blackness, his beloved wife would be sealed forever; she, who had shared his dreams and his youth and his beginnings, and so many of his endings.

As I watched his lonely figure, his shoulders took up a trembling and the tremors became heaves. Then I heard the most heart-wrenching sounds I shall ever hear in my life: choked sobs from a man famed for his deeds of valor and his inherent strength. At the foot of his wife's tomb, surrounded by his nobles and the prelates of his realm, King Richard, who had stood fast through the loss of all his kin and the death of his only child, broke at last and, covering his face with his hands, he wept.

CHAPTER 10

The Parting, 1485

WITHIN DAYS OF QUEEN ANNE'S FUNERAL, ON THE AD-
vice of his councilors, Richard issued a proclamation denying that
he intended to marry me. He didn't tell me himself; I heard it from
my little cousin, Edward, Earl of Warwick.

"Are you s-sad about Uncle R-Richard?" he asked as I pored
over the war banner I was helping him design as a gift to the
king.

I regarded the lonely little fellow with the deepest pity. One of
King Richard's first acts as soon as he took the throne was to send
for orphaned Edward of Warwick and welcome him—and his sister, young Margaret—into his own household. The only happiness
the boy had ever known was with Richard and Anne. What would
become of him if Richard lost the battle?

"I am sad for King Richard, for he suffers much," I said, keeping my eyes on his emblem of the dun cow that I traced for him
on the while silk.

"I m-mean, about n-not wedding the king?" Edward explained.

I hesitated for a moment, at a loss for words. "Why do you ask
such a thing, Edward?" My heart pounded as I spoke.

"J–J–Johnnie told me," he said, as if he were going to cry. "I'm sorry, Lizzie—"

I wrapped my arms around him and held him close to me, smoothing his soft golden curls. "It's all right, Edward," I soothed. "It's all right."

But it wasn't. My heart was breaking.

Soon it became clear that a written proclamation wasn't enough, and Richard would have to denounce the marriage rumors in person. Summoning the mayor, aldermen, and chief citizens of London, his lords temporal and spiritual, and leading the officers of his household, he rode to the hospital of the Knights of St. John in Clerkenwell. He had chosen it deliberately, for it was a place where students were schooled in the law, and the law was the foundation of his rule and dear to his heart. In a loud, distinct voice, he stood before them and denied the rumor spread by Tudor.

❖

WE WERE NEVER ALONE AGAIN AFTER ANNE'S DEATH, but our hearts were one each time our eyes met. On an April morning, as spring burst into leaf and flower around us, Richard summoned the family to his royal suite. He looked as if he hadn't slept in days, and dark circles ringed his gray eyes.

"I have decided that this battle with Tudor shall be my last," he said. "I have done my best for England. 'Tis for God to judge me now. And for us to bid one another farewell."

A wave of panic assailed me. I didn't understand what he meant, but I asked no questions and waited patiently like the rest.

Richard stared at us as if he would commit our image to memory. The countess wore her dark robes of mourning. Beneath her wimple her face was aged, deeply etched by sorrow, but she held herself gracefully erect with the same dignity she had always shown. Little Edward stood at her side, dressed in black velvet. He was ten now, and nothing in his face or manner resembled George of Clarence or the Kingmaker's daughter, Bella, or his proud grandfather Warwick, for there was nothing gay, or proud, or bright about him, and he did not dream great dreams. But his heart was gentle and would always remain so, because it would forever retain the blessed innocence of childhood.

My eyes followed Richard's gaze to his son. His love child, Johnnie of Gloucester, would be fifteen in May. He had his father's dark hair and strong square jaw, but his eyes were green, and if his broad shoulders and long muscular legs did not lie, he would be tall, maybe as tall as my father.

Richard brought his eyes to me, but only for an instant. Then he averted his gaze. I bowed my head and smoothed the green fabric of my gown, my heart filled with woe.

"You must go to Sheriff Hutton, you will be safe there," the king said, his voice thick. My lashes flew up. I opened my mouth to speak. Surely he didn't mean me? Surely it was enough to deny the rumor of marriage? Surely he wasn't sending me away as well? But no words came. He read my expression, however, for he added, flushing, "All of you."

I almost choked on the sob in my throat.

Somehow I managed to nudge little Edward forward. He fumbled with his hands shyly. "Uncle, I would s-seek . . . a favor of you."

Richard looked at him with soft eyes. Gently he said, "Dear nephew, whatever it is, you know I will try to grant it."

"I w-w-wish I c-could fight for you—" Edward drew a deep breath and made fists with his hands in an effort to suppress his stammer. He succeeded, for the words poured forth like a waterfall, "I wish I could fight the bastard Tudor, dear lord uncle, but as I am too young to help you slay him, will you take my banner into battle instead of me—?" He hung his head, embarrassed by his emotion and the effort it had taken him to get the sentence out.

I placed my arms around his little shoulders and nodded to a servant in the corner of the room. The man brought the folded banner to King Richard, knelt, and unfurled it. A blaze of gold tassels and golden embroidery on white silk shot across the carpet. In the center stood a nut-colored tartan cow.

King Richard winced as he gazed at the Dun Cow of Warwick. I knew his thoughts. The last time he'd seen that emblem, it had been in the fog of Barnet and he had fought on the opposing side.

"We've been working on it all winter," I said gently. "Cousin Edward helped in the design. He is talented in things artistic."

King Richard knelt and took the child's hands in his own. "I shall bear your banner at my side and my thoughts shall be of you, Edward, and of your noble grandfather, the Earl of Warwick, and all those of the House of Neville whom I loved so well."

A loud sob escaped from the boy as he stood with bowed head, staring at the floor. Richard pulled him close in a last embrace and rose stiffly. "Go now, Edward. Worship God devoutly, remember to apply yourself to your studies, and never forget knightly conduct. For there is wisdom in prayer and learning, and a great lord has need of both." He gave the boy's hand to the manservant and watched him leave. Suddenly, he called out after him, "May God be with you, fair nephew!"

One sad, lingering backward glance and Edward was gone.

Richard regarded Johnnie. "You have nothing to fear, my Johnnie. You have no lands, no titles, nothing, my son. You are a threat to no one. No one will hurt you, no matter what happens to me—"

"Father!" his boy cried. Richard clasped him to his breast for a long moment. Then he loosened his grip. "Fare thee well, my dear son," he said, his voice cracking. Johnnie fled his arms, stifling a moan as he ran.

The countess stepped forward. They gazed at one another for a long quiet moment. "Dear lady, whom I have loved as a mother," Richard whispered, taking her hand tenderly into his. "I thank you for the comfort and the love you have ever shown me."

Tears sparkled in her eyes and rolled slowly down her cheeks. "You were the son I never had, Richard." Her voice trembled. "I shall pray for your victory."

He bent his head and stood motionless as she left him, and the rustle of her skirts sounded in my heart like the great sighing of a wind that sweeps away the dying leaves of autumn.

He bit his lip. Then he looked at me. He had to know from my red, swollen eyes that I'd been weeping. With a motion of the hand, he dismissed the servants and waited until the door thudded shut behind them.

He said thickly, "I regret the death of your Uncle Anthony and your brother Richard Grey. I know they bore me no ill will and were but unwilling pawns."

"Aren't we all?" I whispered, but it was not a question.

"Can you—can you forgive me, Elizabeth?"

I swallowed hard and bit back tears. "I forgive you, Richard. Because I love you."

"No!" he said roughly, sharply. "No, don't—I'm old, finished. God has taken everything from me, left me alone, barren. But you are young. You have your life before you. You'll change. You'll forget me."

"You can't believe that!" I cried on a sobbing breath. "This is no childish infatuation. I'm a grown woman and I love you, Richard. Anne wanted us together—she made me promise—"

Richard held up a hand and averted his face. "You must not say these things. I must not hear them."

"Don't send me away, Richard! My heart will break without you."

He turned and looked at me again. "It's impossible, Elizabeth," he whispered hoarsely.

We stared at one another until, without warning, we were in each other's arms. He held me close, my cheek against his, and I could taste the salt of our tears. Exquisite joy and profound despair swept through me, all at the same moment, and I felt my grief like a burning in my blood.

Then he thrust me from him.

This is the last time I shall ever see him. The thought struck me so forcibly, I almost reeled where I stood. I cried out in panic, "I crave a favor, my lord!"

He waited.

"I wish a portrait of you. It would be a comfort to me."

I couldn't bear the suffering look that came into his eyes. I dropped my lids. I spoke again, my voice a tremulous whisper, "—and your book, *Tristan and Iseult*."

He held his back rigid, then gave me a nod. There was silence for a long moment. I bent forward and caressed his cheek with my lips, lingering there for a fleeting second, trying to imprint its feel, its memory, on my soul.

"I'll never change," I whispered. "I'll go to my death loving you, Richard."

And then I left.

❖

AS I CAST A BACKWARD GLANCE TOWARD LONDON, MY vision blurred with tears. This was what Anne had feared: leaving Richard alone and vulnerable, with no heart to win the fight for his life and throne. I tore my gaze away and nudged my palfrey forward.

Our journey to Sheriff Hutton took several days; how many I did not know, for one folded into the other. Once again we passed through the villages, the hamlets, and the small towns, and I saw the gilded Maypole across the fields. Strangely, the sight sent despair flooding through me. Yet despite the revels, a great listlessness hung over the land in the warm days of May. The entire realm seemed to be waiting. Few smiles greeted us at the abbeys and the inns; no laughter came from the thatched roofed cottages where sharp-tongued mothers chased their children; no song issued forth from the men working the fields, and in the taverns, the chatter was subdued and patrons sat thoughtfully silent, staring at us and the royal blazon of the white boar. There had been too many kings in too short a time; too many wars; too many rivers of blood, too much horror of betrayal and beheadings. In my mind's eye, I saw Tudor waiting at Harfleur, preparing for invasion, and Richard waiting at Nottingham, checking for allies, searching each man's face to see if he could pry open his heart.

Waiting, in his castle atop the black rock where the tidings of Ned's death had come; where the tidings of Tudor's invasion would be brought.

Waiting, in the place he had named his "Castle of Care," from his book, *The Vision of Piers Plowman;* the grand poem that had once fueled his hopes and dreams of carving a new, just world.

I looked at Johnnie and Edward, my two charges, riding silently beside me. Richard had sent us to his old northern friends of York-shire, the comrades of his youth, for safekeeping. His instructions to us were simple. To wait.

To wait.

For the victors there would be life and a throne; for the losers, there would be death and calamity. God's judgment would decide all.

We received a warm welcome from the servants and keepers at Sheriff Hutton. But the days bore down heavily on me. Sheriff Hutton, with its eight mighty towers of stone, magnificent wall hangings, hallways, and stately stairways, was a lonely place. I spent my time in silent companionship with my two cousins, grateful that Edward's innocence and weak mind protected him from fully comprehending the misery of our situation.

"W-what are you doing, Lizzie?" he asked me one afternoon as I sat before my mirror.

"Plaiting my hair, Edward," I replied gently.

"I l-love y-your h-h-hair. 'Tis s-so soft, l-like an a-angel."

"Thank you, Edward." I gave him a hug and left for the stables. Along the way, men-at-arms fell in behind me. I wished I could be alone, but I knew it wasn't safe. I mounted my white gelding and broke into a gallop. I rode low in the saddle, over meadows of flow-ers, beneath vast gray skies laden with silver-edged, frothy clouds. The wind whipped my face, and I found its touch cool and sooth-ing. From behind me came the thunder of hooves. It was Johnnie. He drew to my side on his chestnut, but he didn't speak, and we rode on together in silent companionship. Finally, out of breath, I drew rein, and Johnnie helped me dismount. We sat down on a blanket of wild red poppies. I mulled my thoughts for a long time before I spoke. "What is going to happen, Johnnie?"

He inhaled a long, audible breath. "No one dares guess, but I fear the worst. Father has no heart for kingship any longer."

I nodded miserably. "I know."

"What will you do if he loses? Have you given it thought?"

"I have thought of naught else." I plucked a poppy and twirled it in my hand, staring down at its black heart. "I want to flee. Oh, how I want to flee! But I fear I must stay."

"You will be made to wed Tudor if you stay."

"I know, Johnnie. But this is larger than me. It is about England. If I flee, the war continues, and more will perish. But if I stay—"

"You shall be queen."

"Aye, queen. And England will have peace." My grief was a huge knot inside me, and all at once the flower seemed a heavy weight in my hand. I dropped it into the sea of red at my feet. "My sisters are in London. What will become of them if I leave? As queen, I could protect all who depend on me—not only my sisters, but little Edward. 'Tis what Richard wants. He wants me to accept the outcome of the battle with Tudor as the judgment of God, whatever it may be."

Johnnie took my hand, his gray-green eyes dark, brimming with sorrow. "Elizabeth, I shall pray for you, my fair cousin."

"And I for you, my dear Johnnie."

SOMETIMES, IN MY DESPAIR, I ROAMED THE GAR-dens, rode through the fields and parks, and sought the wind in my face, but little helped to lift my despondent spirits. In the evenings, I played my lute and sang for Johnnie and Edward. But the songs were all laments, for the merry tunes would not come. Richard was everywhere around me.

News came to me in dribbles, none of it good. Tudor had given Sir William Stanley and his brother, Lord Thomas Stanley, bribes to draw them to his side. The month of August arrived steamy with heat and thunderstorms, and the tension in the castle rose to unbearable proportions. *August is when Tudor will invade,* said the whispers.

Many times during the early days of August, Johnnie, Edward, and I ran to the window as horses galloped into the courtyard. Then, not waiting for the tidings to be brought to us, we rushed downstairs to receive them.

"On August seventh, Henry Tudor landed at Milford Haven in Wales, the land of his fathers!"

"King Richard has left Nottingham for Leicester, the point of muster for his army!"

"King Richard has permitted Lord Stanley to leave his side! No one understands why."

This last report was devastating, and astonishing.

"Sir William Stanley and his brother, Lord Thomas the Wily Fox, are powerful in Cheshire and Lancashire. Now the king will have to do without them," someone exclaimed, echoing my thoughts. "What is he thinking? Does he wish for death?"

"King Richard knows the Stanleys' motto is 'a foot in each camp'!" said another.

"The old fox is too clever to commit until he sees which way the cat jumps," a different voice added to the medley.

My head ached, and the sick giddiness behind my eyes swelled. I turned away, unable to view the look of horror in the eyes around me, a hand over my lips to smother my cry. *Is Richard vainly seeking for loyalty and trust? Is he leaving his fate to Fortune? Is he courting death and relief from the agony of his memories?* I had no answer.

A week later, we had more news.

"A wise woman has prophesied King Richard's defeat! When the king crossed the bridge at Leicester on his way to give battle, his spur struck the wall and the wise woman said that where his spur struck the stone, his head would strike on the way back."

I went back into the castle. In my room, I closed my eyes and sank down into a chair, my legs suddenly too weak to sustain me. A vision of Richard on his white courser leading the way from Leicester flashed into my mind, his men ranging around him, his crown on his head. Joyless, restless, waiting for battle.

No more news came until the twenty-third day of August, when shouts and cries drew my attention to the window. Wounded men were clattering into the courtyard. I dropped the book I was reading to Edward and we ran down the tower stairs together, nearly tripping. I drew up short at the sight of the soldiers. Stunned and disbelieving, clutching their bandaged limbs, leaning against one another for support, they were relating their tale of disaster. I emerged from the tower staircase. They all broke off and turned to look at me. But the last words I'd heard from them reverberated in my mind with the tumult of clarions.

"—Henry Tudor—king—"

I gave a cry; my legs buckled beneath me. I reached out for support and felt Johnnie take my arm.

Gently, a voice said, "My lady, permit me to take you inside."

"No!" I cried. "No—tell me what happened! I need to know what happened—"

The man hesitated. Then he said quietly, "My lady, battle was joined yesterday at Bosworth Field on Monday, August twenty-second. King Richard is dead."

I clenched my teeth hard, balled my fists, and willed myself not to fall, to keep erect. I threw Johnnie a glance. He had gone pale. Edward began to wail. A man took him by the hand. "Come my little lord, this is no place for you." I watched his small figure recede into the tower.

The messenger resumed his report.

"After two hours of battle, King Richard attempted to single out his enemy by himself and rode down the hill accompanied by those knights willing to die with him, for a suicide charge it was, my lady. He went behind enemy lines to get at Tudor. It was as if he sought death."

Someone else broke in. "William Stanley, who had been watching the battle from the sidelines on a neighboring hill, brought the full weight of his army to bear on the side of Henry Tudor."

I tried to focus on the man's face, but it was blurred. Another voice drifted to me softly, ever so softly that I thought for a moment I had dreamt it. "King Richard and his seventy knights fell fighting valiantly, outnumbered eighty to one."

"Eighty to one—" I repeated in bewilderment, trying to understand. My head throbbed with pain. "Eighty to one? Eighty to one—" As the words exploded in my mind, I raised my hands to cover my ears. Dimly, I saw him exchange a look with another man, and then a woman touched my sleeve.

"Me lady, let me take ye inside. Ye 'ave 'ad a shock ... We all 'ave, dearie . . ."

I learned the full story as I sat silent as a statue in my chamber. It was Johnnie who told me.

Richard had gone into battle wearing his crown. It had made him an easy mark for the enemy, as if his white horse weren't enough to single him out. Even then, he didn't die, and so he demanded death by riding behind enemy lines to slay Tudor. Sir William Stanley found Richard's crown in a thistle bush and crowned Tudor to the cheers of his men, who cried, "King Henry! King Henry!"

So Richard was dead; Tudor was King.

What now?

As footsteps raced along the corridors—those of servants, pages, armed men undone by the news of defeat—the world swam before my eyes. Where would I go? And what did it matter? Richard was dead. Richard was dead—

Someone pulled me to my feet, drew me outside. A horse whinnied before me. "No!" I heard myself say faintly. "I must stay. To end the bloodshed. Don't you see, 'tis the only way!"

A group of dark figures moved closer, on horseback. I saw shadows in the twilight. They clattered into the courtyard and dismounted. One of them, darker than the rest, came forward and bowed low. I blinked to clear my vision, but it did no good. I could not see the shadow's face, for it was dusk.

"Sir Robert Willoughby, my lady," he said.

By force of habit, I extended him my hand.

"You are welcome," I said, and I did not know my voice, which came to me like a stranger's.

"You are welcome . . . welcome . . . Eighty times welcome . . . eighty to one . . . welcome . . . welcome," I said. "King Richard is dead."

CHAPTER 11

The Victor, 1485

MY HEAD ACHED. I PRESSED A HAND TO MY BROW TO ease the throbbing hurt. Raising myself to an elbow, I looked around. It was dark, and I was rocking in a litter. Thrusting back the curtains, I looked out. Two strangers were riding beside me, a man and a woman.

"Who are you? Where are John of Gloucester and the Earl of Warwick?" I demanded. "Where are we?"

They exchanged glances with one another. The woman said, "We're nearing London. Just passed through Barnet a half hour ago, I'd say."

Nothing seemed familiar. My eye went to the red dragon blazing on the man's tunic. What emblem was that? I'd never seen it before. I peered ahead. All the men-at-arms sported the same insignia.

"Where are we going?" I asked them. Odd memories twitched in my mind through the ache in my head, and the confusion. And the fear. For now I remembered dreaming that Richard had lost the battle. I blinked.

"Where are we going?" I repeated, fear rising in my throat.

After a hesitation, the woman gave me a reply. "To the Tower." Her voice was chilling in its softness.

I regarded her blankly. "But the king prefers Westminster."

"Not this king," came the woman's retort on a chuckle. Again, she exchanged a look with the man cantering at her side. He gave her a knowing smile.

"Where are my cousins?" I demanded, trying to quell my panic.

Silence. Then the man said, "Best you rest now, my lady. It's been a hard journey for ye. Ye've been ill, and ye'll need your strength, I dare say." He had an accent both strange and familiar at the same time. It reminded me of someone—but who? Like a bolt of lightning on a clear day, it came to me. *Dr. Lewis!* The Welshman from sanctuary. Margaret Beaufort's physician.

With a trembling hand, I let the curtain drop. Inside, alone in the dark, I shut my eyes on a breath and bowed my head. Always in the past months when I had prayed, my thoughts were of Richard. Now, for a moment, I saw his face, but it was very far away, and his gray eyes held a sorrowful expression. A sword rose above him, glittering like a crucifix. Then it bore down. My head throbbed again. I moaned and closed my eyes.

When I dared look, it was nearly sundown. Church bells were clanging, and the white towers of the Tower of London glowed with a rosy light in the fading rays of day. Behind the castle, the Thames sparkled with a deepening sapphire hue. My cart drew to a clattering halt in the cobbled court. I thrust back the curtains and moved to disembark.

"You are not staying here," the woman said.

"Then why are we stopping?"

" 'Tis for the Earl of Warwick and John of Gloucester that we stop."

I hesitated. Why for them, and not for me? Nothing made sense. I strained my eyes into the distance ahead, where a group of armed men were dismounting, and spied Edward's golden hair and diminutive figure. "Edward—Edward!" I called. He turned to look at me. One of the men at his side said something to him, and he seemed crestfallen. He nodded, went inside. *Oh, dear God, I* thought of a sudden, *Edward is a Plantagenet in the direct royal male line!* I made the sign of the cross.

At least Johnnie was safe. He was a bastard and no threat to anyone. I looked around for him, but I didn't see him. Maybe if I went inside—

"I need the privy," I said, climbing out of the litter without assistance.

"I'll go with you," the woman said hastily.

"You may wait here for me. I know the way." I took a step forward, but she blocked my path squarely with her body. "Nay, lady, 'tis not permitted."

"What do you mean?"

"Orders, me lady."

"Whose orders?"

"The king's."

"The king?"

"King Henry. He has bid us bring you to Westminster."

King Henry.

O, Blessed Mother . . .

The pounding in my head rose to a shattering pitch. I shut my eyes and dug my nails into the palms of my hands. Silently, I cried out for help to the Blessed Virgin, and as if Heaven heard my plea, a thought blossomed in my heart. *But Tudor has vowed to wed me. I shall be queen. Edward shall be safe when I am queen. They shall all be safe, for I will unite the white rose with the red and end the bloodshed, as Richard had wished.*

Recovering my composure, I gave the woman a nod. She turned and followed me to the privy.

❀

ON THE WAY TO WESTMINSTER, WE PAUSED FOR RE-freshment at Baynard's Castle.

Where Richard accepted the crown, I thought. I refused wine and remained in my litter. As I sat there, alone with my memories, a horse's whinny pierced my thoughts and the curtain was drawn back. It was Sir Robert Willoughby.

"My lady, I trust the journey has not been unduly harsh?"

I cast my eyes down. "I have no memory of it," I said softly.

"The king is already here at the bishop's palace, but he will not meet us." After a pause, Willoughby added, "Your entry is not to be marked. He wishes no ceremony at this time. You are to proceed to Westminster to be placed into the care of your mother. Later, the king will send for you."

He had said nothing about the wedding, I noted. *Thanks be to the Virgin. A little more time—I have a little more time.*

At Westminster, I was escorted to my mother by a cluster of armed guards. My reunion with my family was bittersweet. "Mother!" I cried, embracing her. She had changed; always robust, she now had a frail quality about her. But then, she had suffered much. Pity and love swept me and I embraced her again. "O Mother."

Then I spied my sister. "Cecily!" I cried. I released my mother and hugged her too, my heart gladdened by the sight of her. " 'Tis so good to see you. I didn't know I could miss you so much," I said, laughing through tears.

Cecily laughed back, "Nor I, sister," she replied, holding me close.

I turned to the others, all standing with faces upturned to me. "Anne, how you've grown! And Kate, my sweet Kate, my beautiful Kate—" I swept her into my arms and covered her cheeks with kisses. "And Bridget—" My youngest sister stared at me with round cornflower eyes, her expression one of uncertainty, for five months is a long span in the life of a four-year-old. " 'Tis so good to see you again!"

My mother took my arm. "You look terrible, Elizabeth. You've lost weight. We must fatten you up for King Henry, my dear." She sent for hippocras and food, and over a repast of olives and the sugared fried bread slices I loved so well, she whispered the details of what had transpired on the twenty-second of August, and it plunged me into a desolation and sorrow of mind I had not known before.

After the battle, Henry Tudor, wearing Richard's battered crown, rode to Leicester. Richard's body, naked, bloody, wearing a felon's halter around the neck, was thrown over a horse. It moved across the bridge at Leicester, and as the wise woman had proph-

esied, Richard's head struck the stone wall of the bridge where his
spur had scraped on the way to battle. His body was handed over
to the monks of Grey Friars Church, but no money was granted
for the burial and he lay in a pauper's tomb, with no headstone.
Tudor had entered London two days earlier than I, on the third of
September—a Saturday, for he was superstitious and considered
Saturday his luckiest day of the week. Borne in a cart, hidden by
dark blue velvet curtains, he peered out at the people from behind
the slit.

"He is an odd fellow," breathed my mother, "for he wishes to
see without being seen. What is the point of that, I ask you?"

I smiled inwardly. By nature my mother preferred to flaunt, not
hide, for she had always loved to be admired and envied. But, indeed, it was strange. The kings I had known enjoyed greeting their
subjects. "Were there any crowds to receive him?" I inquired.

"None to cheer him. But none to challenge him either."

'Tis why he wished me to enter London unnoticed, I thought. *How
humiliating, if a multitude had welcomed me and not him.*

"How many died at Bosworth?"

"Three thousand, almost all on Richard's side, including Lord
Howard, Duke of Norfolk."

I wanted to ask about Sir Thomas Stafford, but I knew my
mother didn't have that knowledge. No one did, not yet. Thomas
was not important enough. "What about the others—Lovell, Ratcliffe, Catesby—and Sir Humphrey Stafford?" I asked.

"Ratcliffe and most of Richard's knights went with him into
that suicidal charge he made against Tudor—against *King Henry,*"
she corrected herself, lowering her voice and throwing a glance
at the servants moving about the chamber. "Lovell escaped, but
Catesby was hung right after the battle."

"Without trial?"

"It seems there is no need for trial in this new world of ours,"
she went on. Her voice was so low, it was barely audible. "They
say Tudor has dated his reign from the day before Bosworth so he
could attaint and hang for treason all those who fought for Richard
at Bosworth."

I stared at my mother. Surely this could not be? Attaint and hang men *because they fought for their king?* With a sweep of the arm, Tudor would send crashing to the ground the rules of chivalry and the code of conduct that had governed men's actions for centuries. Holy Mother of God, if he was capable of this, what was next?

My mother reached out and with a gentle motion, she pushed against my chin, for my mouth had dropped open in shock.

"The world has changed, my child," she said under her breath, "and we must change with it. Now get some rest. I'm expecting the king's mother shortly, and I don't want her to see you until you look better."

Lady Margaret Beaufort proved a frequent visitor to our quarters. I had no wish to see her, and so I disappeared before each visit, but she spent much time discussing matters with my mother, who, after her initial tender welcome had reverted to her true, critical nature. I was not gay enough for the king, she feared, nor fat enough; my cheeks were not rosy enough. Her chatter and promises to Margaret Beaufort formed a dim rumble in the background of my days as I spent time at my prie-dieu, praying for Richard and all those dear to me, now lost.

As the days progressed, I learned from the palace whispers that people in the streets were wondering where I was, since they didn't see me, and that they spoke lovingly of me, for they treasured me for my father's sake and also for the memory of happier days. Some claimed I was already in London, others said I was preparing for my wedding, and still more were skeptical that the marriage would ever take place.

I listened quietly as my sisters gossiped about King Henry.

"They say he's secretive and reveals nothing," said Cecily, turning to me.

I gave her a shrug from the window seat, where I sat poring over Richard's book, Boethius's *De Consolatione.* Boethius had been thrown into prison in the year 800, and, wishing to help others in their time of great travail, he'd written the book to explain God's purpose in allowing evil things to happen to good people. Knowing how much the volume had meant to Richard, I studied its pages, especially the labors of Hercules, and made notes in the margins. One day, moved by my memories, I copied Richard's motto on the flyleaf at the back of the book, in an unobtrusive place where it wouldn't be noticed. *Loyaulte me Lie*, Loyalty Binds Me. I signed it "Elizabeth." He had never sent me *Tristan*, or the portrait I had requested of him, but I had the book that had helped him bear his fate. Now it would help me bear mine, whatever that proved to be.

"How do you feel about marrying Tudor?" Cecily asked.

"I've no feelings about it," I said wearily, "and best that I have none. We are all pawns to family ambitions."

"Not me. I was a pawn to no one's ambition but Ralph Scrope's," Cecily retorted, with a bitter edge to her tone. After a pause, she added, "Do you think you can grow to love him?"

"As much as you have grown to love Scrope," I replied.

"What's 'love'?" demanded Kate.

"I'm not sure," replied nine-year-old Anne.

Anne turned to the young nurse brushing her hair. "What's love?" she asked.

The girl paused in her strokes, a faraway look in her eyes. "They say love can make you believe cinders are flour and old iron is glass. That a felt hat is a jeweled beret, and leeks give honey."

I looked down at the gloomy scene below. *Love lights a fire that turns dismal gray into sparkling silver,* I added silently.

"What tripe!" Cecily exclaimed. "If that's what love is, then it's merely a form of madness and I've no need of it."

"But they say that when you are in love, you are content with life, no matter how little you have."

"Psht!" Cecily retorted. "Only a madman is content to be mad, and in want."

Mother overheard Cecily's remark as she entered the room. "Your Uncle Anthony had a favorite line he often repeated, heaven knows why. 'But Venus, who runs the tavern of love, offers hippocras tainted with gall. Half-drunk on love, we are lured to our destruction.' He always was a romantic fool."

A tide of desolation washed over me. *Uncle Anthony was right,* I thought; *the apple I picked from Love's shining tree has turned to ashes in my hands.*

Gently, I fingered Thomas's sapphire brooch that I always wore, and turned the page of Richard's book, my remnant of love.

WHEN OCTOBER ARRIVED, IT BROUGHT TO MIND A thousand thoughts of Richard when last the leaves had shone gold and fallen from the trees, for the second day of October was his birthday. There had been feasting, and the poor queen had come to the table though she could barely sit for agony. Dear Anne, sweet Anne, she had wanted me to wed Richard. *Only love can save him, Elizabeth*, she had whispered.

I laid my head against the window pane and closed my eyes, seeing again the wax candles flickering that night, the torches flaring against the crimson and olive of the wall tapestries; remembering the emotion that had lifted my heart above the grief as I looked at Richard's dark head across the hall.

He would have been thirty-three years of age, had he lived.

I put down his book and drew away from the window. Richard was dead. The living must accept the life God gave them.

During this month of October, Tudor gathered the reins of government to himself. He summoned his trusted advisor, Bishop Morton, back from the Continent, appointed him Lord Chancellor, and sent Archbishop Rotherham back to York. Plague was rife in London, forcing Tudor to postpone his coronation. This the people took as an ill omen.

" 'Tis a token that the reign shall be laborious, they say," my mother told us, "because it began in sickness."

By midmonth plague vanished, and the city was abuzz with talk of Tudor's coronation, set for the thirtieth day of October. I heard my mother and Cecily chattering together. "For his coronation Tudor has created a personal guard of fifty yeomen in the French custom," my mother marveled.

What surprise in that? I wondered. After all, Tudor was a quarter French, and reared in France for half his life. More French customs were sure to follow.

"They are clad in royal scarlet and gold, and heavily armed to protect him against those who would do him harm," my mother added.

Aye, he must have been terrified when Richard cut around the army of three thousand men that shielded him from the fray, slew four of his bodyguards, and came within a sword's reach of killing him as he turned to flee. *Maybe now,* I thought, *with his French-style guard, he'll rest easy.*

During this time, my weariness became a silent retreat as Mother complained and paced whenever we were alone in our chamber.

"The wedding has been postponed. It seems Tudor will be crowned alone, and govern alone. *Alone*—" She stressed the word, and turned blazing eyes on me. "You know what that means, don't you? He's decided not to claim the crown through your right to it! He fears not to be seen as a true king, but king only as long as you live." She quickened her frenetic pacing to and fro. My head grew dizzy watching her. "Nor has he claimed the throne by Lancastrian descent, for all know his claim is stained by bastard lineage on both sides. Nor does he claim it by right of conquest. For that would encourage others to do the same."

"So how does he claim it?" I asked, bending my head to my lyre and plucking at a wrong note.

"It defies belief—he claims the throne by the fact that he possesses it!"

I lifted my head. "Simply because he is king? That is novel."

" 'Tis all Morton's idea. He's a crafty one, that Morton. He's behind everything Tudor does—Morton and his mother both. The two of them shit out of the same arse."

"I thought Morton had your favor, Mother," I said, barely suppressing my smile.

"He did, when he was on my side. But Morton's kind always finds the mountain peak as surely as water flows downhill. He's run to the Tudors now, for that's where power is." She paused to gaze at me. Then she drew near and lowered her voice to a bare whisper. "By legitimizing you, he has legitimized your brother. Well he knows that if Dickon lives, he is a usurper. I fear Tudor may try to hunt him down and kill him."

I took her hand in mine. "Have you heard from him?" I whispered.

"Nay, not a word. But that could be because Tudor's spies are everywhere and the time is not right."

I inhaled a deep breath. *And it could be because something has happened to Dickon and they have not the heart to tell us.*

"Mother, it troubles me that I do not have the password. Can you tell me what it is?"

She withdrew her hand from mine. "So you can tell the Tudor?" she hissed.

"Oh Mother, how can you think such a thing?" I whispered, wounded to the core. "So I can know Dickon, if something should happen to you!"

She rose abruptly.

"Wishing me ill, are you? I should have guessed!"

I looked up at her helplessly.

She bent down and snarled in my ear, "You pretend you've no wish to be queen, but you would betray my son in order to protect your position!"

She turned and swept out of the room. I watched her leave, my heart twisting in my breast that she could think such evil of me. But I did not call after her, for what good would it do?

❀

HENRY TUDOR'S CORONATION WAS EXTRAVAGANT, and the tumult of the festivities reached us in our suite at Westminster as London glittered with sunshine, pageants, plays, and song. I watched from the windows of Westminster Palace. Bonfires were lit in the streets, and the entire city turned out to catch a glimpse of the new king being rowed by barge to Westminster Abbey. The blare of trumpets came to me from the river. I strained my eyes to see the purple-clad figure, but I could tell little from the distance before he disappeared from view. The splendor of the coronation service at the abbey could only be imagined. Amid the hangings of white and green cloth of gold, and red velvet roses and dragons, the man dressed in purple would be anointed and crowned King Henry VII.

Soon the details were brought to us.

"His mother, the Lady Margaret, is said to have wept most marvelously," Bridget's nurse related.

I suppose Margaret Beaufort's cup overflowed as she watched her son crowned, I thought. I couldn't help but wonder what it felt like to have one's cup overflow with joy; to see cherished dreams realized; to achieve the heart's greatest, most impossible desire. As I contemplated Lady Beaufort's happiness, my own losses, my captivity, my anguish, and the uncertainty of the years since my father's death struck me with the force of a steel blow.

"Come to me, Kate." I held my hand out to my precious little sister. She climbed into my lap, and I tightened my arms around her sweet body and laid my head against her fragrant golden curls. "I love you, my little Kate," I whispered. "I love you so much."

ON THE SEVENTH DAY OF NOVEMBER, THE NEWLY crowned King Henry met his first Parliament and shocked the land by enacting into law what had previously been a rumor: he did indeed date his reign by one day prior to the battle of Bosworth, and attainted for treason all who had fought for Richard—including Sir Humphrey Stafford.

"But it makes no sense," I said from my window seat. "If someone challenges Henry Tudor, who will show up to fight for him?"

My mother paused thoughtfully in her needlework as she sat in a chair near me. Leaning close she whispered, "That is good for us—when Dickon returns." She made another stitch and added, "Henry's act repeals Richard's statutes. You, Elizabeth, are no longer a bastard, but recognized as the king's daughter."

"I have always been my father's daughter," I murmured absently, the memory of Papa's return from the French war stirring in my mind. I saw him again bending down to swoop me up in his great arms as I ran to him.

My mother's voice roused me from reverie. "Aye, indeed you have always been your father's daughter," she murmured bitterly.

Cecily, who was plucking her eyebrows, turned from the mirror and went to Mother's side. She draped an arm around her neck, and Mother drew her down and kissed her. Cecily smiled at me like a cat.

O Mary, I cried inwardly, *how I miss you, my sister!*

I rose, fetched my lyre, and returned to the window seat. Night was falling. I bent my head and strummed a few chords, forcing Mary from my thoughts, for I didn't wish to weep. Inhaling deeply, I raised my voice in song. Sir Humphrey Stafford had been attainted, Mother had said. I took heart in the knowledge, for it meant he had survived the battle. Maybe it meant that Thomas was safe, too. I touched my sapphire brooch. *O Thomas, those were good days in sanctuary, weren't they?*

I ended my song when I heard Mother discussing the estates that King Richard had confiscated from her.

" 'Tis my great hope that King Henry will restore them to me. I particularly miss my London residence of Cold Harbor."

"If he does, Mother, would it mean we could leave Westminster?" I asked.

"Why would we wish to leave?" Cecily demanded. " 'Tis comfortable here. We have fine clothes, good food, and the guard has been lifted."

"I'm talking about freedom, Cecily, not clothes. We can roam the palace, but we take our meals in our chambers and are not permitted into the gardens or the streets. We're still captives."

Cecily scowled at me. "Nothing's ever enough for you!" she cried. "Not even being queen!"

"I've no desire to be queen. I'd rather be free. Then I could wed a squire and live a contented life far away from court."

"Wed a squire?" Cecily said, shocked.

"Fool!" cried my mother, rising to her feet. "What nonsense are you spouting now? Do you not realize our predicament? What lies at stake? There's no assurance you will be queen! I am working my fingers to the bone to arrange it, and instead of helping me, all you do is whine about being free—whatever that is supposed to mean."

"I'm nineteen years old," I said, almost to myself, knowing they would never understand, "and my life is ebbing away in confinement."

THE MIST SWIRLED AROUND ME LIKE A CLOUD, HIDing the world, and I knew not where I was. The only thing clear to me was that night had fallen. I risked a step forward. The whiteness shifted to reveal a glimpse of something—but what? There, it came again! A glint of silver—a shimmer in the distance. Cautiously, I peered ahead and took another step. All at once the fog parted. Galloping toward me was a knight in white armor on a shining pale horse! He emerged from behind the veil of mist, and I saw the circlet of gold on his helmet. A gasp escaped my lips and I gave a joyous cry. I put out my arms to him. *"Richard!"*

I awoke to darkness.

I could not sleep for the rest of the night, but lay in my bed watching the glittering stars in the sky through the window, his name echoing in the black stillness of my mind.

PARLIAMENT CONTINUED TO SIT THROUGH NOVEM-ber, but for all the talk of coronation, there was no mention of marriage, which distressed Mother deeply.

"Though the king took an oath to wed you," my mother fretted, pacing, "he seems to lack desire for this marriage. I fear he might yet find a way to evade it. Lady Beaufort tells me he would prefer to wed Lord Herbert's sister, whom he knew as a boy. There's more to it than that, I am sure."

The days dragged on, and Mother grew more frantic. She bribed and cajoled until she got to the heart of the matter.

"It appears King Henry is jealous of your right to the crown." Mother wrung her hands as she paced. Her confinement was not as strict as mine, and somehow she knew everything, whether secret or not. "But so much depends on this marriage for him, too. Surely he sees that? What in God's name is he waiting for?"

"For me to show if I am with child," I said, unable to help myself from lashing out at her. I wished to wound her, to watch her writhe. Of late, I had become convinced that by going against Papa's wishes and fleeing into sanctuary, she had brought about the very thing she'd feared. Had she reached an accommodation with King Richard, all would have been different for us. Now, I might even be wed to Thomas. She was the cause of my misery, and sometimes I felt I loathed her.

My mother swung around. "What?" she snarled.

"He's waiting for me to show if I am with child," I repeated. "With Richard's child." I clarified, giving her a smile.

"How dare you taunt me?" my mother screamed. "How dare you make light of our situation? Our future depends on you. And you, disgraceful girl, may have undone us all! We must set aside that fear immediately—" Mother turned and left the chamber.

As I watched her swiftly retreating figure, sudden apprehension seized me. I dropped my mending and ran after her. "What are you going to do?" I cried at the top of the tower stairs. But Mother was gone, and I heard only the echo of her footsteps as they faded away.

I gave Kate and Anne their singing lesson, and their French lesson, and waited anxiously for Mother's return. For I knew that look in her eyes; she was up to something and I feared what it might be. Had I gone too far? If I didn't wed Tudor—if I didn't become queen—what would become of my sweet little sisters? We had to survive until Dickon returned. *If he returns*, I added to myself on a breath. *For we live in dangerous times, and who knows what might happen to a child?*

Mother returned hours later. "I have dug deep and now I know the truth." She glared at me.

"The truth?"

"King Henry has been repulsed and incensed by your rumored affair with Richard and is most reluctant to wed you."

"That suits us both then," I challenged, lifting my chin. "For the thought of wedding the man who killed King Richard incenses and repulses me."

My mother slapped my face hard. I nursed the stinging blow, but I didn't raise my hand to her as I had in sanctuary. This wasn't so important; nothing was so important anymore.

"We have to keep a foot in both camps," whispered my mother. "Until Dickon returns. 'Tis the only way."

Pity flooded me. She still hoped. *But what can a boy do against a man?* I thought. *And by the time Dickon is grown, all might be changed.*

Remembering Richard, who had died accepting the judgment

of God, I spent many nights at my prie-dieu seeking strength from the Almighty to endure my fate, whether that meant confinement, or freedom, or life as Tudor's consort. While I worried about my sisters, I was not displeased by Tudor's reluctance, for it bought me time to sing at my lyre and nurse the hopes of my heart: marriage to someone not high-born who would pose no threat to this king; a good man who would care for me and heal my heart.

Sir Thomas Stafford.

How lovely that would be. To retire to the country, to gallop across the moors with the wind in my face, as I had done while Richard lived. But then, what about Edward of Warwick and those I'd vowed to help once I was queen?

Awash with guilt for my selfishness, I silently asked God for forgiveness. Whatever God willed, I would accept with an open heart.

Thus I tried to drown out my mother with my lyre, and gave my sisters their lessons; I darned my dresses, and dreamed my dreams. But I often caught a triumphant gleam in my mother's eyes as we did needlework together; the kind of look she had when something she was plotting was about to come to successful fruition. I found it disquieting.

"Prepare yourself," my mother informed me one cold night in December. "Tonight the king comes to test your virginity."

I pushed myself to my feet slowly, barely conscious that I did so. "You'll stop at nothing to get what you want, will you?"

"Oh, don't play the pope-holy saint with me. You wish to be queen as much as I wish it for you." But she was unable to suppress the triumph shining in her eyes.

"By all that is sacred in Heaven, I shall rejoice the day you destroy yourself, Mother, as you surely will do."

Mother smiled. "What difference if the bedding comes sooner rather than later? You know it has to come." She leaned close to my ear. "Put a good face on it."

Aye, there was nothing I could do. I had to submit, for little Edward's sake, and for the sake of my sisters. What would become of them if Tudor didn't wed me? Though women were never imprisoned in the Tower like men, they could be confined in a nun-

nery against their will and grow old, bereft of all joy. For royal
blood pulsed in my sisters' veins as surely as in young Edward of
Warwick's. I shut my eyes.

❖

DESPITE THE POSSET I TOOK, I WAS TREMBLING WHEN
Henry Tudor entered my bedchamber. Slender in build, and of me-
dium height, with pronounced cheekbones, limp blond hair and
small eyes of undetermined color, Tudor might have been pleasant
looking but for a long, pointed nose that brought to mind a ferret.
I stood in my shift, my hair loose around me, shivering for cold. He
seemed taken aback at the sight of me for a moment and halted in
his steps. Then he resumed his pace and drew near. After all, this
was business—for both of us. I braced myself not to recoil at his
touch, which was icy; at his breath, which was stale; at his scent,
which was musty. I felt cold, so cold . . . If only it were—

If only I could close my eyes and pretend it was—

No. I couldn't. Such a thing was sin. Thomas, then—*O Thomas—
I could have been happy with you, Thomas* . . .

I couldn't help myself; Tudor touched my cheek, and it was
Richard's touch I remembered. I closed my eyes.

O Blessed Mother, help me now, help me in the depth of my despair!

The vision of a frozen lake rose before me; I watched the ice
water drain slowly, inexorably, into my veins, drop by fated drop.
Strength, I told myself; *strength is what is needed to endure life . . . I do
this for my sisters . . . so they don't end in misery . . .*

I lay back on the bed, in the darkness, and held my breath. The
sound of panting came to me, and into my mind flashed the image
of a winded wolf, his red eyes glowing as he chewed on his prey. A
short, sharp pain stabbed my groin, and I cried out; then another
stab. Was this what poets had in mind when they wrote of love?
Surely not; this was something repellent; disgusting; an awful business; naught but pain . . .

I turned my face away from the one who crouched over me,
and I held my breath, for a vile smell assailed me each time I took
in air. *When will this end, Blessed Mother?* Time passed and the horror of Tudor's body in mine finally ceased. He rolled off me with

a sigh of satisfaction. I heard movement on the bed; movement in the chamber. But I didn't open my eyes. I lay there like a corpse, for dead I felt. A shadow stirred at my bedside, and I stiffened; I clutched the sheets to my chin. I held my breath. The shadow bent down and planted a kiss on my cheek.

Tears welled up behind my eyes and rolled slowly down my cheek. I felt the shadow recede. I opened my eyes then, and watched the shadow leave in the moonlight.

CHAPTER 12

Consort of the King, 1486

AT THE COCK'S CROW, AS DAY BROKE OVER LONDON and church bells ran for Prime, my mother burst into my chamber to inspect the bloody sheets.

"You have made our fortune, Elizabeth!" she exulted. "Now you will be queen, and Henry will pay the ransom for your brother Dorset's release from France, as he promised me."

I was overcome with a deep revulsion for her. As haughtily as I could manage, I requested a hot bath. Maybe soap and water would wash away the smell of Tudor and cleanse me of this feeling of filth.

My mother turned as she reached the door, and threw me a long look. "Queen already, are you?" She left, laughing loudly.

I stayed in the water all day.

It seemed that all in the land were anxiously awaiting the moment when Tudor would fulfill his promise and wed me, because as Yule approached, my mother came to me.

"There is news—great news!" she cried, enraptured. "Parliament presented the king a petition asking him to take you to wife and Tudor agreed to comply!"

Cecily swished her skirts around from the looking glass where she had been admiring her image. "Now we shall live at court and go to feasts and disguisings and pageants!"

"What is the matter with you, Elizabeth?" my mother asked, noting my dour expression.

"She's going to a funeral!" Cecily laughed.

"More like a birth," I replied, rising from my seat at the window.

My mother approached me, then took my arm and swung me to face her.

"You're with child?" she breathed, her eyes alight with exultation.

" 'Tis too soon to know for sure."

Mother wasted no time. She fled the room, and I realized she was going to Margaret Beaufort. She returned but an hour later.

"Lady Beaufort agrees that the marriage must take place immediately—there is no time to lose!"

"And the dispensation?" I asked absently. "Tudor and I are both descended from John of Gaunt and Katherine de Roet, in case you've forgotten."

"Lady Beaufort declares you will need to wed without one. A verbal assurance from the pope shall suffice until the written dispensation arrives. The wedding date is set for the eighteenth of January."

To Mother's great joy, Dorset arrived back in England in time for Christmas Day, and wedding plans rushed ahead. Everyone was jubilant except me. Lady Margaret Beaufort and Mother were in deep consultation, heads together as they planned my wedding.

The eighteenth day of January, 1486, dawned sunny and cold, the brightness lit with icy light. After I'd been bathed and my hair had been washed, Lady Beaufort arrived to give eagle-eyed scrutiny and critical supervision to my final preparations. Now that her son was king, she had abandoned the austere black she had previously worn for colorful silks that blazed with gems. The red dress she had donned this morning was trimmed with sable, and her dark hair was hidden by a jeweled, embroidered headdress. She had mapped out minute instructions for the wedding ceremonies, even as to the yardage of material that nobles could use in their apparel, so it would not exceed hers.

"How many strokes for the hair?" she demanded in her shrill voice, enunciating every syllable with precision.

"One hundred fifty," the clerk read, consulting her instructions.

She started the counting, "One . . . two . . . three . . . ," and the maidservants went to work. I stood still as a wax statue as they brushed.

"How many drops?" demanded Lady Beaufort of her clerk, when I was to be anointed with the fragrance of lavender.

"Fourteen," he replied.

"One. Two. Three," she began.

"The hair loose around her in token of virginity," advised Lady Beaufort.

I allowed myself a faint smile at this.

"Where is the gold netting? Six ounces is what is needed. And the pearls? Fifty, I believe."

The counting began anew.

As I stood quietly before them, my heart was cold. I had two choices: to accept my fate, or to fight it every step of the way. This was my destiny. I had known it from babyhood, and I had accepted it—until I met Thomas. And Richard.

I accepted it now for the sake of those I loved, who depended on me. And because God had willed it so.

By the time we were commanded to go downstairs, I found myself counting the number of tower steps. *One, two, three*—

In the snowy courtyard, Henry Tudor, clad in green brocade and cloth of gold and wearing an ermine mantle, stood by the litter that would take us to the abbey. As a wedding gift, he had given me Johnnie of Gloucester's freedom and an allowance for Johnnie to live on, though, for reasons of state, he had refused to do the same for Edward of Warwick. *He is not a bad person,* I thought.

He inclined his head; I bobbed a curtsy. As I approached the carriage, my eye went to the four milky horses decorated with blankets of red and white roses, symbols of York and Lancaster. It occurred to me then that Henry was as much a pawn in this as I.

Sympathy softened my heart. We climbed into the litter and drove through the gates of Westminster and into what seemed a sea of white roses.

A thunderous roar of excitement erupted from a thousand throats, for huge crowds had turned out to greet us. The streets, doorways, and balconies were mobbed with people waving the White Rose of York, fashioned of cloth and of paper. Boys raised their roses high on poles, maidens wore them in garlands, women pinned them to their hair and men to their collars. Young lads perched on snowy rooftops and stood on walls to get a better look at us. The flowers they flung into the air were born by the wind and fluttered down like butterflies, a summer caress over a winter scene. Here and there I spotted both the red and the white rose intertwined as a symbol of peace, celebrating the lines of York and Lancaster that were, after thirty years of war, finally united together.

This was the first time the Londoners had seen me since the death of my father. They danced around the bonfires they built in the streets and broke open barrels of beer, toasting me wildly as I passed. "Elizabeth, Elizabeth!" they called, running after me. "Daughter of the king!" Their emotion bathed me in a warmth that thawed the ice in my veins. On impulse, I gathered in my arms the white silk roses that were heaped into my litter and cast them to my well-wishers. These people were good people; they were my people; and their love would sustain me through all that lay ahead. Along with the white roses and the kisses I threw, I made them a promise in my heart: *Never will I betray you. Always will I try to help you. May God bless you, each and every one of you, my beloved people.*

I thought of Henry Tudor sitting stiffly beside me. Surely in his twenty-nine years he must have loved someone once, as I had loved. Was he thinking of her now? Was there an ache in his heart that echoed my own? I turned my head and smiled at him, but he didn't look at me. Neither for his entry into London after Bosworth, nor for his coronation, had the cheers been more than civil. *He resents the love they bear me for my father's sake.* I settled back into my seat. Our marriage was born of necessity, and nothing could change that, for either of us.

When we reached the confines of the abbey, we climbed out of the carriage, and the crowd exploded with cheering. *Elizabeth! Elizabeth!* they cried. Tudor took my hand, but his touch was frosty.

Inside the abbey, surrounded by Lancastrians and away from the embrace of the people, the warmth that had come to me slowly slipped away. Throughout the wedding ceremony, my eyes remained fixed on Archbishop Bourchier's bejeweled hands. I occasionally forced a smile to my lips, but it was a smile that could not reach my eyes, for my heart had frozen over again. Dimly, I heard the sound of muffled sobbing; it came from Margaret Beaufort, overcome with joy.

The banqueting that followed the wedding ceremony was subdued, though the Great Hall glittered with music and color. It had been a long time since I'd dined there, and nothing was as I remembered. Court seemed lit with a false light now. The jugglers, the animal tamers, the troubadours who sang of love all seemed on edge, and the edginess was everywhere, even in the laughter.

Was it always this way? I wondered. *Or have I changed?* Could this really be what my mother had dedicated her life to—this vacuous ceremony, these fleeting, hollow pleasures? This mock pageantry where people danced, and bowed, and grinned at one another like gem-studded skeletons?

I remembered the old prophecy that had so troubled my father, and I saw his face again, and heard his voice: "It says, my dear child, that no son of mine shall be crowned king, but that you shall be queen and wear the crown in their stead."

O Papa, Papa, I thought. *Forgive me!*

THROUGH JANUARY AND FEBRUARY, HENRY TUDOR shuffled his court from Westminster to Sheen, from Greenwich to the Tower. As I crossed the turf to this last, I glanced up at the Beauchamp Tower where Edward was imprisoned. *Maybe he sees me,* I thought. I raised my hand to my lips and stealthily blew a kiss in his direction. I had to be most cautious, for spies were everywhere. Well had Tudor learned the value of them, for he owed his life to a warning of the agreement made between Richard and Brittany. Fleeing to France, he had escaped his pursuers with only minutes to spare. Since then, both mother and son had made it their business to employ an army of spies, who reported back to them on everything that was being said and done in every corner of the land. One morning, approaching Henry Tudor's privy chamber where I had been summoned, I overheard his mother tell Henry, "Trust no one, my son. A trusting king is easy to bring down." I pulled up short, an ache in my heart. *Richard had been a trusting king.*

No doubt these spies were armed with Margaret Beaufort's ordinances on what to look for in the households of those they surveilled. *One, two, three—*

Sometimes at night, while Henry claimed his marital rights, I counted to myself the number of his thrusts: *One, two, three—*

Soon reports came to us of unrest in the north that was teetering dangerously close to rebellion. This region, still smarting from Richard's defeat, still bearing Yorkist sentiments, was angry that an upstart of bastard descent sat on the throne of England. One gusty March morning, leaving me in his mother's care, Henry Tudor departed on a progress. I stood on the mounting block outside to give him the stirrup cup, for he wished the people to witness a display of affection between us. Not long afterward, a missive arrived for us, which Margaret Beaufort read to me.

York, the city that had loved Richard best, had presented him with the most elaborate of all the pageants. The city was decorated with tapestries, and from the galleries and windows were tossed down great quantities of tiny cakes stamped with red and white crosses, in rejoicing of his coming. They had also asked for favor, because they had not fought for Richard, and I was reminded of the betrayal of Henry Percy, Earl of Northumberland, who had not informed the city of Tudor's landing. The men of York had been on the road to Bosworth when news reached them of Richard's defeat.

On the heels of this report arrived another. Margaret Beaufort stood before me, reading aloud in her shrill voice. On the Feast of St. George, the twenty-third day of April, as he went around his masses, prayers, and banquets, Henry narrowly avoided being kidnapped by Francis Lovell, Humphrey Stafford, and his brother Thomas—

I gasped, then reddened, fearing I'd given myself away. But Margaret Beaufort must have thought my concern was for her son. She paused before she took up the missive again, and there was a tremor in her voice as she read.

"They had gathered an army," Henry Tudor wrote, "but I sent my Uncle Jasper, that seasoned warrior, to quell their rebellion. He offered every man who would desert Lovell's cause a royal pardon, and so many did that Lovell and the Staffords were forced to flee. Lovell got away and is in Burgundy with Richard's sister, Margaret, Duchess of Burgundy. The Stafford brothers took refuge in sanctuary. After I had a few words with the abbot, my men were permitted to go inside and seize them. They are condemned to hang at Tyburn and—"

My breath froze. Margaret Beaufort kept reading, but I no longer heard her words.

Tyburn.

Blessed Virgin—Almighty God—no, not Tyburn! Men were gutted alive at Tyburn—

O Thomas!

I did not sleep until Henry's return. I could not speak to him during the day, for his mother's presence shadowed us everywhere. Now that I was with child I feared he would not come to my bed-chamber, and I was overjoyed when he did. Taking his arm, I led him to the fire, for the night was cold. I sat him down in a velvet chair and presented him with wine and his favorite dish of snails, prepared in the French manner, with garlic. When he had eaten, he sat back, well contented. Then I rose and knelt before him.

"What's this?" Henry Tudor asked with surprise.

"Sire, I come to you a supplicant, requesting favor."

"What is it you wish?" he said, his voice alert, instantly suspicious.

" 'Tis a most serious request that involves life and death."

"Speak then, queen," he demanded coldly.

I lifted my head and looked at him. "I request the life of Sir Humphrey Stafford and his brother Sir Thomas Stafford."

Henry Tudor leapt to his feet. "Never!" he shouted, a look of such wrath on his face that I shrank back. "Do you have any idea how close they came to killing me? A hair—that's how close! But for the grace of God, I would not have lived to return. And you ask for their lives?" He threw me a look of disgust.

"Sire, Sir Thomas Stafford was my guard in sanctuary. He was kind to . . . us." I dared not take nay for an answer, and I raised my moist eyes to his face. "My lord, I thank God for your safety, for I bear your child in my womb, but I must ask for their lives, for honor demands it of me." I saw him soften, and I rushed on. "Anyone can take a life, but only the great can give it. It would show you as merciful, my king. It would endear you to your people. I plead for mercy for Thomas, and for Humphrey."

I bowed my head, and waited. *O hear me, Almighty God! Help me! Help Thomas—*

He spoke then, and his voice was deliberate, cold. "One of them must die. You may choose."

❖

THE NEWS OF HUMPHREY'S AWFUL DEATH STRUCK me hard. Giving out that I was unwell, I took to my bed, clutching Thomas's brooch. Mulling my failure to save both brothers, I came to see that Henry's nature was streaked with a savage vengefulness. He'd been terrified when Richard had nearly killed him, and since he was unable to exact revenge on the living man, he had taken his fury out on Richard's corpse by mutilating his body, throwing a felon's halter around his neck, and dumping it before Grey Friars for a pauper's burial.

Whenever I heard the door latch click, I turned over and pretended to be asleep. Naturally it was always Margaret Beaufort. Truly, the woman was insufferable. She never left my side, and she tormented me continually with questions about why I had not yet used the privy, insisting that I go according to her appointed schedule. I even dreamt she followed me there and stood over me counting: One wipe, two wipes, three wipes . . .

She forced me to eat and drink and counted the number of times I chewed. "For the babe's sake," she explained. "We don't want you to choke yourself, or swallow something large that might injure him."

. To her, and her son, power was the breath of life itself. She saw to it that I was confined mercilessly. I had to request permission to go to the chapel or the library, and she escorted me there. If she gave me permission to walk in a corner of the garden, she sat on a nearby bench, watching like a vulture. I understood the reason. Though I wasn't crowned, in the eyes of the people Henry Tudor's claim rested on my right as the king's daughter, and now the king's daughter was about to deliver him a dynasty. With every look Henry Tudor and his mother cast my way, fear stood in their eyes—fear that something might happen to me before I delivered the child; fear that I might be rescued from their clutches. The Beaufort woman kept me in total seclusion. No one could see me unless she gave permission, nor could I see anyone without her approval. None of my missives were delivered, just as none were given to me. I longed for word from my grandmother Cecily, or even from Queen Anne's mother, the Countess of Warwick. But contact with my Yorkist past was forbidden to me. Yet I had learned a strange truth. The tears Margaret Beaufort wept when overcome with joy stemmed as much from her dread of a future reversal of fortune. Though I might be her captive, she herself was enslaved by fear.

I spent much of my time in prayer, begging God for strength to bear what I must, and I read the book I had taken from Richard's library, Boethius's *De Consolatione*. Meanwhile, my sister Cecily was always angry and complaining. "What do you wish me to do?" I asked her.

"I want you to get my marriage to Scrope annulled. I don't want to go back to miserable Yorkshire. I want to stay here at court where there's dancing and pleasure. I hate it up north!"

"I can give you a gown, Cecily, but more I can't do. Do you not see how powerless I am?"

"Welladay, if you can't, I know who can!" she cried, swiveling on her heel and leaving me for Margaret Beaufort's side. She gave the crabby woman a kiss on the cheek and murmured to her. I saw the stern features relent beneath her charm. Cecily threw me a sly smile, and I thought how much she resembled my mother, and how strange it was that the Beaufort woman should like her so well for it.

From then on Cecily was always at Margaret Beaufort's side, laughing and being merry. They walked together arm in arm, and I thought what odd allies they made. Not surprisingly, Cecily got her wish, and her marriage to Scrope was annulled on some pretext. Then she married Margaret Beaufort's half-brother, John, Viscount Welles. Certainly he was rich enough, and he had a title, but so did many men half his age. I couldn't fathom why Cecily had chosen to wed him.

In these days, my mother was my most welcome visitor.

"You're smiling broadly, Mother. Come sit by me, and tell me what good thing has happened." Smoothing my skirts closer, I made room for her on the garden bench while Margaret Beaufort busied herself with chastising the gardener for missing a patch of weeds.

"Though King Henry has kept my London residence of Cold Harbor, he has granted me the lordships for life of Waltham, Badowe, Magna, Masshebury, Dunmore, Lieghes, and Farnham—and"—she grinned broadly—"and one hundred two pounds per annum from the fee farm of the town of Bristol!"

"That is indeed much to smile about," I said, though my heart ached that we had so little in common.

One dismal morning, watching the rain fall, I began to weep. For Richard, for Anne, for all that might have been. *Anne had not wished to be queen, either,* I thought. When Ned died, Richard had sat at her bedside, begging forgiveness. He'd blamed himself for accepting the crown that Anne had pleaded with him to refuse, for it was the crown that had claimed their child's life.

"Why these tears?" my mother said gently. "What is the matter, child? Here you are queen, and you weep?"

I had not noticed her enter the room. I wiped my eyes with the back of my hand and realized that the Beaufort woman was not around. "I never wished to be queen," I said. "I don't love Tudor, Mother."

A silence.

"You think I loved your father?" she replied.

I looked up sharply at her words.

"You marry for power, for riches. That's where happiness comes from."

"Mother, don't delude yourself," I said roughly, retreating back into myself. "You were never happy, though you had what you thought you wanted. Nay—have no fear, I shall do my duty and be a good queen to Tudor, though 'tis not for wealth and power and pretty dresses. None of these things mean much to me. 'Tis to give you and my sisters a better life."

"Ah!" my mother exclaimed. "You can put your nose up at fancy clothes and jewels and a crown because you have never known what it is to go hungry. Or to see others with barely a fraction of your beauty ride by in rich gowns and sneer at you. You know not what it is to be ridiculed and disrespected, to have people despise you, to be powerless to strike back. The crown I wore gave me the chance to set things right—to get revenge for the humiliations my family suffered. You are princess now because of me. Queen, thanks to my sacrifice."

"So now it's a sacrifice, not happiness? Pray, Mother, make up your mind."

My mother gave a muffled sound of aggravation, and quitted the room.

But in domineering Margaret Beaufort my mother had met her match, for Henry Tudor's mother was as strong-willed as my own. Margaret Beaufort always had the final word in the control of my household, and this brought about many clashes between her and my mother, until the erstwhile allies soon became foes.

"Don't turn your back on me!" my mother cried after a particularly heated argument with the Beaufort woman.

"I do as I wish with the likes of you," retorted Margaret Beaufort, lifting her brows.

"With the likes of me?" my mother repeated in disbelief. "Dare you give yourself such airs—I am queen, my daughter is queen! You are no queen, and signing yourself 'Margaret R' doesn't make you one! It only exposes your foolery in thinking yourself royal."

"If you wish to debate queenship with me, then I say this," replied Margaret Beaufort. "You, madame, lost a kingdom for your sons which I, by my ingenuity and intellect, won for mine. My Henry is king now, and I, as his mother, wield great power. Through your insatiable greed and recklessness you obtained advancement for your family, but at what cost? You drew upon yourself, and on them, the great hatred of the land—and this loathing, upon the death of King Edward, brought about the doom of your brother and three of your sons and the fall of House of York. Need I remind you that your title, your lands, indeed, all your property, has been granted you by our grace? Beware, lest we deprive you of it as surely as we gave it with a wave of our *royal* hand."

She looked up at my mother from her diminutive height. "You have only yourself to blame for the loss of a kingdom, madame." She rustled out of the room. At the door, she turned back. " 'Tis not I who am the fool."

After she left, my mother stared at me. "Welladay, are you going to sit there and watch me take this abuse? Have you nothing to say about it?"

"And what would you have me say, Mother?"

"Anything! Something!"

"Then I say that she is right."

"What?" Mother whispered on a breath. "What did you dare utter to me, you insolent girl?"

I sighed and laid down my mending. "She is right, Mother. Can you not see that? All that has come to pass is because of you. Good King Richard is dead, Henry is king, I am captive here. Dickon and Edward are who knows where, whether alive or dead only God knows; and little Warwick spends his days alone, imprisoned in the Tower. My Uncle Anthony, whose sound advice you never cared to heed, is dead, and with him my brother Dick Grey. 'Tis your doing. 'Tis what you have wrought. I have resigned myself to it. Best that you do the same, Mother."

"I have had enough of you, and that horrid woman!" Mother shouted. "I am queen dowager! I don't have to take this, and I won't!"

One evening, in front of Henry, they went at it again.

"What do you mean I'm not permitted to wear a surcoat?"

demanded my mother. "I am queen dowager and can wear what I wish."

"My ordinance makes it clear. Only I, as the king's mother, am permitted to wear a surcoat and other attire like the queen," replied Margaret Beaufort.

My mother, who was especially tall for a woman, and almost as tall as many men, strode up to the Beaufort woman and looked down on her. Many times I had seen two hounds of vastly unequal size challenge one another in just this manner. I couldn't help myself; it was such a comical sight, I was almost unable to suppress the laughter that bubbled in my throat. I stole a glance at Henry and was surprised to find he had the same reaction. Our eyes met and we smiled at one another in shared understanding.

"I've had enough!" my mother exclaimed suddenly. "I shall retire from court and live elsewhere."

I leapt to my feet. Despite all our difficulties, I had no wish to see my mother leave court. "But Mother—where will you go?"

"Cheynegate. There's a mansion up for lease. You may visit me there, Elizabeth—if you are granted permission, which I doubt."

"Mother—" Panic seized me. I watched her incline her head to Henry and sweep out of the room. A sickening knot formed in the pit of my stomach. She would take my sisters and leave me truly alone.

Over the next weeks, I stole many glances at Margaret Beaufort. I could well understand why Humphrey and Thomas had joined Richard's cause against the Tudors. For Margaret Beaufort, a relative, was devil enough to inspire fervent hatred to the death, especially by those who had the misfortune to know her well.

Poor Humphrey. That he suffered so horribly at Tyburn. Dear God!

A vision of him flashed into my mind on our last Yuletide together: "Look!" he'd said with a grin. "Someone has had his fill of marchpane—"

❋

ONE DAY, WHEN MOTHER CAME TO VISIT AND MARGAret Beaufort was called away by Henry, I confided my misery to her.

"There is only one thing you can do to ease your lot. You must seize control of your household away from her."

"Mother, don't you understand? We are captives, you and I. Though you may roam more freely than I, we are both watched by Tudor spies, and they report back on everything we say or do. I cannot take back the reins of the household from Henry's mother. I have no influence with him. He hates the House of York. 'Tis only his mother and Morton he trusts. Their advice has been to give me honorable captivity, but tighter than what Henry received in Brittany, for in the end he escaped. I am not even permitted to write letters—though whom I would write to is a matter for consideration. Everyone I would wish to write is dead."

Mother looked at me with soft eyes, and my heart flowed to her.

"You have to do something about that awful woman," she said abruptly.

"Hush, Mother. She has spies everywhere."

My mother turned and shouted to the far ends of the room, "Do something about that awful woman! Aye, that's what I said, you accursed eavesdroppers!"

I felt myself turn as red as the root of a beet. The servants scattered, heads down. The room emptied. She turned back to me.

"And what, pray, can I do?" I demanded angrily.

"If you had some spirit, I wouldn't have to tell you. You'd know what to do—you'd get into bed and lick that king of yours until he stops listening to his mother and turns to you."

"Henry is not my father," I retorted icily, flooded with disgust. But if I had thought to shame her, she was impervious.

"All men are the same, you fool. They all want the same thing. You could free us from that witch, if you so chose. But you choose not to."

"Aye, 'tis my decision. Henry is my punishment. Your gift to me, Mother."

"Beware, daughter, lest your humility makes you invisible, forgotten, and despised. Of no use to anyone. *Dispensable.* You do know what happens to dispensable royalty?"

I chose not to address her last charge; it was too frightening. "And your arrogance makes you offensive, Mother."

"At least I shall not be a forgotten queen, for I was never help-less like you."

"Indeed, you are too reviled to ever be forgotten, Mother. I have no intent to walk in your shoes. I have chosen my path and 'tis the opposite of yours. I choose to be humble."

"Humble you certainly are. As vulnerable and humble as a peasant."

"I may be vulnerable, but I have acquired a wisdom you never had. Greed is the root of all evil, and your greed has been our de-struction, Mother."

"How can you be so insipid? Such a mouse? So without ambition."

At the word *ambition*, such rage seized me that I trembled, for it was my mother's ambition that I blamed for my predicament. "I need none! You have enough for us all," I screamed. "Now leave me."

She swept out of the room, her yards of silk rustling angrily. I sighed with the agony of my despair. I wanted her love, her respect, her advice, but never would I have it.

The next day tidings reached me that the Bishop of Worcester had concluded his sermon on Trinity Sunday by reading the pope's bull of confirmation concerning my marriage to Henry. He sent me a copy and I received his messenger in the Painted Chamber. As always, Margaret Beaufort stood at my right-hand side.

"In appreciation of the long and grievous division between the Duchy of York and the Duchy of Lancaster," his messenger read, "and with the consent of our College of Cardinals, we approve the marriage made between King Henry VII of the House of Lancaster and the noble Princess Elizabeth of the House of York to beget a race of kings—"

My purpose from birth has been to supply an alliance through marriage with the highest bidder, I thought; *my function to provide an heir, and to give him brothers and sisters to be sold for more marriage alliances . . .*

"Furthermore the Pope confirms that, if it pleases God that the said Elizabeth should decease without issue, then the issue of her who afterwards shall join King Henry shall inherit the crown of the realm of England."

The babe in my belly kicked. *And if I fail in this, if I die trying, then someone else shall take my place, and it shall be as if I never was.*

A sick bitterness flooded me. I thanked the bishop's man as graciously as I could, with a smile that hid what lay in my heart. As soon as he was gone, I turned and retched in a gilded bowl.

CHAPTER 13

A Rose Both Red and White, 1486

BUT INTO ALL GRIEF FLUTTERS THE BREEZE OF HOPE.
As the months passed, my belly grew large. I caressed it day and night, wondering if my babe would be a boy. A son; a king, to rule over England with wisdom and justice, as Richard had done. Such a one could only have the name *Arthur.* Determined to end oppression, Richard, like legendary Arthur, had ordained that justice be blind and his laws dispensed without regard to a man's rank. Henry had set aside Richard's laws, but his son— my Arthur—would return Richard's dream to English hearts.

I fingered Richard's book, the Boethius. God had released him from this brutal world and reunited him with all whom he had loved here on earth: Anne, Ned, the Nevilles, his daughter Cat. I tried to imagine them in Heaven, golden clouds of joy encircling them as they laughed together, while angels sang choruses of joy.

If we have a son, I shall get Henry to name him Arthur, I thought. He was away in Bristol, but was returning shortly to Sheen, and wrote us that we should meet him there.

" 'Tis time for celebration," he announced on his arrival. "Rebellion has been thwarted, and the people of Hereford, Gloucester, and Bristol cheered my path. But the poverty of Bristol troubles me. I have promised to ease their pain by reactivating their shipyards."

My heart warmed at his words, for it meant he cared for the people. I'd not had evidence of that till now, and I grew hopeful for the future.

Henry's gaze touched on my stomach. "Perhaps a son in the fall, eh, Elizabeth?"

I inclined my head, and gave him a smile.

❖

AS THE BABE DEVELOPED, MARGARET BEAUFORT GREW more insufferable. I endured her presence by praying for the day when she would leave to visit her own estates and her husband, Thomas Stanley. But she never did. She remained at my elbow, shadowing my steps. From my embroidery frame, I stole glances at my mother-in-law, dictating her rules for the making of the king's bed. The scrivener read them back for her final approval.

"The Making of the King's Bed. Rule Number One. Testing the Mattress."

He looked at Margaret Beaufort, who nodded.

"In the making of the king's bed, the first rule is to test the mattress. This shall be done thus. One yeoman shall leap upon the bed and roll himself around on the mattress to test for lumps and soft spots. Upon finding such, a new mattress is to be brought in and tested in the same manner. Then the mattress taken from the king's bed shall be sent for immediate repair and kept in abeyance until needed."

He looked at her again; she nodded once more.

"Rule Number Two concerning the King's Royal Pillows," he read. "The yeomen are commanded to take the king's pillows and beat them with their hands. When they have been beaten for no more than ten minutes, and no less than—"

I closed my eyes; I wanted to scream. She hounded everybody with her rules, dominated the entire court with her petty "ordinances." From peeling potatoes to fluffing pillows, she had rules. Rules about how to mourn; when to retire to the bedchamber; when to take a drink or go to the privy.

"The pillows should be cast up to the squires of the body," came the scrivener's voice, "who shall place them on the king's bed in the manner he is known to prefer. The queen's bed is to be made only with gentlewomen, in the manner directed for the king's bed. Rule Number One—"

I could understand Henry's devotion to his mother, for he owed her his crown, but the woman was a scourge on everyone, with the possible exception of the scholars and universities she patronized. Power had gone to her head. Not only had she put aside the black she used to wear and the Psalter she used to carry, but now she dressed herself in copies of my gowns and wielded my scepter as if I didn't exist.

I noticed that Margaret Beaufort had moved on to dictating rules about the nursery.

"The royal infant shall have a wooden cradle set in a fair frame decorated with red, purple, and gold paint," she said. "For state use there shall be a great cradle, covered with crimson cloth of gold and garnished with fringes of silk and gold and trimmed with ermine. There shall be layers of velvet upon velvet." She turned to a page standing against the wall. "Fetch the chamberlain," she said.

The man arrived minutes later, breathless from running. He bowed deeply.

"I am preparing my ordinances for the rule of the nursery, which are to be read to the staff four times a year," Margaret Beaufort said, "and I wish to go over them with you personally."

"Aye, my lady Margaret."

"The nursery attendants are to be chosen with the greatest care. They are to be sworn in by you. They must be supervised in the strictest manner. At every meal a physician must direct the nurse to make sure she feeds the royal child correctly."

My mother's angry voice made me turn to the door.

"I have just been informed that you are planning to be godmother!" she exclaimed, addressing Margaret Beaufort without ceremony. "That position is mine, not yours!"

But Margaret Beaufort did not give in.

"You are good at usurping the positions of others, aren't you?

Do you know what they call you out there?" Mother pointed to the window. "England's 'Usurper Queen'—that's what they call you! Then they laugh into their beer."

For once, I sided with my mother. They went on to argue about everything, and agreed on nothing: not the furnishings of my chamber, nor my lying-in arrangements, nor the program for the christening, nor the feeding and nursing of my child, and certainly not the design of my baby's cradle.

"And why purple, red, and gold for the cradle?" my mother demanded.

"They are my favorite colors," replied Margaret Beaufort.

"What about my favorite colors? What about Elizabeth's favorite colors?"

"I know what's best."

"Has it ever occurred to you that your taste is not perfect, that you make mistakes?"

"I never make mistakes. I take my direction from God, and He is never wrong."

"Aye, indeed, I forgot. God told you to choose handsome Tudor over boring Suffolk as your husband. How convenient."

"That was not God. That was Saint Nicholas."

"Very clever. I should have thought of that myself. Instead of taking old Mayor Cooke to trial three times before getting the verdict I wanted, I should have declared that Saint Nicholas appeared to me in a dream and told me to have Cooke locked up. That would have saved us all much trouble."

"Are you accusing me of something, madame?"

"I'm accusing you of suffocating everyone around you with your surety of purpose. Of trying to breathe their very air for them! You say you know best, yet 'tis not true. You are strong-willed and domineering, madame. Everything has to be your way, and nothing is right unless it is."

I became aware that Henry stood at the threshold of the chamber, listening. On his face was a smile that reflected my own. Our eyes met, and we shook our heads to one another. I rose to greet him, and taking him by the elbow, brought him to sit at my side on the settle.

"May I sing for you, my lord?" I asked.

Henry understood. "Indeed, that would be most soothing. My ladies—" He turned and inclined his head to our mothers. Acknowledging his nod of dismissal, they swept out of the chamber, one fighting with the other to lead the way. Henry and I watched them, and when the chamber door shut, we burst into laughter.

It was a good moment for me to request the control of my own household, for his mother was truly driving me mad with her preparations for the "coming of the prince." As if there were no doubt it would be a boy. But I decided against it. One day, perhaps, a peaceful household would be mine, but now a more urgent matter needed attention. I went to my lyre. Strumming the chords of a popular melody, I raised my voice in song while Henry gazed thoughtfully out the window. I decided the time had come to broach the subject close to my heart.

"My lord," I said when the song was done, "have you ever wondered how remarkable it is that you came to be king? Surely, 'tis God's plan and the fulfillment of the dream of Cadwallader eight hundred years ago."

"The prophecy of the angel that the English would be displaced from power," he mused. "That the line of ancient Britons preserved through the Welsh would take back the crown. Aye, it does seem so, does it not?"

"Indeed. Have you thought to trace your lineage to the greatest king of them all—Arthur?"

"What a fine idea, my lady," he exclaimed. "Worthy of Morton's own exemplary brain, I dare say. I shall inform my lady mother."

"Then perhaps it would be good to have the child born in Winchester, the ancient seat of King Arthur." I added hastily, "In case it is a son."

"You are a veritable fountain of splendid advice, dear lady."

"And to name him Arthur," I said.

"Arthur," Henry murmured. "*Arthur.* How apt. My lady, you outdo all my advisors with the excellence of your counsel this evening."

He came to me and took my hand. As he raised it to his lips, I gave him a gentle smile. This was my first victory; it meant there could be more. I would cherish each one, no matter how small, for each would give purpose to my loveless life.

Over the next weeks, I caressed my enlarged stomach, and my prayers grew more fervent. *Father in Heaven, grant me a boy-child. If You see fit to answer my prayer, I vow to dedicate my life to raising a son worthy of England, one who will care for his people, and seek to do Thy will always.*

And if it's a girl, whispered a small voice at the far reaches of my mind, *a girl as helpless and useless as you are—as we all are—what then?* I shut my eyes and banished the thought. I would await the judgment of God.

✿

ON THE TWENTIETH DAY OF SEPTEMBER, 1486, AT ST. Swithin's Priory in Winchester, the birthplace of King Arthur, I gave birth to a boy. Henry nearly went mad with joy. He sat at my bedside, holding my hand and kissing my fingers. I was grateful to him, for by his presence Margaret Beaufort withheld her shrill barking at the servants.

"I wish to make you a gift, my dear Elizabeth. What is your heart's desire? Emeralds, diamonds, rubies—"

"A fool," I replied sleepily. *I know he will be a spy,* I thought; *but if a spy can bring me relief from your mother's ordinances and make me laugh, I shall welcome him.*

"A fool? That is all?"

" 'Tis all."

"Consider it done, Elizabeth. You shall have the cleverest fool in all England." From inside his breast pocket, he removed the little black memorandum book he had taken to carrying around with him of late and wrote himself a reminder.

Margaret Beaufort departed for the privy, and I heaved an inward sigh of relief. The very air seemed lighter without her. Henry, too, finding me drowsy, left my side. I was about to close my eyes and let myself drift into slumber when my mother's voice came to me near the threshold of my chamber where she had accosted Henry.

"Sire, are you king?" my mother said.

My lids flew open.

"What have you just said?" Henry demanded, stiffening.

"The people are declaring openly that you are ruled by the Lady Margaret, and it is she, not you, who wears the crown."

"That is preposterous."

"There is a way to put these rumors to rest once and for all, sire."

"What way is that, madame?" Henry said warily.

" 'Tis for me as queen dowager to stand as godmother to Prince Arthur. However, the Lady Margaret has informed me of her decision to take the place that is rightfully mine. I thought you would wish to know, so that you, as *king*"—she laid a heavy stress on the word and paused before continuing—"can show the land that you are not ruled by your mother."

Henry's back was turned to me, so I did not know his answer until I saw my mother's broad smile. She inclined her head and gave a curtsy. Henry left, the footsteps of his throng of yeoman guards resounding behind him. Before my mother and I could speak, however, Margaret Beaufort returned from the privy. I turned my gaze on her.

She stood for a moment, her glance moving from my mother to me. "What has just happened?"

Mother and I exchanged a glance. *Thank goodness for the privy*, I thought.

"Nothing, Lady Margaret," I replied sleepily.

"Nothing," my mother echoed, staring at Margaret Beaufort with a triumphant gleam in her eyes.

Henry was so proud of his new son that he barely left my side during the week after Arthur's birth. We spent much time admiring our child. He was a healthy babe with dark hair, light eyes, and long fingers who ate hungrily, slept much, and rarely cried.

"He shall be a warrior king," I murmured. *Like Richard,* I added silently to myself.

"He shall have no need of arms, for I shall rid the land of all his enemies," Henry replied.

Messengers were sent to the far reaches of the kingdom with the happy news. Bonfires were lit in the streets and butts of wine opened in the crossroads. People sang, and drank, and cheered. I heard them celebrating every night.

"All is proceeding splendidly for Prince Arthur's christening at Winchester Cathedral," Margaret Beaufort announced, sweeping into my chamber one morning. "The work is nearly completed."

"And how does it look?" inquired Henry absently, smiling at Arthur.

"The walls are covered with tapestries, and I have commanded a special platform be built with seven steps covered in red carpet. The baptismal font is of silver, lined with fine linen. Over the font, from a large gilt ball, hangs a richly fringed canopy. The entire event will be a glittering pageant, one worthy of a new dynasty, dear son."

"Very impressive," murmured Henry as Arthur grabbed his finger, gurgling sweetly.

Sunday, the day of my babe's christening, dawned bright with sunshine and noisy with birdsong.

" 'Tis a good omen," Lucy Neville noted.

Lucy, niece to the late Warwick who had caused my father such grief all those years ago, was my principal lady-in-waiting among the horde of thirty the Beaufort woman had appointed to keep me under firm control. Her father, John Neville, Lord Montagu, had died with his brother fighting for Lancaster at Barnet, but he was found to be wearing the colors of York beneath his armor, for he and his family had ever been Yorkist and would never have left the fold had it not been for my mother's enmity. Some at court still called him a traitor to Lancaster, and for this reason, Lucy had not many friends. She had joined my household when her husband died in Henry's cause at Bosworth. I had thought her merely another spy, but I quickly came to realize it was an injustice to dismiss her this way. She went about her duties quietly and never participated in the gossip of my other ladies. Her kindness to others, especially the servants, was remarkable.

I extended my hand to King Richard's sister, Elizabeth, duchess of Suffolk, who had just arrived. Her husband had not fought for Richard at Bosworth, though his oldest son, Jack, Earl of Lincoln, was his heir. Jack had sought Henry's pardon, and she and her four sons were welcome at Henry's court. "Dear Liza, how are you?" I asked.

Liza cooed to Arthur, who was wrapped in a rich mantle of crimson cloth of gold lined throughout in ermine. She reminded me of Richard and I would have liked to converse with her, but my uncles, Edward and Richard Woodville, entered with many other guests streaming behind them. The room filled with a cross-current of greeting and salutations.

Clarions blared. "Everyone, take your places!" called Margaret Beaufort.

A glittering procession began to form in the Prior's Great Hall.

"Where is John de Vere, Earl of Oxford?" Margaret Beaufort demanded, casting a look around. "He is to stand as godfather, and was supposed to be here an hour ago."

She sent a page to search the castle and paced to and fro as she waited. My mother watched her with an expression of arrogant disdain. When Margaret Beaufort had discovered that Henry had set her aside as godmother, there had been a huge scene. She had accused her son of ingratitude, and my mother of living up to every name the land had ever called her.

"They care not for you either," my mother had replied, "my dear usurper queen. At least, no one can deny I am a true queen."

I had hidden my face from them both, for a wide smile had come to my lips.

One of the yeoman of the guards appeared with a messenger from the Earl of Oxford. The man entered and strode up to Henry.

"Sire, the Earl of Oxford was caught by surprise at the prince's unexpected birth a month early. He is hurrying from his own estate in the west and expects to be here shortly. He begs you to delay the ceremony and wait for him."

Leaning against a tall gilt chair, Henry regarded the man a long moment. Along with William Stanley, Oxford was the prime reason for his victory at Bosworth, yet he had not received any significant reward for the service he had rendered. Henry had no wish to ennoble supporters with titles and wealth that he regarded as coming from his own pocket. This honor of godfather he'd bestowed on Oxford was meant to keep him satisfied for a very long time.

Finally, Henry gave a nod. "We shall delay the proceedings as long as possible."

Everyone wiled the time away as best they could, playing cards, throwing dice, and reading. One hour passed; then two, and three. They began to fidget; women fanned themselves and men loosened their collars, for the day was warm, and their jewels and finery grew heavy.

"We've waited long enough," Henry announced at last. He turned to his father-by-marriage, the newly created Earl of Derby. "Lord Stanley, will you accept the honor of standing as godfather to our firstborn son, Prince Arthur?"

Stanley gave a low bow and took up his position beside my mother. The others fell in behind them two by two. Flanked by knights, my sister Anne bore the chrism, and after them walked Cecily, carrying in her arms my little prince. They filed out of the chamber, trumpets blaring.

I moved to the window to catch a glimpse of them crossing the court, where they were joined by Henry's henchmen, squires, gentlemen, and yeomen of the guards, each bearing an unlit torch. But I grew fatigued, and returned to bed.

My sister Anne was the first to arrive back from the baptism.

"Lady Margaret wept again, nearly ruining the ceremony," she whispered before assuming a normal tone. "Yet all went well. Stanley accompanied our mother to the font where Arthur was christened. Torches were lit, and hymns sung. Then Oxford arrived. He took Stanley's place. He held him as the Bishop of Exeter confirmed him. Everyone sang a *Te Deum*." Anne dropped her voice again. "Mother missed Dorset, but she was proud of taking precedence over Lady Margaret."

I nodded sadly. My brother Dorset was not welcome in Henry's court.

Trumpets blared, and the yeomen entered with their flaming candles. Anne moved to the side, and Cecily laid my babe in my arms. Arthur received the gifts of his godparents. My mother gave him a cup of gold, and Oxford a pair of gilt basins. From Margaret

Beaufort's husband, Stanley, he received a saltcellar of gold. My mother beamed with joy from ear to ear. Not only had she prevailed over the king's mother, but the birth of Arthur had secured her position. In addition, Henry had begun negotiations for her marriage to King James III of Scotland. She bent down to me.

"Next is your coronation," my mother whispered. "And then my royal wedding."

I looked down at my babe, seeing my own victory and fulfillment in those tiny fingers, that tiny mouth. *One day he will be king, God willing; I need nothing more than this.* Suddenly, my brothers' faces rose up before me. I closed my eyes and added, *Pray God Henry lives long enough for my child to reach manhood.*

Reluctantly, I gave my babe up to be taken away to his nursery, where he would be fed and rocked by three nurses under the supervision of a doctor. *At least I don't have to worry about him,* I thought. Yeomen and squires who had sworn oaths of allegiance to Arthur would reach out to rock his cradle each time he cried, and everything would be done according to the directives of Margaret Beaufort. She would stand guard at his cradle against all harm, except that sent by God.

CHAPTER 14

Of Roses and Thorns, 1486

HENRY SURPRISED ME BY ASKING WHERE I SHOULD like to spend my churching, for I was sure he would decide this with his mother. I chose Greenwich Palace.

Standing on the banks of the Thames with its semioctagonal towers newly faced in red brick, its emerald parks and grand vistas, its graceful pillared hall and terra-cotta floor tiles adorned with the white daisy emblem that had belonged to Marguerite d'Anjou, Greenwich echoed with the soft sound of lapping water and cries of river birds diving for fish. From my childhood, it had been my favorite residence, and it welcomed me now with the warmth of memories. On these lawns Papa had run with me on his great shoulders, pretending to be my horse, while I had lashed him and urged him on. There, beneath a shady elm, I had frolicked with my pup, Jolie, and learned to ride my palfrey.

Away from the noise and smells of London, life was simpler at Greenwich. I was not restricted to the use of a walled garden, and Margaret Beaufort relaxed her stern eye on me, for no one could approach unnoticed as they might at Westminster. There was less ceremony of court; the political intrigues were distanced, and the outside world seemed far away. In quiet and privacy, we took our leisure as a family. While Margaret Beaufort and my mother argued about the treatment and nursing of my baby prince, Henry hawked and rode to the hounds, or played a game of tennis with a stuffed pig's bladder to serve as a ball; I strolled in the parks amid serenity, free from reminders of Richard. For Richard had never found time for Greenwich; only the troubled halls of Westminster had been his haunt as king. Even so, the day of his birth, the second of October, still proved difficult. I watched the leaves wither and fall from the trees, and thought of him, felled in the prime of life.

Before I realized it, the hourglass had emptied again and the lawns turned white with a November snowfall. My churching was over and we left for Westminster to celebrate Yule.

❁

WHEN MARGARET BEAUFORT WASN'T GUARDING ME, she watched my babe. She tried to curtail my time with Arthur and dictate when I could see him. *The woman is a born jailer,* I thought with disgust. She had removed Arthur from my side after my purification sixty days after his birth, and now he lodged in his nursery. A few days before my coronation, I went to his room.

"He cannot be disturbed at this time," Margaret Beaufort announced when I appeared. "He has just been fed and shall take a four-hour nap."

I glanced at the physician, Arthur's three nurses, and the two women rockers who stood waiting against the wall. Then I looked at my babe. He was cooing joyfully and waving his little arms and legs in the air. My heart melted to see him, and I knew that if I didn't take a stand, Margaret Beaufort would as happily strip me of my mother's rights as she had of my queenship. But this child, England's future king, embodied my sole purpose for living, my entire reason for enduring a loveless existence. I stood my ground.

"Am I to be kept from my son?" I seethed, closing the distance between us. Though I was slow to anger, and preferred to suffer in silence rather than engage in confrontation, this was too important to ignore. Such a fierce wrath had seized me that I trembled.

"For his sake you must abide by my ordinances."

"He is *my* child, and if you want any more grandchildren from my Plantagenet blood, you'd better step aside now." Though I hated argument, I had reached the end of my tether with Henry's dreadful mother. I preyed on her deep-seated fear that as long as there were no more children, Henry's dynasty would be left hanging by a single thread and could be toppled as easily as Richard's. She made no reply for a long moment, then stood aside and let me pass. I strode over to the cradle and took my child into my arms. From the corner of my eye, I saw her leave.

I dismissed the servants with a wave and sat down. Rocking my babe in my arms, I laid my cheek to his. "You are born to be a king, my little one," I whispered in his ear, "and kings have much to learn. Soon you shall be taken from me. Only now, in these precious days of infancy, do you belong to me. I have only a short time to teach you to be loving and kind, to be a gentle master to the animals you hold, to be pleasant to those who serve you, to do your best, to do your duty."

As King Richard had.

A tear trembled at the corner of my eye. I saw him again in my mind's eye, his sad, gentle face. He had tried to defend the poor, but in bringing them justice, he had alienated the powerful nobles on whose support his throne rested. Henry didn't care a reed for justice, or for the happiness of the people, and he had no use for the nobles who posed a threat to him. But they had killed one another off in these Wars of the Roses, and few remained to trouble him; no doubt they slept uneasy in their beds, for they could see that power had drained from their hands into Henry's fists. And Henry had made it clear that he would take the opposite tack from Richard. After all, Rome had lasted a thousand years.

My lips curled at the thought of Henry's contrived lineage. Now he suddenly went all the way back to Aeneas, the founder of Rome, which with the coming of Caesar was ruled by terror and tyrants. Aye, Henry knew his history, and he would not repeat the same mistake that had brought down his predecessor. He would be Caesar.

I looked at the babe sleeping in my arms, his head on my shoulder, his arms outstretched, his tiny fingers splayed. A rush of warmth dissolved my bitterness. I set him down in his cot. Here lay England's future king, another Arthur who would shape a golden age of peace and justice, as Richard had wished to do.

All shall be put right in the end, I thought. This little treasure was my great gift to England. I arranged his blanket around him with a gentle touch.

Sleep, tiny King Arthur; sleep and grow strong, my darling one.

CHRISTMAS AT COURT WAS GALA, AND HENRY SPARED no expense on it. Recognizing the importance of royal magnificence and display, he entertained more than six hundred people at his banquets, which offered as many as sixty dishes of confections in addition to the other courses of pheasants and swans, jellied eels, and pies of turtledoves and larks. We dressed in purple velvets and cloths of gold tissue furred with ermines and sables and adorned ourselves with jewels, and golden crowns, and collars that dazzled in torchlight.

Powdered with a light snowfall, 1487 was ushered in with much revelry. Outside, great bonfires lit the streets and people skated on the frozen Thames. Inside the castle, feasting and religious services filled the hours from dawn to dusk with spectacle and pageants. Surrounded by Henry's attendants clad in his colors of green and white, and mine in wine and blue, our minstrels played while Henry and I distributed to our courtiers and servants bountiful gifts of money, silver and gold goblets, cups, dishes, capes, and cloaks as if we had not a care in the world. The gifts, like the celebrations, grew more lavish with the passing of each of the twelve days of Christmas until they reached their finale in the Feast of the Epiphany on Twelfth Night, the most glorious celebration of all. Then Henry presented his Yuletide gift to me.

"My queen," said Patch the Dwarf with a courtly bow that jingled all his bells, "I am your fool, and you may rest assured that never was there such a fool as I in all the world."

I laughed heartily.

Thus drew to an end the blessed year of Arthur's birth. But nothing is ever as it seems, and no one knew that our joyous displays hid the shadow of uncertainty. Rumors of rebellion clouded the air, and behind the lavish extravagances I darned the hems of my garments while Henry pored over his accounts each night, inspecting and signing his treasurer's account books. Avoiding needless spending, he doled out to me an allowance so niggardly it never failed to prove short of my needs, no matter how I cut costs. On occasion, I was forced to borrow from my ladies-in-waiting and to repay them when I received my next portion from Henry, so that I was always in arrears. But I knew it was hopeless to ask for more money. Henry was saving for a battle he did not intend to lose.

Richard's friend Francis Lovell and my aunt, Margaret of York, fanned the discontent of the people and fueled rumors through the land. *Why had Henry Tudor not crowned his queen? Why was young Warwick held a prisoner in the Tower? Was Henry plotting the death of the child?* With the birth of my Arthur, I had proved fruitful, and they knew that Henry was intent on establishing a dynasty, for he had resumed his visits to my bedchamber as soon as I had been churched, never missing a night unless I was unwell. Henry's enemies realized that with his relentlessness, and my fruitfulness, there would be no end to the number of Tudors to fight them for the crown, and they had decided to strike now, before Henry became too entrenched on the throne.

But they had shrewd, cunning, unconscionable Morton to contend with. Henry had raised him to be Archbishop of Canterbury on old Bourchier's death the previous year and appointed him Lord Chancellor. No man had done more to bring down York, and now Morton set his devious mind to securing Henry's throne. I had come to know him well, and time had confirmed my perception. Here, behind this rotund belly tied with a red sash, dwelled all seven deadly sins. Whenever my eye rested on his brutal, fleshy face, I wondered if he had murdered my brothers and poisoned Richard's son, all in the cause of Lancaster.

Because of the threat of rebellion, Henry and his mother increased their watch on me. The Beaufort woman never left my side and dominated me in small ways and large, ordering me about and telling me when to sleep and when to rise, and demanding we dress alike for state occasions.

"The olive shade does not suit me. I shall take the emerald silk," I told the Master of the Wardrobe as I inspected fabrics for a new gown. I could scarce call him *my* Master of the Wardrobe, for like everyone else around me, he had been appointed by Margaret Beaufort.

"But olive is *my* color," Margaret Beaufort called out from across the chamber, where she was discussing a new book with the printer, William Caxton, whom she had taken under her patronage. "Since your dress is a copy of mine, you must wear olive, Elizabeth."

I almost snickered aloud. *Your dress is a copy of mine—when I was queen, and she wished to parade as one!* Surely, Heaven had laughed as it handed me such a mother-in-law. Even when she was not at my elbow, she remained within earshot. I turned away so she would not see the hatred that must surely light my eyes. My mother, I knew, would have challenged her, for she thrived on confrontation. But I hated argument and comforted myself with the solace God had granted me—my little Arthur. I glanced over at my mother-in-law chastising a nursemaid until the young girl burst into tears. *Let her fuss about the nursery,* I told my babe, rocking him in my arms; *one day you shall be king, and set things right.*

Serenity came only in those rare and treasured moments when I was alone in Arthur's company, for whenever my mother visited, she fought with Margaret Beaufort, or harangued me.

"How can you just sit there and take their abuse?" she demanded one afternoon when Margaret Beaufort left the room. She closed the door against the ladies-in-waiting milling in the antechamber. "These Tudors are nobodies—their claim to the throne is too delicate to raise! Without you, they're usurpers, and all the land knows it. You are the old blood. You give them legitimacy—"

Repairing the lining of my skirt, I smiled as I listened. The same charge had been leveled against her when she'd wed my father, but, thanks to her determination, all those of ancient lineage who'd spoken out against her were dead.

I drifted out of my thoughts, knotted the thread, and broke it with my teeth.

"—you are the true queen," she was saying, "yet you remain uncrowned. You must demand to be crowned! I don't understand why you are content to be treated in this humiliating manner."

"I have no power to demand anything, Mother."

"Then find it," she breathed in my ear.

"I don't know how," I said absently, threading a needle.

She looked at me with disgust. "I told you how! You get it by charming Henry every way you can. You sing like an angel, surely even you know that? That helps. And you have great beauty. I gave you that. Use it to your advantage—in bed."

I thought of Henry's breath in my face, vile from a mouthful of decaying teeth, his saliva and runny nose dribbling down my cheek as he moved over me, winded with passion. I held my breath and turned my face away.

"I cannot, Mother."

"What do you mean, you cannot? You do it to get what you want—what you need!"

"Henry is not like Father. It takes all my will just to submit. 'Tis all I can bear."

"Submit! 'Tis all you understand.'

"Would that you might have understood years ago, Mother. Maybe it would be a different world now. You have given us the misery we must abide."

Her eyes lit with hatred. "You're such a fool! So damned humble, without pride. All you know how to do is pray!"

"Mother, I have chosen my motto. Do you care to know what it is? *Humble and Reverent.* Humble, because you're arrogant. Reverent, because you're not." I rose to my feet, unable to keep spite from my tone. At this moment I believed I loathed my mother as much as she despised me. "And see what your arrogance has wrought for us? What pass your stupidity has brought us to? You never could foresee the consequences of your actions or learn from your mistakes. Naturally, for that takes intelligence. But I've learned from *your* mistakes, and I am loved, while you are hated."

"And what good does it do you being loved?" my mother sneered. "Let me remind you that these same people who love you today will forget you tomorrow. In the meanwhile, you're a captive and must ask permission to go to the privy."

"Do *you* not understand, Mother?" I exclaimed, forgetting to keep my voice down. In a bare whisper, I added, "What is more stupid than handing Dickon over to Margaret Beaufort to be murdered like Richard's son—which you almost did."

A gasp of horror escaped her lips "How do you know they did away with Ned?"

"He died quickly. He died after eating. He died in great pain. *He died on the anniversary of Papa's death."* I stressed every word. "It doesn't take a seer to fathom what happened. Why do you think King Richard risked everything to go behind enemy lines and kill Henry himself?"

"You are wrong," she inisted. "It cannot be true. You are being a fool."

But her tone lacked conviction. She didn't want to concede to me, for that meant admitting her own extreme folly in almost trusting Dickon to Margaret Beaufort. But we had mulled this same road time and again, and I was weary. She was the only one I could confide in, the only friend I had, yet we seemed to always battle like foes. I hated contention, and she loved it. I wanted her affection, and she despised me. When I was little, she never took my hand, or offered me an embrace. Yet she had doted on my two brothers. Now I was grown and we couldn't even hold a discussion when our interests converged.

"Mother, I pray you, let me alone. There's no point discussing this any further. We shall never agree on anything." I turned to leave the room.

Then she spoke the words I would never forget, or forgive.

"I should have let you rot by wedding that humble knight of yours!"

I froze in my steps, and swung around. "What did you say?"

"That knight. That nobody—Stafford, I think his name was."

Stunned, I retraced my steps. "How do you know about Thomas? What did you do?"

"One word answers both questions, my dear. *Letters.* I had them destroyed."

"He wrote me? When?"

"In the early days, when you were first received by Richard and Anne."

I lunged at her with a scream, my fingernails bared to draw

blood. "I could have wed him then! Richard would have let me wed him!"

My mother grabbed my wrist and bent it backward until she had me down on my knees. I felt the pain all the way up my arm to my chest where Thomas's brooch lay pinned to my black velvet dress. Mother's eyes glittered with triumph. Smiling coldly, she released me.

I rose to my feet unsteadily. "I loved him, and you destroyed my one chance at happiness."

"Happiness? With a squire?" She stared at me and burst into derisive laughter.

"Have you never loved?" I cried out. "Do you even know what love is?"

She ceased her laughter. Her eyes, moist with revelry, took on a strange look and I thought I saw reflected in them the flicker of a memory: Sir John Grey, young and handsome, standing in his armor, his helmet under his arm, a breeze stirring his hair, a pained smile on his face as he gazed at her for the last time before leaving for Northampton, where he died. In that fleeting instant, I knew beyond doubt that my mother had once loved, and loved passionately, and when she had lost that love, a depth of bitterness had shriveled her heart until nothing remained but a gnarled knot of scars.

The misty look left her eyes, and her voice came again. "Forget love. It's here one day and gone the next. What matters is what you can grasp in your hand—power, money, riches. Take it, and hold on to it with all your strength, and it will comfort you in the cold, and the dark."

I reached out and touched my mother's sleeve, tears stinging my eyes.

THE COURT MARKED HENRY'S THIRTIETH BIRTHDAY on the twenty-eighth of January, and merriment filled the palace halls. But he continued to put off my coronation with excuses. Now it was for the threat of rebellion. Jack, Earl of Lincoln, Richard's heir to the throne, who had accepted Henry's pardon, escaped to Francis Lovell's side in Burgundy in January, and word reached England that Lincoln and Lovell were preparing to invade, and claimed to have Edward, Earl of Warwick.

I found this very strange. Edward was a captive at the Tower, so the other child was an impostor. Everyone knew that. Why would Francis and Lincoln purposely give the lie to their rebellion? Henry was deeply troubled, for to him it meant only one thing. *One, or both, of my brothers still live.* Because they were too young to be revealed until the rebellion succeeded, Lovell and Lincoln had the impostor child front for them. I was torn by this knowledge now that I had Arthur, and I spent much time praying for strength to accept God's will, whatever the outcome. For their success would plunge my son's life into jeopardy.

"What news?" I asked when Henry came to my chamber after his birthday feast.

"The rebels have met with success in Ireland," he said grimly. "The boy claiming to be Edward of Warwick was crowned with a diadem borrowed from a statue of the Virgin in Christ Church Cathedral in Dublin. They hail him as King Edward VI."

Patch the Dwarf assumed a haughty expression and, turning himself upside down, swaggered forward on his hands. "King Edward VI—make way for King Edward VI!" he cried, his bells jingling.

He made such a ridiculous sight that we both laughed. Then Henry took a seat. "Sing to me," he said.

I chose my lute and raised my voice to a sweet melody. Henry closed his eyes.

During the troubled week that followed, I learned much from Patch, some of which I wished I had not known.

"King Richard's bastard son, John of Gloucester, has been taken to the Tower." Patch threw up his little arms and grimaced to mime the pain of being tortured.

It seemed to me that a cold blast of wind knocked the air from my lungs. *Johnnie, that fine young boy, an orphan of no means, of no power—the child Richard had thought safe from danger!*

"On what charge?" I breathed.

"Treason. He received a letter from Ireland."

Dear God, they took him for receiving a letter?

My legs trembling beneath me, I lowered myself into a chair. This had to be the work of Morton and Margaret Beaufort, for Henry had some scruples, and they had none. Since the birth of my babe, I had not slept well, my sleep troubled by bad dreams. Johnnie was no threat to anyone—or so we had thought—for he was a bastard. But Henry was of illegitimate descent himself, and the old rules no longer applied. In this new world, a bastard was no threat to anyone except another bastard. And that meant no one was safe.

A chill ran along my spine. I feared that Johnnie would never see the light of day again, for Henry could not afford to let him live. The blood of kings ran more closely in his veins than in Henry's own. I moved to my prie-dieu. Clasping my hands together, my heart breaking, I prayed for young Johnnie.

⚜

THE LAND WAS RIFE WITH PROPHECIES OF THE WHITE Rose blooming again and the Tudor dragon slinking away, bloody and beaten. My aunt Margaret of York was reported to have called Henry "a most iniquitous invader and tyrant." But Henry, aided by his mother and her nefarious helpmate, Morton, devised a reply to Margaret.

I learned it for myself when I went to see Henry on a money matter. My ladies-in-waiting had informed me that my household needed to make various sundry payments for garments sewn and materials procured, and that the merchants we owed were unable to extend me further credit, for they themselves were in desperate straits. I chose my moment. Margaret Beaufort was absent on an errand, and so I did not need to request permission and risk being denied.

"I am going to see the king," I told my chamberlain, the Earl of Ormond.

"I am happy to accompany you to his chambers, my lady."

I did not argue. He did what he was commanded to do. Words had never come easily to me, and so we walked along in silence through the palace halls and across the garth. A strong wind blew, displacing my hood, and I was reminded of my stroll with Richard through this same garden on my nineteenth birthday, for today was my birthday, the eleventh day of February, and I had turned twenty-one. How much had changed in only two years! Tonight there would be a banquet in my honor, but I wasn't certain if I'd have time alone with Henry to discuss my personal finances, hence this visit. My accounts were in such arrears that I was finally driven to ask him for money.

Henry's chamberlain greeted us at the entrance of the royal suite and bowed courteously. "His Grace is with his lady mother and Archbishop Morton in the council chamber. Shall I announce you, my queen?"

"Pray disturb them not. I will wait in the anteroom."

Everyone present rose to their feet, and the room filled with the rustle of silk and clink of gold chains as they withdrew. A steward closed the door. I went to the window seat where I could hear what was said in the privy chamber.

Morton's voice drifted to me. "Your royal poet, Bernard Andre, made an interesting remark at the French ambassador's banquet, sire."

"Remind me what it was." Henry's voice.

Margaret Beaufort answered in his stead. "He repeated the court opinion that Margaret of York spends all her days thinking of new outrages to damage you. Like Juno hurling storms at Aeneas, she lashes and rails at you."

"Spite never dies; a woman's anger is eternal," Morton recounted. "Sire, listening to his words, a new idea came to me." He fell silent. Margaret Beaufort's voice picked up again.

"You know how the land keeps talking about your paternal heritage, dear son? Morton has suggested a way to make them forget it, and I agree with him."

Morton seized the opening she'd given him. "Sire, you need a royal lineage traced not only back to Arthur, as you suggested, but through Arthur to the Trojan Brutus who ruled Britain during the Dark Ages. Then, may I suggest that from Brutus, the legendary founder of Britain, we proceed to his ancestor, Aeneas himself?"

"I like the idea, Morton, but can this be done? The people remember that my—"

He didn't finish the sentence, but I knew what it was: *The people remember that my grandfather was a groom of the wardrobe, and his father a man wanted by the law for debt and murder.*

"The people have a short memory, sire, like children. That which is often repeated is believed, especially when it is accompanied by the rod. If I may be so bold, my liege?"

"You may speak freely, Morton."

"Put terror into them, and people will not dare give offense, no matter how audacious the lie."

In my mind's eye, I saw Morton giving Henry the lopsided sneer he considered a smile.

Henry snickered. "Indeed, 'tis a splendid idea, well worth attempting." Then he moved across the room to his desk and caught sight of me.

"My lady, to what do I owe this pleasure?" he demanded.

"I fear you shall not find it pleasurable that I come to ask you for money."

He exhaled an audible sigh.

❧

SOON AFTERWARD HENRY CALLED A COUNCIL AT Sheen and brought the real Warwick out of the Tower. Dear Edward was twelve years old now, never having known a day of liberty since Bosworth. Henry paraded him through the London streets to prove the falsehood of Lincoln's claim, and ordered John de Vere, Earl of Oxford, and Jasper Tudor, Duke of Bedford, to prepare for invasion. Then he left for a progress to secure the land, traveling quickly through Essex, Suffolk, and Norwich, and to Coventry with Morton. Along the way Morton read a papal bull of anathema and excommunication against the rebels, for which Henry had paid the pope a great sum of money. This had been yet another of Morton's ideas, hatched in the solar as I played the harp and they conversed over a game of cards following my birthday banquet.

"What we need is a papal bull recognizing your right to the crown and cursing with bell, book, and candle all those who go against you."

"Will the pope issue us such a bull?" Henry had inquired, laying down three knights.

"He will issue anything for a price," Morton had replied, smiling as he presented three kings over them. "No matter how high the cost, it shall be worth paying. There can be no surer sign of God's approval than the papal censure of all who threaten you, Your Grace."

Henry commonly called Morton "a clever devil," and it had occurred to me listening to them that truer words were never spoken. In Morton, the cloth was a disguise of the devil.

MY MOTHER CAME TO VISIT AS FEBRUARY DREW TO a close. As soon as I glimpsed her, I knew something was wrong. She entered without fanfare and took a seat by the window, where she fell into thoughtful contemplation. Accustomed as I was to her parading in with her demands, bursts of temper, fits of weeping, and angry recriminations, I was deeply unsettled by her behavior. I sent for wine, which she didn't touch, and I sang her a song that was the rage at court. But she sat drooping and said little, though she smiled at me once. At length, I rose and went to her. Kneeling at her feet, I took her hand into mine. She turned her eyes on me. "Mother, what is wrong?"

She gave me a barely perceptible nod and glanced over at my ladies-in-waiting chattering before the fire. I understood; we were being watched. Though the women seemed engaged in gossip, they had trained an ear on us and would report back dutifully to Margaret Beaufort, or Henry, or Morton. Tudor spies were everywhere through the land, and even beyond, in Spain, Burgundy, Scotland, and France. Yet there was a time when she hadn't feared them. I brought her hand to my lips and kissed it tenderly. Settling down close beside her on the window seat, I draped my arm around her. She laid her head on my shoulder, and I glimpsed the sparkle of tears on her lashes.

Then she raised it to look at me. "Growing up in uncertain times," she said, "all I had to rely on was family. I tried to do my best for them all. When you were born, I obtained for you the best I could . . . *queen* . . . Life is better on top, Elizabeth."

"Mother, not everyone wants the same thing. I would have liked a different life, if I could have chosen."

"You are young; you know not what is best," she sighed. "You know not what it is to go hungry and to worry about money." She dug her fingers onto my hand and lowered her voice to a bare whisper. "But know this now—everything I do is for you and your sisters and br—"

I felt myself blanch at the dangerous slip of her tongue. She broke off, then bowed her head. A silence fell. I looked up, fearing that someone had overheard, and to my dismay, I found that people were looking at us. They resumed their conversation and busied themselves, but my unease grew to unbearable proportions. I stared at the top of my mother's jeweled headdress with heavy dread. Was she plotting again? *Plotting against Henry?* If so, there could only be one reason. The scene in sanctuary rose before me: my mother and Dickon whispering together in a corner. *Dickon has sent her the password.* The knowledge sent me reeling where I sat. I raised a hand to my brow. *My brother lives! Dickon has sent her the sign. She is torn between us. She has had to choose, and she has done so.*

I didn't need to ask which of us she'd chosen.

She lifted her head and gazed at me fully. Under her breath she said, "No matter what happens, you and Arthur will be safe. Never doubt that. Now I must go."

Steadying myself with a hand against the rough stone embrasure, I rose to my feet and watched her leave.

My uncle Edward Woodville broke the news to me two weeks later when he came to see Henry by slipping me a note that I burned after I'd read it. As March stormed in with violent winds and black clouds that released a deluge of rain over London, my mother was abruptly stripped of all her goods and sent to Bermondsey Abbey. I placed a hand to my dizzy head and sank down into a chair. *This is the day I promised my mother would come when she'd destroy herself, and I would rejoice at her destruction.*

But rejoice I did not. Despite everything, she was my mother, and I could not help but love her. Henry was still away, and for once I regretted his absence. I could learn nothing about the banishment until he returned, and I knew Margaret Beaufort would tell me naught. Nevertheless, after breaking fast the next day, I confronted her.

"I understand my mother has retired to Bermondsey Abbey. I wish to see her."

Margaret Beaufort looked up from the document she held in her hand. To my surprise, without further ado, she said, "It shall be arranged."

We took a barge across the river. The water stretched before me, murky and forbidding. At Bermondsey we followed the abbess to the royal residence where my mother was installed. The room was not unpleasant, but the idea that my mother, who loved the gaiety and color of court, would be confined here in this drab grayness with nothing but silence and the prayers of the nuns for the rest of her life cut me to the core.

Mother sat listlessly at the window. She had seen us disembark, but she had not risen. I knelt by her side as she turned her head slowly to gaze at me. But she would not speak, and the nuns took us away.

Palace whispers claimed that she was caught throwing her support to the rebellion and had written the Earl of Desmond in Ireland to put his faith in Lincoln and Lovell. The dread tidings, and the fearful emptiness that engulfed me on the loss of my mother, sent me to prayer. But the angry Fates were not done with me yet. From my jester Patch I learned that my brother Dorset had been taken to the Tower.

On the heels of this report, I received a missive from Henry that Margaret Beaufort read to me in her stern fashion, commanding me to join him at Coventry with Arthur. There we maintained our court and sat through the pageants of welcome, indulging our subjects with spectacle and the royal presence, seemingly unruffled by rumor or rebellion. But beneath this deceptive display of tranquility, my heart churned in my breast day and night. I knew the feigned boy was not Edward, Earl of Warwick, and he was standing in for my brother who was too young to be brought forward yet—if he was still alive. But clearly, my mother believed one of them had survived. Was it my younger brother, Dickon? All the rumors held that he was alive, but no rumor had given out that Edward still lived. *Poor Edward, God grant him rest.*

Henry came to my chamber on the first evening of my arrival at Coventry. He stood, waiting for everyone to leave. His mother was the last to depart.

"I am giving you the properties I have confiscated from your mother," he said. "But in so doing, I must remind you that it is now your obligation to support your sisters."

This did not surprise me. Henry was not one to give away something for nothing, and he always had the better of the deal. Remembering my mother's words, I tried to please Henry in bed that night, though his breath was as foul as a dragon's and he took inordinately long to reach his climax. When he was finally done, I found courage.

"Henry, my mother—"

Before I could broach the subject that weighed down my heart, he flung back the sheets. "Do not meddle in my affairs, lady! I am not your father to be twisted around by a woman in a bed." Then he stormed out of the room.

I turned my face into the pillow and sobbed.

CHAPTER 15

Trumpets of War, 1487

WHEN THE REBELS LANDED IN LANCASHIRE, HENRY sent us to the safety of Greenwich. Tidings dribbled in, none of the news good for the Yorkists. Francis Lovell could gain no support from the people; they were all terrified of Henry. Tudor spies were everywhere, and in any case, after thirty years of fighting, they'd had enough of war.

It was when I heard Margaret Beaufort's loud weeping outside my privy chamber that I knew the rebellion had failed. Francis and Jack invaded England with the Earl of Kildare. They brought many Irish followers and two thousand Germans financed by Henry's bitter enemy, my Aunt Margaret, Duchess of Burgundy. The battle took place on the sixteenth day of June at Stoke, and Francis was soundly defeated.

Jack, Earl of Lincoln, was slain.

Pain shot through me when I heard these words. I rose and went to my bedchamber so no one would see my anguish. There, at my prie-dieu, I remembered Jack's laughter, his joy in placing wagers, the pleasure he took performing sleight-of-hand tricks for the children, and I bowed my head in tearful prayer.

Henry remained in the north for a few weeks to secure the region and then returned to London like a conquering hero. Margaret Beaufort and I went by barge from Greenwich to a private London house near Bishopsgate to observe the pageantry of London's greeting, but we didn't meet Henry in public. Margaret Beaufort was adamant that the triumph was his to enjoy alone. I noted that the greeting of the mayor and aldermen was more effusive than after Bosworth; the banners in more profusion; and more citizens lined the streets to cheer. We watched him pass, and as sunset threw jewel colors across water and sky, we took the barge back to Greenwich.

Henry arrived the next evening. " 'Tis unfortunate about Lincoln," he murmured. "I would that he were captured alive, so we could get to the bottom of the trouble."

I had been grieved by the tidings of Jack's death, but now I rejoiced and thanked God that He, in His mercy, had spared Jack the horrors of torture. Later, I pondered Henry's words, for it meant he himself was not certain of the fate of at least one of my brothers.

I was struggling to determine if one or the other was still living when Margaret Beaufort came to me with an announcement.

"Henry wishes that you go on a royal progress and be seen by the people. It would settle the land. Naturally, I shall accompany you. If your progress goes well, it shall go well for your mother at Bermondsey, and for your brother Dorset in the Tower. They are both ailing, as you may know." Margaret Beaufort gave me a hard, meaningful look.

"If . . . if there is difficulty . . . with the progress—" I stuttered.

She gave me a look that left me in no doubt. "They may not recover from the sickness that has gripped them. I dare say your mother, at least, will not leave behind many mourners. There is not a woman alive who has contrived to make more personal enemies."

A silence fell. I laid aside my mending and rose stiffly. I searched my mother-in-law's face, and as I did so, realization washed over me. Hard and resolute, her wolfish features bore a cruelty I had not fully appreciated until this moment. *She is a woman capable of murdering babes with her bare hands,* I thought with a shudder. *And now that I have given birth to a son, I too am dispensable, along with my entire family. She would not flinch to do whatever it took to keep the crown on her son's head.*

These Tudors were made of steel. I dropped back into my chair and turned my face to the window. I stared at the cold and dreary Thames and the oppressive clouds, my mind utterly stripped of feeling and thought. Dimly, I heard Margaret Beaufort's footsteps tapping against the glazed tile as she left my chamber.

Lifting the lid of the coffer by my chair, I reached for Richard's book. Boethius's *De Consolatione*. I opened it, and bent my head to his words.

❀

ON A WARM AUGUST MORNING, WHEN WE WERE TO leave on my progress, I awakened to find I had been crying in my sleep. I knew I had been dreaming of my childhood. In my dream, I'd been with Papa again, playing Hoodman's Bluff in a sunlit chamber. He chased me through the room and out to the passageway, along the hall and to the tower stairs. There was laughter all around, and smiling faces wherever I looked. Down I went; down the steps, shrieking with joy, his footsteps clicking on the stone behind me, his laughter filling my world. Then I couldn't hear him anymore. I stopped and looked around; it was dark and quiet. I was alone. I called out his name, but there was no answering reply from the silence; I stretched out my hands for him but touched only emptiness.

It had rained in the night, and the wind rattled the shutters. The fire had died in the hearth, leaving behind a pile of gray ash. Wearily, I rose from bed and went to my prie-dieu as the castle began to stir. Under Margaret Beaufort's eagle eye and a myriad of instructions read by her clerk, my ladies-in-waiting prepared me for my journey. Accompanied by the usual escort of men-at-arms, servants, and baggage carts, we left London for Nottingham.

I had forgotten how beautiful the world was. Enjoying my first taste of freedom since Bosworth, I saw golden haystacks crowning the farmlands, sunny orchards laden with ripe plums, and the lovely green gloom of woods damp with the smell of earth and dense with willow and elm. We emerged from terrain covered with fern and pine needles into bright fields blanketed with crimson poppies and fireweed, a strange plant of rugged loveliness that grows only on the scars of ruin and flame. We passed serene lakes and rushing waterfalls, stone cottages and hillsides pastoral with sheep. Nightingales sang to us from thickets, and turtledoves screeched, and everywhere we went, we were greeted by smiling faces.

I loved meeting my people. From far and wide, in rain and cold, they came to the market squares and castle gates with gifts of pike, dried fruits, pies, and carvings they had made. They showered me with compliments and told me of the love they bore my father. I gave them presents in return: a few yards of woolen fabric, a silver trinket, a flask of wine and fine cheeses, ale and a pheasant, and a few small purses of coin. Margaret Beaufort stood guard at my elbow, grumbling under her breath at the expense, but she knew what an important service I rendered her son, and dared not curtail my expenditures.

Since the Beaufort woman supported the universities of Oxford and Cambridge and ran a home for poor scholars, some thought her a generous person. That was not so. She kept a sharp eye on expenses and was as tainted by avarice as Henry himself. With the army of lawyers she retained, she persecuted tenants and farmers, taking away their carts and plows as punishment for trespass and minor offenses. She even sued the widows of her most loyal servants for small debts, some going back a hundred years to her paternal grandfather, John, Duke of Somerset, sending them to prison when they were unable to pay.

Only my mother matches the Tudors in love of money, I thought. Hastily, I crossed myself and begged God's forgiveness for the disloyal thought. Mother's faults seemed insignificant now.

Sometimes in the silence of the night, I tossed fitfully as I considered how vulnerable my sisters and I were; how we could be murdered with impunity. In the end, who was there to protect us? They were all powerless, my people. Henry had modernized the Tower with implements of torture imported from France that instilled terror through the land. Morton's words hammered in my head: "We have made torture an art, sire." I bit down hard against the thought. No longer was the Tower known for the beauty of its residence and its royal menagerie, but for its chambers of horrors, and men trembled to enter its gates of Hell. Many of Richard's loyal followers, good knights with whom I'd laughed that last Yuletide of Richard's life, had disappeared into the Tower. Of them all, the one that burned my memory was young Johnnie of Gloucester. At least Edward, Earl of Warwick, lived; I could take comfort in that. *But Johnnie—*

He was surely dead. I made the sign of the cross and offered a prayer for his soul as I rode.

Everyone in the land knew someone who had disappeared. Fear kept them in check and made Henry's throne more secure. Petitioners shrank and grew silent before Henry's mother, and it was only when they turned their gaze on me that they forgot their cares and broke into smiles. I reminded them of the old world, the world of chivalry that had belonged to Papa and died with Richard at Bosworth Field. Morton's advice to Henry rang in my ears: "King Richard with his mercy and his justice was here one day and gone the next, but Rome lasted a thousand years, for it was built on terror."

I shivered, remembering.

Now here I was, alone in this frightening place, clinging to the past for strength, struggling to endure the present, so I could banish the darkness of Henry's court with the light of a future King Arthur. To this end, I felt an awesome responsibility to survive. Under Margaret Beaufort's tutelage, without me to teach my babe the ideals of my father, he would grow up into another shrewdly calculating, power-hungry tyrant.

Thus did my thought ramble as we rode to Nottingham. The next morning, at the castle, after we had broken fast and attended chapel prayers, I received petitioners in the Great Hall, dressed in one of my black silk gowns with Thomas's brooch pinned to my collar, as always. And, as always, Margaret Beaufort admonished me for not standing on the dais.

"You forget you are queen. You should not be in the center of the room like a common peasant," she said.

"Pray, my lady Margaret, allow me this one liberty. My wish is to mingle with the people."

She gave in reluctantly, a sour look on her face as she took up her position at my elbow. The doors were opened and the common folk filed in. I noticed her recoil as the room filled with the stench of unwashed bodies, and I took a certain pleasure in her discomfort. These people were my people, not Henry's, and I loved them, washed or unwashed. For me, hearts counted more than the weight of gems or titles.

One after the other, they filed in, and I delighted at their pleasure in seeing me, in their love, which warmed me, in their small gifts: oranges, cheese, a pair of doves, a clavichord. Some begged for my aid: a widow pleaded for money to rebuild her cottage, which had been destroyed by fire; a metalworker asked for patronage to make religious vessels; a man beseeched me for money to pay a physician for his sick son.

I stole a glance down at Margaret Beaufort. She stood silently beside me, not uttering a word, a look of disdain on her face. Aware how much she valued pomp and royal ceremony, I took a secret joy in her misery. After an hour had passed and there was still a crowd of folk pressing in the antechamber, she whispered that she would be gone for a few moments. I gave her a smile and remembered my mother's words: "Thank God for the privy!"

Aye, it offers us relief in more ways than can be counted, I thought wryly.

At this moment, an older man with white curls stepped forward. He knelt before me and bowed his head. "My lady queen, I failed to bring you this long ago when it was entrusted to me. My horse went lame and you were gone by the time I arrived." His voice was low, meant for me alone. He handed me a book.

My body began a fierce trembling at the sight of the worn brown leather volume, and my hands shook as I took it. I kept my eyes lowered to hide my emotion, but I could scarcely speak, for my throat had closed up.

It was Richard's book, *Tristan*.

The last time I'd held it, I'd been in a small chamber at Westminster, leaping from the window seat as King Richard entered the room. Again I saw his gaunt face, his eyes alive with unspoken pain as they fixed on me, and again my heart took up a fierce pounding and I dropped the book.

"My lady queen," the man said, jolting me into the present as he picked it up and inserted back into its pages a small painted image that had fallen out, "forgive my clumsiness."

"Nay, forgive me mine," I breathed. "What is your name?"

"John Hewick, my queen."

There was so much to say and so little time! Margaret Beaufort would return at any moment. "How did you come by this?"

"It was given me by a wounded knight with instructions to bring it to you at—in August—after—"

I met his eyes as I took his hand and raised him to his feet. *Aye, I understand only too clearly what you are trying to tell me.* "My good man, you have done me more service this day than you can ever know. Here is a gift for you of a purse, and this ring—" I slipped off my gold ring wrought in the shape of a rose that my father had given me. "I would that it could match the value of your gift to me, but that is impossible. Tell me, what living have you?"

"I was Yeoman of the King's Crown."

"Was?"

"No longer, my queen."

I did not delve.

"Why did I not see you at the palace?"

"You are well guarded, my lady queen, and permission was always denied."

"I know it—"

"What is this?" Margaret Beaufort had crept up on us so stealthily that neither of us had noticed. "John Hewick, what do you here, taking up the queen's time, be gone, man!"

As she chastised him, I hid the book in a small basket beside me, beneath a handkerchief embroidered crudely with white roses. My thoughts were a tumult in my mind. I wanted only to get away with my book and see if the painted image was what I hoped it was—the portrait I had requested of Richard.

Later that morning, before Margaret Beaufort had a chance to search its contents, I retrieved my book from the basket, hid it in my skirts, and stole into my privy. A fierce wind whistled through the arrow slits, fluttering the curtains and nearly putting out the candle that lit the gloomy garderobe. With a thundering heart, I removed the painted image from within its pages and held it up to the light. My breath caught in my throat.

O Richard, Richard! To see your face again, even here, in this place, even for a moment—

Tears stung my eyes, and I gave vent to an uncontrollable fit of sobbing. At length, drained of emotion, I dried my eyes, smoothed my dress, and left the sanctuary of the privy. Hiding the book in a hidden compartment of a small coffer, I locked it with the key I wore around my neck and lay down on my bed. The chanting of the monks from the chapel drifted through the open window, and I stared at the dismal sky, flooded by memories. Too soon my rest period was ended by a knock at the door.

"Your Grace," said Lucy Neville, my lady-in-waiting, "Lady Margaret the king's mother wishes to leave for Kegworth in a half hour. May we prepare you for the journey?"

"Pray first send Patch the Dwarf to me," I said, rising. I needed a moment of humor to soothe my nerves.

Patch entered with a sweeping, courtly bow. He leaned close and whispered in my ear, "I heard what the man called Lady Margaret when he left you—"

I stared at him, not comprehending. "What man?"

"The one who gave you the book."

I froze. "You saw?"

He nodded.

"Anyone else see?"

"I doubt it, my lady. They don't notice things the way I do."

"So, my dear Patch, you see things and hear things that others don't. You would make a good spy." I threw him a knowing look, and he gave me an affectionate grin in return. Margaret Beaufort had hired Patch to spy on me, as she hired everyone to do, but I'd detected a change in him in recent weeks and I dared to hope he'd transferred his loyalty to me. "So tell, what was it?"

"A friend of his asked how he'd done, and he said he'd seen you and would have talked more with you, but for 'that strong whore' who chased him away!" Patch sallied across the room, swinging his hips, and ended his sashay with a kick. I giggled at his sly jest, and Patch smiled as he watched me. *Have I found a friend at last?* I wondered. "Patch, would you be willing to do something for me?"

He knelt at my feet and turned his head to me. "By the faith of my heart!" he whispered, pressing both hands to his breast as he gave voice to Lancelot's favorite oath.

I bent down to him. "I wish you to get someone to take marchpane to Edward of Warwick in the Tower. And find out what else he would like."

"Consider it done, my lady queen."

❂

HENRY SEEMED WELL PLEASED WITH ME WHEN I RE-turned. That same night he came to my privy suite. After dismissing everyone present, including his mother, he requested that I sing for him. I ran my fingers over my lyre and raised my voice above the rippling chords. When the song was ended, he patted the chair beside him. I sat down and smoothed my skirts apprehensively.

"You seem curiously disinterested in power, Elizabeth," he said.

I turned his question over in my mind. *Aye*, I thought, *I know well the dangers of power.* Power had driven Marguerite d'Anjou into exile, where she'd died in poverty, homeless and childless. It had destroyed my mother and sent her into Bermondsey a pauper, deprived of the comfort of her children and friends, with nothing to sustain her but God; she, who had worshipped wealth and ceremony and paid God little heed for most of her life. All I wished was to be safe, to raise my son so I could give England a worthy king.

"I do not seek power, my lord. It destroys the queens that wield it. In the end, they are always hated. When I stand before God, I hope to say I left the world a better place than I found it." I lifted my eyes to his face. "What do you hope power will achieve for you?"

Henry sighed and slapped his knee. He rose from his seat and went to the window. "I wish to give England peace through settled rule," he said. "I wish to make England great. But more important than all else, I wish to make my son safe on his throne, and that means I must be safe. To that end, I will sacrifice all."

I felt a shiver run along my spine. Henry had lived the life of a hunted animal, known hunger and cold, danger and desperation, and thrice escaped the clutches of death. Would he ever feel safe? I closed my eyes and the image of little Edward rose before me, surrounded by a thicket of armed men as he disappeared into the Tower. Motherless, fatherless, a descendant of the male Plantagenet line that had ruled England for nigh on four hundred years, the child stood in Henry's way. I had thought I could keep him safe once I was queen; now I knew I could not. *What will become of him?* I wondered.

Henry spoke again. "About your coronation."

I blinked. I realized that I hadn't expected to ever be crowned. If Henry had waited long enough, I might have died and he'd have been spared the expense. I searched his face, but it was as impassive as always: the thin lips pressed tightly together; the hooded gray eyes hard as marbles. Was this offer now an olive branch to his persecutors, the Yorkists, or merely a ploy to appease the people and quell future revolt? Was he no longer jealous of my superior claim to the crown, or had he satisfied himself about my ambitions? I would never know; Henry didn't open up his heart to anyone except, perhaps, his mother.

And what about *my* mother, who had so desired my coronation?

"Will my lady mother have the honor of carrying my train?"

"I shall decide the details later, but frankly, I doubt it. She has been feeling unwell lately. As you know, she wishes no visitors, or even to venture out from Bermondsey."

"Or even to write to me?"

He didn't flinch at my sarcasm. "Apparently so. And now, lady, with your permission—" He threw me a nod and withdrew. I rose and bobbed him a curtsy.

CHAPTER 16

Queen of England, 1487

HENRY SPENT LAVISHLY ON MY CORONATION. HE SAID he wished to oversee the planning of the entire occasion personally, but it was difficult even for him to go against his mother, and her hand was evident in every detail.

On Friday, the twenty-third of November, 1487, two days before my coronation on St. Catherine's Day, in the cold sunshine of a wintry day, I left Greenwich for the Tower of London by river. For this occasion, I abandoned the black wide-sleeved gowns I had come to favor for attire of white satin and a velvet cloak trimmed with ermine. Escorted by minstrels and the blare of trumpets, with banners streaming behind us, my flotilla of colorful barges sailed along the shining waters bearing my noble lords and ladies, the mayor and aldermen of London, and other city fathers. One, called *The Bachelor's Barge,* was fashioned in the image of Henry's emblem of a great red dragon and outshone all the rest as it belched flames into the Thames.

Margaret Beaufort stood at my side, coordinating her wave with mine as I greeted the cheering crowds assembled along the shore, but I scarcely noticed her, for my thoughts were with my mother.

She had been excluded from my coronation, as I had feared. I strained my eyes in the direction of far-off Bermondsey, along the curve of the river, and wondered how much, if anything, she could see from her window. Then I turned my attention to my sisters, Cecily, Anne, Kate, and Bridget, standing behind me.

Cecily held herself very still and regarded me impassively. I gave her a cold glare. Soon after I returned from my progress, in a light moment, I had confided to her about the man who had called Margaret Beaufort "that strong whore." Then I learned from Patch that a charge of treason had been levied against the man from Nottingham for speaking ill of the king's mother, and he had been assessed a ruinous fine. I knew then that Cecily had betrayed my confidence. Never would I trust her again. I glanced away.

My younger sisters threw me bright smiles, and I thought how lovely they were: Anne, twelve, with her golden hair and azure eyes; sweet eight-year-old Kate, with gilt hair and large fern-green eyes; and seven-year-old Bridget, who stood solemnly, clearly awed by the significance of the occasion.

My eye rested on Richard's sister at the side of the barge. Liza, Duchess of Suffolk, sitting on a tapestry-covered bench, in conversation with her daughter, Eleanor de la Pole, one of my ladies-in-waiting. Liza had already lost one son for Richard's cause. *Does she know her other sons are giving Henry restless nights?* Though her boys were descended from the second son of Edward III in a maternal line, the blood in their veins, in contrast to Henry's bastard lineage, ran indisputably royal. Her husband, the Duke of Suffolk, had failed Richard at Bosworth, and I wondered if Jack's death and Henry's taxation had caused Suffolk to regret his betrayal of Richard. If not, he surely would in the future. I had seen the names of his other three sons in Henry's memorandum book where, among other reminders, he noted those to be watched.

I banished the dismal thought and turned back to the crowds. I was one of *them* now. A Tudor queen. The first of a long line to come, if Henry had his way. I could not change what God had ordained, but I also knew that what Henry did for his throne would secure it for my own beloved Arthur. I had not sought queenship, nor did I relish it, but I was a pawn of Fate, and queenship was mine by destiny. Though I was an accessory to Henry's sins by virtue of my marriage, I had been a most unwilling participant with no power to alter the flow of events. All I could offer England was my best efforts in raising her future king and in teaching him the ideals in which I believed.

We drew up to the Tower wharf. Henry's glittering figure in crimson velvet and jewels awaited me, surrounded by his attendants and fifty armed yeomen. As I alighted, he gave me his royal welcome and an embrace. A most joyous cheer went up. *Henry has calculated this for effect,* I thought. But if reminding the land of the union of York and Lancaster brought my people comfort and allayed their fears, where lay the harm? They had known three decades of suffering and death, and it was time for peace.

Side by side, Henry and I entered the apartments of the Tower, where we were greeted by the newly created Knights of the Bath. All day and night, as bells rang throughout the city of London, banqueting, disguisings, and dancing marked our hours. On Saturday morning, I was left alone to meditate in privacy and seclusion. Kneeling at my prie-dieu, I lifted my eyes to the celestial sky, the residence of God. After offering my thanks to Him and beseeching His blessing, I turned my thoughts to one who lived in my heart.

Richard, I make thee this vow: I shall be the queen you wished me to be, not for Henry's sake, but for yours, and for Arthur's, and for the sake of our people for whom you died, so that war might end.

After I broke my fast, my ladies dressed me in a rich gown of white cloth of gold. A mantle of the same fabric furred with ermine was fastened over my bosom with intricately woven gold lace and silk tasseled with knots of gold, and my yellow hair was arranged to flow loose below my knees, sparingly covered by a circlet richly garnished with gems and a net woven of golden threads.

"How do I look, Lucy?" I asked, for I knew her to be the most truthful of all my ladies.

"My lady queen, you are luminescent. You seem to walk in a golden pool of light, and to gaze on you is to look on a bright summer's day."

I remembered thinking the same of Queen Anne when I stood by her as Lucy stood by me now. I had sought to emulate her in

every way. *Perhaps I am succeeding*, I thought. Resting my hand on
Lucy's sleeve, I smiled my thanks.

I took the Tower steps down to the courtyard, accompanied
by a great number of people and much ceremony. The procession
of lords, ladies, city fathers, and Knights of the Bath had already
formed and was waiting patiently. Clad in furs, velvets, gold chains,
and jewels, and mounted on steeds caparisoned in cloth embroidered with their emblems of roses, dragons, and lions, the lords
dazzled in the sun. I threw my sisters a smile as I climbed into
my litter cushioned with gold damask pillows. They were seated
directly behind me, in chairs decorated with my father's blazon of
the White Rose and Sun in Splendor, beside the duchesses. The
baronesses, in matching gowns of crimson velvet, trailed them on
their gilded horses.

Then Margaret Beaufort appeared. Wearing a replica of my
gown and a glittering coronet, she took a seat beside me. At her
nod, we proceeded through the gates of the Tower. A joyous thunder erupted as we emerged. From a sea of white roses, the ecstatic
crowd called "Elizabeth, Elizabeth! God bless you, Elizabeth! God
bless the king's daughter!" Their excitement was contagious and
my heart soared in response, for everywhere I looked, the White
Rose was in evidence among the throng, reminding me how madly
they had cheered for my father wherever we had gone.

I stole a glance at the Beaufort woman. She sat as still and silent as alabaster, waving when I did. Not one person called her
name. *She knows that the people only accept her son as king for my sake,*
I thought. I would have to pray for forgiveness later, but for now I
couldn't help taking satisfaction in her discomfort—not for my ego,
not for my moment of fleeting glory, but simply because she was a
mean and petty woman who reveled in her power over others.

I was touched to see how hard the Londoners had worked to
make my coronation perfect. The city glittered. The streets along
my route had been washed and hung with tapestries and banners
of velvet and silk that streamed and fluttered in the wind. Rotting
traitors' heads had been taken down from the bridge, and the guilds
of the city lined the way to Westminster Abbey, every man dressed
in the livery of his craft. People had climbed rooftops and walls

and stood on balconies to gain a better view, wrapped in blankets against the cold. Their eager faces smiled down at me. Each time my procession rested, the sweet voices of children sang for me, some dressed as angels, others as saints and virgins.

At Westminster, I was entertained with many pageants and marvelous spectacle. Later that night, I took my place at the table in the Painted Chamber for the banquet on the eve of my coronation. The hall was fragrant with the scent of ambergris and rose petals. But the feast drained me. I missed Arthur, and my mother.

The Archbishop of York arrived for my coronation on the following day. It was the first time I'd seen Rotherham since Richard's court, for he'd left London when Henry had deprived him of the chancellorship. And my memories of him were not fond. I gave him a civil nod and was relieved when he was lost to my view by a throng of spiritual lords and monks who appeared between us. With stately pomp, to the music of minstrels, I proceeded to Westminster Abbey on the path laid out by the carpet of gold, Suffolk bearing the scepter before me, Cecily holding my train, and Jasper Tudor following with the crown. Duchesses in scarlet velvet studded with pearls streamed behind.

Suddenly, a terrible noise filled the air. The men-at-arms had given way and the excited crowd had broken through the barricade. Eager to have a share of the valuable coronation carpet that was the traditional gift to commoners, they rushed forward. Fighting one another for a piece, they tore it into shreds and turned their hands to the hems of my ladies. The duchesses screamed, and everyone fled for safety. Swords flashed, and those who had snatched bits of gold cloth were cut down.

I shut my eyes on an anguished breath, averting my gaze from the bodies being thrown into a cart like trash. The procession reorganized itself and I moved on with a heavy heart, murmuring prayers for the souls of those who had died on my coronation day.

Passing through the west door, I led the way past the choir, toward the pulpit and the royal seat where Morton awaited to celebrate the mass. I had dreaded what lay ahead, but it no longer seemed so terrible in light of what had just happened. I approached the high altar and prostrated myself before him. After he had prayed over me, I rose and opened my gown ever so carefully so that his fish eyes would not see too much as he anointed me first on the breast, then the head. The touch of his fleshy fingers, fat as veal sausages, was clammy, and I had to force myself not to recoil. *"In nomine Patris, et Filii, et Spiritus Sancti, prosit haec tibi unctio—"* he intoned, spreading a bejeweled hand.

As the ceremony progressed, my gaze went up to a latticed stage between the pulpit and altar in a far corner high above. There, like two bats in a cave, hidden from all eyes, Henry and his mother watched my coronation. No one understood why they had chosen to do so this way. Only I knew Margaret Beaufort preferred to be absent if she couldn't share the glory. Yet, in keeping with her character, secretive and sly, she wished to see, and to know, without being seen, or known. It was the new Tudor way. Henry and his mother spied on me now, as they spied on all my people. *Is this not the man who came to London after Bosworth peering at his subjects from between the curtains of his litter, shielded from them by a thicket of armed guards?*

There had been death this day. Tragedy had marked the triumph of my coronation, as it had marked my life, and once again I'd been powerless to interfere. The sight of the valuable gold cloth had proved too much for the poor. Fearful of the precious item eluding their grasp, they had fought and died for it. I found a cruel similarity between these unfortunate folk and the nobles who had killed one another over power and lands. They, too, had grasped, and snatched, and seized, with no thought to what was right, and it had cost them everything.

That night Richard came to me again in my dreams, swirling in mist. *I shall make you proud of me, Richard,* I murmured. But he seemed so distant now, and whether he heard or not, I did not know.

As I learned over the next few days from the hushed whispers of the men-at-arms, the tiring maids, my ladies-in-waiting and the scriveners, clerks, varlets and other servants, Henry's money proved well spent, for my coronation helped him secure his hold on the throne.

"The heir is already born," they murmured.

"The line of descent clear—"

"The land is gladdened to see King Edward's daughter honored—"

"Maybe now God will see fit to lift our penance, His scourge of war inflicted for the deposition of kings."

"Amen to that!" someone whispered.

And a chorus went up, *Amen, Amen*.

CHAPTER 17

Henry Tudor's Court, 1488

WE KEPT THE YULETIDE THAT FOLLOWED MY CORO-
nation at Sheen, Henry's favorite palace. To the Lancastrian emblems
of swans, antelopes, and daisies that abounded on the ceilings and
cornices, Henry added his own personal touch. He carved his motto,
Dieu et Mon Droit, God and My Right, into the stone of the cloisters, and decorated the entire palace with the entwined roses of York
and Lancaster. The "Tudor Rose" was visible on the tiled floors and
stonework, the bosses of the wood ceilings, the gilded harnesses of
the royal horses, and the green and white tunics of his guards. It even
embellished the pages of manuscripts in the royal library. The theme
was picked up quickly by courtiers who, anxious to show their loyalty, stamped it into the designs of their gold collars.

Amid feasting, revelry, and music we celebrated New Year's Day
of 1488 with a pageant and a disguising, to which Henry came as
Sir Lancelot. Though he had won both Bosworth and Stoke, he
had never personally fought in, or guided, a battle, and he lacked
the chivalrous demeanor and warrior quality needed to give his
role credibility. But fear made people pretend to forget the truth,
and elicited gushing praise of his disguise.

A hush fell over the court as Henry's favorite poet, blind Bernard Andre, took his place in the center of the hall and prepared to recount yet another poem about King Arthur, who had ruled over Britain. Torches were snuffed out to dim the room; candles flickered, smoke drifted in the air, misting my sight. My lids began to close, for the day had been tiring, and I knew what to expect. Aye, there was the first of the prophecies of Merlin that the true heir of Celtic kings would come from Wales, as Henry had done to rescue England from the "tyrant." I laughed inwardly at the farce of black painted white; and white, black. *Has everyone forgotten that when St. George slew the dragon, he was slaying the Devil? Now they pay homage to the dragon . . .*

I must have dozed off, for the finale jolted me awake. Welsh harpers and rhymers, well paid and well rehearsed, had joined Andre's side, and a medley of voices rose to proclaim Henry's greatness as torches were relit around the chamber and guests applauded.

On Twelfth Night Henry and I wore our crowns. Margaret Beaufort, who had grown more obnoxious now that the danger to her son had lessened with my coronation, showed herself again in a mantle and surcoat that was a copy of mine. Since my crown couldn't be duplicated, however, she wore a coronet instead.

One afternoon as I embroidered a silk gown for Arthur, Henry's voice sounded in the passageway. "Come, Lancelot," he said, appearing in the threshold of my chamber and waiting for his hound to come to him.

"I thought his name was Piers."

"It was," replied Henry. "I changed it."

"Why?" I asked, pretending I didn't know. Since Lincoln's rebellion, everything Henry did was designed to make people forget his bastardy and to link him with King Arthur. But all he said was, "Lancelot suits him better."

That evening at dinner, after the tables had been cleared and the dancing began, I noticed Margaret Beaufort and Morton in deep conversation with a little man in black. "Who is that?" I asked Henry.

"Polydore Vergil is his name."

"And this Polydore Vergil, where is he from?"

"He is in the employ of the Duke of Urbino."

"An Italian scholar, then? What does he in England?"

"Nothing yet." Henry's voice had a sharp edge to it.

"Why your reluctance to discuss him with me, my lord?"

"Why ask so many questions?" he retorted.

"I was merely making conversation."

"Then make conversation with Patch."

I smothered my frustration. My husband was a rude, impossible man. Infinitely suspicious, he considered every question a trap. Something was going on here, and I was determined to find out what it was. Taking Henry at his word, I asked Patch.

"Do you know anything about a man named Polydore Vergil?"

"The Italian with the spindly legs, who always wears black and has an obsequious smile? King Henry is considering having him rewrite English history, my queen."

"But why an Italian?"

"An Italian can be made to change English history with less difficulty than an Englishman." He grinned and stood on his head, looking at me quizzically.

I laughed, but not as merrily as I would have wished. Patch was my only friend, and I worried about his loose tongue, for so many others dear to me had been taken from me in one way or another.

On a cold January afternoon, after receiving petitioners, I sought Arthur in the nursery. I was playing Catch Me If You Can with him, and he was running merrily away when Henry surprised me. I caught Arthur and swept him up in my arms, suddenly anxious. "Pray, my lord, I hope 'tis good tidings that bring you here at this early hour?"

"Indeed. I wished you to know that I have decided to arrange a marriage alliance for Arthur."

"Marriage?" I echoed in bewilderment. I clasped my babe tightly to me and smoothed his hair. "But he's not even two years old!"

"Do not fret, Elizabeth. Nothing will change. They need not marry until Arthur is grown, nor does the chosen princess need to come to England till then. But a betrothal will secure us an alliance with a foreign power that can only benefit England."

"Have you given thought to which princess it shall be?" I asked more calmly.

"Who can say what union shall be best for England years from now? But I have gone over the prospects with Morton and my advisors—"

Your mother, I thought bitterly.

Henry made himself comfortable in a chair by the hearth. Clearly, he wished to arrange his thoughts aloud, and for once I was the beneficiary of learning what they were. "A minor sits on the throne of France, and his throne seems none too secure at the present time. Italy is in total confusion. Spain seems the nation most secure. It is growing more powerful, and its royal family has many daughters."

I gazed at my little one sucking his thumb, his head against my shoulder. I offered him my finger, and his fist closed tightly over it. I kissed his sweet face and looked up at Henry. "I make only one request. Let it not be too soon."

Henry rose, placed a hand on my shoulder, a tender expression in his hooded eyes as he looked at me.

We kept Easter at Windsor. Once more, Margaret Beaufort replicated my dress while I pretended not to notice. Not long afterward, the Spanish ambassador, Doctor Rodrigo de Puebla, requested a formal audience. He was a one-armed man with a kindly face who wore his empty sleeve tucked into a leather belt. Naturally, Margaret Beaufort was there when Henry and I received him in the State Chamber at Westminster. De Puebla strode in and made us a deep bow. "Sire . . . Your Grace . . . My lady," he said, rolling his tongue on the *r* in the Spanish manner and flourishing his plumed cap to each of us in turn. "I am delighted to inform you that I am the bearer of splendid news destined to make our nations most powerful across all Europe."

Henry leaned forward in his throne.

The ambassador resumed, "Their excellencies King Ferdinand and Queen Isabella of Spain have accepted your marriage proposal for the hand of their second eldest daughter, Katarina of Aragon."

Unable to control his joy, Henry leapt from his throne. Doffing his hat, he embraced the Spanish ambassador. *"Te Deum Lauda-*

mus!" he cried. God be praised! By this acceptance he had won recognition as a legitimate monarch by one of the most esteemed houses of Europe.

✿

I STEPPED INTO THE NURSERY. EIGHTEEN-MONTH-old Arthur dropped his toy soldier and toddled to me, shrieking, "Mama! Mama!" I swept him up in my arms. Pressing him to my heart, I twirled around the room with him, both of us laughing. "Oh, my precious, how I miss you when I don't see you! Oh, how good it feels to have your little arms tight around my neck!" I covered him with loud, smacking kisses. The nurses and young rockers in the room smiled, and the men-at-arms at the door turned to watch us with soft eyes. Into my mind flashed the memory of the nobles at the council table when my father had chased me around just before Warwick's rebellion. I gazed at the dear child I held in my arms.

How much has changed since then! And how much is eternal.

As often as I could between my queenly duties, I sought Arthur's hugs and listened to his sweet babble that I found so soothing. I was glad I'd stood my ground with Henry's mother when he was newly born. Settling down in a chair by the window, I fussed over my child, kissing his soft dark hair, his bright gray eyes, his chubby red cheeks. He pointed to the window and told me something impossible to understand, and I told him how much I loved him. "You, my sweet babe, are everything to me, did you know that?" He chuckled at me in a way that delighted my heart.

Not as monarch did I reign, not for ambition either, but to stand as an example to my babe. To teach him the ideals I believed in. To raise a king of strength, honor, and courage; one that would govern our people well.

I kissed the top of his silken head and gave him over to his nurse. It was time to receive petitioners.

✿

"UNCLE EDWARD!" I CRIED, RISING FROM MY SETTLE in pleasant surprise. The last time I'd seen my maternal uncle, Sir

Edward Woodville, was at my coronation, and we'd been given no chance to speak privately. I suspected my Uncle Edward was deliberately kept from my presence, like everyone else of my blood except my younger sisters, who posed no threat to Henry. This, despite the fact that he enjoyed Henry's special favor, for unlike Dorset, he'd never tried to reconcile with Richard and had fought for Henry at Bosworth. But Henry, ever wary of losing his throne, ever suspicious of everyone, still kept us apart.

" 'Tis so good to see you." I took his elbow and we moved to a window seat. I smoothed my black silk skirt beside him. "How are you?" I examined his face, lined by time and experience of war and exile. "Why have you not come to see me before? I've missed you."

He avoided the last part of my question, and I knew that I was correct. He had been prevented from visiting me. Now I tensed, wondering what urgent matter had secured him permission to see me.

"I am here to bid you farewell, dear niece," he said.

A surge of panic swept through me. "Where are you going?"

" 'Tis a little hard to explain, and a secret, so you must not tell anyone."

"Uncle, whom can I tell? I see no one but servants hired by Henry's mother, and petitioners whose gifts to me are examined."

He took my hand. "I know, Elizabeth. These are difficult times. Maybe one day it will be different for you."

I gave him a nod.

"Elizabeth, I'm going to war."

I gaped at him is disbelief. "War? We're at peace!"

"Officially. But the king is indebted to Brittany for offering him safe refuge during the hard years of his exile, and also to France for funding his invasion of England. Now hostilities have broken out between them, and both seek his aid. He has given them excuses why he can't take sides, but he feels honor bound to help Brittany. So I go secretly with four hundred men to discharge his debt. The king knows, of course, but when it comes out, he will pretend he didn't."

"Oh, Uncle—" I didn't know what to say. Not coming to visit

was one thing, but it was quite another to face death in battle. I might never see him again. Sometimes life itself felt like one long war. Nothing but losses, one after the other.

His voice came again, soft and low. "I saw your mother."

My lashes flew up. "How is she?"

"Holding up. It's not easy for her, surrounded by nuns."

"I know. I pray for her." The irony of my words was not lost on either one of us, and we smiled at one another.

"She has no visitors, you know."

"None? Not even some old servants?"

" 'Tis considered dangerous to see her. No one wishes to take the risk."

"What of my brother Dorset?" I asked. "Any news when he might be released?"

"It has been almost a year now, but God be thanked, his release is imminent. Be not too hopeful," he added. "He is not welcome at court and needs to keep his head down for the foreseeable future."

I bit my lip. We sat in silence for a while, and then we both rose together.

"May God be with you, dear uncle," I said, with a heavy heart.

"And with you, dear niece."

As I watched him stride to the water gate and board his barge, I was assailed by an acute sense of loss. I must have had a foreboding, for a few months later I received word that the battle had been lost. The army of Brittany was destroyed, almost to a man. My uncle, Sir Edward Woodville, perished along with everyone he had taken with him.

Henry had to explain himself to the French, who accused him of breaking their treaty, and to the English, who screamed for war against France now that English blood had been spilt. One evening, deeply troubled by his predicament, he came to my chamber without his mother.

"Sing to me, Elizabeth," he said, drooping in a chair, a hand to his brow, his limp fair hair hiding his face.

I chose the lyre over the lute, arranged the folds of my black gown over my knees, and launched into a rippling melody. The sun was setting over the Thames, drenching the blue water in golden color, and a flock of blackbirds squawked from a nearby chestnut tree, providing a rich chorus for my song.

"You have a lovely voice," Henry said, lifting sad eyes to me when the last chords had echoed away.

"What ails you, my lord?" I asked, dropping my hands, though I knew well his troubles.

He let out an audible sigh. "As you know, the boy king Charles VIII of France and the twelve-year-old Duchess Anne of Brittany have declared hostilities, and Brittany is on the brink of destruction. I am loath to see the once mighty duchy absorbed by France, and am torn between my conflicting loyalties to both Brittany and France. Meanwhile, Isabella and Ferdinand of Spain are urging me to attack France."

"What will you do?"

"I shall take the funds Parliament gives me for war and try to maintain peace," he replied. "I believe your father did that once."

I reached out and laid a hand on his sleeve. "Pray, my lord, be gentle with the people. They suffer much, and many go hungry to pay their taxes. It may also—God forfend—bring revolt."

"Nay. I have shown them what happens to rebels."

"My lord, the English are unlike the docile French. We are a spirited people of an independent nature."

Henry rose to his feet. " 'Tis a favor I do you to tell you of my affairs! I am not ruled by women as your father was, madame!" He strode angrily from the room.

He forgets he is ruled by his mother, I thought. *But perhaps he is right. Margaret Beaufort is no woman.*

With a chuckle, I took up my lyre again.

Henry convened Parliament and demanded an exorbitant sum in taxes; Parliament, cowed by fear, granted the funds. I sighed to myself. What could I do but pray? Pray for Henry's soul—for well he needed my prayers—and pray for the poor people who had to make the payments. *And pray for myself, not to hate my husband.*

"I fear there shall be trouble," I whispered to my thirteen-year-old sister, Anne, who was old enough now to understand such things. "The commons prize their rights, and will not give in easily to such heavy taxation."

I was not long in being proven right. The people of Durham and Yorkshire refused to pay the tax collectors. Henry Percy, Earl of Northumberland, the great traitor of Bosworth, went out to enforce the levies. Led by a commoner, John a Chamber, the mob pulled him down from his horse and slew him while his retainers watched.

Welladay, what surprise in this? I thought. Percy was a hated man. The people of the north had loved Richard and had never forgiven Percy his heinous betrayal of their beloved king.

"Even here, confined in my chamber, I knew it would happen," I told Anne, "for I understand my people as Henry cannot. French and Welsh blood course in his veins more closely than English, nor does he know England because he spent much of his life in France."

"He sent Thomas Howard to help his father, the Earl of Surrey, put down the rebellion in the north," Anne replied, dropping her head.

Cupping her chin, I searched her upturned face. "Do I detect worry in your tone? You blush!" I broke into a smile as realization dawned. "My fair sister, you care for Tom Howard."

"Tom cares for me, too," she replied, darkening to deeper rose.

"Do you wish to wed him, dear sister?"

"More than anything in the world, Elizabeth."

"Then we shall have to see what we can do about that," I said, smiling. "But on one condition."

"What is that?" my sister asked.

"That you not wed for many years yet." She was too young for the duties of a wife, no matter how much she thought she desired them.

Tom Howard returned safely from York with his father, the Earl of Surrey. Following Henry's orders, they hanged the leader of the rebellion, John a Chamber, on a high gibbet with his accomplices symmetrically placed on gallows below him.

"Surrey is a good man," Henry told me one evening in my chamber.

"He has proven himself," I said. "And should be rewarded."

This was met with silence. A wry smile twisted my lips. "But not with money and lands," I added.

"Then how?"

"My sister's hand in marriage to his son, Tom. The boy loves Anne. She has nothing to bring him, but he'd take her anyway, and Surrey would see it as a great royal benefice."

My plot worked. Henry agreed to the Anne's betrothal to Surrey's son.

"I'll miss you when you do marry and leave court, dear Anne," I sighed as we sat together in my chamber, embroidering.

She covered my hand with her own. "I promise to come and visit often."

I threw a glance at my ladies in the antechamber, laughing and chattering with Patch in an abnormally unrestrained fashion. "There is much to celebrate now that Margaret Beaufort is gone to visit her estates in Woking," I smiled.

Anne grinned broadly.

I wove my needle through a complicated stitch, as my thoughts returned to Anne's future family. "Tom Howard's father seems devoted to Henry," I said.

"Nay, he cares little for him," she whispered under her breath. "But he is loyal to the death because he blames King Richard for his father's death, and for the years of imprisonment he himself endured at the Tower."

I jerked my head up. "How is that?" I exclaimed. Surrey's father, John Howard, Duke of Norfolk, had died at Richard's side at Bosworth, the only one of Richard's nobles who didn't turn traitor.

"Tom says King Richard delivered his people into Henry's hands when he led that suicide charge behind enemy lines. He cast away his life, his crown, and the lives of everyone who put their faith in him. For that, his father will never forgive King Richard. Tom said that when his father was freed from the Tower, he vowed to accept whoever sat the throne, even if it was a bramble bush."

A vision of Richard rose before me, cutting his way to Henry, killing Henry's bodyguards, raising his sword arm to slay the cowering Tudor. But for William Stanley's traitorous redcoats, Richard would have had him.

I blinked to banish the image. *It is as it is.*

But there was some truth in what Surrey said. At the end, Richard had been a man crazed by grief; he had not wished to live. He'd only wished—like King Arthur—to get at his Mordred, the one he held responsible for the destruction of all whom he had loved.

I was swept with sadness. I knew Thomas Howard, Earl of Surrey, to be a good man, and I regretted that he felt so bitterly about Richard.

Patch was watching us from across the room. His eyes had taken on that sad expression I often caught when his gaze rested on me. I reached out a hand to him and he left his group of ladies, crossed the antechamber, and came to me.

"Make me laugh, Patch," I said on a sigh.

CHAPTER 18

The Ostrich Feather, 1489

THE OLD YEAR OF 1488 GAVE WAY TO 1489. WINTER struck hard the year I turned twenty-three. And then came spring, and with it the knowledge that I was expecting a child in November. Margaret Beaufort curtailed my hours for receiving petitioners, but I did not mind, for I found myself more tired than ever, and I wondered at the cause of my listlessness in the brightness of May Day. Instead of lifting my spirits, the revels oppressed them further. Maybe it was due to my condition, or maybe to the fact that my time with Arthur was drawing to a close with the passing of his childhood. He would turn three years old in September.

"Arthur is ready to be created Prince of Wales and leave for his own household in Wales," Henry told me one day in August. "He is an exceedingly bright child, far older than his years, and shall progress well under the tutelage of my lady mother's appointees from Oxford and Cambridge universities, I warrant."

"May I not have a little more time with him, my lord?"

Henry regarded me with soft eyes. "Best to let go now, Elizabeth. It will only get harder to give him up the longer he is with you." He inclined his head, and departed my chamber.

The month of September arrived too soon. We celebrated Arthur's birthday that fall with a feast that featured a masterpiece of the confectioner's art after each course. There was a red knight with his sword fashioned from red sugar and licorice; a fierce golden dragon sculpted from marchpane; and the most exquisite wall of edible stained glass ornamented with Arthur's blazon of three ostrich feathers that was the insignia of the Prince of Wales. But my stomach churned with dread with each bright smile I threw Arthur. How would I manage without him to lighten my days?

Quitting my chamber, I took the tower stairs to where he played in the garden.

"See what I have—a bird!" Arthur exclaimed jubilantly. He jerked the string tied to the creature's feet, and pulled it along.

I knelt before him and forced a smile to my lips. "I do see that, my sweetheart. Come, let us sit here on the ground together." He took a cross-legged position, and I lowered myself onto the dry grass. Placing my arm around his tiny shoulders, I drew him close and kissed his curls. " 'Tis a pretty blue thrush you have there, dear heart."

"I caught him all by myself!" he exclaimed. "He was in the bushes—" He turned and pointed to a clump behind the bed of roses. "I saw him moving. I knelt down like this—" He crouched on all fours. "And Master Bowman gave him to me."

I gave the archer an unsmiling look. The man colored.

"He's a nice bird, Arthur, my love." I stroked the little thrush whose heart pounded fiercely. "Do you know why he is so frightened, my sweet?"

Arthur shook his head.

" 'Tis because he fears he will never be free again. Free to fly where he wills, free to feel the wind on his feathers. He fears captivity."

"Is captivity bad?"

"Let me see . . . Would you like to be told that you could never again see your friends? Or play ball? Or shoot your arrows? Or run wild across the grass with your arms out pretending to be a bird like him?"

He shook his head vehemently.

"Would you like me to place you in a dark room where you would never again feel the sun on your skin? A room so small where you could barely walk a few steps?"

"No!"

I stroked the little bird, gripped by an inexplicable sadness. "Now that he is captured, he fears all these things. Freedom is his breath of life, my sweet." A tear threatened. I rose to my feet before Arthur could notice. "You may keep him captive, if you so choose, for you are a prince, and yours is to command. But I hope that you will give thought to this little creature that God made to be free, and show him mercy."

With a nod to the archer, I left my son holding the bird tightly in his lap. When I reached the tower entry, I looked back. Arthur was untying the string. He held the thrush in his hands a long moment, and then tossed it high into the air. The little creature flapped its way skyward. And I smiled.

❁

ARTHUR LEFT FOR WALES AND I WENT TO WESTMIN-ster Palace for my confinement. At the threshold of the chamber Margaret Beaufort had prepared for my lying-in, my steps faltered. A dense gloom hung over the room. A fire burned in the hearth and candles flickered all around, but the windows had been shrouded by thick tapestries to blot out light, fresh air, and noise, according to Margaret Beaufort's ordinances, for she had decided these were detrimental to the health of a newborn. *It feels like a tomb,* I thought.

I inhaled a sharp breath and stepped inside. Here I would be confined for the next four weeks, like a queen bee breeding in her hive, sealed away by wax from all intruders. There was naught to do but pray, and read, and sew. And wait. *The last time I was buried like this,* I thought, *at least I had my mother.* Overcome with yearning for her, I sought comfort at my prie-dieu.

God must have heard my prayers, for within twenty-four hours of my confinement, Margaret Beaufort entered with an announcement.

"Your mother is being brought to court to receive her kinsman,

Francois de Luxembourg, who heads the French embassy from Charles VIII."

"My mother?" I breathed, my eyes widening. "Here?"

"Fret not. She will not stay long," Margaret Beaufort said spitefully.

I trembled with expectation as my ladies dressed me in one of my black gowns with wide, hanging sleeves, and covered my hair with a jeweled gable headdress and veil. My breath caught in my throat at the sight of my mother, whom I had not seen but once since the rebellion in 1487. She looked gaunt and frail, and now walked with the aid of a cane.

"Mother," I whispered hoarsely, embracing her.

"Daughter . . . queen," she murmured. "I greet thee well."

My heart pounded; I looked down in an effort to recover my composure. I barely noticed Francois of Luxembourg doffing his hat or heard what he said, for it was all trivial against the weight in my heart.

I'd hoped to have a few private words with my mother, but the Beaufort woman never left my side during the entire audience. Too soon, I had to bid Mother farewell. I embraced her for a long moment, and when I released her, I found tears glistening on her lashes. I watched her leave my presence, walking slowly with the aid of her plain wooden stick, and knew with a finality I could not bear that I had looked my last upon her. Now she would be returned to her abbey and locked away, and I would remain here, locked away.

Swept with sorrow and emptiness, I lay in bed that night, listening to the monks' chant and the church bells that tolled the hours. *If we could undo a single error of our past, what would it be?* I asked myself. The answer flew into my mind. *If Mother had not gone into sanctuary, if she had made her peace with Richard as Papa had wished, all would be different now.* Nor was I blameless. *If I had fled Sheriff Hutton, all would be different now.* But the past could not be changed, and a sea of tears would not wash out a word of what Fortune had written. Looking back did no good; we had to keep going forward.

A few days before the twenty-sixth of November, 1489, Arthur was brought from Ludlow to Sheen to be created a Knight of the

Bath, and also Prince of Wales. In their own barges, Henry and Arthur crossed the Thames to an elaborate reception in London.

"He waited on his father through all the public dinners and ceremonies, holding his towel, offering him dishes," Margaret Beaufort reported to me. "He did very well."

How weary my little one seemed as he stood beside his father in the doorway, stiffly formal in his heavy robes, an ostrich plume in his cap. He was too well raised to shift his feet or duck behind his father, and merely stood there, awaiting my invitation to enter. Unable to stem my euphoria at the sight of him, I sat up in bed and opened my mouth to speak welcome, but my joy was so great, I could not find voice, and so I put out my hands instead.

Arthur ran to me and jumped up on the bed, crying, "Mama, Mama!" I enfolded him in my arms, choking with sobs as I covered his sweet face with kisses. Aye, there was loss in the past; but there was such hope in the future!

"Mama, I am going to become a knight!" he exclaimed when we finally parted to look at one another.

"My sweet, I know you will make a fine knight. A knight with a heart that is pure and true—" A spasm in my belly made me cry out.

Arthur scrambled off me. "Mama, pray forgive me! I didn't mean to hurt you."

I forced a smile through the pain that seized me.

My labor began that night, and in the morning, I gave birth to a daughter. I gazed at the child through a blurred fog, dimly aware that Margaret Beaufort spoke. " 'Tis a girl. She shall be my namesake, and I will stand as her godmother."

I remembered the nasty fight she had put up over Arthur. Now my mother languished in an abbey and was not permitted even to attend her grandchild's christening.

I laid my head back on the pillow. Suddenly exhausted, I closed my lids and knew no more. When I opened them again, it was dark, and by the flare of candlelight, I saw Henry sitting at my bedside.

"Arthur—?" I asked anxiously, raising myself up on an elbow. He was only three years old! The long day would have taken a toll on him.

"He is doing splendidly," Henry replied. "The two ceremonies have been tiring, but he held up well. I invested him as Prince of Wales, and the feasting and celebration began. When I left, he was sitting at the center of the table, raised high on a chair that brought him to table height. I checked on him from behind the curtain, and he was presiding over the hall like a little king."

My King Arthur, I thought, smiling.

A noise drew my attention to the door. It was Margaret Beaufort. At her side walked the nurse with the new babe in her arms. "All is well," she said. "My godchild is now christened Margaret."

I shut my eyes.

CHURCH BELLS CHIMED FOR VESPERS. I STRUGGLED up in bed. I felt better, though still weak. "How long have I been asleep?" I asked.

"All night, and through most of the day, my lady," Lucy Neville replied.

"Can you send for Arthur? I wish to see my son."

Lucy retired with a curtsy. Servants came in and out, straightening the room, bringing a basin of water, a tray of sweetmeats. And then a babe's cry came from the alcove. My daughter!

"Tell Nurse to bring my babe to me," I said.

The woman entered with my child in her arms. I gazed at the small bundle, but I didn't have the strength to hold her yet. "Lay her in the cradle, and bring it close so I can see her," I said, surprised I felt no emotion.

At that moment, Arthur entered my chamber, and I felt as if a shutter had been thrown open to sunshine. My fatigue vanished. "Come, my little love—" I held out my arms. He ran to me. The sickness that always seemed to be with me relinquished its hold. I held him close for a long moment. "This is your sister," I said as I released him. "What do you think of her?" He hovered over the cradle. I laughed at his shrug. "Here, come and sit beside me. Tell me all that has happened."

He talked excitedly of events, but I barely heard his words, for I was drinking in the sweetness of his face, the light in his eyes, the joy of his voice. "—the tumblers, and then the troubadour—" he was saying. His days might be filled with serious matters of state, but our evenings would be like this: quiet, precious, kept in my chamber, at least until Twelfth Night, when he went back to Wales.

"Would you like Patch to do a jig for you?" I asked when he had finished telling me about the exciting things he had witnessed. "Or shall he read to you the adventures of the great King Arthur?"

"No, my fair lady mother. I would like to play with the wolf-hound, Percival."

Patch did some hand somersaults and then sat down cross-legged and made a farce of weeping in the corner of the room. Arthur went over to him and laid a gentle hand on his shoulder. "I am fond of you, Patch. But Percival can balance a stick on his nose."

Patch couldn't suppress his smile. He looked up at Arthur and dried his pretend tears. I laughed, and Arthur ran back to my arms. I smoothed my child's soft locks, filled with gratitude for Heaven's bounty. No one had to remind me how precious and rare these moments were; how much I had to be grateful for in this child I had borne. My greatest fear was that he should catch some illness.

"I hear there is an outbreak of measles in the city, my lord. I would like to leave London and complete my churching at Greenwich," I told Henry that evening.

"I am of the same mind. Several members of the court have come down with the disease. 'Tis not safe in the city."

We left for Greenwich by water. It was a quiet Yule. Due to the epidemic, we had no disguisings and few pageants, though an "Abbot of Misrule" made much sport. Too soon Christmastide was over.

Arthur left for Wales the morning after Twelfth Night. From my chamber high above the water's edge, I watched as my tiny son was lifted into the boat. As he turned, searching for me at my windows, my heart twisted in my breast. Could he possibly sense the longing I felt as I stood behind the glass pane? Did he feel the same? But he must not be allowed to become dependent; he was a child with the responsibilities of a man and had to learn to do his duty. I wiped the tears from my eyes. And I must learn to endure the farewells, and the absences. *God grant me strength*, I thought.

With Arthur's departure, I lived with loneliness. Solace came from my sisters' company in the evenings, my music, and the occasional letter from Bridget, who had taken well to her religious studies at Dartford Priory. That I was kept from court for all but important occasions did not disturb me one whit, and I scarcely missed it. Its glitter and beauty hid dangers for those who did not take care where they trod, and my absence meant I would not forge affections for those who were here one day and taken away the next for some careless remark. I had become accustomed to my captivity, and I valued the quiet that was my companion. Aye, I could not deny that I was lonely, but so were many others who had their freedom. And I had Patch, and my sisters, and my memories. It was a sin to complain.

In the meanwhile, Henry had grown morose and irritable, for the new year brought distressing news. A new pretender had emerged in Europe, claiming to be my brother Dickon, and Blind Fortune teetered on her globe once again. The news blazed and thundered through the land, breathing new life into the belief that King Richard had smuggled my brother abroad to safety with instructions that he return and claim his crown when he was grown. Terror gripped England, for men who received letters from Burgundy or Ireland were rounded up and taken to the Tower to be tortured for more information, as Johnnie of Gloucester had been before Stoke. I closed my eyes and willed the images gone. I could do nothing to help them, so I must banish their fate from my mind, or I would be crazed.

As I sat with my new babe in the solar, I sang a lament and watched Henry at the window, silent and morose, deep in his troubled thoughts. The young pretender had landed in Ireland in hopes of gaining support for his claim, but the Irish nobles heeded Henry's threats of reprisals and he found little succor there. He accepted Charles VIII's invitation to shelter in France. Charles had informed Scotland's King James IV that my aunt, Margaret of York, had secretly preserved Richard of York for many years. Petitioning the pope to accord him apostolic recognition, she said the prince had been snatched away from those who would kill him and brought up under her protection, but was moved across Europe to keep him safe. I dwelled on the words of Molinet, chronicler of the court of Burgundy, who wrote that my aunt Margaret had lost her brothers, her husband, her nephews, and most had died by the sword—but of her nephews one was alive.

It was said he was the exact age, and made in the image of my father, except for his height, for he was not exceptionally tall. I did not allow myself to ponder the truth of this, for whichever way I turned the matter, only pain greeted me. On the one hand, I wanted him to be Dickon, for that meant that Dickon lived; but if that were so, what would become of my Arthur? *To be a king you have to kill a king.* First uttered by my father about Henry VI, it was something that had tormented King Richard when he'd learned of the disappearance of my brother, Edward. He had never meant harm, yet harm had come because he took the throne.

I swallowed my anguish and turned my eyes on Henry, delighting in our children's laughter. For me, joy and sorrow had always walked hand in hand.

Isabella and Ferdinand of Spain, and even my Aunt Margaret's son-in-law, Maximilian, King of the Romans, who had recognized the pretender as England's true king, urged Henry to attack their common enemy, France, for harboring the pretender. But Henry had no wish to start a war that would weaken his hold on the crown. Instead, he hired more spies—spies to spy on spies—and sent them fanning out all over Europe to learn whatever they could about the pretender. On the home front, he set himself to getting me with child again, and as the new year of 1491 blew in on a hailstorm, I learned that I was *enceinte* once more. The babe was born on the twenty-eighth of June, and it was a boy. Margaret Beaufort named him Henry.

CHAPTER 19

Fortune's Wheel, 1492

THE MORE I LEARNED ABOUT THE PRETENDER, THE deeper his mystery grew. His very name suggested he was not who Henry claimed—the son of a boatman in Tournai, on the border of France. For Perkin Warbeck was the anglicized version of *Pierrequin Wesbecque,* and those who knew French and Flemish could readily catch the play on words: the Flemish *wezen,* "to be" or "to be real," and *weze,* the word for "orphan."

Aye, there was much to ponder in this pretender. Henry was tormented by the "feigned lad." His triumph in begetting two sons to inherit his throne did not ease his insecurity, and his determination to establish a dynasty grew more urgent than ever. Losing no time, he had me with child again within two months of my churching. My wifely duties were anathema to me, and each night I braced myself for what was to come. As Henry fumbled and panted, I lay beneath him, helpless, penitent, praying for strength to endure my destiny, and forgiveness for ranting inwardly against my fate—praying all the while that the pretender was Dickon; and praying that he was not.

Though childbirth was excruciatingly painful, I embraced the months of my pregnancy, for Henry let me alone during this time. Even so, God found reason to punish me, for in April of 1492, as I prepared for the delivery of my babe in July, I received word that my mother had been taken seriously ill.

"I would like to see her," I told Margaret Beaufort.

" 'Tis not advisable," she said, standing with arms folded across her chest.

"I beg you to let me see my mother before she dies!" I pleaded.

"Have you forgotten you are *enceinte*? The risk is too great. No one knows whether her illness is infectious. 'Tis best you stay away, for the sake of the child."

It was a legitimate reason, but the truth was that Henry and his mother trembled to consider that my brother Dickon lived, as rumor claimed he did. Somehow, they feared, my mother would manage to confide it to me, and I would find a way to send him aid. When news of my mother's illness was quickly followed by the somber tidings of her death on the eighth of June, the Friday before Whitsunday, it was brought me by Margaret Beaufort, who could scarcely suppress her elation.

"Did she die alone?" I asked, trembling to consider the thought. Everyone needed tenderness at the beginning of life, and at the end.

"She was attended by King Edward's illegitimate daughter, Grace, and by the Lady Cecily."

The two from whom Margaret Beaufort feared naught, I thought bitterly. Grace had no rank, and Cecily she could trust implicitly. In addition, both Grace and Cecily could not be ignorant that their every move was watched by spies reporting back to Henry and his mother. No doubt even they were never left alone with her.

"Your mother dictated this will on her deathbed," Margaret Beaufort said, handing me a parchment. I bent my head, and read:

In the name of God, I Elizabeth, by the grace of God Queen of England, being of sound mind and seeing the world so transitory, and no creature certain when they shall depart from here, bequeath my soul to Almighty God and beseech him to bless

our lady Queen with comfort. I bequeath my body to be buried in Windsor beside my lord, without pomp or costly ceremony. Since I have no worldly goods to leave my children,
I beseech Almighty God to bless Her Grace and all her noble
issue, and with all my heart I give her my blessing . . .

Memories flooded me. I forced my mind back to the testament
in my hands, and remembered my mother's final request. *I will that
such small stuff and goods that I have be used to pay my debts, and if there
is anything left that my children wish to keep, I ask that they be granted
these in preferment and permitted to have them after the payment of my
debts.*
    She had appointed her doctors as her executors, and asked me
to see her wishes carried out. She, whose sole aim in life had been
to gather riches and power, had died with nothing to leave anyone,
powerless, and nearly alone. *Fortune must have laughed as she spun her
wheel to lift my mother high, and spun again to plunge her down.*
    Clutching the will in my hand, I lowered myself into a chair,
and wept openly as Margaret Beaufort left the room.
    That night I lay awake, turning over many dark thoughts in my
mind.
    Did Mother give Cecily the password? I wondered.
    She would not have dared, for Tudor spies were everywhere.
Besides, Cecily had said naught about it.
    I found the timing of her death sinister. Margaret Beaufort
would not hesitate to use poison, and she had hated my mother.
How convenient that she died just as the pretender perched in Europe, awaiting his chance to invade. Now no one would ever know
if he was truly my brother Dickon.
    On Monday evening, Patch gave me the details of my moth-
er's internment; they'd been reported to him by someone who'd
learned of them in a tavern near Windsor Castle.
    "The witness was a merchant. He saw the entire affair with his
own eyes," Patch whispered. "On Whitsunday, the tenth of June,
the queen was conveyed in the darkness of night by riverboat to
Windsor without the ringing of any bells. Only the prior of the
charter house of Sheen was with her, and one of the executors

of her estate, Edmund Haute. From there, her body was drawn by cart, such as the common people are brought in, with a pall of black cloth of gold over it, and a few gilt candlesticks, each bearing a cheap taper. She was received into the castle by King Edward's bastard daughter, Mistress Grace, a few gentlewomen, a clerk, and a priest. She was buried privately at about eleven o'clock at night, without any solemn mass done for her obit. In the morning the Bishop of Rochester gave a service. Some royal servants of the household attended, but nothing else was done for her."

Rage filled me as I listened. Margaret Beaufort never left anything to chance, and this disgraceful treatment of my mother bore her hand.

"Patch, I need you to get word to King Henry that if he cares for my well-being, and that of his unborn child, he must come to me immediately on a matter of great urgency! He must tell no one, not Morton, and not his lady mother."

I paced in my chamber as I waited, wringing my hands. When next I looked up, Henry stood at the threshold of my chamber door.

"What is so important that I must be drawn out of a council meeting?" he snapped.

"Pray, shut the door," I called out to the man-at-arms. But before he could do so, Margaret Beaufort appeared in the doorway.

"What's this I hear?" she fumed. "You summoned the king? On what matter?"

"My lord, this is between you and me. Send your mother away, I pray you."

"What do you mean—send me away? How dare you?" Margaret Beaufort exclaimed, rustling forward.

I clutched Henry's sleeve. "If you wish to save me and your unborn child, send your mother away!"

Henry took a moment, then turned to her. "My dear lady, whatever it is, we shall not know until we are alone with our queen."

"Well, indeed, am I to be excluded now that I have plucked you a crown? After all my suffering and sacrifice, is this how I am to be treated?" She looked angrily from Henry to me.

"Madame, pray, I beg you, let me have a word with the queen in private."

Margaret Beaufort glared at him a long moment. Then she swished her train and swept from the room.

"Thank you, Henry," I said when she was gone.

"What is this about?"

I braced myself and lifted my chin. "I have been a dutiful wife to you, my lord. I have been fruitful. Rarely have I asked you for anything. I mend my own gowns and never complain or beg you for money, if I can avoid it. But my mother is dead, and her body has been borne to her resting place in the darkness of night, on a cart, like a common felon. I beg you to remember that whatever she was, whatever she did, however much your mother hated her, she is still *my* mother. Your lady mother believes you owe your throne to her and that you must abide by her wishes in all things, but it is you and I who shall be blamed for my mother's shameful treatment. I demand that you, as king, and as my lord husband, rectify this dishonor. If not, I fear God may see fit to punish us for it."

Henry stared at me in disbelief. This was the first time in my marriage that I'd spoken out forcefully.

"What do you wish me to do? She is already buried."

"I would like you to give her a funeral mass and allow my sisters and me to attend."

Henry mulled this for a moment in his cautious manner. Then he nodded his head. I sank into my chair and laid a hand to my brow with relief as he left me.

In the presence of Cecily, Kate, and Grace, a mass was conducted at Windsor on Wednesday for the repose of my mother's soul, and her body was laid to rest in St. George's Chapel, beside my father. In the end, I had not been allowed to attend. I was *enceinte*, after all, and the health of a royal heir was at stake. In this, Margaret Beaufort had her way.

On the second day of July, 1492, I was delivered of a girl that Henry named Elizabeth, after me. She was a small babe compared to Arthur, Margaret, and Henry, and her cry was more a whimper than a full-fledged wail. But she seemed healthy, and for that we offered many thanks to the Blessed Virgin.

In September, after my churching, Henry gave me permission to visit my mother's tomb. I knelt at the foot of her marble vault, bowed my head, and spoke to her silently in my heart. *You were a fatal queen, Mother, and many came to mourn your elevation—your father, brothers, sons, and your husband. Even I, Mother—I, who live, yet am not alive. If you could speak, what would you say now? Have you learned wisdom? Would you say that early death is happiness? That favored are they who are not left to learn that length of life is length of woe? Is that what you would say, Mother?*

I pressed the ground with a light touch. *Here lies a broken heart at rest,* I thought, wiping a tear from the corner of my eye. I rose to my feet and returned to Margaret Beaufort, who stood in the arched entrance, watching, waiting.

✦

THE OCTOBER MORNING WAS DISMAL, LADEN WITH memories of brighter times, and in my depressed spirits, I turned to music to bring back the past that lived in my heart.

"The Spanish ambassador requests an audience, Your Grace," Lucy Neville said softly, when I had ended my song.

"With me?" I set aside my lute in puzzlement. No one ever wished an audience with me, for they knew that I was helpless and real power lay with Henry's mother. And de Puebla was an important and busy man: the ambassador not only from Spain, but also from the pope, the Catholic kings, and the emperor of the Romans as well. Recovering my composure, I said, "Pray, have him enter."

I rose, moved to the fireplace, smoothed my black velvet skirt, and fluffed up the fur of my collar to hide a worn edge.

"Your Grace," Doctor de Puebla said, flourishing his plumed cap. "Forgive me, my queen, but I must say that to visit your chambers is to enter Heaven, for angelic beauty is everywhere to be seen"—he looked around at my antechamber, crowded with the thirty-two attendants Margaret Beaufort had set to watch me—

"and the most exquisite voice greets one's ear on his approach." His gaze rested on my lute, and then again on me. "Your beauty is such that a man may be forgiven if he forgets the urgent matter that brings him into such a royal and heavenly presence."

"Doctor de Puebla," I laughed, "is this how you won over my lord husband, King Henry, who is not given to easy friendship? He meets with you in his private quarters when no one else is present, and you assist in the deliberations of his council. I know of no other man in whom he places such trust."

"Now I am being flattered, Your Grace."

"What may I do for you, my dear Doctor de Puebla?"

"I have received a letter from my sovereigns, King Ferdinand and Queen Isabella of Spain. 'Tis addressed to you."

"To me?" No one ever wrote to me. They wrote to Henry, to Margaret Beaufort, to Morton, even to Reginald Bray, that ardent and ruthless Lancastrian. But never to me. I was the invisible queen and could do nothing for them.

" 'Tis expressly for you, on a matter of great importance to the Christian world, and I come to request a state audience to read you the missive they have sent you."

I was baffled and flattered at the same moment. Isabella and Ferdinand considered me so important that they addressed their letter to me! The reading of such a document from one monarch to another was a state occasion, and all the court would witness the honor they did me. I raised my eyes to de Puebla, and sudden realization dawned. *'Tis at his request that his sovereigns write me!* The dear man was attempting to rectify Margaret Beaufort's rude treatment of me by offering the court—and Henry—a discreet reminder that I was the true queen. He was doing what he could to elevate my standing with Henry and his nobles.

The warmth I always felt in his presence washed over me in a flood. We had a bond, he and I, for we were both outsiders: I, for my Plantagenet blood, and he, for his Jewish blood, if not his deformity. For I had long suspected that de Puebla was of Jewish extraction, perhaps even a *converso.*

My eyes grew moist. "My honorable Doctor," I replied, "I pray you to advise King Henry that I await with great pleasure the royal letter to me from your noble sovereigns, King Ferdinand. 'Tis my hope that we may receive it tomorrow evening in the State Chamber before dinner." Rumor had it that the ambassador was always pressed for funds, for his royal masters often forgot to pay his salary, obliging him to take a room at an inn of ill repute and his meals in a tavern, for that was all he could afford. "Pray, stay to dinner this evening, Doctor de Puebla?"

He gave me a low bow of acceptance. And I wondered why it was that in this world of ours, good men were made to suffer, while the wicked flourished. Then I chastised myself, for only God had the answer, and it was not for us to ask.

IN THE CROWDED STATE CHAMBER, SEATED ON OUR thrones and surrounded by our nobles and archbishops, as Henry's mother stood at my right-hand side, looking dour, I received Doctor de Puebla. The flare of torches reflected off the colorful glazed tiled floor as the good doctor unfurled the letter from his monarch. After addressing me as the most serene and potent princess, in formal language with many flourishes to denote respect and affection, de Puebla came to the thrust of the missive his king had sent.

"The very high and powerful prince, King Ferdinand of Spain, our lord and master, has made great progress in the war against the Moors and has conquered the town of Baca, in the kingdom of Granada. As his victory must interest all Christian monarchs, he considers it his duty to inform Her Majesty Queen Elizabeth of England."

There was a great murmuring, and then loud applause. De Puebla gave a deep bow of acknowledgment. After thanking him formally with the same elaborate language he had used for me, I lifted my eyes to his in a special thanks all my own, from one heart to another. The old ambassador, his empty sleeve tucked into his belt, gave me a smile of understanding.

"If I may be permitted your indulgence for one moment longer, Your Highnesses," de Puebla said in his most ambassadorial tone, "I have here someone who has come from the court of Spain amid much travail but with the blessing of his majesties, King Ferdinand and Queen Isabella, to seek your favor for a great enterprise, one that holds promise of fabulous riches in reward." He turned to Henry, and waited.

Henry gave a nod, and amid a blare of clarions the herald's voice called out "Bartholemew Columbus!" A stout, broad-shouldered man strode into the hall, clad in modest dress of brown wool, scantily furred, with a belt and dagger of simple silver and high leather boots, much worn with use.

"Your Majesties," he said, kneeling before us. "I am glad of heart to be here before you, for I have braved shipwreck, storms at sea, and a bout with pirates that made me doubt I would ever see the shores of England."

He presented his credentials to Henry and told of his brother, Christopher, on whose behalf he came to seek Henry's financial backing for a great voyage of discovery to what he called "the New World."

"Such a voyage is expensive," said Henry.

"To secure great riches, a king must sometimes incur expense," replied Columbus. "Were it not for Marco Polo, we would not have the Silk Road and the wealth it has poured into royal coffers, sire."

"Indeed, you make a good point," Henry replied. "I shall consider your brother's venture with my council." Clarions sounded again and a name was called that stirred vague memories.

"Father John Rouse, chantry priest of the Earls of Warwick!"

I glanced at Henry, and saw that his face had darkened. This was the priest whose praise of Richard during his lifetime as England's noble monarch had so angered him. The man must have good reason to show his face at Henry's court. Curiosity moved me forward on my throne.

"Sire . . . my queen," the monk said, bowing before us. "I come to present to you a new history I have written titled *The History of the Kings of England*. I have seen the errors of my ways and have corrected much of what I wrote during King Richard's reign. Those earlier volumes have been destroyed, and this new account replaces them with the truth."

"Indeed? What truth did you find that might gain my favor?"

"I have amended my description of Richard III to clarify him as a monster born. Sire, if I may read——"

Henry gave a nod.

Rouse flourished open a large manuscript: "King Richard III was born after two years in the womb with a set of gnashing teeth, hair down to his shoulders, a tail, talons, and a hump." He looked up at Henry nervously.

"You outdo yourself, Rouse, with the charms of your new book," Henry said, a sly grin on his face.

Rouse broke into a broad smile. As he bowed obsequiously, I was reminded of the little Italian whom Henry was planning to engage for a new "history" of England.

"You may place your new version in Archbishop Morton's hands. I am certain he will find a use for it in the new history of England's kings that we shall undertake shortly."

My heart sank in my breast. Richard had gone to his death believing he had nothing left to lose but the crown he had never wished to wear. Now he was losing his good name and the honor for which he'd sacrificed all his life. For Morton's account of Richard's reign was sure to be malicious and thick with lies.

At the feast later that evening, a troubadour related tales of love and sang a song he called "October"——

> *'Tis October, when falling leaves remind me of you . . .*
> *'Tis October, when I wait, cold and alone*
> *For love to find me.*
> *But love shall never come again,*
> *For you are gone forever*
> *And forever 'tis October for me.*

Overcome with emotion, I closed my eyes. When I opened them again, I saw de Puebla regarding me with an expression of infinite compassion. *Aye, my dear ambassador, you know too much of the griefs of this world——*

I gave him a smile, and then I shut my eyes again, plagued by a depth of weariness. It had been another long day.

✦

"YOUR AUNT HAS OFFICIALLY RECOGNIZED THE PRE-
tender as your brother," Henry grumbled to me in my chamber.

"For hatred of you, she recognized a scullery knave as my
cousin," I replied, referring to the impostor who had impersonated
Edward, Earl of Warwick, in Lincoln's rebellion. "Do not fault
me, my lord. There is naught I can do about it. She hates me and
returns my letters unread." *The letters your mother dictates to me,* I
added to myself.

"I don't wish to fight. 'Tis expensive, and avails us naught, for
there is little chance of victory."

*No, you would not wish to arm your subjects with weapons that might
be turned against you,* I thought.

"Perhaps you should do as my father did. Make a pretense of
war, invade France, get Charles of France to sue for peace and offer
you riches to return to England." I made my comment absently, half
in jest, more intent on my embroidery than on the words I spoke,
for I had almost completed the Order of the Garter sash that was to
be Henry's Yuletide gift. I examined the motto I had stitched: *Honi
Soit Qui Mal Y Pense.* Evil to him who thinks evil. The golden letters were clearly visible against the blue silk. I smoothed the fabric,
wondering if Henry wished to remind everyone that the evils of
the Tower awaited those who thought evil of him.

Henry rose from the window seat and gazed down at me with
eyes alight. I realized I had used the magical word *riches.*

"What a splendid idea! A pretense, aye. It need not cost much.
A few skirmishes, a siege or two. That might be all it takes. I could
even demand that Charles pay the cost of my invasion and eject
the boy pretender from his court." He pressed my shoulder with a
gentle touch.

Within two weeks Henry was ready to leave for Calais. He had
me garnish his helmet and place it on his head in full view of the
public, for such doings delighted the people. After a few skirmishes
and sieges of Boulogne, he sued for peace. Charles VIII, more anxious to invade Italy than fight the English, readily agreed to all
Henry's terms, including ousting the pretender from his court. The

treaty was signed on the third day of November, and the war was over before it was fought. The French and the Bretons paid his expenses of seven hundred twenty-five gold crowns in fifteen yearly installments, and renewed the annuity they had paid to my father. The armies were upset that they had no chance for plunder, but Henry had won a victory and much wealth.

"Like my father," I smiled when I greeted Henry on his return just before Yule of 1492. "You have saved lives and made money."

"Indeed, I have. And you have a good head on those elegant shoulders of yours, my dear Elizabeth," said Henry.

It was a grand compliment, one he'd never given me before, and his tone held a note of flirtation. Oh if I could claim just a piece of his heart, how much good I could do! My cousin Edward might be freed from the Tower. A tombstone might be secured for Richard's grave. So much could be done for my people! Hope flared in my breast.

CHAPTER 20

False for True, 1493

"ARTHUR! O MY ARTHUR," I CRIED, BARELY ABLE TO contain my joy. My son had come to pass Yule of 1492 with us at Sheen. He looked such a little man in his velvets and plumes. "See how you've grown! You're so tall now."

"I am six, Mama," he said proudly, drawing himself up to his full height.

Suffused with happiness, in the privacy of my chamber, I kissed his dear face and marveled at his beauty. I gave him my news about King Ferdinand's letter to me, and the Spanish ambassador's many kindnesses, his poverty, and how I wished I could help him, and I told him of the petitioners I had recently seen.

"There was one who sheltered the poor. His house burned down and he begged my help to build another. I found funds to give him, but that meant I had to turn away many others." I thought sadly about those who came begging for work, and the two gaunt nuns in dire poverty whose request for funds I'd had to deny. "I have so little money, and though I mend my own gowns and cut corners every way I can, there is never enough to do all that I wish."

Arthur's gaze went to the tin buckles on my shoes. "When I

am king," Arthur said, "you shall not want, Mama. You'll have silver buckles for your shoes and we'll help all who need our aid."

"My sweet son," I murmured, kissing his dark curls. "Now, tell me: have you studied hard?"

He nodded his head vigorously. "I have learned much, Mama— I finished Livy's *History of Rome*, and I know all about the siege of Troy and the feats of arms of Alexander. I have read Caesar's invasion of Gaul for tactics, strategy, order of battle—" He broke off, trying to remember. "The laying of sieges . . . the management of men. From the *secreta*, I have learned how to behave on the battlefield."

"What is the *secreta*?" I asked, wishing to hear him speak more. His sweet voice betrayed all the tenderness of his years.

"Alexander the Great's own rule book, Mama. It has taught me not to risk my own person and not to follow the enemy when it flees. I am to camp near water, and before giving battle I must check that Leo is in the ascendant, and Mercury in midheaven."

"Very wise indeed," I said in my most admiring tone.

❖

ON TWELFTH NIGHT, I FOUND MYSELF STANDING FOR- lornly at my window, watching my sweet boy depart for Wales. As always, it took me weeks to recover from the loss of his dear presence. In his stead, I was visited by my husband. Henry, in turmoil over the pretender, sought my company often in order to soothe his mind from the ill tidings that streamed to him.

"This is all your aunt's doing," Henry told me one cold evening as eighteen-month-old Harry played at my feet with his toy knights.

He took a seat by the fire. "Charles sent the pretender from France, as he promised to do by the terms of our treaty, but now the feigned boy has disappeared yet again. It shall take months to learn his whereabouts."

Harry, who had been watching us, frowned, almost as if he understood the reason for his father's dismay. Then, with a single forceful blow, he knocked down his little army of enemy knights and yelled, "Bad!" Looking up at us, he flashed us a triumphant grin. Henry and I shook with laughter.

✿

SPRING TWITTERED AND BLEATED WITH NEW LIFE
all around us, and bright fields replaced the muted shades of winter.
One day in April, Henry let out an oath as he read a missive.

"What is it?" I asked.

"Remember that fellow de Puebla introduced to us? His brother
returned to Spain from his voyage west, laden with treasure!"

"How is that possible? In October, he still didn't have
funding."

"When Bartholemew Columbus came to ask our aid, he didn't
know his brother Christopher had already sailed, with help from
Spain."

But news about explorers and the riches then had amassed paled
in comparison to tidings about the pretender. Although Henry and
I had grown close amid the insecurities that preyed on his mind, I
could not get him to consider easing the imprisonment of Edward
of Warwick. Even so, I was able to obtain a precious concession,
dear to my heart, on a matter I had never previously dared to raise:
a headstone for Richard's unmarked grave.

"He was a king, after all," I said. "As you are, Henry."

Summer announced itself with the advent of May. In fields
near Westminster and in the palace garden, young men put up
Maypoles, attaching the gilded wheel with its colored stream-
ers to a stout oak post. That afternoon, a picnic was held on the
banks of the river and people made merry, with revels in the
warm sun. But I was weary and strangely despondent. I went to
my room to rest, and there, in solitude, I watched my sister Kate
and the other maidens twine the ribbons as they danced below
my window.

How happy everyone is.

I remembered my first May Day after sanctuary, a dark time,
drenched in mourning, when love was an ember billowing into
flame, and my blood soared with unbidden memories—

As the dance ended, my gaze went to Kate's shining head. She
had approached a fair-haired, well-made young man clad in tawny
velvet cloth. I recognized William Courtenay, son of Edward Cour-

tenay, Earl of Devon. Even from my high chamber I could tell she blushed as she laughed at something he said and accepted a flower from him. *So that is how it is, sweet Kate; you've fallen in love.* In spite of my low spirits, I smiled.

That evening, when Henry appeared in my chamber, I took his arm and led him to my settle. We were alone except for a minstrel. Patch was in the antechamber entertaining my ladies-in-waiting, Kate had gone for a stroll in the garden with William Courtenay, and I'd sent the children to the nursery.

"I can tell," he said, his mouth twitching at the corner, "that you want something from me, my fair lady."

"I do, indeed, Henry. 'Tis something joyful, to banish care and this dismal talk of the pretender."

"I stand before you all ears, like a donkey, my lady."

"You sound like Patch," I said with a smile.

"As long as I don't look like him," Henry replied.

I laughed. "Indeed, you need have no fear of that."

When I informed Kate that Henry had granted her permission to wed Courtenay, she burst into a flood of tears and hugged me tightly.

"How did you know I love him?" she asked when she could speak again.

"Love is not hard to read, dear heart. But I hold you to one condition. That you not wed until you're at least eighteen."

Kate's face fell, as she burst into tears again.

"That's years from now!" she sobbed. "Who knows if I'm still alive?"

"My sister, time passes too swiftly. Why rush into marriage? Enjoy your maidenhood."

But her sobs grew louder. I could not bear to see her weep, and drew her close in an embrace.

"What if the pretender wins?" she asked. "Then all will change again. I am so afraid, dear Elizabeth!"

What if—

No, I could not bear for her to lose her heart's desire.

"The truth is it would break my heart to see you gone from court, Kate."

She looked up brightly. "Ah, but that is easily remedied! We shall stay here, with you."

Three months later, as Kate turned fourteen, church bells rang in celebration all over England. For there was a royal wedding at Greenwich that summer.

❁

FROM FRANCE, THE PRETENDER RETURNED TO MY aunt's court in Flanders. Aunt Margaret gave him a personal guard dressed in the blue and wine colors of the House of York, and from there, he watched and waited for his opportunity to invade England. Henry was distraught and grumbled ceaselessly; it was not long ago that he himself had done the same in Brittany, and now he sat the throne.

As I listened to Henry's anguished railing, I tried to soothe him the only way I knew—with sweet words and song. "Do not distress yourself, Henry. The land is weary of war and will not rise up for the pretender. All anyone wants is to be left alone to enjoy the precious calm you have restored to them. My lord, there is a merry ditty that may banish care for a while. Shall I sing for you?"

Drooping in his chair, Henry gave me a nod. A soft look came into his eyes as he watched me. It had been there often of late. Perhaps he held his crown so tightly to him not merely for its power and kingship, but for the comfort it had brought him—for a home, a wife, a family. I could never love him, but the antipathy I'd felt for him in the early years of our marriage had dissolved. I'd come to realize how much he had suffered, how alone he had felt all those years in exile, fleeing from one place to another, chased and hunted like a prized animal. He'd lived as a captive at the whim of various monarchs, including my father, and known naught but uncertainty for most of his life. Now, beneath his royal robes trembled a wretched and desperate man.

I often thought that if I could meet my Aunt Margaret, all the strife between England and Burgundy would be put to rest. Her hatred of Henry was manifest and she would support any effort to dethrone him, but she was childless and had loved her brothers dearly. Now all were dead, and the House of York had been dethroned by a usurper. For usurper Henry was, no matter how many poets praised his ancestry. The Italian he had brought to court to rewrite history would give him the most illustrious lineage of all the kings of Europe, and Morton's account would make a villain of Richard, but it could not change the truth. Aunt Margaret hated me for being so fruitful to the one she called "iniquitous tyrant and usurper" and blamed me for not fleeing Henry's clutches after Bosworth.

Oh, Aunt Margaret, can you not understand? I wanted to flee Sheriff Hutton! But marrying Henry was the only way to stop the bloodshed, to bring peace to my people after thirty years of strife. I did it for their sake, and for Richard's. He had commanded me to abide by God's judgment, and God had spoken at Bosworth. Aye, I was the king's daughter, and I held England for Henry because together we united the land; it was the way things had been ordained by Heaven. Richard had given Tudor his blessing by dashing unprepared into battle. He had accepted his fate. Now I must accept mine.

Why can you not understand, Aunt Margaret, and leave us in peace? As I brought my lament to an end, I saw that Henry's eyes were moist. I put my hand out to him, and he rose and came to me.

"We shall get through this, Henry," I said.

He bent down and kissed my hand tenderly.

❀

YULE CAME, BRINGING ARTHUR, AND TWELFTH Night arrived, taking him away again to Wales. The year of 1493 died, and the year of 1494 was born. News of the pretender's doings fueled Henry's days. By October 1494 the pretender, now calling himself the Duke of York, was parading his blue and wine halberdiers at my aunt's expense, handing out silver groats like a king, and answering Henry's charges by issuing proclamations of his own. He did not fear papal anathemas, he stated, for the pure right of his title meant he was protected from God's punishment. But low-born Henry Tudor, who illicitly occupied the throne of England, had offended God by his usurpation.

"My answer shall be to create our Harry the Duke of York. His badge will be of the red rose as well as the white, and his colors blue and tawny," said Henry as we sat in the solar with his mother. "The celebrations for his investiture shall last all month, to the end of November. I leave the planning to you, my lady mother."

"A month long? Then there is time to arrange for a tournament. Tournaments are not only colorful but also appropriate in this instance, since they are martial in quality—"

A knock at the door interrupted us. Henry grew irritable to hear it; all news was bad these days.

We were told that Sir Robert Clifford had returned from Burgundy, and had a report of the highest urgency.

What business does he have with Henry? I wondered. Clifford was a Lancastrian who had defected to the Yorkists the previous year and was cursed by Morton at St. Paul's with bell, book, and candle as traitor to the king. He strode up now, his face somber, and knelt before Henry. My husband's hand shook and his breathing had grown shallow, although he struck a casual pose as he lounged beside me on the settle. As my gaze moved from him to his mother, the reason for his discomfort grew clear. *Clifford is one of Henry's spies!* Morton's curse had added authenticity to his adopted identity. It was a detail so subtle and deceptive that it bore the mark of Margaret Beaufort's hand.

"What is your news, Clifford?" Henry demanded.

"The conspiracy is growing, Your Grace. King James of Scotland and Maximilian of Austria are offering men and arms to Warbeck to launch an invasion." He hesitated, then lowered his voice. "There are some among your royal circle who promise aid."

A collective indrawn breath resounded in the chamber.

"My lord, would it not be best to let the queen retire to her chamber?" Margaret Beaufort said to Henry.

"She is one of us now," he replied. "Do you think she would betray her own sons for an impostor?"

And what if he is not an impostor, what then? asked a small voice at the back of my mind. I drew a deep breath and forced the thought away. *'Tis not possible. It has been a long time. Dickon is dead.*

"They have said that if Perkin Warbeck can be shown to be Richard of York, they shall not raise a hand against him, sire."

The tapping of the rain against the windows seemed to fill the room.

"Can such a thing be proven?" Henry uttered, his lips pale.

" 'Tis said the pretender carries papers signed under the signet of Richard III. In addition, he has the same strange left eye that marked the countenance of several Plantagenet kings—and Richard of York. Without exception, the crowned heads of Europe have accepted him as Richard of England. Even Spain."

Silence thundered in the room. *Even Spain, our greatest ally.* I had half-risen from my chair in shock.

Henry turned to me. "Elizabeth, papers can be forged, you understand? And the eye means nothing. Your father sired many bastards." But there was a tremor in his voice.

I sank back down into my chair, unsure of what to believe. I knew Richard hadn't killed my brothers. I knew Edward had perished, probably at Buckingham's hands. But I didn't know what had become of Dickon after Bosworth. Had my aunt stationed a faithful retainer at Bruges to learn the outcome of Lovell's invasion? Had Lovell taken my brother away with him as soon as that hope disappeared?

Henry's voice broke into my thoughts. "These traitors in our midst, who are they?"

Clifford cleared his throat nervously before he replied. "Chief among these men is one impossible to believe. Your uncle, Sir William Stanley."

My eyes flew to Margaret Beaufort. Her face took on a glazed look. And Henry's own was awash with horror as he stared at his mother.

"My step-father-in-law's brother? My chamberlain?" he murmured through ashen lips.

Though he had become accustomed to bad news, he wasn't prepared for the astounding proportion of these ill tidings. As lord chamberlain, Stanley appointed Henry's most intimate servants: his surgeons, barbers, physicians, Knights and Squires of the Body—those who had the closest access to his person and could slay him with the sudden thrust of a dagger.

Henry rose from the settle, shaken, pale as a phantom. "But he saved my life at Bosworth Field and has been richly rewarded for it—he crowned me with his own hands—it cannot be! He has too much to lose to back a false claimant."

The words he uttered struck a chord of familiarity that mocked me eerily. For Richard had said the same of William's brother, Thomas Stanley. I put a hand to my head to still the clamoring past.

Aye, the accusation was impossible to understand, but one thing was certain. Henry stood in grave danger. His mother, highly placed and honored by Richard III, had led Henry to Richard's crown, and Stanley, highly placed and honored by Henry, could lead the pretender to Henry's scepter. Until now, the conspiracies had no focus; they were small and occurred spontaneously in different corners of England, fanned by discontent with Henry's harsh policies and taxation. For the most part they'd involved old Yorkists united by a longing for the past, disgruntled at Henry's treatment of me and wishing to see the White Rose bloom bright once again. But these were little fires, easily quelled by picking up a local knight. The pretender had to rely on letters, which could be intercepted, and he had no one to speak for him or help organize the plot against Henry, as Margaret Beaufort and the Stanleys had done against Richard. Now all this was changed. The pretender had snared a Stanley—powerful, well respected, and close to the throne.

"Take him to the Tower," Henry said through clenched teeth.

I realized I had followed Henry's own thoughts.

"My son, let us not be too hasty here," Margaret Beaufort interjected. "If only because it shall spoil Harry's ceremony, and we don't wish to give the feigned boy that satisfaction. Let us, instead, make a pretense of knowing nothing, and of celebrating merrily. We can hold Yule at the Tower. Then we'll have all the traitors under one roof. On Twelfth Night, they can be rounded up. We may catch every last one if we lull them into a false sense of security and strike when they least expect it."

Henry, who had gone against his cautious nature by issuing such a hasty command, gave in readily. "Aye, you are right, my lady mother," he said. "As always."

ON THE AFTERNOON OF THE TWENTY-EIGHTH DAY OF October, 1494, our little Harry rode to London from Eltham Palace. According to my mother-in-law's report, he was cheered mightily by the merchants, craftsmen, farmers, carters, students, and apprentices who lined the roads as he trotted briskly past, making his way to Westminster. We met him at the gates. He looked like a tiny cherub with his rosy cheeks, sitting on his richly caparisoned courser, his little figure dwarfed by his escort of noblemen, a massive gold chain around his shoulders and his velvet cap pulled low over his red-gold locks.

Like Arthur, Harry was first invested as a Knight of the Bath. Then he was created Duke of York. A tournament followed the ducal ceremony, and the contending knights wore on their helmets emblems of my livery, the wine and blue colors of York. The November day was unseasonably warm as I sat with Henry on our thrones, surrounded by our children beneath our canopy of estate. Arthur was now eight; Margaret, five; Henry, three; and Elizabeth, two. My eyes dwelled softly on my eldest. He held himself like the king he would be one day. I drew my gaze from him and turned to the others. They were all handsome, bright, attentive children, excited by the noise and confusion, and they reminded me of a faraway time when I'd been their age and sat watching my uncle Anthony Woodville joust. The world had been good then, and my family whole. They had all been present: my golden father, my brothers, my sisters, Edward, Dickon, Mary—

Everyone had admired us. My father, young and strong, seated on the stage, threw us happy looks as he watched the tournament with no suspicion of what lay in store for us, or his dynasty. Did the same danger lurk behind this pageantry and display of arms? As these heralds blew their clarions, were death and tragedy awaiting their turn to make entry upon the stage? I looked around at the cheering crowds. Amid the rejoicing ran undercurrents of unease. Fear had resurfaced that the Wars of the Roses were not yet ended and bloodshed would be renewed. For Henry there was the pretender, just as for Richard there had been Henry.

And for me?

I almost dared not give thought to my unease lest it take on a life of its own. A Tudor heir in England under a Yorkist king would be in danger. The only solution for the one who wore the crown was the arrest and execution of his rival.

It was then that the sound of sobbing came to me. Margaret Beaufort was putting on her display. *Can she not keep her anxiety to herself as I do?* She poisoned every happy occasion with her tiresome tears.

My tortured mind returned to the pretender. From the court of Burgundy, where he remained under my aunt's protection, he'd issued another proclamation. Once he was restored to his rightful crown, he promised to "reestablish the laws of our noble progenitors, the Plantagenet Kings of England," and banish the Byzantine laws instituted by the usurper and tyrant, Henry Tudor. Now the pretender prepared for invasion. Was this young man who had shed the title of the Duke of York and assumed that of King Richard IV of England, truly my brother Dickon?

If he was, and he won England, what would become of Arthur?

I gripped the side arms of my chair, and closed my eyes.

✧

THOUGH WE MADE A PRETENSE OF MERRIMENT, WE celebrated the Yule of 1494 under a cloud of gloom at the Tower of London. I trembled to cross the moat and pass through its gates, for I knew the reason Henry had chosen the place. Yet the choice didn't seem ominous to anyone else. The children loved the Tower's menagerie of wild animals, and the old fortress had been a favored royal residence since ancient times. Now, however, its prison cells and instruments of torture would serve the king's purpose.

Various nobles and officials who had plotted against Henry were summoned to the Christmas festivities and to my sister Anne's wedding two days after Candlemas, on the fourth of February. Despite my heaviness of spirit, the sight of my sister Bridget cheered me enormously. She was fourteen now, and had decided to take vows. I had mixed feelings. A cloistered life meant she would never know great joy, but neither would she taste the bitter cup of loss and sorrow.

The arrival of Thomas Howard, Earl of Surrey, also helped lift my spirits, and I took his arm in personal welcome. No matter what he thought of Richard now, we had both shared devotion to him and remembered the old days of chivalry. That we were loyal to Henry, each in our way, did not lessen our unspoken bond.

Margaret Beaufort arrived with her husband, Thomas Stanley, and never left his brother William's side all during Yuletide, just as she had never left mine in the early years. During the feastings and banquets of Yule, my gaze went often to the Stanley brothers. *Do they suspect what is about to unfold?* I wondered.

As soon as Twelfth Night was over, Henry ordered the arrest of William Stanley and other nobles with whom he'd celebrated Yule. One of those entrusted with the duty was Anne's prospective father-in-law, the Earl of Surrey. I scrutinized Surrey's face as he marched the shocked lords across the cobbled court into the frightening prison of Beauchamp Tower, but if he felt any Yorkist sympathy or dismay at what he had been charged to do, he knew better than to let it show.

On Candlemas, the second day of February, as frost covered the windows of the Tower, we celebrated the Virgin's purification. But everyone present was aware that one familiar face was missing from the intimate circle. William Stanley lay under sentence of execution in the Beauchamp Tower, in a room not far from young Edward, Earl of Warwick. Henry made a display of enjoying the entertainment. He also made an extraordinary payment of thirty pounds to a young damoiselle who had delighted him by dancing in the Saracen fashion, with bared midriff and gauzy veils. Henry had an eye for pretty women. I know I should not care, but I did. It made me feel as if I wasn't there, and I resented his disrespect, and hated being reminded how little I mattered.

After the feasting, Henry and I retired to my privy chamber for a brief rest before joining our guests for dicing and games of cards in the solar. My ladies-in-waiting leapt to their feet at our approach and dipped into their curtsies. My sister Kate and Lucy Neville were already waiting for us, and they moved to follow, but I gave them a shake of the head. We retreated into the quiet of my private bedchamber, for Henry was troubled and needed a few moments to recover his composure. At the banquet a wise woman had been brought forward to tell fortunes, and she'd warned Henry that his life would remain in great jeopardy throughout the year of 1495.

I was surprised how much the prophecy unsettled me. This man I had wed was not my choice, and many times during my marriage I'd had cause to grieve my fate. But in the shadow of threat from the pretender, I realized that I'd come to care for Henry. He was ruthless as a king, avaricious as a man, yet his suffering had drawn my sympathy and touched my heart. He was a dutiful son to his mother, a caring father to his children, and in recent years he had shown me kindness. And we both wanted the same thing for England. *Peace.* And Perkin Warbeck would bring war.

The night was chill, and tapestries fluttered in the wind that seeped through the stone cracks around the windows, but a welcome fire burned in the hearth. Henry went to warm his hands at the fireplace while I removed my cloak and hung it up on a peg. Before we could say a word to one another about the prophecy, a knock came at the door. I exchanged an anxious look with Henry before calling for our visitor to enter.

"A missive for you, sire," a messenger declared, as he fell to a knee. "From Ireland."

Henry almost snatched the letter from the man's hands, but he waited until the door was shut before he broke open the seal. The blood drained from his face as he read.

"The pretender?" I asked when he finally looked up.

He nodded curtly. "Funded by *your* aunt—" Again came that accusing tone I heard whenever he spoke of my Aunt Margaret. "He attempted to land in England, but his forces were small and he was obliged to retreat almost immediately."

"Why does that displease you?"

He threw himself into a chair. " 'Tis not all. He went to Ireland, received support from the Earl of Desmond, and laid siege to Waterford. Meeting resistance, he fled." After a pause, he added bitterly, "Now he's disappeared again. No doubt he's on his way to Scotland. James IV would spring at a chance to harass me."

"What do your spies say?"

"They know nothing. Last week, in desperation, I paid the exorbitant sum of five pounds for a letter about a mere rumor—" He raised a hand to his brow.

I remembered what Henry had put out about Richard murdering my brothers, and now here he was, sleepless with fear that my brother Dickon still lived. One of my brothers had eluded Margaret Beaufort's grasp. Had she and Morton succeeded in murdering both, Henry would not be so anxious at the whisper of a pretender, so tormented by doubts.

A shudder ran through me. *The pretender could be Dickon.*

"You are cold, my dear," Henry said. He rose, removed my furred mantle from its peg in the corner of the room, and set it on my shoulders. " 'Tis a chilly night."

I took his arm, and we made our way to the solar.

MY CHILDREN'S VOICES FLOATED TO ME FROM A SMALL alcove off the royal library as I passed along the hall. I drew near to listen. Arthur had stayed longer this year in order to attend his aunt's wedding, which had brought me great comfort. He sat at a table with a book open before him, while Maggie lounged on a window seat and Harry sat on the floor, cross-legged, strumming the lute his father had given him for Yule. In a corner out of my line of sight, Lizbeth was cooing to her puppy.

"Treason is when you try to kill the king," Arthur was saying.

"Why did Uncle William try to kill father?" asked Harry.

"He had his own ideas about who should rule," Arthur replied, throwing an uncomfortable glance at the varlet sweeping ash from the fireplace.

"What's going to happen to him?" Harry asked.

"He'll be executed," Maggie said from the window seat. "Isn't that right, Arthur?"

"We don't know yet. It depends on what Father decides."

"Why wouldn't Father want to kill him, when he wanted to kill Father?" demanded Harry.

" 'Tis not always so simple, Harry," Arthur said. "A king must consider mercy whenever he can, especially with family."

A screech of delight erupted from Lizbeth as she chased her

puppy across the room. "Mama!" Lizbeth cried, catching sight of me. She ran to me, grabbed me tightly around the skirts. "I love, love you, love you! I love Father, too."

Her wide blue eyes, blue as periwinkles, gazed up at me. I knelt down and hugged my sweet two-year-old daughter to my heart.

We learned Henry's decision soon enough. *Execution*.

✦

LORD THOMAS STANLEY'S PLEAS FOR HIS BROTHER'S life fell on deaf ears. Henry was not Richard, and he was too well aware of the Stanley policy of survival through the Wars of the Roses: *divide and conquer*. Place one brother on one side, the other on the opposite side, and the winner would extract the loser from his troubles. It was a strategy that had paid handsome dividends. The Stanleys not only had survived nearly forty years of bloodshed, but had thrived and grown rich where better men had perished.

Yet Sir William Stanley evoked my sympathy. *Turncoat and traitor* might aptly describe his brother, Thomas, but not him. He had remained true to his Yorkist roots through good times and ill, ever since the first troubles with Lancaster. He withdrew his support of Richard when my brothers disappeared, for he came to believe that Richard had murdered them. Only then did he transfer his loyalties—but not to Lancaster and Henry. *To me.* With my brothers supposedly murdered, he saw me as the true claimant of the House of York.

One evening after Kate's wedding, as Henry sat by the fire in my bedchamber with his head in his hands, I touched him lightly on the sleeve. "Is there anything I can do for you, Henry?"

He looked up with anguished eyes. "I honored him, and he betrayed me. Now I understand how Richard felt."

I was taken aback. This was the first time Henry had called Richard by his name instead of an epithet. "Pardon William, Henry," I pleaded. " 'Tis sin to take a life, and how will it go for your lady mother if you execute him?"

"I am inclined to follow your counsel, my dear, were it not for one thing." He gave me a wry smile. "My lady mother urges me to execute William."

I stared at him. William was family to her; many dinners had they taken together, many a cup of wine had they shared! But why should I be surprised at such callousness in Margaret Beaufort? Had she not given me cause to know her well?

"She tells me mercy is a weakness a king cannot afford, and I must execute Stanley. If I do not, I place myself in danger, like Richard whose pardons encouraged treason and toppled him from the throne." Softly, he added, "After all, had he executed my mother after her first treason, I wouldn't be here, would I?"

I lowered my lashes. "Henry, you owe William for Bosworth. Grant him pardon. A life for a life."

Henry inhaled a long, audible breath and let it out slowly. He rose, went to the fireplace, and stood with a hand on the mantel, staring at the flames. "In executing William I chop off the head of the beast. The pretender has no one to speak for him now, and his venture is doomed."

"All the more reason to grant William his life. He can't harm you in prison."

"Ah, you have a short memory, my dear. The Earl of Oxford was imprisoned for ten years in the Fortress of Hammes before he escaped to win me the battle of Bosworth. 'Tis but another example of Richard's reluctance to take a life that in the end cost him his own."

"I—"

Henry held up his hand. "No one will dare partake of rebellion when the king executes a member of his royal family. Morton put it most aptly—in terror lies my security. Besides, William Stanley is a rich man, and there is his fortune to consider."

I looked away so Henry would not see my aversion to this last thought. An image of my darling Arthur rose before me; he, who held such great promise of goodness, generosity, chivalry, kindness. I could not save England from my husband, but I would save it with my son.

On the sixteenth day of February, 1495, at six in the morning, Sir William Stanley was publicly beheaded on Tower Hill to the shock and amazement of the crowds, who felt certain there would be a last-minute reprieve. Harry had begged to be allowed to watch, and he did so with excitement. I had argued against it, for Harry seemed to revel too much in the heads of traitors dripping fresh blood, and always pointed out with glee the ones he had known. But Henry said it would make him a man.

As I passed the nursery later that day, I heard Harry's nurse, Anne Oxenbridge, whispering to a companion, "Why in Heaven's name would Stanley risk all to encourage an impostor? It makes no sense!"

I drew to a halt and tried to crush the thought that came to me. *Unless he is not an impostor.* My mother's espousal of the rebellion had cost her everything she had valued on earth. Now William Stanley had given all he owned to my brother's cause. They had both been convinced that he lived. I felt faint and giddy, but forced myself to inhale deeply. Summoning all my courage, I steeled myself against the doubts and resumed my steps forward.

CHAPTER 21

A Divine Prince, 1495

"WHICH GOWN WILL YOU WEAR TODAY?" LUCY NEVILLE asked.

"My black velvet," I sighed. Almost without exception since my marriage, it was one of the black ones; I had no heart for anything else. Henry had gone on a relentless killing spree. He executed my father's bow-maker, a clerk of my father's jewel house, a nephew of one of my long-serving childhood nurses, and Richard Harliston, an old servant of my father's for spreading word that Richard of York was alive. The poor old man had been hung and disemboweled at Tyburn. In Suffolk and in the Cumbrian Fells, several Knights of the Body to my father were also rounded up and executed, men I knew well.

Some of the conspirators had sent money to Flanders. They had secret signs and code words to recognize one another: bent ducats, silver lances, pairs of gloves. Several of the attainders issued were for receiving letters from the pretender, and some for writing back. A vision of Johnnie of Gloucester rose up before my eyes, struggling in the grip of Henry's men, his young face contorted in terror as they took him to the Tower, never to be seen again. What had he done indeed? Naught, yet enough. A letter from Ireland had been delivered to his door.

Others consigned to hang came from my grandmother Cecily's household. One of them had connections to the royal nursery maids—women who, as my Aunt Margaret had told the pope, would know Richard, Duke of York, without a second thought. My grandmother had turned eighty in May, and many who served her were as old as she.

I yearned to hear from my grandmother's own lips how she had borne the travails of her life, for prayer did not always dispel my heavy spirits these days. Her ancient years proved only one thing to me: *length of life is length of woe.* After burying eleven of the thirteen children born to her, including all of her sons and the husband she had adored, she had embraced the Benedictine order and remained in seclusion at her castle of Berkhamsted. I wished to visit her, but knew it was as useless to go to Berkhamsted as it had been to Bermondsey. We would not be able to talk in private, nor would she wish to see me, after what Henry had done.

In these days, I often wondered, too, about the Countess of Warwick. Old, poor, and alone, deprived of all whom she had ever loved, she had resorted to the laws courts to get back Middleham, that stone repository of her happy memories. When she won, Henry made her sign the property over to him. That was the last I knew of her. I drew a long sigh. Henry always left a trail of tears in his wake for those whose lives touched his.

To secure his mind, Henry relied on spies and torture and sought comfort in Morton's assurances that the people had a short memory, and those that dared snort at his ancestry would be silenced forever in the dreaded Tower. Morton was cardinal now, and a man reviled in England for his evil deeds. Each time I saw him together with Henry, I had the strange sensation I was gazing on the devil and the soul he was luring into his lair.

I understood that behind Henry's ruthlessness stood a terror of losing what Fortune had dropped there, and behind his avarice a fear of being in want. But I hated his ruthlessness, and despised his avarice.

Queen Anne's words came back to me across the years. *You have to decide what you will stand for, fight for, die for . . .*

And Henry had decided.

"You are ready, my queen," Lucy said, stepping back. She had pinned my sapphire brooch to my bodice and had arranged my hair with a gold headband and a veil.

With a nod, I led the way to the hall where my petitioners awaited me.

❀

AS THE CONSPIRACIES GREW, HENRY WATCHED THEM, cautiously and keenly. He had perfected the network of spies that had helped him win the throne, and these infiltrated every corner of England. They were monks, friars, trumpeters, pursuivants, even noblemen. Irish, Scots, English, even French, they swarmed over England and over foreign soil, invisible and nameless.

But each time the pretender's name came up, Henry could not restrain an emotional outburst. Ten years after Bosworth, he still could not be sure he would not end as Richard had, his corpse treated foully, thrown on the back of a horse, dumped into a horse trough and buried in a nameless grave. Henry had said he would sacrifice all to keep the crown, and he had. He had sacrificed his soul.

"Majesty," de Puebla said one day, bowing low, "my sovereigns instruct me to tell you that bearing in mind what happens every day to kings of England, 'tis surprising they should even consider giving you their daughter."

"Our throne is secure," cried Henry. He pressed both hands to his heart as Lancelot was said to have done. "By the faith of our heart, the pretender is no prince, but merely a boy from Tournai. My spies have confirmed it."

But I knew this was bluster. I exhaled an audible sigh as I made my way along the passageway to the royal chapel, aware of the emptiness at my elbow, the space normally occupied by my jailer, Margaret Beaufort. She had instructed her servants to pack her household, for she needed to return to her husband, Thomas, at

Latham Hall before Lent. Torn by emotion, she had buried herself in prayer since the revelation of William's treason.

I turned into the chapel, walked quietly up toward the altar, and knelt beside her. When she threw me a look of surprise, I gave her a kindly smile. I should have been celebrating her departure, but I could never withhold compassion from those who suffered. She gazed at me a long moment; then she nodded, her eyes misting.

I know she thought I sought God's blessing on those I'd loved and lost. She didn't realize that it was for her son's immortal soul I came to pray.

✿

FROM MY WINDOW HIGH AT GREENWICH, I WATCHED my son, four-year-old Henry, romp in the sunshine with his nurse. Heavyset, with reddish-gold hair and a happy demeanor, my "divine prince" as he was often called, bore little resemblance to the father for whom he was named. Yet he troubled me. Often, when he turned his gaze on Arthur, I caught an unpleasant expression in his eyes that reminded me of my Uncle Clarence.

"Everyone says Harry resembles our father. Is that true?" Kate asked, moving to my side at the window. I drew my skirts back to make room for her, and regarded her tenderly. She'd been but a babe when Papa had died, and never tired of hearing about him. I said softly, "Time will tell."

Kate turned to watch him as he ran after a ball across the green, and I moved to my embroidery frame. I had not made many stitches before she gave a cry and leapt from the window seat.

"You'd better come and see this!" she exclaimed.

I rushed to her side. Harry stood before a gardener, laughing uproariously. The man's clothes and shovel lay at his feet, for he had taken off his shoes and stripped down to his undershirt. Harry said something to him then and he, with evident reluctance, removed his undershirt so that he stood naked to the waist.

"God's teeth!" I cried.

Running out of the chamber, I fled down the tower stairs and raced across the green, past the flower beds to where Harry stood with the gardener and his nurse. The fellow was as red as the root of a beet.

"My l-lord," he was stammering, "I beg you—"

"What is happening here?" I demanded breathlessly.

The man dropped to a knee. "Your Grace, Prince Harry requires that I—I—"

"Take off his hose!" laughed Henry.

It was my turn to blush. I swung on Harry's nurse for an explanation.

"Your Grace, I tried to stop Lord Harry from issuing such commands, but he would have his way!"

I looked at my child. "This shameful behavior must end, Harry. This time you shall indeed be punished. Bring him to my chamber and send for the whipping boy. Dress yourself, Master Gardener."

The whipping boy arrived in my chambers a few minutes later. He was a fair-haired, frightened child of four chosen for his resemblance to Harry. I gave a nod and he was made to bend over. The man-at-arms laid bare his rear and took up a thick bundle of rushes tied at one end. He struck the child's tender white buttocks. The boy screamed; I winced. Once, twice, three times—

The little fellow wept and pleaded for the punishment to stop, and Harry watched intently. I found the boy's tears hard to bear, but steeled myself to sit through the punishment. When it was finally over and he was back on his feet again, I turned to Harry for his reaction.

"What have you to say?" I demanded.

"More!" Harry cried, pointing to the boy and laughing. "More, more!"

I rose to my feet in shock and dismay, unable to comprehend his lack of empathy. "Leave him with me," I told his nurse. "And give the whipping boy marchpane."

I knelt down, took Harry by the shoulders. "This is not entertainment, Harry. You are a prince, but the behavior you have exhibited is not noble. 'Tis important that a prince show concern and respect for others. Do you understand?"

"I want to play!" Harry cried. "I want marchpane, too!"

"You may not play for the rest of the day, and you shall not have marchpane. You shall sit here with me and read with Master Giles." At a nod from me, the man-at-arms went to fetch his tutor.

"No, no!" Harry screamed, hurling himself at me and punching my legs with his small fists.

"Stop it, Harry!" I cried, struggling to grab his arms. Harry squirmed, screaming, and kicked at me with his boots. I loosened my grip as pain flashed in my knee. He wrenched free and threw himself on the floor, flailing and hurling his legs in the air, his face livid with anger, crying and screaming, "I want to shoot arrows! I want marchpane."

I watched him with dismay. How different was this child from my beloved Arthur. I saw him in my mind's eye, standing in the gloom of my doorway at three years of age when I was awaiting the birth of Margaret. He'd worn a plume in his little hat that day, a pure little prince from head to shiny toe. I had to admit to myself that I did not love Harry as I did Arthur. Everyone took him to be made in the image of my father, but my father must have been an affectionate, good-natured child. Harry, though beautiful, with a winning smile, was willful and had a fearful temper.

"I hate you!" he screamed at me, a look of pure venom on his little face.

Not long afterward, I caught him kicking his pup down the steps of the keep at Sheen. "Harry!" I cried, picking up the yelping dog that was trying to limp away from him as fast as it could. "Why did you strike this little pup?"

"I commanded him to sit, and he wouldn't," he said with a sulky expression.

I gave the pup over to a maid, who cuddled him against her bosom and carried him away. I took Harry's hand in mine and led him to a bench in the garden where Lizbeth examined wildflowers in the grass while her nurse stood watch behind her.

"The pup is too young to know what you are saying, dear son. He must be taught gently," I told Harry.

"He'd best make haste and learn if he knows what's good for him," Harry replied.

Lizbeth smiled at me from the lawn. Then she toddled over, her fists tightly pressed over something hidden. She collapsed against my skirts, laughing, and opened her hands to drop her cargo on my lap. It was a posy of purple flowers. "Mama!" she said, her sweet little face shining with pride.

"For me? Thank you, my darling child." Suffused with love, I gave her a tight embrace. But in my chamber that night, it was Harry who filled my thoughts.

"What troubles you, my dear?" Henry inquired.

I heaved a sigh. "Harry."

"What has he done now?"

"He injured old Lady Fogge."

"How did he manage that?"

"He shot an arrow straight into her backside."

Henry laughed. Then he recovered his gravity. "Is she all right?"

"God be thanked, she shall be well in a week or two. She is recovering in the east wing. I have placed Dr. Nicholas at her disposal."

"How did you punish him?"

I rose and moved to the window. "I didn't, Henry. I have tried to talk to him, appeal to his conscience. But I cannot reach him. I don't know what to do. He is no Arthur."

"Does he not heed when the whipping boy is chastised in his place?"

"He laughs, Henry. 'Tis more than I can bear. He seems not to have a care in the world for anyone but himself. I can't make him heed."

"By God, he shall heed me!" said Henry, rising angrily. "Bring Prince Harry in," he told the man-at-arms on duty at the door.

"What are you going to do?" I asked, suddenly anxious.

"You shall see."

Harry was delivered to our privy suite and everyone else commanded to leave. Henry waited until the door had shut behind them before he turned to his son.

"I am told you injured the aged Lady Fogge and that you will not apologize for your behavior. Am I correct?"

Harry nodded vehemently. "She's naught but an old woman. I am prince, and need give her no apology."

"What if I demand you apologize?"

"No!"

Henry sat down and took Harry by the shoulders. "Will you reconsider?"

Harry shook his head defiantly. "I will not. I am prince!"

"You may be prince, but I am king, and those that defy the king merit punishment of the harshest measure. Therefore, because you insist in engaging in outrageous behavior and you do not heed your tutors, your nurse, your mother, or your king, there is naught else to be done but to chastise you in a way that you will understand."

He pulled Harry across his lap and drew down his hose. Holding him firmly as he protested and squirmed, Henry lifted his hand and struck him a hard blow on his buttocks. I gasped; Harry screamed. Slowly, a red welt took shape on his tender white skin. Henry lifted his hand again, and again.

"Henry, stop! I pray you, stop!" I cried.

But Henry was relentless. Not until Harry wept and begged for mercy did he halt the punishment. "Will you apologize to the lady you wronged?"

Harry nodded through his tears.

"Then you shall have mercy." Henry drew up Harry's hose and set him down on the floor. He rose and straightened his own gown. "But remember this. Each time you do not heed your mother, you shall be taught by me more strenuously than before."

With a nod to me, he left the chamber.

Harry glared at his father's back. "I hate you!" he sneered when Henry was out of earshot.

"Harry!" I exclaimed. He threw me an accusing look. Then, abruptly, his foul expression melted into a smile of the sweetest tenderness. He came to me and placed his little arms around my neck. "I love you, Mother."

"And I, you, my dear child," I soothed. But I could not entirely banish my misgivings.

AS OFTEN HAPPENED IN THESE DAYS, GOOD TIDINGS arrived hand in hand with sorrowful ones. That summer Kate gave birth to a son she named Henry. He was a sweet child who barely ever cried. But within days of his birth we learned that my grandmother Cecily had died. Again I donned black; again, I sought my prie-dieu.

Another explorer came seeking Henry's aid who claimed he knew a better route to the riches of the Orient, and Henry leapt at the chance to fund him. Heading west like Columbus, John Cabot left with a small ship from Bristol, and Henry went back to tracking his demon, the elusive pretender.

Ever watchful, ever cautious, he sent trusted servants to spy on his spies and check the truth of the rumor that claimed the pretender was in Scotland. The strain was telling on him, for he was often morose and preoccupied, and he shed so much weight that he grew gaunt. To drown his fears, he thrust himself into activity. Each morning, he indulged in a game of the tennis he loved before closeting himself with his councilors, and regularly each week he rode out from the castle with a falcon on his wrist and his yeomen of the guards around him to hunt deer in the royal forest. Every evening before supper, he went over his books meticulously, making notations in the margins of questionable charges and taking pleasure in his growing hoard of treasure. After dinner he gambled at dice with his nobles, or sat in my chamber listening to the songs I sang for him.

But his riches were never enough for him. He raised taxes continually and curtailed expenses with a ferocity he had not shown before. Beset with night sweats, he came to my bed more frequently in order to avoid having his discomfort witnessed by the attendants of his bedchamber, but he slept fitfully, and often he cried out and bolted up in bed.

"Is it the dream again, my lord?" I asked one warm August night, placing my arm around his shoulders.

He nodded.

I checked his forehead. His brow was damp and feverish. Pushing back the heavy bed curtains, I alighted from bed. By the flame of the candle that burned in the wall sconce in the alcove, I made my way to the side table where a ewer stood ready. I poured rosewater into the golden basin, wetted a towel, and returned to mop Henry's brow.

"Is it the same dream?" Yesterday had come news that my Aunt Margaret and her son-in-law, Maximilian, had written the pope for his blessing on the pretender, calling Henry a tyrant without sufficient title, sprung from adulterous embraces.

Henry sighed. " 'Tis always the same. I am being chased to the death by hounds in a dark forest. This time I saw your aunt's face, and Maximilian's as well."

I gave him a cup of wine and took up my lyre by the fire, where a few embers still smoldered. Strumming the chords of a soft melody, I raised my voice in song. Even in the darkness, I saw that the lines on Henry's forehead and at his mouth had grown ever more pronounced, his sunken cheeks more hollow. The strain of kingship was etching into his flesh. Pity flooded me. I was planning to wait before telling him my news, but I decided to do so now. As the last notes of the song faded, I dropped my hands from my lyre.

"Henry, I am with child again."

He rose and came to me, knelt at my feet, and took my hand, then kissed it tenderly.

"Amid all the troubles that beset me," he said hoarsely, averting his face, "by God's grace, there is one sure light. One blessing that never falters." He lifted his gaze to me. "You, Elizabeth."

❀

SOON ALL THE LAND KNEW THAT THE PRETENDER had surfaced in Scotland and was well received by James IV. Then came astounding news. It was Kate who broke it to me. I had just returned from receiving petitioners in the audience chamber. Patch had greeted me merrily and I had taken up my lute to practice a new version of a favorite old song when she burst into the room without knocking.

"The pretender is getting married!" she cried.

"What?" I rose to my feet, stunned.

"To a royal cousin of King James IV—Lady Catherine Gordon, daughter of George, Earl of Huntly, the most powerful lord in all Scotland after the king himself!"

I opened my mouth to speak but no words came. " 'Tis not

possible," I managed at last. Marriage was always a financial affair, entered into without emotion by the bride's father, and there was nothing in this union to advance, or even secure the interests of the Earl of Huntly. Far from it; he had much to lose. Further, the marriage now bound King James to the pretender as surely as it bound Lady Catherine.

" 'Tis said the pretender gave James's privy council a most heart-rending account of his life—how his brother was slain, how King Richard had given him papers and sent him to the Continent on the eve of Bosworth with orders not to return until the time was right," Kate went on, wide-eyed. "Lovell was supposed to contact him, but after Lincoln's rebellion, no word came from him. So Aunt Margaret of Burgundy hid him with a trusted retainer and moved him around Europe to protect him. Now James has wed him into his own royal family. Surely that has to mean he is who he says he is— our brother Dickon?"

Though Kate had married and was a mother now, she didn't comprehend the full implications of her words; she was still too young, her head filled with the ideals of romance. I clenched my fists to still my pounding heart. "It just means that James believes it, not that he is really our brother," I said.

Patch sauntered before us. He turned to the minstrel who sat on a stool in the corner with his gittern and gave him a nod. As the man launched into a melody, Patch puffed his chest like a troubadour and screeched out a ballad in his high voice.

> *Once there was a baron's daughter*
> *Who fell in love with a juggler*
> *Who conjured a fine steed from bits of old horse bone and cloth.*
> *He pranced so alluringly—*

Patch imitated a man riding a horse in such a ridiculous fashion that Kate couldn't stop laughing.

> *That she bedded him, thinking him a duke, or at least an earl.*
> *At dawn she looked again—*
> *And what did she see, my ladies?*

"What?" Kate demanded with excitement.

"What?" I asked absently, still trying to digest the news.

"A bleary-eyed churl."

"But they say she is as desperately in love with him as he is with her," Kate persisted. "And that she is the most beautiful maiden in the land of Scotland, with eyes like stars. Her father firmly believes the pretender is our Dickon."

I raised a hand to my throbbing head. Commoners didn't wed royalty for love, and when they did—as in the case of my own mother, or my distant ancestor, Katherine de Roet, who had wed the Duke of Lancaster—they caused worldwide scandal. Yet this marriage had not elicited a murmur of reproach. Clifford's words echoed in my ears: *Without exception, the crowned heads of Europe have accepted him as Richard of England. Even Spain.*

Blessed Virgin, who is he?

Is he my brother?

I don't want him to be my brother!

"Henry's spies say James will go to war against us on behalf of this Richard, and that 'tis James, not the pretender, who is pushing for invasion," Kate said.

Patch fell to one knee before me and swept his feathered cap from his large, malformed head. "The pretender has no thirst for battle! He wishes only to kneel bareheaded before the one he loves, murmuring words of endearment."

"Patch, you fool, what do you know of love?" Kate laughed.

I left them abruptly and went to the window. The minstrel in the corner of the room picked up the rippling chords of melody I had been playing earlier. "October." Even in the heat of August, the melody suited my mood.

'Tis October, when I wait, cold and alone, he sang. *For love to find me.*

Love . . . Never would I know wedded love. To feel so close to someone that my flesh seemed to contain both our hearts. To be undressed by the one I loved, to have him unpin my headdress, to loosen my hair, to unfasten my bodice, to lift my kirtle over my hips. To have my hands loosen his princely trappings and let them fall away, robe, surcoat, shirts, points . . . To lay together inside our drawn bed curtains, in the thick of the labor of love, in the tender darkness of the night, to work by touch, to close our eyes at the height of pleasure, and lose ourselves in the rapture of our bodies. To have the one I loved abandon himself to me, and to cry out to him in love.

To be his; and to have him mine.

My sense of loss was beyond tears; I drew a long breath and let it out slowly. The pretender had sought a crown, and found something far more precious.

Dickon, if it is truly you, take what you have won, and let the crown be!

Kate came to me and placed an arm around my shoulders. She led me to the settle and sat me down beside her.

"All the world believes he is Dickon, Elizabeth. Except here in England, where Henry rules." She hesitated, added on a sigh, "Because they dare not."

She took my hand in hers, and I dropped my head on her shoulder wearily.

❀

OVER THE LAST OF SUMMER DAYS, IN OUR GORGEOUSLY hung rooms in Windsor Castle with their views of the river and the scattering of houses beyond, we carried on with our daily lives and tried to pretend all was normal. The cobbled palace courts rang with jingling horses and greetings of welcome for the lords and ladies who were our invited guests. At banquets we clapped for the feats of tumblers and a man who ate coals. Other evenings, we laughed at Diego the Spanish Fool, who cavorted about as a horse to entertain us, and at the antics of my fool, Patch, and Henry's fool, whom he had named Dick the Fool in a slur on Richard. The children went fishing; they rode at the hunt with us and chased hares; they played tennis with their father. Whole nights were spent at tables with games of cards. Losing at Triumph or Plunder, Henry would borrow money from his councilors to continue.

But he could no longer hide his dismay beneath a casual dismissal of the pretender, whose wife, Catherine Gordon, had given birth to a son. Before he granted his approval to such a marriage,

King James IV must have been offered incontrovertible proof that Perkin Warbeck was my brother Dickon. This plunged me into a depression of spirit that forced me to take to my bed. Again I was in an agony of mind, remembering the days in sanctuary and the sorrow of my little brother's parting from my mother. I kept seeing my uncle Richard standing in the chapter house, and Dickon, disguised as a grimy stonemason's boy helper, stepping through the door behind him. *"Dickon!"* my mother had cried, stumbling toward him, her arms open wide. *"Dickon!"*

Was this pretender my brother? If he was, and he won the throne from Henry, what of my Arthur? My mother's words echoed across the years: *No matter what happens, you and Arthur will be safe. Never doubt that.*

But good intentions meant little when weighed against reality. My father had never wished to destroy Henry VI, but in the end, he did. Shutting my eyes against the agonizing thought, I tumbled into fitful sleep and a turmoil of confused dreams.

CHAPTER 22

Rebellion, 1497

AS SEPTEMBER ARRIVED, THE NIGHTS GREW LONG and cold, but never more so than now, in this year of 1495, for great heartbreak was mine. My little daughter Lizbeth, the precious darling who loved to bring me flowers, whose kisses had always been so abundant and whose laughter and sweetness had delighted everyone that beheld her, fell ill. She died on the fourteenth of September, aged three. The palace went as silent as a tomb. My pain could not be eased, nor grief stifled. I fell into a deep despondency. As the October day approached that had been Richard's birthday, the heaviness that always bore down on me in this season reached oppressive heights. Leaves turned, painting the earth in glorious color, but I knew their bright triumph would prove brief and transitory, for soon they would fall to the ground and crumble into dust.

"Let us make a pilgrimage to Walsingham," Kate urged me. "It will do you good, dear sister."

To my surprise, as Margaret Beaufort was not at court to dissuade him, Henry approved my request, though I was four months with child, even lamenting he could not come with me. I left for

Walsingham on my white palfrey, for I wished to see the people and have them see me. Only when I tired did I take to a litter. The outpouring of love in all the hamlets and villages, in the towns and cities that we passed through brought me solace, for I realized once again how much I meant to my people. "Elizabeth, Elizabeth!" they cried, dropping their burdens in the fields where they labored. They emerged from their small dwellings with babes in their arms and children at their skirts as they rushed to greet me. "God bless King Edward's daughter!" they shouted, lining the roads—merchants, craftsmen, farmers, carters, students, and apprentices. "God bless Elizabeth the Good! Elizabeth the Good, our queen, the king's beautiful daughter—"

Many times I had to avert my face to hide my tears, so moved was I by their love. They brought me gifts of pudding and spices, fresh fruit, dried cherries, even birds in cages. I never accepted their presents without giving back others of more value, for I knew how poor they were and how much sacrifice their small gifts represented to them.

On our journey to Walsingham, we stayed a night at Lucy Neville's family estate of Burrough Green. The spires of the little church pierced the sky, and as we approached, bells rang melodiously. The rolling fields were ringed by woods of bright gold poplars and orange aspen shimmering in the sun. Enfolded in the serenity of the place, I was reminded that I was not the only one who had drunk from life's cup of sorrow; others had trod these roads before me who had known love and loss. I glanced at Lucy, riding beside me. Her father, Lord Montagu, had been brother to the Kingmaker, and had died with him at Barnet.

"Your parents, Lucy—I hear they wed for love against daunting odds, because they came from the enemy camps of York and Lancaster. Is that true?"

"Indeed, it is, Your Grace. My father paid a thousand pounds for my mother's hand, for she was the ward of Queen Marguerite, the sworn enemy of my grandfather, the Earl of Salisbury, and my uncle, the Earl of Warwick."

"A thousand pounds. 'Tis a king's ransom. Your father must have loved her very much."

"He did. And she loved him. I remember the way she ran to him each time he came home from battle—the way he touched her. The way they gazed at one another—" She broke off, tensing visibly.

I caught the glint of tears sparkling on her lashes in the sunshine. "What is it, dear Lucy? What ails thee?" I asked softly.

"Nothing, my queen. 'Tis nothing important. Merely a memory."

"Lucy, I believe we honor those we love by remembering them, though the memory brings us sorrow rather than joy in the speaking of it."

She must have accepted my words, for after a pause, she said in a hushed tone. "I remember the last time they ever saw one another before Barnet . . . They each knew they were bidding farewell forever. They tried to be brave and to pretend that it would come out all right, but my mother broke at the last moment and threw herself against my father's armor—" She bit her lip and averted her gaze. "And he stood stiff as a lance, gazing out over her head."

Anguish engulfed me as I listened. In my mind's eye, I saw Richard's face in that small room at Westminster before I left for Sheriff Hutton. *I too remember the last time I saw Richard on this earth. We both knew it was final and forever.*

I gave Lucy's hand a squeeze, and closed my eyes against the sorrow. *We think the wounds of the past are scars, long since forgotten, but one scratch, and they bleed.*

That night, I dreamt of Richard. He came to me out of the mist, carrying a red rose in his hand.

❀

I RETURNED TO SHEEN IN EARLY NOVEMBER. THE pilgrimage to Walsingham had not lifted my despondency, for Lizbeth's loss was too keenly felt. But God, in His grace, had bestowed new life on us, and every week my belly grew larger, reminding me that amid sorrow came blessing.

Many times during these weeks, I sought refuge in memories. Alone in my chamber, I unlocked my coffer with the key I kept around my neck and drew out Richard's book, *Tristan.*

You said I'd forget you, Richard, I said, gazing at his likeness. *But I haven't. I never will.*

By late November unsettling omens arrived to give us notice that Fortune was not done with us, for London was visited by a mysterious sickness and a storm of hailstones as large as plates. There was heavy thunder in the night and strange winds. As Yuletide approached, we learned from Margaret Beaufort that she had separated from her husband, Thomas Stanley, and taken the vow of chastity. Now she donned the black and white attire of a nun, with the lower part of her headgear well up to her chin. It was a fashion that did nothing to flatter her, but it was one that her ordinance forbade to anyone below the rank of baroness. Beneath her garments she wore a hair shirt. With her time, she took up scholarly pursuits at Oxford and Cambridge and devoted herself to the education of "brilliant Harry" and "tempestuous Margaret," the grandchildren she adored. She had also taken to washing the feet of the poor and comforting the dying.

"I hope to learn from them how to die well."

She is fifty-two now, and trembles to meet her Maker, I thought, crossing myself.

Arthur came for Yule and brightened up the weeks until he left again. The terrible year of 1495 that had carried off my little Lizbeth finally died away.

When I was close to my confinement, Margaret Beaufort returned from her estate in Woking to prepare my birthing chamber at Sheen. On the bed she laid feather pillows and a rich coverlet of scarlet velvet, furred with ermine and embroidered with gold crowns and roses. The room was dark, for all the windows had been covered with tapestries, according to her ordinances, and only floral scenes were permitted, for she believed representations of human figures would adversely affect the newborn child. I smiled vaguely to myself; Margaret's ordinances would be the death of me yet.

Outside, the wind howled and whipped about the palace. The Thames churned and tossed its boats, and the screams of sea birds pitched against the chilling rain. The day of the birth drew near. I knew the signs well. Had I not been with child for half my married life? Five births in ten years. On the eighteenth of March, I took to my bed as Margaret Beaufort fussed around me. After many hours of hard labor, the pains finally ceased and the cry of a child pierced the fog that engulfed me.

" 'Tis a girl," whispered Margaret Beaufort. "A beautiful girl-child." She held her up to me. She was a lovely babe with fair hair and well-defined little features. As Lizbeth had been.

I nodded, closed my lids. A tear trickled from the corner of my eye.

At my request, she was named Mary, for my beloved sister who had died in May of 1482.

❖

WINTER PASSED. THE LAND SHRUGGED OFF ITS SHADES of dismal gray for the bright palette of spring, and Kate gave birth to her second son, named Edward. We moved to Greenwich, that castle on the banks of the Thames that had always been a symbol of joy to me through my childhood. There, we indulged in our games, our horses, and the hunt. Young Harry displayed his talent for sports by shooting at the crossbow and let out glad whoops of joy to learn he would accompany our guests fowling after dark with nets and lights. Summer faded into the golden wheat fields of August. Then followed September, and inevitable autumn.

Henry, in fearful dread of being ousted from his kingdom by the pretender, took no chances and did not stop mobilizing for war with Scotland. The occasion offered him an excuse to levy enormous taxes on the people. He collected three hundred thousand pounds and readied nearly fifty thousand men for a spring march north on Scotland.

"James can have war if he wishes," Henry said to me as we played cards together in the quiet of my bedchamber. "Or he can give up the feigned lad and have peace."

"Surely there are other ways to resolve the situation?" I asked. "It doesn't always have to be war." Maybe, if given a chance, the pretender—*Dickon?*—would choose to retire with his love into peaceful seclusion, someplace in the world that wasn't England.

Henry wrote James Ramsey, Lord Bothwell, his chief spy in Scotland, asking how he could avoid war.

"James is set against you," his spy wrote. "There is naught you can do, no means you can employ, either by persuasion or gold, to separate him from the pretender. King James is firmly on his side."

Henry even prepared a plot to murder the "feigned boy," Perkin Warbeck, but his Scottish spy advised him against it. "It would only inflame James with more determination to avenge himself on England," the man wrote back.

While James spent a fortune on guns, cannonballs, arrows, and armor and continued to busy himself on the border, checking his forts and preparing his men, Henry paced in confusion and dread, listening to the reports his spies sent. *James wants war with England; James doesn't want war with England. The guns are good, can shoot straight; the guns are a jest and nothing need be feared from them.*

Henry's spies were thorough. They even wrote that James had paid one hundred and ten pounds for a new cloak in his favorite velvet, lined and embroidered with crimson satin to wear to war, and sent him details that could be known only to the most intimate counselors of King James and the pretender. Camped in a pavilion on the border of England on a dewy, cold morning, after sleeping on pallet beds, between trips to the outdoor privy across a field of snow, King James and Richard the pretender had hammered out the terms of their agreement. James demanded Berwick castle, several sheriffdoms, certain lands, and seventy thousand pounds for services rendered. The pretender refused these terms. They argued long into the night. In the end, the pretender agreed only to half the terms that James wanted.

"He acts like a man who cares for England," wrote Henry's spy.

The embroidery that busied my hands blurred before my eyes. I raised a hand to my aching head. Could this "boy," as Henry called him, truly be who he said he was? My brother, Richard of England, the rightful king?

No, he is not, I told myself. *Dickon is dead.*

AS I EMBROIDERED A SILK BANNER FOR ARTHUR IN Henry's privy chamber, a messenger came with the pretender's latest proclamation, shouted by common criers at the gates of a handful of English border towns. He cleared his throat nervously and read:

"Whereas we in our tender age escaped by God's might out of the Tower of London and were secretly conveyed across the sea into other diverse lands there remaining as a stranger, while Henry Tudor, son to Edmund Tudor of low birth in the country of Wales—" The man's voice shook, for there was danger in displeasing a monarch.

The pretender went on to accuse Henry of manifold treasons, abominable murders, manslaughters, robberies, extortions, and daily pillaging of the people by taxes. Henry grabbed the proclamation from the messenger and scanned it. He swallowed visibly. "He signed his proclamations *Ricardus Rex.*"

The words knocked the breath from my lungs. I pushed myself to my feet. "Henry, forgive me, I feel unwell of a sudden."

He nodded, and I fled the chamber.

The invasion soon followed.

Henry greeted me in his chamber with a rare smile. "The people of Northumberland did not rise to join the feigned boy." He nodded to the messenger as I took a seat on the settle.

"King James," the man said, "furious at the betrayal of the English, laid waste the fields, pillaged the houses, and burnt the villages. Those who resisted, he killed. The pretender, in tears, begged James to stop savaging his country and his people. Lordship was worth nothing to him, he said, if it was obtained by so piteously spilling the blood and destroying the land of his fathers. 'How can my heart not be moved by the destruction of my people?' he demanded. To this King James replied, 'But they are not your people. And though you call England your country, far from recognizing you as king, they don't even recognize you as an Englishman!'"

Henry laughed as merrily as I'd ever seen him do, but I could not smile.

"They have done great violence to the border region," he added. "After all, they are Scots."

This was the news that Henry commanded be proclaimed all over the land. The border was sparsely populated, and I knew the "great violence" was on a tiny scale. Yet it was more than enough to turn the pretender's stomach.

"He seems a gentle man," whispered Kate to me when we were alone in the solar. "He was shocked by the blood he saw. Shocked into pity."

I picked up the sketch of the pretender's likeness that had been sent to Henry by one of his spies, and which he had forgotten on the scrivener's desk.

"How handsome he is," Kate murmured over my shoulder.

"He has the mark of the Plantagenets in his left eye that Dickon had. What if he is truly our brother, Kate?"

Kate embraced me, and we held one another close for a long moment.

"Come," said Kate, taking my hand. "We need to pray."

❂

ARTHUR CAME FOR YULE, BRINGING WITH HIM A TU-mult of rejoicing to my heart, and left after Twelfth Night, taking the sun with him, as the year of 1496 gave way to 1497. The explorer John Cabot returned. His voyage had been successful, and he brought back gold and many wonders. At the banquet Henry threw for him, he presented to me three strange men in animal skins who tore their raw meat and relished its gore, and who spoke no language ever heard before. I marveled at the men, and at Cabot's courage.

"They are Indian, the native people of the New Land," he said. "Finding the waters open, I would have sailed farther, but my sailors grew afraid."

But once more, the pretender banished our joy. In my privy chamber at Sheen, Henry paced to and fro as dusk settled on the day.

"I need money for war, and the men of Cornwall refuse to pay! They rose up against me the day after I dispatched my chamberlain, Lord Daubeny, north with the army to fight the Scots!"

I sighed heavily. Henry had disregarded my warning that there might be trouble collecting the additional heavy taxes. "The Cornishmen are poor, Henry. They scratch out a living mining tin, and fishing, and farming. They have no money to give you."

"The devil take their souls, they *will* pay! I'll send Morton and Bray to collect it. That shall put the fear of God in them!"

I shut my eyes on a breath. When it came to money, Henry was like a man crazed.

Not long after their departure, Morton and Bray scurried back to report that the measures they'd taken had only infuriated the people, and now a mob of eighteen thousand men was marching on London. Inexplicably, the nobleman John Touchet, Lord Audley, had joined their cause.

"Let them come," Henry told Morton. "They will tire themselves marching, and we'll make short shrift of them. Meanwhile, send to Lord Daubeny to return from the Scots border. I myself shall take a force to Woodstock to block the rebels' path to London."

The next morning, Henry entered my chamber before the cock's crow. I saw that he hadn't slept. I threw back the covers and leapt from bed, instantly awake. Gathering my night robe around me, I searched his face. "Henry, what is it?"

"For your safety and the safety of the children, I am sending you to the Tower."

"The Tower?" I echoed in bewilderment. My mother had been sent to the Tower when Warwick's cousin Lord Fauconberg attacked London after Barnet. I had been five years old then, and never had I forgotten those frightening days. Conveyed secretly by barge with my sister Mary, I was hustled up the water stairs and through the gates of the Tower to hide in terror for days while the gun battle raged between Fauconberg and my uncle Anthony Woodville. Now the nightmare was repeating itself, and I would be retracing my steps there with my own children.

The pretender is marching into the land to seize the throne from Henry, and if Henry, then Arthur. I felt nauseated. Reaching for a chair, I fell into it. With difficulty, I lifted my eyes to Henry's face. He had been right.

Now I was indeed one of them.

※

AT THE TOWER, WE ANXIOUSLY ALIGHTED AT THE river entrance. Darkness and evil seemed to hover there, and I gave a sigh of relief when we emerged into the sunshine of the courtyard.

"Is Edward, Earl of Warwick, the true king of England?" demanded Harry as we rushed hand in hand past the Beauchamp Tower, where Edward was imprisoned.

I ignored his question, and so did Kate.

"Which room is he in?" Harry insisted.

"I know not," I replied to my son, exchanging a glance with Kate.

"You do indeed! You send him sweets and books to read!" Harry shot back.

My breath froze. He must have heard me instructing Patch. *Then Henry knows, too.* He must have decided it did no harm, since he had not spoken to me about it. *Foolish of me, to think I could hide anything from him and his spies.* I halted in my steps. "Harry, you must not ask about your cousin of Warwick. 'Tis not a matter for discussion, understood?"

He nodded. I tightened my hold of his hand and resumed my steps, but he craned his neck back toward Beauchamp as we rushed along.

The Cornishmen arrived on the thirteenth of June and pitched camp at Black Heath, four miles away. In the capital there was great fear. The gates were closed and guarded; the walls were fortified with timber, manned, and armed; and buckets of water were distributed around the city, to quench both thirst and fire.

"What will happen to me if Father dies?" Maggie asked. "Will they kill me, too?"

"No, my sweet," I said, drawing her close. "They won't harm you."

"Will they set up Edward, Earl of Warwick, as king, if they win?" she pressed.

"If they win, they will," Harry replied before I could answer Maggie. "But they're not going to win, are they, Mother?"

I hesitated. Life was full of uncertainties. Who could be sure of anything? Looking into my children's anxious eyes, I said, "Have no fear. Your father will prevail."

I tried to provide a normal life for Harry and Maggie by keeping them at their studies during the day. In the evenings Patch entertained us. We played cards with Kate, and I had the children read aloud to me and practice their musical instruments of lute and harp. Sometimes we watched the high-sided sailing ships passing up and down the Thames, and I'd explain to Harry about trade.

"See that painted ship coming in? It carries silks from Italy and Saracen carpets from Turkey."

"And spices, monkeys, and parrots from China!" chimed Harry. "The ones leaving carry our good English wool to their lands and make us rich."

"You are quite right, Harry. Master Giles has taught you well. Now, would you care for some dancing?"

Harry scrambled down with a cry of delight. Maggie relinquished her mirror to take the floor with Harry, but Harry said, "May I dance with you, Mother? I'm tired of dancing with Maggie."

Red in the face, Maggie stomped her foot. "What's wrong with dancing with me? I'm a good dancer, aren't I, Mother?"

"You are, Maggie, and I like you well enough," Harry said before I could reply. "But I always dance with you, and I never have a chance to dance with Mother." He turned his angelic face to me. "I pray you, Mother, just once? Then I'll dance with Maggie without complaint."

I fought to keep a straight face. "Very well, Harry. Aunt Kate can play the lute for us."

We took our positions on the floor and Kate broke into a popular French tune that had been sweeping court, "*L'Amour de Mai*." We took the tiny steps of the *danse*, first bending our knees, then rising on our toes, transferring weight from one foot to the other while dancing slowly side by side across the room.

The tune ended. I clapped for Harry. "Well done, my young prince! You have mastered the *basse danse*. We shall have to arrange for you—and Maggie—" I added hastily, "to give us a display at court."

Harry rewarded me with a smile and a courtly bow from the waist.

As I filled the hours of waiting, I tried to push back the specters and shadows of the past that crowded my own mind. But I could not forget the Beauchamp Tower, and my gaze often strayed there.

"Patch, did you never find out what else I can send Edward of Warwick?" I asked him softly one day.

Patch hung his head. "My queen, no one returns with his reply. I can never get the same person to go there twice."

I regarded him closely. *Everyone is terrified of offending Henry.* "Patch, it seems my lord king knows I have been sending him marchpane, and does not mind. Would you be willing to go to the young earl for me?"

He nodded.

"Here, take this letter to his guard," I said, scribbling a few words on a piece of paper. "They will give you his answer."

It was barely an hour later that Patch returned, pale and tense.

"I gave your missive to the guard, and he took it to another guard who went upstairs with it. I waited in the courtyard and they finally brought me the answer."

"So, what is it? What does Edward ask for?"

Patch shifted his weight on his feet and averted his face. "Soil."

"What did you say? I didn't hear you."

Patch raised moist eyes to me. "He requests a bit of soil. To plant a seed. To watch it grow. He misses the smell of the earth."

I turned away, a hand to my mouth to stifle my cry.

ONE DAY AFTER A BRIEF RESPITE IN THE GARDEN, I returned to find Harry and Maggie gone, their lesson books open on the table.

"Where are they?" I asked Kate, my heart jumping in my chest.

"I thought they were with you," she replied, rising from the window seat where she had been reading.

I turned to the man-at-arms at the door. "Surely you saw them leave?"

"Your Grace, they weren't here when I came on duty. I took up my post at three o'clock."

"Gather men—find them!" He spun on his heel.

I sank down on the settle, a hand to my aching head.

Kate squeezed my shoulder in sympathy. "Fret not, sister. I doubt our enemies have penetrated into our midst with all the fortifications Henry has set around us. The children may be visiting the animal menagerie, or the armory."

Assailed by a tumble of confused thoughts, I regarded her bleakly. "I fear Harry has gone to find Edward of Warwick."

"I'll see if they're at the Beauchamp Tower."

She returned half an hour later with both children, one in each hand. Swept with relief and joy, I leapt to my feet and kissed their faces, laughing in my delight. "Where were you?" I remembered to ask at last.

Harry's face lit up. "I saw the prisoners!" he cried. "They're all in iron chains!"

I stiffened. "Fetch me Harry's nurse, Kate."

A quarter hour later she returned with a chastised Anne Oxenbridge, who had been visiting in the kitchen with one of the cooks. I received her in a far corner of the room and spoke softly so Harry would not hear. "I fault you for his ways, Anne. You should curb his obstinacy and teach him to obey you. It also troubles me that he appears to take pleasure in the suffering of others. You are with him most of the day. You could guide him better than you have done."

"My queen, I have tried but he will have his own way. He does not listen to me. He has more respect for Master Giles. Perhaps if you spoke to him . . ." Her voice trailed off. But I had caught the lack of conviction in her tone. It appeared that Harry needed a new tutor, someone of a lofty stature who might be able to instill ideals in him.

"Let the children play in the garden for a while," I said wearily. "Make sure there are plenty of guards around you."

She curtsied. Taking Harry and Maggie by the hand, she led them from the chamber.

"You're as white as a phantom, Elizabeth," Kate said. "That was quite a fright they gave you."

"With all that's going on, it's hard not to think the worst."

I sank into the settle, and she came and sat beside me. "You're right to be concerned about Harry. When I found him, he was tormenting the wretched prisoners through the bars of their cells."

"I don't know what to do, Kate. He seems to delight in human misery. I've spoken to him about it until I weary of my own words, but I can't seem to get through to him. Though he will not be king, he shall wield great power one day, and it worries me."

"Speak to Henry. Maybe he can think of a way to reach Harry."

There were no more escapes after that, for I chastised all the household and doubled up the guard. I also commanded Patch never to leave them alone. Now that they couldn't run away, Harry and Maggie held vigil at the window, watching the glow of campfires by night and the smoke by day. Early one morning, as we were preparing to break fast in our chamber, Harry let out a loud cheer. "Father has arrived! He's moving the royal army into position on the south bank!"

We all rushed to the window.

"What's going to happen to Father?" asked Maggie anxiously.

"He's going to win," Harry replied before I could reply.

"How do you know?" Maggie demanded.

"Because it cannot be any other way," Harry said.

"And then what?" Maggies demanded.

"Then he's going to chop the traitors up into teeny pieces while they're alive."

"How do you know?" Margaret asked.

"Because that's what I would do if I were king," he said.

Gently, I took Harry aside. With my arms around his small shoulders, I explained about mercy.

"That's foolish," Harry said. "They're only going to rise up again."

"Maybe they won't. Maybe your kindness will win their hearts, dear son."

Harry laughed. "Who cares about their hearts? If they're dead, they're done."

Again came that disquiet as I regarded my child. He charmed everyone with his winning smile, his laughter, and zest for sport; his musical talent, dancing ability, love of poetry, and brilliant mind, so advanced for his years. He looked angelic with his rosy complexion and red-gold locks. But blood held a macabre fascination for him.

He is young yet. There is time to correct his failings, I told myself.

At dawn the next morning we were awakened by shouts and screams and the far-off boom of cannon and neighing of horses.

"The royal forces have attacked!" cried Harry, running to the window. "Father has attacked!"

I gave Harry permission to watch the battle from the turrets after extracting his solemn promise to come directly to me once the outcome was known. Taking Maggie and Kate, and accompanied by the women of my household, I retired to pray. The fighting continued for hours. Then Harry came running to me at noon with the announcement.

"Father has won! The rebellion's been crushed! Black Heath is covered with dead bodies and we are all safe!"

At two o'clock in the afternoon, amid much rejoicing and the blaring of trumpets, the gates of London were thrown open to the royal army. I went down to the court to meet Henry. Smiling broadly, he took my hand in his own.

❀

LORD AUDLEY, THE ONLY NOBLE TO CHAMPION THE cause of the rebels, was taken to Newgate the next day. Dressed in a torn paper tunic with his arms reversed, he was drawn in a cart through the city to Tower Hill and beheaded.

"Can I watch, Father?" Harry demanded.

" 'Tis not a sight for a child's eyes," I interjected.

"But I'm a man—I have the heart of a man! I saw Uncle William die. Why should I not see Audley get his head chopped off?"

I turned to Henry. "I am most decidedly against it, my lord."

Henry ruffled Harry on the head. "Your mother is right. You have seen enough blood already."

Later that same day, I found Harry in the presence chamber, seated on the throne, his short, sturdy legs sticking straight out over the edge of the chair. Maggie was bowing and scraping at his feet. "More!" he yelled, laughing. "I want more homage or I'll send you to the headsman!"

"What are you doing?" I demanded.

Both children scrambled to attention before me.

"He's king, and I'm a traitor," Maggie said. "And I'm going to be chopped into pieces by the headsman."

"Leave us, Maggie!" I commanded, trembling with anger. "As for you, Harry, 'tis best to remember that you shall never be king, for that estate belongs to your brother. Never let me catch you at such pretense again. 'Tis a serious offense."

Harry went off, downcast. I joined Henry in his privy chamber. He lay down his papers and met me with a kiss on the cheek, and then a sigh.

"What is the trouble?" I asked.

"I have to decide what to do with the rebels. I'll give the leaders a trial, but the rest—"

"Henry, show them mercy!" I saw his face harden. I was always preaching mercy. I added hastily, "Their punishment can be severe nevertheless."

He regarded me in puzzlement for a moment, then his face lit. "Fines, you mean? Take their money instead of their blood? 'Tis an excellent idea."

I smiled inwardly. By appealing to Henry's avarice, I had reached his heart.

The rank and file of the Cornish rebels were sent home unharmed, except for the massive fine he levied. Over the next few days, trumpets sounded through London as Henry's proclamation was read to the crowds. "All men who took prisoners at the battle shall bring them to the Tower. For each prisoner the lord king will pay twelve pence a peasant, more for those of higher degree."

A procession of dejected prisoners made their way through the grounds, accompanied by captors anxious to collect their money.

Henry presided over the trials of the rebel leaders personally, and Harry was permitted to watch. They were condemned to a traitor's death and disemboweled at Tyburn. Pieces of their bodies were impaled on the Tower gates, while their heads went to London Bridge.

"See, I told you," I heard Harry whisper to Maggie as we rode out from the Tower to Sheen. "Father chopped them up into little pieces."

CHAPTER 23

Fortune's Smile, 1497

UNCERTAINTY WAS CASTING A SHADOW OVER OUR comfortable lives.

Perkin Warbeck was rumored to have sailed for the south of England. Henry prepared for invasion and distributed placards all over the land, offering a reward of a thousand pounds for his capture. While he waited, he went hunting at his palace of Woodstock to give the impression he was unconcerned—I remembered how Richard had done the same at Nottingham—and at night, he gambled at dice and cards, losing great sums as if to appease Fortune. When a messenger came to report that the pretender had captured St. Michael's Mount, Henry turned to the poet Bernard Andre, smiled sarcastically, and said, "So this prince of knaves is troubling us again."

Not long afterward, news arrived that the pretender had departed the Mount, leaving behind the two most precious to his heart: his wife, Lady Catherine Gordon, and his small son, another Richard. I thought of the daughter of the Earl of Huntly, so young, so vulnerable, possessed of such great beauty, now alone in a foreign land, separated from the one she loved, facing the extinction of her world. And I prayed for her and her child.

"Wherever the pretender goes, men flock to him," Henry complained bitterly. "They say he has charm."

Like my father, I thought.

Henry threw the dice as we gambled together in the solar while a great fire blazed in the fireplace.

"You lose," I said, gathering my winnings.

"He who wins, loses," Henry said, referring to the name of a favorite card game. "And he who loses, wins." He relaxed into his chair and gave me a sly smile. "I pay Fortune off, and she rewards me by drawing to my side."

That Henry was superstitious, I knew well. He had lost at cards the night before Bosworth, and had emerged victorious in a battle that he had neither fought in nor directed. Ten years later, he still couldn't believe his good fortune: how he, with a few adventurers at his side, had won a kingdom from the one who held in his hands the resources of a nation. What he didn't know was that Richard had not cared to keep what he had and chose not to wield his power, whereas Henry would fight for his crown with fists of iron for as long as he should live.

"Fortune will be yours," I said.

Over the next week, messengers galloped in and out of the palace, bearing news and carrying back Henry's orders.

"The pretender has traveled east and taken Castle Canyke, sire," they said, and Henry sent a force of twenty thousand Cornishmen against the pretender's eight, outnumbering them by more than two to one.

"Sire, the royal troops approached the castle, but they stopped and would go no further. They turned and fled, sire."

"Perkin Warbeck entered Bodmin, sire, and was greeted as King Richard IV by heralds and trumpeters who proclaimed him the second son of King Edward."

"The pretender has set out for Devon, sire. He has with him three thousand archers." And Henry commanded that the sheriff of Devon prevent his march to Exeter.

"Sire, the troops, awed by the sight of the pretender, refused to fight. They have fled, my liege."

Henry turned from the window with his hands clasped behind

his back. " 'Tis time for Lord Daubeny to march against him with the royal army," he said. "And for you, Elizabeth, to go to the Tower with the children."

The pretender must have learned of the forces massing against him, for he had his wife, Catherine, transferred from the Mount, which had no privilege of sanctuary, to St. Buryan, eight miles to the west. A strange and dismal place, virtually abandoned by the clergy, St. Buryan was built of brown granite on a bleak plateau with views of nothing but gray sky. It was said that the dark church was the gloomiest in England, its rood screen decorated with depictions of black demons devouring blue and gold birds, hounds tearing down gold-antlered deer, and most fearful of all, a winged dragon, its jaws open, about to seize a unicorn by the throat. Amid these fearful scenes the young bride and new mother waited with a few servants, and a few priests, for news of the man she loved.

He has no chance for there is no one left to speak for him, I thought with a stab of great sorrow. All who had championed his cause were dead or rotting in the Tower. Others who would gladly have deserted Henry, like my brother Dorset, released from captivity but staggering under an enormous fine and threatened with the disinheritance of his son, were too terrified to do so. Dragging myself to my prie-dieu, I opened the triptych of the "Virgin and Child Enthroned" that my Uncle Anthony had brought back for me from Florence and bowed my head in prayer for Lady Catherine Gordon and her babe.

❂

KATE'S FATHER-IN-LAW, EDWARD COURTENAY, EARL of Devon, shut the gates of Exeter and repelled the pretender on St. Lambert's Day, the seventeenth of September.

Over the next week, the pretender's army lost heart. Five hundred rebels had died in battle since the Cornish rebellion, and many more from sickness traced to the tainted grain used to brew their ale and bake their bread. It was said they fell as if poisoned, cut down by the papal curses of excommunication issued against them. But I suspected Henry's hand in the rumors, and Margaret

Beaufort's in the deaths, for she and Morton never left anything to chance. What better way to thin the ranks of their enemies than by poisoning their bread and ale? Now Henry was on the march from Woodstock with ten thousand troops equipped with knights and many guns, and Lord Daubeny had left London with the highly disciplined royal army, both descending on the pretender from the northeast. Meanwhile, Perkin Warbeck had no nobles at his side to give him credibility, and no generals to advise him; he had no money, no armor, no weapons save a few swords, pitchforks, and bows. He was outmanned and outgunned, and while Henry's coffers overflowed with six million in gold, the pretender had no coin even to buy food for his army.

I thought of Buryan and the winged dragon with its jaws open, about to seize the white unicorn by the throat. The tidings of the pretender's defeat came as no surprise to me.

A messenger knelt before me. "The pretender, cornered by the royal army, fled east to Beaulieu Abbey where he took sanctuary disguised as a monk, deserting his army in the dead of night like the base coward he is," he reported.

Pressed against my skirts, Harry threw a glance up at me to smile his triumph. But I thought of my uncle Anthony Woodville, the heart of bravery, who had fled the retinue of Charles the Rash just before a battle with the Swiss. And I thought of Henry himself, who had abandoned his troops on the eve of Bosworth, struck in the heart by terror of Richard's great army. Like the pretender, Henry had lost his nerve. But Henry had returned, offering as excuse something about having lost his way in the night. Since he had won Bosworth, no one dared call him a coward.

Shortly after this messenger, de Puebla paid me a visit.

"Pray, Doctor de Puebla, take a seat," I said, always pleased to see his kindly face. I indicated the hearth where a pair of tapestried chairs stood on either side of a small table. Servants brought us wine on a silver tray and set cheese, bread, and sweetmeats before us, for I knew de Puebla had few comforts at the inn of ill repute where he was forced to lodge for lack of funds. Like Henry, King Ferdinand was a miser. He didn't pay de Puebla the wages he owed him, just as Henry had not paid the maker of Richard's marble headstone. Neither of them parted with money if it could be kept in their pockets.

"Your Grace," he said, accepting the wine, "I have here a letter from King Henry, who has apprised me of events that transpired on the thirtieth of September. He requested that I pass this news on to you, as well as to the Venetian and Milanese ambassadors."

I nodded.

"The pretender, surrounded by the king's men in sanctuary, and cut off from all escape, was most anxious to accept the king's pardon. King Henry writes that he knows you shall be glad to hear this."

Glad? Am I glad to hear this young man might have been dragged from sanctuary by sixty or more armed men, as Thomas and his brother, Humphrey Stafford, had been from Culham in 1486? Henry had a long history of violating the ancient laws of sanctuary, but he would make sure to let out that the "feigned boy" had requested to surrender, trembling with fear and racked with weeping, and Henry, the "most merciful" of kings, had granted his request.

I understood Henry's need to keep what he had. But sometimes I wondered how he could live with the cost.

❖

I WATCHED HENRY'S TRIUMPHANT ENTRY INTO LONdon from the gabled window of a house in Cheapside with Kate and the children at my side. Only Arthur was absent, for he was still in Wales and had remained there throughout the ordeal. Henry had deemed him safer in Ludlow than elsewhere in the kingdom. The November day was cold but bright with sunshine, and the chill wind that blew did not deter the crowds.

The pretender came into view, and I gasped. Richmond Herald had said that he had worn his robes of cloth of gold when removed from sanctuary, but now he was attired humbly. Even so, shabby clothes could not hide the pretender's resemblance to my father, or the elegance and dignity of the way he sat his saddle and held his head. Unbound and unfettered, golden haired and blue eyed, even in drab dress he had a royal demeanor about his person that was bred into a prince from babyhood. The crowds jeered, mocked, and hissed. "Low-born foreigner!" they cried, "How dare you?" "King are you—king of the rubbish heap!" They threw rotted garbage at him. He didn't flinch, but rode past as if he didn't see or hear them.

My heart went out to him in pity, and a tear rolled down my cheek.

"Why do you cry, Mother?" Harry said. "Be not afraid, he can't hurt you anymore."

Kate placed her arm around my shoulders.

"I cannot watch," I said, raising a hand to my head, which now throbbed with unendurable pain. Kate led me away.

At Westminster that evening, Henry poured me wine in my privy chamber. I declined, but he pressed the goblet into my hands. "Drink, it will do you good."

He stood at the fireplace, deep in thought, a hand on the mantelpiece. I forced myself to take a sip of the wine he had offered.

"What of his wife, Lady Gordon?" I managed, unable to get the image of the pretender—Dickon?—out of my mind.

Henry took an audible breath and let his hand drop. "She came out of sanctuary and gave herself up to Daubeny."

He lied. I had heard him dictating a letter as far back as the sixteenth of September, making it clear he intended to extract her from sanctuary.

"Why is she not here with her husband?"

"She gave birth to a child at Buryan. The child is dead. She has remained behind in Exeter and is shuttered in a house for the requisite seven days of mourning."

I shut my eyes on a breath. *Woe, such woe!* When I could speak again, I said, "What of her other son, the babe that is a year old?"

"I have sent him away to be raised by a trusty couple."

She has lost her entire world—the man she loves is captive in his enemy's hands; her child is taken from her; her babe is dead. She bears far worse than ever was my portion, and God knows how I suffered, how I grieved after Bosworth.

"What will you do with her?"

"I haven't decided yet. Probably keep her here for a while. She makes a worthy bargaining chip against her husband. As long as I have his wife and child, I can make him say——" Henry broke off, bit his lip. "The feigned boy is not your brother, Elizabeth. Make no mistake about that."

I heard a threat in his words; but whether that was so, or merely my imagination, I could not be sure. "By your leave, my lord, I should like to have Catherine Gordon as my lady-in-waiting for as long as you have her stay in England."

He regarded me thoughtfully, and I saw his mind turning over the implications of such a move. How much would she dare tell me? Would she confirm Dickon's birthmark, the red mole high inside his right inner thigh? When Henry had brought the "feigned boy" to his council and asked him to identify those he knew from his youth, the pretender had not even looked up before replying that he didn't recognize anyone present. He knew he had to be Perkin Warbeck now, if he valued the life of his child. And those who should have known him—if he was Dickon—knew what they had to say. One of these was my brother Dorset. He had already served one long tour at the Tower; he would have no wish to return, and would choose his words carefully.

Another was John Rodon, the servant who had turned down Dickon's sheets as a child, who had brought him his wine and laid out his clothes. He, too, knew what to say, for he had no desire to lose his pension and the position of royal sergeant at arms that Henry had conferred on him. Everyone involved understood what was expected. Especially Catherine Gordon, who trembled for her babe, and her husband.

As for me, I would never know the truth because my mother had not seen fit to trust me with the password.

Henry smiled. "Indeed, that is a fine idea. To have you take his poor wife under your protection not only displays great compassion, but it shows all the world that he is a fraud."

We received Lady Catherine Gordon in the state chamber, seated on our thrones, with our nobles gathered around on either side of the room and Henry's favorite greyhound, Lancelot, beside him on the dais.

Henry looks well, I thought. Clad in his favorite crimson cloth of gold, he wore a rich collar with four rows of large pearls and rare, costly jewels around his neck that blazed in the light of the torches. His freshly washed, graying hair no longer hung limp beneath his crown, for he had bathed and spent the day preparing for this moment. The subject of Catherine Gordon's beauty had been a matter for long discussion with his Scottish spy, James Ramsey, Lord Bothwell. No doubt he wished to make a good impression on her.

A herald called out her name, and she was hustled in to us, tied like a bondswoman. I looked at Henry in shock, for this could only have been on his orders. Tall and slender as a willow, Lady Catherine had the neck of a swan, thick glossy black hair, and perfectly arched brows set over huge blue eyes that sparked like sapphires in her oval face. *She is,* I thought, *a vision of female loveliness more exquisite than any I have ever seen.* Henry was staring at her in disbelief.

"Untie her!" he demanded, scowling as if he had never given the order to have her fettered. He loved drama, and I knew this scene was meant to be a spectacle for the people to mull and marvel over in the taverns.

"My dear lady," said Henry, "from now on, we shall personally make certain that you are accorded the dignity of your rank. You shall have money, clothes, and servants. You shall lack nothing. We shall provide all that your husband, who wed you in falsehood and deceit, cannot provide you." Pressing both hands to his breast, he added Lancelot's favorite oath, "I swear this to you by the faith of my heart."

My gaze went to him. Abruptly, I realized that he viewed this girl as a damsel in distress and wished her to see him as her rescuer. Henry could hardly play Sir Lancelot to her Guinevere, but he could, if he wished, burn her at the stake, and she knew it, for fear glittered in her beautiful eyes.

With the look of a man besotted, he gave the young beauty a gap-toothed smile that revealed his blackened teeth.

❖

ON THE EIGHTEENTH OF NOVEMBER, WE SET OUT FOR Sheen in a colorful procession, accompanied by the entire court. Musicians played as we rode with our entourage of lords and ladies, councilors in velvets and plumes, and knights in breast armor. Hounds barked and children laughed in their open litters, trailed by household officers, squires, grooms and pages, and the yeomen of the chamber and the guard. In carts at the back sat the men of the pantry and scullery, their pans and kettles clattering. Behind them rumbled many wagons of furnishings, clothes, state papers, and reliquaries. Some of the army accompanied us, rolling their guns. I was reminded of Richard's progress north to York in 1483. He had no armed men with him. His voice echoed in my ear: "I rest my rule on loyalty, not force," he'd said.

Amid the neighing of horses and shouts of men, the procession drew to a sudden halt. A pretty maiden selling roses had caught Henry's eye. She drew up to him and gave him a rose. There was a burst of excited tittering.

"What happened?" I inquired, and the answer came back down along the line. "The king gave her a pound for her rose!"

A pound for a rose. The generosity of a stingy man was always cause for marvel.

We moved again. A thunderous cheering went up at the sight of me. "God bless King Edward's daughter!" they cried with one voice. "God bless our queen, Elizabeth the Beloved!" The inevitable tear rose to my eye. I raised a hand to thank them. Ahead, Henry turned in his saddle to cast me an unsmiling look. My appearance had trumped his once again. In a way, I pitied him almost as much as the pretender. He had brought a measure of calm to English life, yet the land did not care for him, and fifty armed guards had to protect him everywhere he went.

All the guard I ever needed was his mother, I thought.

I watched his thin figure bobbing as he rode. He was not such a hard master at times. He loved music, could be affable, gave compliments to pretty women, and could occasionally be moved to charity, as with this maiden, but nothing he did endeared him to the people. *Not like Richard, who had been beloved by those who knew him.* But then, Henry and Richard stood at nearly opposite ends of the human spectrum.

It had been more than ten years since Bosworth, and I couldn't help comparing the two kings. At the gates of the cities he'd visited, Richard had refused the proffered gifts. "I would rather have your hearts than your money," he'd told his people. That could not be said for Henry. *He wants their hearts, aye,* I thought; *but he also wants their money.*

Henry wished to be seen as merciful; instead, he was regarded as ruthless, for he had put to death William Stanley, the man to whom he owed his crown. Richard had failed to see threat in anyone until it was too late; Henry suspected everyone before they committed a crime. Richard had won the goodwill of the north by dispensing justice, but there was only terror in Henry's courts, especially the Star Chamber, where verdicts were predetermined and punishments decided; whether guilty or innocent of the charge made no difference.

For when a bastard sits the throne of England, everyone is a threat and no one is safe, not even another bastard, as Johnnie of Gloucester has proved. The boy had disappeared into the Tower and likely died under torture, for he was never seen again. Many had shared his fate over the years, and more than anything else, it was fear that kept people from joining the pretender's side. Henry's reign had become one of terror.

I threw a glance behind me, at the carts. Somewhere back there, hidden away and surrounded by Henry's men and weapons, rode the captive Perkin Warbeck, Henry's rival in love and war. No doubt Perkin welcomed the brief respite. Every day in London he'd been led out through the streets to be cursed by the people. Kate told me he bore his misfortune with courage.

Sheen opened its gates to us. Set on a broad bend of the Thames, seven miles from London, the palace beckoned. Here on its lawns and amid its orchards, I had passed many pleasant summer afternoons with my brothers Edward and Dickon in the long grass alleys as they ratcheted the bucking crossbow or batted leather balls with the flat of their hands.

Is Dickon the one who now rides as prisoner?

I bit down hard against the sudden, searing anguish.

We settled into the palace and took up our games once again, but it became evident that Henry was still troubled.

"I know not what to do with Perkin," he confided in my privy chamber. "Maximilian has written begging me to spare him and send him back to Burgundy. In return he offers to give me any assurances I wish, any pledges I demand, to establish that he and Margaret and Perkin renounce in perpetuity all their rights to the English throne for themselves and all their heirs."

I was stunned. He and my Aunt Margaret were truly convinced that the young man was Dickon! Though their interests were no longer even remotely served by this pretender, he meant so much to them that they were willing to abandon all their claims to the throne merely to have him back. It was incredible, past belief, for it was not the way of royalty. But it afforded a miraculous resolution— one that would relieve great grief and sorrow.

"Oh, my lord, if you do this, all the world will hail you as the most merciful of kings!"

Henry threw me a sardonic smile. "Or the most foolish. There is Spain to consider, and Arthur's marriage." He fell silent for a long moment. The logs in the fireplace hissed. "I will do nothing to jeopardize it."

"Perhaps de Puebla can find out Spain's advice on the matter," I suggested, desperately clinging to hope.

We returned to Westminster Palace three days later for the Scottish ambassador to present his credentials.

"I wish Lady Gordon to attend my reception for the ambassador after the banquet," Henry said as we rode. "Pray see to it that she is brought to us."

I couldn't help wondering at the purpose of his strange request.

From gossip I learned what had transpired. After the feast, the Milanese and Venetian ambassadors accompanied Henry to a smaller chamber for more intimate conversation, and there they encountered Perkin and his wife standing in a corner, his arm around her waist. "He is twenty-three years old," one ambassador told the other, "a most noble man, and his wife a most beautiful woman. The king treats them well, but does not wish him to sleep with his wife."

Perkin and Catherine did not speak to the envoys but merely nodded to them as the ambassadors departed the reception.

The next morning, as I breakfasted in my privy chamber surrounded by Kate, Lucy, and my many other ladies, I gazed over at Catherine eating quietly at the end of the table. Her lustrous black hair was tied in a headdress of black ribbons, and she looked singularly beautiful in the black satin gown Henry had given her. She sat lost in thought amid the chatter, engulfed in a cloud of profound sorrow. Pity twisted my heart once again. She was the highest in rank in the land after Henry's mother and my two little princesses, and royal blood coursed in her veins. Everything was still possible for her. But she had refused to divorce Perkin. No matter what he confessed publicly, she believed he was who he claimed. For she loved him.

Love . . .

I shut my eyes on the memory.

AT YULETIDE MY BELOVED SON, ARTHUR, AGAIN RE-turned from Wales. He had grown taller since we last met, and he had the maturity that belonged to someone far older than his mere eleven years. I took his arm in the cobbled court at Sheen, and we walked together along the wide riverbank.

"What of this pretender—Perkin?" asked Arthur. "Father still seems rather unsettled by the whole business."

"He is," I murmured softly.

"But Perkin is a pretender, is he not?"

I heaved an audible breath. "Your father is unsure. There are—there are indications that he might be your Uncle Dickon. You know of Maximilian's offer?"

He nodded.

I regarded my dark-haired boy strolling languidly at my side. *How much he reminds me of Richard!* I blinked to banish the flash of wild grief that swept me. "What would you do, if you were in your father's place?"

" 'Tis not an easy place to be, and I cannot say for sure, you understand? But I would probably demand the most favorable trade terms for England that I could obtain from the Low Countries. To further assure Maximilian's good faith, I would seek a large annuity. This, in addition to the letters patent of assurances and oaths he has already promised renouncing all claims to the English throne, should prove sufficient. Then I'd send the pretender and his wife back to Burgundy."

"Oh, Arthur, my sweet son," I whispered. "What a fine king you shall make one day."

Yuletide festivities drew me to court more often now that Arthur was here, for I had no wish to miss a moment in his company. I clapped and laughed for the mummers, tumblers, and troubadours in a way I had not done for a long time. Yet my eye kept stealing to Henry's golden, strangely elegant captive strolling about the halls with his guards at his side. Unarmed, they resembled servants, which was Henry's intention. Crushed and beaten, the pretender was being exhibited at court as a token of Henry's utter confidence that no one would take him for anything but a fraud. He had given Perkin a trumpeter, and every so often, the man would sound his notes as if the king were coming. Then Perkin would appear, and all the court would laugh.

Many times I caught Harry and his friends tormenting the young man. I always put a stop to their cruelty, but I never spoke directly to Perkin. I knew Henry did not wish it, and besides, something held me back. For the same reason, though Catherine Gordon tended me and was at my side daily, we remained formal with one another and avoided mention of her husband. He was a dangerous subject for her, and I had no wish to stir more uncertainty for myself than I already felt. Sometimes at night I'd resolve to ask her about Perkin's birthmark. But in the morning, sanity always returned.

What if she lies to protect him?

What if she tells me the truth?

What if it has faded with adulthood so that she never knew of it?

Or Henry has burned it off, or cut it out, so it can no longer be proven?

No, 'tis best to leave the subject untouched.

If Mother had trusted me enough to give me the password, I could have known the truth.

It is as it is, I sighed in my misery.

THERE WAS MUCH TO CELEBRATE IN THIS MONTH
of December 1497, and the palace halls rang with merriment as we
drank to Perkin's capture, to Arthur's proxy marriage to the princess of Spain, and to Henry's truce with James IV. Though Margaret Beaufort took my right at banquets, and Arthur sat on Henry's
left, I could hear my son's voice, and the occasional glance he threw
me from around his father filled me with delight.

Arthur was a grave and serious boy, much given to books. I
thought again of Richard, who had driven himself mercilessly, always striving to do his best for his people, depriving himself of
much joy of life in order to tend his duties. I didn't want that to
happen to Arthur.

"Idleness is not a sin, Arthur," I told him, as we sat in the solar
with the family and friends. "We must enjoy life, my sweet son, for
time has a habit of flying from us. 'Tis good to sit in reflection and
contemplate God's creation. If you bury yourself in work all day,
you have no time for what is necessary to your soul."

I looked at six-year-old Harry spinning a four-sided disk like
a top as he played a game of All or Nothing with Maggie on the
colorful tiled floor. *No such worries about him,* I thought. *'Tis all
about pleasure for Harry.* He loved his lute, loved to dance, to ride
his horse and best his brother at jousting. He wrestled the servants
to the floor to the delight of his sisters, but he didn't know they
didn't wish to win, for that would incur one of his famous fits of
temper.

No concerns, either, about Maggie, I thought. She was already tall
at eight, and in addition to the love of gambling she had inherited
from her father, her favorite delight was flirting with boys.

As we feasted on dishes of trout, roasted pheasant, mutton richly
garnished in sauce, and eel in gelatin, I stole a glance at Henry's
new pet monkey with the white-whiskered face, which he led
around by a leather collar and chain. It was full of amusing tricks
and had become Henry's constant companion, especially when he
played at cards and dice, for Henry felt it brought him good fortune.
For this banquet, the monkey he called Prince had appeared in a

crimson velvet doublet. Everyone knew the intent was to mock the pretended "prince," Perkin. I thought it was a particularly cruel jest, and my heart went out to the young man, and to Catherine Gordon, who seemed near tears all through dinner.

That same night, as we sat in the royal apartments at Sheen, around Compline, suddenly servants yelled, "Fire in the king's chambers! Fire—fire!"

We dropped our games and books, gathered our pet dogs, and raced to the hallway. I turned toward Henry's chambers and gasped. Flames were sweeping the rushes on the floor and crackling up the costly wall hangings. Already smoke choked the room as carpets and tapestries caught alight.

"The children!" I screamed, running to the nursery with Kate at my side. We reached the threshold breathlessly. Men-at-arms roused Harry and Maggie from their beds, and Kate grabbed her children, Edward and Henry, and we all fled into the garden. Standing in the darkness, we watched the flames soar as men climbed to the roofs with buckets of water.

"Is someone trying to kill us?" Harry asked sleepily.

I smoothed his tousled hair. "No, Harry, of course not," I said. But I couldn't help wondering.

The fire raged for three hours, and plumes of black smoke billowed forth from the windows. Much of Sheen was destroyed. Standing beside me, Henry watched it burn.

"I shall rebuild an even more splendid palace," he vowed, "and name it Richmond."

CHAPTER 24

The White Rose, 1498

WE CELEBRATED HENRY'S FORTY-FIRST BIRTHDAY IN January, and in February, my thirty-second. On Shrove Tuesday, the day before Lent, we feasted on puddings, pastries, and exotic delicacies served with flourishes of the clarion between courses. In the royal park and the village green, as they had done for centuries, boys spent the day in cockfights, and also "throwing at cocks," a game in which they hurled sticks at their target from a distance until they killed it. Seven-year-old Harry, whose arms and chest were unusually strong for his age because of his consuming passion for sports, slew more birds than any other child and was proclaimed the winner, to his great pride.

Maundy Thursday followed Ash Wednesday, and as was my custom, I distributed to poor women the shoes I had collected for them all year. A week later, tender spring broke into splendor across the land. Birds twittered in the branches and the earth shrugged off its dismal gray for the lime palette of glorious rebirth. To celebrate the advent of May, we decorated the palace with hawthorn branches and watched maidens dance around the gilded Maypole. In the evenings we played dice and card games of Triumph, Torment, and Who Wins Loses. It was the season of tournaments, and as June neared, the blare of trumpets and clash of steel could be heard around Windsor.

All the while Perkin was with us: free, yet captive, for invisible silken chains bound him as securely as iron fetters. He strolled around Westminster Palace at apparent liberty, his two guards that passed for servants at his side, but he could not escape the mockery and disdain that followed him wherever he went.

At Greenwich, after breakfast in the Great Hall, as I gave my orders for the day to my steward, my glance kept stealing to Perkin standing with Catherine Gordon in a far corner of the Great Hall by one of the tall mullioned windows that lay open to the breeze from the cool river. The splashing of a fountain and melodic notes of a lute could be heard in the garden below, but Perkin and Catherine Gordon seemed oblivious to everything except one another. Then Perkin lifted his hand and gently tucked a stray lock of hair away behind Catherine's ear. She smiled up at him.

They are like a pair of turtledoves in a gilded cage, I thought. Perkin had to be in torment. He could set his eyes on the woman he loved and hold her hand, but he couldn't provide for her as a husband should, or make her his again in the way ordained by nature. He did not know what had become of their little son, and he was a jest at court, as much as Dick the fool, or Patch, or Henry's monkey. Children laughed and threw rotten fruit in his direction before running away, and servants scowled and spat after him as he passed. Yet he endured his humiliation with dignity.

As for Catherine Gordon, she remained true to her husband through all Henry's efforts to woo her. Again, Henry had offered to obtain a divorce for her, but she declined, saying Perkin would always have her heart. Henry had a riding cloak made for himself in tawny velvet edged with black satin, and sent her a matching gown with a kirtle of black worsted, and ribbons for her girdle. He even gave her a set of hose lined with soft white gauze, a gift of the most intimate nature. She had returned all his presents with fair words, explaining that she expected to remain in mourning forever. The implication was clear. She would have none other than the captive who was her husband, though a king sought her heart.

Another round of painful memories assailed me, and I recalled the days of my youth; that time of hope, dreams, and darkness when I felt my blood warm, when I ached with longing for what I knew was impossible to have and had better never mention.

I realized with a start that my steward had asked me a question. "What did you say?" I asked him, for the servants made much noise as they cleared the room, and one had dropped the trestle table he was removing.

"You will receive petitioners after luncheon until Nones, my queen? Is three hours not tiring for you?"

"I thank you for your concern, but I can manage it today." I gave him a smile and added, "Pray, request Doctor de Puebla to come to me."

He withdrew with a bow. I moved to the window. As I waited for de Puebla, I stole sidelong glances at Perkin and Catherine Gordon, far down along the wall, turning over in my mind my conversation with Kate the previous morning.

"Henry's besotted with her," Kate had said. "Anyone can see that. He follows her around with lovesick eyes."

"He had Bernard Andre write an account of his meeting with her," I had replied. "In Andre's version, he is the powerful and compassionate king rescuing a grateful royal maiden from the clutches of the lying wastrel who abducted her. He's over forty now, and 'tis clearly the pathetic fantasy of an old man. He carries the scene around with him hidden in a plain brown leather book, and reads it as I play the harp for him in my chamber, thinking I do not know what it is."

Kate regarded me with pained eyes. "How do you feel about that, Elizabeth?"

And how did I feel about it? "Grieved, naturally." And angry. *Angrier than I cared to admit.*

"But you don't love him. You never have. Doesn't that make a difference?"

I gave a sigh. Kate was right; not loving Henry should make it easier to bear, but it didn't. "Aye, but we have shared much together, and now I am forced to watch him make a fool of himself—and of me—over this poor girl."

Kate had placed her hand gently on mine. "I don't know how you bear it all."

I endure it as I have endured all that has come my way, I thought; *I seek comfort in prayer, and somehow find strength to abide what God has chosen to send me.*

I tore my eyes from the young couple down the hall and forced myself to focus on de Puebla, who approached. He bowed before me, and I gave him my hand to kiss.

"Doctor de Puebla, the matter I wish to discuss is this," I said. "I have spoken to my lord King Henry about your money troubles, dear ambassador, and we believe we have found a way for you to dispose of them permanently." I gave him a smile. "Doctor de Puebla, King Henry wishes to offer you a bishopric. A rich diocese would provide you the means of living as well as any lord."

As I awaited de Puebla's answer, from the corner of my eye I saw Harry's new tutor, John Skelton, appear in the arched entry at the opposite end of the room. He was Margaret Beaufort's appointee, a poet whose credentials from Oxford and Cambridge had brought him to her attention. He had been a fixture around court since 1495, writing and reciting his rhymes along with Andre. In his black gown and round cap, with his darting eyes and sharp little movements, he reminded me of a bat. Catching sight of Perkin and Catherine Gordon, he swooped around and dived on them, a dark look on his face.

De Puebla gave me a low bow. "Your Grace, your offer is beyond generous. I know not what to say—"

I took his hand in my own. "Accept, Doctor de Puebla."

"How I wish I could, beloved and gracious queen! But first I must seek the permission of my masters, the King and Queen of Spain. I cannot offend them."

"Absolutely, my dear doctor. We shall await your decision." I intended to leave, but my eye fell on Skelton. Unaware of my presence at the far end of the hall, he was shouting at Perkin. A fragment of what he said reached my ear. "How dare you—naught but a fart!"

I blushed at his words. De Puebla turned to look down the

room at him. Nearby, my ladies-in-waiting ceased their chatter. I called to Lucy. She left the group and came to my side.

"Pray inform Lady Gordon that we much enjoyed our game of cards last evening and wish her to sup with us tonight in our private chamber," I said.

A knowing look came into Lucy's eyes, for it was a way not only to alert Skelton to my presence, but also to remind him of my favor toward Perkin's wife. She gave me a curtsy and departed on her errand.

"Your Grace," de Puebla said softly, "I have never met a more tenderhearted and kinder queen." Hastily, he added, "Excepting my own Queen Isabella, of course. I am certain it shall greatly comfort the princess Catherine of Aragon to know what blessing she shall find in you when she is far from Spain."

"I look forward to welcoming her as my own daughter." I smiled.

My gaze went back to Lucy. She had approached Lady Gordon, and now the entire group turned to me. Skelton colored and threw me a low bow before quitting the room. Lady Gordon fell into a graceful curtsy. Perkin's face I could not read, but I thought I saw anguish in his gaze, reflecting my own feelings when I looked at him. De Puebla waited with me while Lucy spoke to Perkin and Catherine.

"What was the problem?" I asked when she returned.

"It appears that Perkin was teaching little Henry Courtenay the skill of harping the other day, and Master Skelton did not take kindly to that. He regards music as his purview and feels that Perkin overstepped his abilities and the bounds of propriety by so doing."

"I thank you, Lucy," I said. "By your leave, Doctor de Puebla, I must prepare for my duties this day." I inclined my head to him.

Troubled by Skelton, I made a detour to my chambers past Harry's schoolroom. Coarse and petty, filled with his own self-importance, Skelton was kind and complimentary to those he liked, but spiteful and vindictive to those who displeased him. In a quarrel with a fellow poet, he'd dedicated a verse to him that said, in part:

Hidden in my hose,
I have a rose
that is perfect for your Scottish nose.

As I approached, I heard Harry asking a question to which Skelton replied. But I did not know what they discussed until I drew near.

"There shall always be plots and rebellions as long as your cousin, the Earl of Warwick, lives. Indeed, as long as Warbeck lives! Repeat what I have told you."

" 'Tis better that one man die," Harry responded dutifully, "so more do not perish."

"Exactly."

I gave a gasp and halted my steps. *Skelton condones murder. He is teaching Harry how to kill with a clean conscience, and never feel the blood on his hands!* I was reminded of his scathing poem to another of his many enemies in which he said he would exult to see him butchered at Tyburn. I willed myself forward. As I came into view, Skelton, Harry, and Henry Courtenay all scrambled to their feet. They bowed, and I set my gaze at a point past Skelton's head, so that I would not have to look at him.

"Your Grace," Skelton said, "Prince Harry is a brilliant pupil, superior to any I taught at Oxford or Cambridge. He is a delightful small new rose. One who is half god, born of kingly stock."

Harry beamed, but Skelton's effusive flattery offended me. Brilliant Harry certainly was, but he already had an exalted opinion of himself and such words only fanned his resentment of his secondary place in the order of things. Skelton presented Henry to him as the divine instrument to end a century of conflict, and Harry was growing up to believe his father's propaganda that the Tudor children had a unique relationship with God and were the offspring of a miracle. He was jealous of Arthur and extremely competitive with everyone else, and these were worrisome traits in a prince who would wield the kind of power Harry would inherit.

"You speak of ideals and you have instilled a delight of literature in Prince Harry, but much of what children learn is by example," I said pointedly.

He bowed again.

He knew I was without influence, and though he caught my meaning, he would likely not change his behavior. I left them, more troubled than before. This man of low virtue did not make a suitable tutor for a prince. I debated whether to complain to Henry. There would be a confrontation with Margaret Beaufort naturally, and unpleasantness would surely follow. No it was best to remain silent and have peace. *Besides, what good would it do? My opinion is ignored when it conflicts with hers.* He had given her the responsibility of educating our children, for it kept her too busy to meddle in his affairs of state.

My helplessness weighed on me all day, and in a state of despondency, I took to my bed immediately after dinner. Even so, the next day, Trinity Sunday, the ninth of June, broke too soon. Before I was ready, as if in a dream, I heard sounds of confusion: voices calling, the patter of running feet, mumbling, and weeping.

Someone shook me. "Wake up, wake up!" they cried.

I opened my eyes. Kate was gazing down at me urgently. I raised myself to an elbow. "What is it? What's happened?"

"Perkin! It's Perkin! He's escaped!"

Henry seemed strangely unconcerned when he came to visit me in my chamber later that evening.

"How could Perkin escape when he sleeps with two guards in your wardrobe on a high floor?" I inquired, trying not to seem suspicious as I embroidered at my loom.

"Someone was careless," Henry replied. "They left the window open."

"Why would he even try to escape? Where can he go? He has no money, no friends. He knows it's hopeless."

"He always runs away. From Tournai, from Ireland, from Scotland. 'Tis what he does."

It was a particularly unsatisfactory reply, and Henry knew it.

"To run away in his circumstances is stupid, and Perkin is no fool," I persisted. "He speaks Latin and four other languages; he writes and reads, and plays three musical instruments. He rides well and knows how to handle knightly weapons. That would make him a genius for a boatman's son."

"He knows these arts because your aunt trained him!" Henry exclaimed, leaping to his feet. "I will thank you to keep out of my business, madame." He swung on his heel and left my chamber.

I gazed after him. There was something sinister about Perkin's escape. Henry was in love with Perkin's wife, and he had the power to rid himself of his rival. Why would he not use it? Especially as Isabella and Ferdinand had finally sent back their reply.

Their advice to Henry was that as long as Perkin Warbeck and Edward, Earl of Warwick, lived, they could not send their daughter to wed Arthur.

✦

PERKIN WAS RECAPTURED FOUR DAYS LATER AND taken to the Tower to be lodged in the cell directly beneath Edward, Earl of Warwick. After a private audience with Henry, Catherine Gordon was deprived of all her servants save one. The general consensus held that she'd had something to do with helping her husband escape. I knew that was not so. Henry was punishing her because she rejected his advances even now, when her husband was lost to her forever.

I was swept with sorrow for the young beauty.

In July, a delegation arrived from my Aunt Margaret, headed by the high-ranking Bishop of Cambrai. In a corner of my chamber, with the door and windows closed to eavesdroppers, de Puebla confided to me what he had witnessed.

"On Monday morning, July thirtieth, King Henry himself conducted me and the bishop to the Tower. The bishop asked for Perkin to be brought out, so he could see him and talk to him. It seems your aunt, the Duchess of Burgundy, wished to find out how he was. 'Tis said she is so restlessly unhappy about Perkin's plight that she is willing to do anything, make any promises, to persuade King Henry to return Perkin to her. Her only hope is that Cambrai can still save her White Rose."

"Was he brought out?"

De Puebla nodded, but fell silent.

"Did you see him?"

De Puebla nodded once again.

"How is he?" I pressed, swept with a terrible sense of unease.

De Puebla heaved an audible sigh and let it out slowly. "He is much changed, my queen. I almost didn't recognize him. He is . . . He is *desfigurado*. They have broken his face."

My eyes widened with horror.

"He cannot live much longer," De Puebla added softly.

I made my way to a chair, and collapsed.

De Puebla averted his gaze from me. "He was brought in wearing foot shackles and the kind of neck and hand manacles wild animals have when performing." He hesitated a moment before he went on. "In the Chapel of Our Lady he was made to kneel in his chains and solemnly swear before the Bishop of Cambrai that Duchess Margaret knew—as he himself knew—that he was not who he said he was—" He broke off.

I bit my lip. Perkin was repeating what he'd been told to say.

"It serves him right," de Puebla finished.

He, too, was saying what he was expected to say. I dropped my hand from my brow and looked at the old man through my tears.

"YOU DIDN'T NEED TO TORTURE HIM!" I CRIED TO Henry that night, pacing to and fro, wringing my hands. Never had I been so agitated, so furious, or felt my helplessness so wretchedly. "You can make him say or do anything you want merely by threatening harm to his wife and child!"

"It was necessary," Henry said calmly.

I halted my steps and whirled on him. "For what purpose? Give me one reason!?"

"Because the world thinks he is your brother." He looked at me coldly, with a piercing gaze. "And because you think so, too, do you not?"

I opened my mouth to deny it, but I closed it without a word. There was nothing more to be said.

Or was there?

Yet one more reason remained for such brutality; one he had not mentioned. More than anything else, he wished to destroy the face that Catherine Gordon loved. I lifted my eyes back to his, and what I saw there sent a cold shiver racing along my spine. I could not breathe and my chest felt as if it would burst. A ghastly thought took shape in the far reaches of my mind and, fed by fear, grew into appalling proportions; like a shadow, it stole forward and loomed over me.

"You believe it, too, don't you?" I breathed. " 'Tis why you destroyed his face! Before you kill him, he must be stripped of his resemblance to my family, so you can do the deed!"

Henry said nothing. Behind the opaqueness of his eyes, something stirred.

I tore my gaze from his and sank into a chair, feeling as if I were devoured by blackness. My mother's words of long ago clamored in my head. *Well he knows that if Dickon lives, he is a usurper.* Dimly, through the tumult in my head, I heard my husband's footsteps fade away on the tiled floor. The door shut. A terrible silence engulfed me.

I looked up at the empty space he had occupied before me, a single thought thundering in my ears, my heart, my soul. *Perkin must die because he is Dickon.*

⚙

THERE WAS TALK OF RESCUE, BUT THE PLOT WAS DIS-covered before it could bud. Henry told my Aunt Margaret and Maximilian that he would not release Perkin, but if they agreed to cease all efforts on his behalf, he might not kill him. He told James IV of Scotland that if he agreed to a truce and a marriage with our daughter Maggie, he would ensure the safety and honorable treatment of his cousin, Catherine Gordon.

A letter arrived for Henry from Aunt Margaret; it was the first she had ever written him. In a most civil tone, she offered an apology for her behavior of the past and promised not to make any more trouble. Maximilian did the same. I knew this was their last hope of saving Perkin, and I wondered at the strength of their faith in him, and at their willingness to humble themselves before Henry to beg for his life.

Was he my brother, Dickon?

He has to be my brother.

He must not be my brother.

Oh, Blessed Virgin, help me to accept what is!

I feared that worse was yet to come. Henry wanted this marriage between England and Spain desperately, for the alliance
would stamp his kingship with legitimacy, and he would no longer
be seen as a usurper, but as the founder of a proud new dynasty.

With the advent of October, a heavy listlessness settled over me
and all I saw when I looked around me was darkness. I was pregnant again and I couldn't help wondering how many more babes I
would have to bear before God permitted me rest. Then Yuletide
came, and Arthur appeared, shining before my eyes like the sun at
the zenith of a bright day. Tearful with joy, I embraced my beloved
son. Before I realized it, the new year of 1499 was blowing in on a
ferocious storm that shook the ground beneath our feet. Twelfth
Night followed swiftly on its heels. I bid him farewell once more,
and the sun faded from the sky as I watched him leave.

In February, I received the news of the death of Cecily's husband, Viscount Welles, with little emotion. I did not know him
well; he was merely one of the faces that came and went at court.
Nor does Cecily seem to mourn him deeply, I thought, watching her
laugh with friends, dressed in her black widow's weeds. One day
she disappeared from the palace, and all I could learn about her was
that she'd gone to Lincolnshire. Even Kate didn't know more. I put
her from my mind; she would be back when it suited her.

CHAPTER 25

Blood of Roses, 1499

TEN DAYS AFTER MY THIRTY-THIRD BIRTHDAY, WHICH
I spent in the darkness of my bedchamber under the watchful eye
of Margaret Beaufort, I gave birth to a third boy-child, who was
named Edmund, for Henry's father. Margaret Beaufort was elated,
but Henry barely rejoiced and merely patted my hand and murmured that I had done well. He had been morose and irritable
all winter. No doubt Warbeck and Warwick weighed on his mind,
along with Catherine Gordon, who still rejected his overtures. As
for me, I felt weary, listless. The days bore down heavily on me, and
I wished only to sleep through the grayness of February.

"I have asked my astrologer, William Parron, for a reading on
Warwick," Henry announced to me one day in mid-March as he
sat at my bedside. "I shall take it here, in your chamber."

Candles flickered in the iron candelabras and on the large table
but failed to cheer the room, for the day was gloomy, filled with
shifting shadows. I accepted my seat with trepidation and watched
the bearded man in the long brown gown lay out his charts.

"I have examined at great length the signs at the birth of a certain man not of base birth—"

My cousin, Edward Plantagenet, Earl of Warwick.

"It is difficult to describe how hopeless his stars were at the time he was born. All the triple lights were unlucky, set firmly in the house of death." He pointed to an intersection of lines on the chart. "See here—Mars in conjunction with the sun signified the execution of the father and the destruction of his property. For the young man himself, it meant the clash of iron and combustion of fire."

"War?" said Henry.

"Indeed, sire. The positions of Saturn and Mars spelled utter destitution and prison. The movement of the moon between them meant that nothing he desired would come to pass. See this aspect—" Parron turned the chart toward Henry and me. "It means he is imprisoned. Shackled. Troubled."

I averted my eyes from the hideous chart. His words meant nothing to me. I had never put great store in omens or astrology, and I suspected Parron was telling Henry what he wished to hear. And Henry wanted me to bear witness so I would absolve him of the crime he was about to commit.

"The young man is unlucky not only in himself, but also, despite his impotence, for England. He shall be a lasting focus of unrest and rebellion"—Parron met Henry's eyes, but glanced away from mine, as I did from his—"until death removes him."

"Am I justified in keeping him in prison?" demanded Henry.

"Absolutely. A prince may imprison another prince for fear of insurrection. That is without sin."

"What if I put him to death?"

I tensed; beneath the table I tightened my grip of my chair.

"That, too, is not necessarily an evil act. A judge who condemns a man to death for a crime does not sin unless he revels in the death."

"What if the condemned is innocent?" Henry demanded.

"Christ was innocent, and His death was the most evil act of all, yet God ordained it for the good of mankind. Considered in this light, Christ's death was an act of charity and mercy." The astrologer looked at his charts, and added, "It is undoubtedly good for the land that this one man die in order to preserve the peace."

Henry inhaled a long breath and let it out thoughtfully. " 'Tis what Caiaphas said of Jesus, is it not?"

The astrologer nodded.

The words were those Skelton had made Harry recite, and instantly I knew it was no coincidence. Behind Henry stood Parron and Skelton, and behind them both Margaret Beaufort and Cardinal Morton, working the strings of their puppets, turning their actions from black into white and making their policy seem as if ordained by God Himself.

I rose from the table and went to the window. The winter frost lay thick as glass on the panes, and I could see nothing. From behind me came the sound of parchment being folded, of pen and ink being put away, and the click of a door closing. I did not turn. I merely fixed my gaze on a small pitcher of intermingled white and red roses set on a coffer by the edge of the window. *If I had fled Sheriff Hutton all those years ago, would this be happening now?*

Henry appeared at my side.

"You understand that it must be done?"

"I do not understand."

Henry said roughly, "Did you follow his explanation?"

I looked at him. "I followed it. But I am not fooled. Nor are you. You want me to sanction what you wish to do to Warwick, who is innocent of any crime against you, and whom you have imprisoned since childhood. I cannot condone murder. 'Tis an evil act, whatever this astrologer says."

"For God's sake, Elizabeth, you are not making this easy!" He slammed a fist on the wood chest. " 'Tis either Edward or Arthur! Kill or be killed. One must die so the other can live. There cannot be two claimants in a land. You of all people should know that."

The image of young Edward's little figure surrounded by guards as he disappeared into the Tower flashed before me, and I heard my father's words of long ago. *Sometimes a king must do what he knows is wrong, what is hateful to him. For the peace of the land.*

"I pray you leave me, my lord. I cannot listen anymore." Swept with desolation, I closed my eyes and leaned my head against the stone embrasure of the window.

Henry strode to the door and slammed it shut behind him. My

glance returned to the vase of white and red roses, and the emotion I had held back by force of will flooded me all at once. I grabbed the vase and hurled it against the wall.

❀

AS WE PLAYED DICE IN THE SOLAR WITH HARRY BY torchlight, while frost still lined the garden paths of Westminster, there came news of a young man on the borders of Norfolk who claimed to be Edward, Earl of Warwick, escaped from the Tower.

"He is a youth named Ralph Wulford, the younger son of a shoemaker who lives in Bishopsgate, Your Grace. Apart from a priest who preached his cause, he has no adherents," said the spy.

"Pick him up and hang him for treason," replied Henry.

"Henry, I pray you to reconsider!" I pleaded. "What threat can he pose?"

Henry pushed to his feet angrily. "The rebellions never stop! Must this procession of pretenders go on forever? Shall I be made to end like Richard, dispossessed of everything I own? I care not about his youth or that he has no adherents. He must be made to hang—to hang until he rots!" Henry glanced at Harry before returning his gaze to me. "Think on it, madame. Is this what you would have for your son?"

I put a hand to my throbbing head.

Weeks later, as April glimmered, a man-at-arms came to Henry.

"Sire, Wulford was hanged on a gibbet at St. Thomas Watering. He has dangled there in shirt and hose since Shrove Tuesday. The stench has grown so foul that passersby complain of annoyance. My liege, may we have permission to take down the rotted corpse?"

Henry nodded assent.

It was at this time that Henry angrily informed me Cecily had married a humble Lincolnshire knight by the name of Thomas Kyme and gone to live on the Isle of Wight without his royal permission.

I set down my Book of Hours and rose to my feet, unable to comprehend what I heard. " 'Tis impossible! Cecily cares too much for wealth and position to wed a humble squire."

"Welladay, she has done it. As of now, she has no wealth or position to concern herself about, because I am confiscating all her lands. Nor is she welcome at court."

I didn't know what to make of Cecily's marriage. It was scarce to be believed, but since she had done it of her own free will, I could not help wishing her well. And in spite of myself, I did miss her.

On a dreary morning at the end of October, Kate came to me as I sat on the bench in the walled garden below my bed chamber, reading Boethius. I looked up at her, and the expression on her face sent a shiver through my body.

"Perkin and Edward were caught escaping from the Tower," Kate said.

She took a seat beside me. I had told her what to expect, and it came as no surprise to her that they had managed such a feat, one never before accomplished in the history of the Tower. No surprise, either, that they were so easily recaptured, and that no one questioned the story.

No one ever questions anything Henry tells them, not if they value their life. Nevertheless, Kate had been weeping and her eyes were red-rimmed. I gave a heavy sigh and took her hand. We sat together in silence, staring at the garden where autumn had turned the leaves to gold.

"Even the trees are dressed for death." I sighed.

❖

WE DIDN'T HAVE TO WAIT LONG FOR THE ANNOUNCE-ment. Perkin was to die on the twenty-third of November, the Feast of St. Clement's. It was a Saturday, the day of the week that Henry considered his most fortuitous. On that morning, the young man, who was believed to be my brother Richard, Duke of York, by all the world save England, was drawn on a hurdle behind a horse for three miles, through muddy streets littered with dung and fallen leaves, to Tyburn, where a huge crowd awaited.

Kate's husband, William Courtenay, and de Puebla witnessed the execution, but only William was prepared to give us the details. De Puebla, with tears in his eyes, begged to be excused. I inclined my head and watched him leave. William stood before us in my bedchamber, which had been emptied of all my ladies except Kate. He took his time before launching into his report.

"A large crowd came to see him die. They wanted to hear his confession, for men do not lie at the point of death." William spoke haltingly, in a low tone. "Wearing the simple knee-length white shirt that is the garb of the condemned, Perkin climbed the small ladder up to the scaffold. His wrists were bound and he had difficulty, so the guards pushed him up. When he arrived on the platform, the executioner placed the halter on him. Perkin didn't say who he was, but he told the people that he was not who he was thought to be. At the end of the confession, he asked for the forgiveness of God, and the king, and all others he might have offended."

William fell silent and took a moment to compose himself before he went on. "Then he gave himself up to the executioners and went to his death meekly, as our Lord Jesus is said to have done. He was granted mercy, and was not disemboweled at the end. He just hung there, by the neck, in his white shirt. He did not struggle but waited patiently for death. The crowd watched and waited with him. It took him an hour to die."

I averted my face and swallowed hard, for a suffocating sensation constricted my throat.

"Some in the crowd still believed he was your brother, Richard of York, though he did not look much like him anymore," William murmured.

A lengthy silence fell.

"May God in His infinite mercy grant him blessing and eternal rest," I whispered, making the sign of the cross, "whoever he may have been."

❁

I HAVE LEARNED THAT THE FIRST DAY AFTER A DEATH is the hardest.

You wake up to a vast emptiness of soul that is as trackless, shoreless, and boundless as the skies that stretch over your head. The dawn is always bleak and gray. Church bells toll, monks chant, and it seems that all the world weeps with you. Yet you know you are alone.

Perkin lay dead at twenty-four years of age, in the summer of his life. I did not know who he was, but somewhere deep within my being I believed him to be Dickon. That he had denied being Dickon meant nothing. Henry had taken his child, and Perkin, to protect his babe, had uttered the words Henry wished England to hear. Probably, too, he had been offered mercy and wished to spare himself the agony of a hand groping inside his entrails while he still lived. He was never brave, had always detested bloodshed.

I thought of Catherine, who mourned Perkin as the husband she had loved and as the father of the child she would likely never see again. Her loss was infinitely greater than mine had been after Bosworth. And still, all these years later, I remember how I'd grieved for Richard, how hard it was for me.

The castle stirred around me but gently; the voices were subdued, the steps quiet, as if everyone walked on tiptoe. I kept to my chamber and gave orders not to be disturbed. Even so, Kate came to me that same night.

"The king is here to see you," she said.

"I do not wish to see the king," I replied.

"What shall I tell him?"

"Tell him I am indisposed and know not when I shall be well again." Then I went to my prie-dieu and bowed my head in prayer for Perkin. *O Christ, my God, O Christ, my Refuge, O Christ, King and Lord; Have mercy upon him; pardon all his transgressions; shelter his soul in the shadow of Thy wings. Make known to him Thy grace.*

I committed myself to prayer for the next day, and the following, and the one that came after that. For death crouched beside me, waiting, and I feared to sleep for the dreams that plagued me, and I feared not to sleep for the thoughts that tormented me. I begged Kate to stay and share my bed. When she agreed, I embraced her tightly.

"O Kate, Kate—how different it would have been had King Richard lived!" I wept, giving voice to my anguish for the first time in my life. "I miss him more with each year that passes, Kate." It was dangerous to speak such things, and dangerous for Kate to hear them. The strength ebbed from me; I let her go and dropped into a chair. I closed my eyes.

Kate rested a hand on my shoulder. "How you have borne it all, I know not."

"Arthur," I murmured on a breath, enfolding her hand with my own.

❖

MY COUSIN EDWARD, THE CHILD I HAD KNOWN AND loved, died by the headsman's axe five days after Perkin, on the twenty-eighth of November, 1499, at two o'clock in the afternoon. He was led out between two guards to Tower Green. It was a private execution. There was no one to watch, no one to comfort him, and no one to weep. As soon as he was pronounced dead, the sky turned black and rain poured down as if it would never cease. Fierce winds, thunder, and lightning shook the palace windows. All over England, there was flooding. It was as if Heaven itself grieved.

A great despair descended upon me. Amid the gilded tapestries of my room, I lay down. I had sent Catherine Gordon a gift of a Book of Hours on Perkin's death, but who was left to mourn poor little Edward but me? In his twenty-four years of life he had run free over the fields for less than two of them, and that was the sweet interlude when Anne and Richard had taken him into their family. All who had loved him were dead now; he, like King Richard and Johnnie of Gloucester, had been born into calamity.

Oh, Richard, if you could have foreseen what would follow, would you still have cast your life away?

But I, too, shared blame for the blood that had flowed since Bosworth. Had I fled Sheriff Hutton, a Tudor could not have remained king and none of this would have taken place. But in my moment of great tragedy, blinded by loss and by grief, I had the misguided thought that I could save a nation. And I had stayed.

I hated this new world I'd helped create; this frightening and sinister place where a groom's bastard grandchild could be a king, and the bastard could send a king's son to meet a traitor's death. Never had Fate reveled so heartily in her jest! I could almost hear her laughter in my ears.

Save a nation.

What arrogance!

All these years, God has been punishing me for my sin of pride, and I never understood until now.

That night I dreamt of Richard on his white horse riding out of shadows and mist, charging toward me, the crown on his helmet glimmering in the gloom, but instead of a rose, he held a battle-axe in his hand. I bolted upright in bed with a scream on my lips.

"What is it?" Kate asked, placing an arm around my shoulders.

"A dream, Kate." I shuddered and drew the blanket tightly around me. "Naught but a dream. Go back to sleep, sister."

But I lay awake in the darkness. Twice before Richard had come to me this way, and both times he'd brought me comfort. This felt different. This time I was afraid.

CHAPTER 26

Lost Princess, 1500

"THE KING HAS TAKEN ILL AT WANSTEAD," KATE whispered, "so ill, there is murmuring of the succession."

I heard her dimly. I didn't wish death on anyone, but I derived little personal happiness from my marriage. I had endured for England's sake, and for Arthur's, yet the blood cost kept rising. It would be a blessing to see Arthur on the throne.

But Henry recovered. Through the fog that engulfed me, I heard Kate tell me that he had returned to Westminster.

I remained cloistered in my chamber until Arthur arrived in mid-December. Donning one of my wide-sleeved black velvet gowns, a heavy fur-lined cloak, and a jeweled headdress, I met him near the entry to the Great Hall of Rufus. The sight of his sweet face brought a smile to my heart, my first since meeting Henry's astrologer.

"Arthur, my dear son!" I took his arm, unable to tear my gaze from his face, my eyes misting as I looked up at him.

"Mother, you have lost much weight. You are not ill, I pray?" he asked anxiously.

I gave him a smile as I clung to him. "No, I am well enough, and even better now that you are here safe at my side. 'Tis Yule, and that is my favorite time of year for I always know I shall see you, my beloved son." I threw a glance at his attendants hovering in the background. "Shall we go to the river for a stroll? I would like to be alone with you before others claim your attention." I hung on him as I walked, for I had not much strength after three weeks confined to bed, and I noticed that he had slowed his pace on my account.

"How is Father?" he asked, as we approached the wide Thames.

A wind blew. I caught at my cloak. "I know not. I haven't seen him since—since—"

Arthur pressed his hand over mine. His gesture gave me courage to broach the subject that had assailed me since Edward of Warwick's death. Henry would never relax his white-knuckled grip on the crown until death pried it loose. And what of Arthur? Would he choose to murder innocents to keep his throne safe?

"Dear son, I worry greatly what lessons your father's actions are teaching you."

He paused his steps and tightened his hold of my arm. He threw a glance around for eavesdroppers, but our retinue followed far behind. "Mother, rest assured I would not have done what Father did. I see the world with your eyes. Mind you, I do not criticize him. He did what he felt necessary, but I would have handled the problem differently. There are always options." After a pause, he added, "I would probably have sent Perkin back to Burgundy. 'Tis no doubt reckless of me."

A tear found its wayward path down my cheek. "Mercy is not reckless, my dear one. To have the hearts of your people is a great thing. It will take time, and it is by far the harder path, but in the end, that is your measure as a king. And as a man."

We walked and chatted, and watched the barges pass, and listened to the screech of the seabirds against the morning cold. The air hung heavy with moisture, and I felt revived by the time we returned to the palace. Oblivious of where we were headed, joyous merely to be near him, I followed where he led, and we turned into the presence chamber. We both came to a sudden halt. Harry, who had arrived the day before from Eltham, stood on the dais, playing a game with his friends.

"Take your positions," Harry was saying. "You're the executioner," he told a friend, "and you're the condemned," he said, pointing to Kate's son, Henry Courtenay, who knelt at his feet.

"I am afraid to die this way. Pray, Your Great Majesty, allow me to live!"

"Traitors must be punished. Therefore, you shall be tied to a hurdle and dragged through the streets to Tyburn where the executioner—"

"Harry!" I cried. "How dare you disobey me? What did I tell you the last time I caught you in here?"

"Mother, I do not disobey you. I am not sitting on the throne this time." He regarded me with his angelic, innocent face.

For a moment, I was at a loss for words. "Nevertheless, I forbid you to play such games. You may leave."

The children scrambled out of the room. I took Arthur's arm again, my head throbbing. "You shall have to watch Harry," I said under my breath.

"No, Mother. These are but boyhood games. He'll grow out of them."

Arthur's words brought me little comfort. Harry was learning ruthlessness, not only from Henry's actions, but from Skelton, and Morton, and especially Margaret Beaufort, who doted on him and filled his head with her ideas. And I could not stop them.

I forced my dismal thoughts gone. This was a precious time, and too brief. I could not afford to waste my golden moments with Arthur. We chatted quietly together as we made our way through the passageway. By the time I took in my surroundings again, we were at the nursery door.

Ten-month-old Edmund looked up at us, surrounded by his nurses. He toddled to me, screeching, "Mama, Mama!" Then he noticed Arthur and stared at him with bright blue eyes as round and wide as cornflowers. "Dah?" he said, grabbing my skirts, pointing.

Arthur laughed heartily. "That probably means 'Who are you?' Doesn't it, Mother?"

I turned my smile on Arthur again, suffused with love. "Probably."

Arthur knelt down on one knee, and grinned. "Edmund, fair brother, 'tis time you met the eldest in your family. So how have you been? Up to a good deal of mischief, I am sure." He rumpled his brother's corn-colored hair, picked him up, and tossed him high into the air. Edmund seemed shocked at first, but after Arthur caught him and set him down on his little legs, he put his arms out to be tossed again.

Edmund's nurses laughed with admiring looks in their eyes as they gazed at my lanky, dark-haired son. *He is handsome indeed, and fortunate is the Spanish princess,* I thought, a pang squeezing my heart.

We bid them adieu and made for Henry's chambers.

I did not wish to see him. I would have been glad never to see him again. But that could not be. I had to make my peace with him and find a way to go forward.

I fell silent as we approached his chamber. He was seated at the table, his head bowed, writing in his little black book. I hung back as Arthur strode into the room and called out, brightly, "Father!"

Henry glanced up, and his eyes lit with joy. He put his book away and pushed out of his chair. Standing in the doorway, I stared at him in shock. He had aged twenty years since I last saw him! He was forty-two years old, but looked sixty. His hair had turned white, and he had lost much weight. His bony cheeks were sunken and hollow; his brow lined with deep furrows; his mouth and eyes etched with lines that had not been there a month earlier. Where he had played a hard game of tennis as late as this past summer, he now drooped over the table, bent and shriveled, and leaned his weight on his hand.

He is an old man! I thought, pity flooding me. *He hates what he has done, and he grieves.* I had covered my lips to stifle my gasp, but the movement caught Henry's eye. The gaze he turned on me was filled with pathos. He held out a hand to me in a gesture begging of forgiveness, and I went to him.

He was not a wicked man, only a man who had done wicked things.

To keep the peace.

To keep his crown.

Surely, there is a difference?

But where is the difference?

It was all too much for my poor mind. *'Tis for God to judge him, not me.* I could only pray for him, as I prayed for his victims. Turning to Arthur, I gave him my hand. He took it and placed an arm around his father's shoulders, and together we stood.

❖

IN THE SOLAR, WE WAITED FOR ARTHUR TO JOIN US in a cup of wine before dinner. I kept my voice down as I chuckled with Kate over the antics of Henry's pet monkey, who now sat at his feet, watching us demurely. He had absconded with Henry's memorandum book a few days earlier. When the book was finally retrieved from behind a coffer, it had been shredded, its precious secrets erased forever. Henry had received the news with good humor, and the court with delighted amusement. *No doubt, to many, the monkey is a hero,* I thought.

"I met Desiderius Erasmus of Rotterdam," Harry announced as soon as he entered, interrupting my chat with Kate.

Maggie and Mary ran to him, and Henry looked up from his ledger, where he was checking expenditures.

"Did you talk to him?" Maggie asked, taking his arm.

"Did you talk to him?" Mary echoed, taking his other arm.

She always repeated everything her older sister said. With a shiver of vivid recollection, I remembered how my brother Dick Grey had done the same with Dorset.

"Naturally," Harry beamed.

"I wouldn't know what to say," Maggie blurted, her bright eyes wide with awe.

"Me neither," Mary added.

"That's because you're girls," Harry replied, standing with his stout legs astride.

"Are we talking about the Bishop of Cambrai's private secretary, the Dutch scholar and priest?" Henry demanded, giving his monkey a chestnut.

"The same," Harry responded.

"How did that come about?"

"Thomas More brought him to see me at Eltham Palace. You know the clever lawyer who is Morton's protégé?" Harry replied, throwing himself into a chair. Maggie and Mary each pulled a stool to sit at his feet.

I thought how grown-up he seemed for a child whose feet could not yet touch the floor when he sat, and I smiled to myself over my embroidery.

"Ah, More. He is a fine young man. Morton thinks highly of his talents." Henry put down the lead rod he used to mark his accounts and turned his full attention to Harry.

"He is a friend of mine," said Harry proudly, helping himself to an apple from the bowl on the table beside him. He took a bite and chewed noisily. "And Erasmus is, too, now that we have met. We spent the entire afternoon together in discussion of many serious matters."

Henry exchanged a glance with me, amusement flickering in his eyes, for Harry had the air of a wizened old man.

"What did you learn?" demanded Henry.

"Something of great interest to you, Father."

Henry leaned back in his chair and waited.

"Erasmus told me of his friend in Italy. The man is a scholar of politics and philosophy and is preparing to write a treatise on how a prince should govern his state."

I saw Henry's mouth quirk with humor, and I bent my head low over my embroidery for I feared to burst out with laughter.

"And what principles does he advocate for his prince?"

"He says it is more difficult for a new prince to rule than a hereditary one. For he must stabilize his newfound power and build a system that will endure. And he may have to do things of an evil nature in order to achieve the greater good."

My merriment vanished. Henry edged forward in his chair. "What else does he say?"

"That the end justifies the means."

His words, cold as ice water, chilled me, and I shuddered.

"The end justifies the means," Henry echoed thoughtfully. "Indeed, 'tis so." He looked over at Harry, who was turning over the core of his apple and picking off the last bit of flesh. "We must invite this Erasmus to banquet with us."

I felt a sudden desperate need to quit the room. "I wonder what is keeping Arthur. By your leave, my lord, I shall go and check for myself."

Everyone looked at me with astonishment, and I wondered if they had forgotten I was there. *I am*, I thought, *the invisible queen, as my mother warned I would be.*

✿

IN THE GREAT HALL OF RUFUS, I RECEIVED PETITIONERS. An old woman entered and knelt before me. She mentioned a name that seemed familiar and hovered on the edges of my mind, but I could not place it.

"I come on 'er behalf to begs your aid, my queen. She was wet nurse to Prince Richard, brother to Yer Queen's Grace. She's feeble now and is bedridden. She's fallen on dire straits, she 'as."

The mention of Dickon's name sent a rush of panic ripping through me. "Take her this material," I said quickly, feeling faint. " 'Tis three and a half yards of the finest wool. She can sell it, and the money will sustain her for some months."

Lucy Neville placed the fabric into the old woman's hands.

"No more petitioners. 'Tis late and I must rest," I told Lucy.

But I could not rest. I stood by the window with Richard's book, *Tristan,* in my hands, gazing at his portrait. The day was dimming outside; soon it would be dark. Deluged in memory, the sounds of the castle came to me only vaguely: the chatter of my ladies in the antechamber, the voices of servants calling to one another outside, the laughter of children.

"Mother, what are you doing?"

Harry's voice at my elbow startled me. I had not heard the door open and I jumped, dropping both book and miniature. I took no breath as Harry bent down to retrieve them. Slowly, very slowly, he reinserted Richard's portrait into the pages of the small leather-bound volume. He rose and returned them to me. His eyes met mine.

"Yours, Mother, I believe?" His voice was hard, edged with steel.

I watched him leave. Now he would tell his father. What did it matter? I'd never give Henry the portrait; I'd hide it away where no one would find it for a hundred years. Henry was good at destroying people, but he wouldn't destroy this last bit of Richard. I turned back to the traceried window with a sigh, and my glance touched on a figure in black in the distance, seated on a bench by the riverbank, her head bowed.

I went to my brocade-covered writing desk, my treasured, worn copy of Richard's *Tristan* in my hand, and took a seat in the carved chair. Opening the book with extra care now that I'd dropped it, so as not to spill the last grains of red earth that still remained from the field of battle, I gently traced Richard's inscription with the tip of my finger: *Richard of Gloucester, Loyaulte me Lie.* He'd had such beautiful handwriting: strong, clear, each letter elegantly formed.

"Richard," I murmured, touching all that was left of him. "Richard—" *Good that you didn't know that day at Bosworth Field how it would all end: your body despoiled; your memory vilified; your friends and those of your blood hunted down and murdered. Jack of Lincoln, Humphrey Stafford; young Edward of Warwick; your own sweet boy, Johnnie, a bastard and no threat to anyone save another bastard. All who loved you are dead now, Richard, except for me, and maybe Francis Lovell.*

I flipped to Richard's portrait in the middle of the book, where Harry had inserted it. Dark hair, wide sensitive mouth, strong square jaw. Eyes looking into the distance: earnest eyes, filled with terrible sadness. His last words to me echoed in the dark stillness of my mind: *You'll change! You'll forget me!*

You were wrong, Richard. I didn't change, and I didn't forget. Nothing can erase you from my heart.

I set down the miniature and drew the book to me, remembering myself at eighteen, at Sheriff Hutton. Removing a pen from a sand cup, I dipped it carefully into the ink and opened the flyleaf. *Sans Removyr,* I wrote beneath his inscription. It was my motto, used only once in my life, when I was neither princess nor queen. *Without changing.* I brought his portrait to my lips, implanted a kiss.

I lifted my face to the bleak winter sky. "Richard, if you have been greatly hated, you have also been deeply loved," I whispered.

I removed my silver chain and key from around my neck and unlocked the secret compartment of my coffer. I put away Richard's book. Withdawing a small breviary, I secured the drawer. Dropping the key back into my bodice, I left my chamber to join Catherine Gordon.

I held my cloak close to my face and slipped through the palace grounds, unnoticed by those I passed. I made my way over the gravelly path to where she sat. It was a cold day. The Thames was drenched in gray mist, and no one was about except a few ferrymen and the mewing gulls.

"May I?" I said, surprising Catherine Gordon out of her thoughts, as Harry had surprised me.

She leapt to her feet. "My lady queen—"

"Hush. Do not alert the guards. Sit back down, I pray you."

She did, and I took a seat beside her on the bench.

"I brought you a gift," I said, passing her the breviary from beneath my cloak.

"I thank you, my queen, but you already gave me a Book of Hours."

"Are you not going to read it?" I asked pointedly.

A look of puzzlement came over her beautiful face, and she turned her gaze to the little volume in her hand.

"Go ahead, my dear," I urged.

She bent her head to the breviary, and it fell open in her hands. She took a quick breath of utter astonishment and gave a sweet, yet achingly painful cry. Tears glistened on her lashes as she lifted her eyes to me. "I know not what to say, beloved queen—"

"There is naught to be said, Catherine." I patted her hand.

"I was so afraid I would forget his face." She spoke in a broken whisper.

My heart twisted. I knew that fear. It had been mine, long ago. "Now, you'd better put the likeness away," I managed. "You don't want anyone to know what you have there."

"Not yet, I pray you! I have not the heart—another moment longer?"

I glanced around. The ferrymen were gone, and though the wind had risen, mist still drifted and dusk had fallen, shielding us from view. I nodded.

She caressed the drawing tenderly, as if she laid her fingers on her husband's own face. She swallowed hard. "How—where—may I know—" Her voice cracked.

"My lord had the miniature of Perkin sketched for him soon after your marriage. It was sent from Scotland by one of his spies. He kept it in his memorandum book."

"But—will he—"

"He will think his monkey ate it, I doubt not," I said, my lips quirking.

Catherine gave a sudden, silvery laugh, and I realized I'd never heard a sound of joy from her before. She turned her gaze on the likeness and grew pensive. " 'Tis almost as if he lives again," she said in a soft whisper. "All I had left of him till now was this—" She opened her palm.

I tore my gaze from her eyes and looked down at her hand. A coin shimmered in the fading light of day. I took it from her.

It was a silver groat, one of the many minted for the White Rose prince in Flanders that bore the profile of a crowned head, encircled by the words *King Richard IV*. I turned the coin over. On the back it carried a prayer—

O Mater Dei, memento mei. O Mother of God, remember me. Beneath, someone had etched, *Long live Perkin, I was from Tournai.*

O, Mother of God, remember me!

O, Mother of God, remember me.

I shut my eyes.

Memories are the only gifts life gives us to keep.

We sat for a long time in silence, and the shrill wind seemed filled with a thousand voices. At last, very softly, I said, "The anger dies away over the years, Catherine; 'tis the loss that never leaves you."

CHAPTER 27

A Twilight Path, 1500

HENRY THREW THE MOST ELABORATE FEAST OF HIS reign to welcome in the new century of 1500. Hundreds of candles flickered on the white-clothed banquet tables, and torches flared around the Great Hall of Rufus as we entered and took our seats at the stone table on the dais. For once, I sat next to Arthur.

Glittering lords and ladies in gold, jewels, and colored velvets and satins rose to greet us with lusty cheers and the loud rattling of horns, shouting compliments. High in the gallery, minstrels took up their instruments while servants began the steady procession of courses between drum rolls. The company dined on hare soup, partridge in spicy sauce, and fat capons in pies garnished with salted olives, but I restricted myself to small bites of a salad of flowers and herbs, a taste of cream fritters, and a piece of sugared bread, for I had not much appetite.

To the fanfare of trumpets, a whole boar was brought in on a silver serving tray, borne on the shoulders of four grooms clad in green and white. A procession of peacocks followed, cooked and reassembled in their feathers of emerald, jade, lily, and cream. The guests stamped their feet in approval. At the first table just below the dais, Doctor de Puebla shifted in his seat to make room for the servers to pile another goodly portion of meat on his plate. Not having heard back from his sovereigns, he had finally declined my offer of a bishopric. Unwilling to give up, I had made him another: to procure him a rich wife. His answer was the same. He had written them, and this time, I hoped they would not forget to reply.

Along the table, Harry chewed noisily as he tore into his capon, smacking his lips and licking his fingers in hearty delight. A servant refilled his golden goblet with more of the sweet malmsey from Portugal that he loved, and which had been thinned with water for him. He drained his cup in one gulp. I smiled as I watched my happy, fun-loving, and absolutely unsinkable son. He had a lusty appetite for all God's gifts, and that pleased me well. *Life should be enjoyed.* He set down his goblet and grinned at me, his face smeared with sauce.

"What's so amusing?" Arthur inquired.

"Harry," I replied.

Arthur turned to look at his brother, and we both laughed. Relaxing into his chair, Arthur draped an arm around my shoulders. Harry's eyes narrowed as he gazed at us, but before I could ponder this, the minstrels gave a drum roll and Patch entered.

"Here's our troubadour!" someone mocked, for Patch had a high-pitched, feminine voice.

Everyone roared.

"My voice is too fine for your hairy ears!" Patch called out, with a courtly bow in his direction.

The company hooted approval. Patch waited until the noise had died down.

"I am here to announce a most special display! Prince Harry, our illustrious and brilliant Duke of York, friend to the great Erasmus"—Patch bowed in the philosopher's direction—"shall hail the new century with the performance of a dance he has designed with his royal sisters, the princesses Margaret and Mary. Then His Grace shall sing a song he has written himself."

Patch withdrew with a bow. Harry took the center of the room, accompanied by his sisters, one on either side. The minstrels broke into a lilting melody, and the children hopped, and turned, and switched partners most delightfully. Then the girls left, and Harry stood alone at the center of the hall, all eyes on him. I was surprised that he displayed such confidence, but then I remembered how he relished the adoration of crowds. A chair was brought. He sat down and was handed a lute. He bent his ear, strummed the notes of the complicated melody he had devised, and broke into song. He had a charming voice, and as I gazed on him, I thought how much he resembled the glorious golden cherubs of the illustrated manuscripts. When he was done, the hall erupted with cheers. I wiped a tear from my eye, so moved had I been by his sweet music, and so filled with pride at my son.

The joyous evening continued with the performances of mummers, jugglers, tumblers, fire-eaters, and men who walked on great sticks so that they seemed as giants. With the wind howling outside, the fire blazing inside, our children gathered around us, and Arthur at my side, I drank wine and toasted to the new century of 1500, my heart filled with gratitude.

"May joy be ours!" Arthur called out, holding aloft his goblet.

The hall echoed his wish, but there was one who set down her cup with barely a sip. Stunningly beautiful in her simple black gown, Catherine Gordon sat at the far end of the dais. Though once in a while, she nodded her head and smiled graciously at something someone said to her, an aura of profound sorrow wrapped her as entirely as the ebony velvet she wore. I had seen little of her since that day on the riverbank, but she had been in my thoughts, and in every prayer I uttered. It did not escape my notice that Henry did not cast any lustful glances in her direction.

At least he is not without shame, I thought; *that much can be said for him.*

❂

THE NEW CENTURY DID NOT PROVE KIND. DEATH HAD grown overfond of me and refused to release its embrace. The plague that had devoured many thousands of lives was over and England was in the full bloom of glorious summer when my babe Edmund fell ill of a strange sickness and died on the nineteenth of June at the age of sixteen months. We took his little body from

Greenwich to Westminster, and once again the mayor and aldermen and the men of the crafts and guilds lined the streets to share our sorrow. Edmund's tiny coffin was borne to the Shrine of St. Edward at Westminster Abbey and buried near his sister, Elizabeth.

So much grief, I thought; *how can I bear it?*

It must be borne, came the answer unbidden to my mind. Excessive mourning always provoked the wrath of God. Richard's queen did not put aside her anguish, and her unabated grieving tumbled Richard from his throne. I lifted my head and gazed at the tiny coffin as it moved forward beneath drizzling skies, almost lost in the procession. *I shall be strong, if not for Henry, whom I have never loved, then for Arthur, who has all my heart.*

Sitting on my bench in the walled garden after the funeral, I bent my head back to the book of meditation that Bridget had sent me. It was by St. Mathilde of Hackeborn, who wrote of reunion with loved ones after death. The little volume had once belonged to Richard and Anne, and it bore their signatures. It had been bequeathed to Bridget by my grandmother Cecily Neville, and she had sent it to me, thinking it would bring me comfort. The timing of the book's arrival almost made it seem that Heaven herself was reaching out to me, and sore at heart, I lingered on the words St. Mathilde had written: *Come and do penance; come and be reconciled; come and be consoled.*

We held court at Westminster, visited Coventry, attended splendid mystery plays, and rested at Windsor with its fine hunting. But each time I passed the knoll where I had sat with Queen Anne after the loss of her child, I averted my gaze, for the sight unleashed a stream of painful memories. I rode again to the barking of the hounds and felt the wind in my face; I raced through the dappled forest, ducking the limbs and branches of graceful trees. It was good to rest in the evenings to the music of flutes, and gittern, and harp, and to awaken in the morning to the sweet voices of children singing in the village.

One evening, as a gentle rose twilight settled over the earth, I returned from a picnic in the woods with my ladies and noticed a tall friar climbing the steep path up to the castle gate. He walked with his head bowed and I saw him from the back, but something

about him struck me as familiar. I slowed my gelding and drew up
to his side.

"Sir Friar," I said, restraining my spirited palfrey. "Do I know
you?"

He lifted his cowled head and looked at me. A silver cross
glinted at his throat. My breath caught in my chest.

"I know not, my queen," he said. "Do you?"

I stared at his face, at the strong square jaw, the dark hair, the
brown eyes. *O Thomas, Thomas.* The years had left their mark on
him, but it was Thomas! How could he think I would ever forget?
Memories flooded me, and again I saw the little pond where we
used to meet; felt the honeyed sweetness of my first kiss; remembered the hopes and dreams of my maidenhood. I swallowed hard
on the memories, thankful I had my back to my attendants and that
I obstructed their view of him, for the heartrending tenderness of
his gaze made my own heart turn over in response.

"I see that I was mistaken," I said. "I do not know you."

A silence fell.

His eye went to the sapphire brooch he had given me, pinned to
my bodice, in the spot he had chosen for it so long ago.

He said, "I heard of your sorrow and came to give you this,
my queen." He took out a breviary from the folds of his robes and
drew near. He held it up to me, and I bent down and reached for
it, but he did not release his grip, nor did I seek to remove it from
his hand. Our eyes met and held.

At last I took it from him. "You are most welcome here, dear
friar, and since our paths have crossed, will you not take my Psalter
in return?" I put away his breviary and accepted my Psalter from
Lucy. I passed it to him.

"I thank you, my queen," he said, taking the book. "I shall keep
you in my prayers always."

I gave him a nod. He stepped back. I jerked my bridle, and my
palfrey jingled forward.

ILL TIDINGS REACHED US AT WINDSOR SOON AFTER
Henry returned from London, where he had gone to attend Mor-

ton's funeral. At eighty, Morton had outlived almost everyone I had known from childhood. *Life is strange,* I thought; *the good die young, and the wicked flourish.* I watched Henry's face change as he read the missive delivered to him in the solar.

"What is it?" I asked.

"Suffolk has fled for Burgundy with his brother, Richard de la Pole. Tyrrell has let them through Calais," Henry said through clenched teeth, a muscle twitching at his jaw.

Welladay, what do you expect? Suffolk stood next in line to Edward of Warwick in the order of succession. To Suffolk, that had to mean next in line for execution.

"He had no reason," said Henry.

No reason, I thought scornfully, *when you set such an exorbitant bond on him that he faced financial ruin paying it!*

Henry had devised a policy that had worked well for him. By keeping his nobles in desperate fear of being penniless and losing the means to support their rank, not only for themselves, but for their children, he kept them in firm check. Edmund, the son of a duke, had lost the family title along with the family money as punishment for his brother's support of the rebellion at Stoke. The loss of rank meant loss of honor, but unlike my brother Dorset, Edmund had pride of lineage and found it impossible to abide the humiliation.

Henry was good at humiliating noblemen. " 'Tis our intention to keep our subjects low; riches would only make them haughty," I had overheard him tell de Puebla.

Henry's voice came again, jolting me from my thoughts. "I am informed that the de la Poles had dinner with the Earl of Devon and Kate's husband, William, on the night before they left. Dorset's son and Stanley's son were also with them."

My blood went cold. *Kate's husband?*

"Surely you cannot suspect William, or his father? They helped you capture Perkin!"

"I suspect everyone," Henry replied, his pale, hooded eyes as cold as steel.

"By your leave, my lord, I shall take some air in the garden," I said.

He nodded absently, and I knew I was already forgotten. At the door, I glanced back. He was writing in his new memorandum book, no doubt adding William's name to the list of those to watch. I gave a shiver.

I did not go to the garden but to the river. There was something about the lapping of water and the mewing of river birds that always comforted me. Bidding my attendants to wait by the water gate, I strolled along the banks of the Thames, alone with my thoughts. The light was draining from the sky, and the clouds glimmered with a soft touch of silver. Geese scattered out of my path with a flutter of wings and loud honking of horns, and on the river a few barges and scarred wooden boats passed in the distance. I inhaled deeply of the fresh, wet air. The evening was bathed in calm and serenity.

But I was deeply troubled. I knew Henry. He would not act rashly, but cautiously, and take his time. Like a cat with a mouse, he would play with his victims first; let them hope for reprieve or escape before he pounced for the kill. I remembered with a shudder the heretic in April with whom he had disputed the true path to God. He had converted him from his error and given him alms. Then he rode away and the man was burned alive.

But surely he will not hurt William Courtenay?

A terrifying realization washed over me. Suffolk's departure left Kate's sons next in line for the throne! I felt as if a hand closed around my throat. "Jesu—!" I whispered. Abruptly, on the wind, came voices. I heard them as clearly as if they spoke in my ear:

"He had a deadly disease, the poor young lad," someone said.

"What's that?" asked another voice.

"Royal blood," came the answer.

I gasped, stumbled in my steps. *They are talking about Edward of Warwick, and know not that they mean all my relatives.* I looked around but saw no one. The oppression in my chest sharpened into panic and my stomach clenched tight. Feeling nauseated, I sank down on a nearby bench. Henry had inverted the natural order of things. Now, that which should have been at the bottom lay on top, and all those who should have been on top had to die to secure the place of the low one who had risen.

I placed a hand to my brow, my head reeling. Henry persecuted my family because he feared them, and he would not feel safe until they were all dead or helpless against him. I lifted my eyes to the heavens. *But what can I do? Tell me what I can do!*

A cloud moved across the sky. I watched it take form and shadow, and it seemed to shape itself into a crown. Somewhere in my mind, across the far reaches of time, the memory of a distant voice echoed— "my best"—and I saw Richard's face as it had been when he had sent me away to Sheriff Hutton, and remembered what he had said: *I have done my best for England. 'Tis for God to judge me now.*

I bowed my head. I had done my best. I had given my people Arthur. The rest was in God's hands. All I could do was pray.

MAXIMILIAN WOULDN'T EXPEL THE DE LA POLE BROTH- ers. At St. Paul's, Henry had them cursed with bell, book, and candle and excommunicated, but he worried that he hadn't caught the traitors involved and turned his suspicion on Suffolk's friends—all his relatives—anyone of Yorkist blood. One of these was Sir James Tyrrell, the governor of Guisnes, who was lured back to England by Henry's safe conduct, which was promptly discarded as soon as he stepped aboard ship. Tyrrell was conveyed directly to the Tower, and no doubt tortured until he confessed to whatever Henry wanted.

I closed my eyes, remembering the kindly knight who loved a good jest. *In this new world of Henry's, even a king's promise is worthless.*

At Westminster, in November, while I was at my embroidery frame, Henry came to me. Though he understood he was no longer welcome in my bed since the executions, he still sought my company in the evenings. That was agreeable to me.

He wore a smile on his face and was in bright spirits. "You know that de Puebla wrote Ferdinand and Isabella about Warwick and Warbeck?"

I nodded. De Puebla had shown me the letter before he sent it, thinking it would please me. Never would I forget his words: *After kissing the royal hands and feet of Your Highnesses, I cause you to know that not a drop of royal blood remains in this kingdom, except the true blood of the king and queen, and above all, that of the lord Prince Arthur.*

I laid down my needle and looked at Henry.

"He has received a reply from Ferdinand and Isabella. They will send the princess Catherine of Aragon to England as soon as we are ready to receive her."

My breath caught in my throat. "How soon?"

"As soon as the wedding preparations can be made."

"No!" I cried, rising to my feet. "Not before he is fifteen—you promised me, Henry!"

"We need to secure this alliance as soon as possible."

"He is too young yet. Surely another year can't make much difference?"

"You're asking me to wait on a matter of such urgency?"

"I am only asking for you to keep your word. If honor still counts with you." My voice had a bitter edge, for I remembered the shame of Tyrrell's false safe conduct.

Henry regarded me for a long moment. "I suppose we can wait a year. The new palace of Richmond will take that long to complete."

Suffused with relief, I sank back into my chair.

"And you, madame, should try to curb your ill nature." Turning on his heel, he left me.

"And you, my cold arse of a lord, should try to find a heart," I hissed under my breath, stabbing my needle through the silk.

❖

HENRY ORDERED WHOLESALE ARRESTS.

"Suffolk's friends and associates must be interrogated. All those who had accompanied him to the coast must be placed under arrest. Any suspicious person found near the coast must be imprisoned," he told Bray.

" 'Tis time you resolved to rid yourself of all possible rivals, my son. Mercy is a weakness, and you have been far too lenient," Margaret Beaufort said.

I looked up with shock from St. Mathilde's book that I was reading on the window seat. *Lenient? Jesu, what perversion was this, to call Henry lenient?* I trembled, for there was no doubt in my mind which rivals his mother meant. I came to my feet angrily.

"I married you to stop the bloodshed, and you keep killing! When will it be enough—when?" I cried.

Henry and his mother turned and looked at me. Clearly, they were unaware I was in the room. Once again, I was the forgotten queen. Neither of them spoke for a moment. Then Henry rose and took my hand.

"My dear lady, remember Arthur," he said. "Remember your son. 'Tis for his sake we do what we must."

We do what we must.

There was no turning back.

I inhaled a deep breath, too weary to argue. I left them and dragged myself to my chamber. As I approached Harry's schoolroom, voices floated out to me. The door stood ajar. I halted in my steps to listen. I heard the name *Suffolk*.

"You've read the Chronicles," Skelton said. "This is an age-old problem that has an age-old solution. Can you tell me what it is?"

Harry nodded his head. "Better that one man die than many perish."

I covered my mouth with my fist and fled past.

I had requested from Skelton that he instill in Harry the ideals of noble and legendary heroes like Alexander and King Arthur. To his credit, even though he knew me to be without influence, he had attempted to do so. He preached to Harry—whose uncontrollable rages were known to all—that his head should rule his heart. But what good did it do when Harry witnessed Skelton rushing at his own enemies with uncontrolled vengeful hate, flinging himself into poetic attacks of utmost brutality and coarseness? Though he was a priest himself, it was said Skelton kept a wife, and, according to Patch, he avidly pursued the youngest, most helpless of the female servants. If they spurned him, he scoured them savagely with invective thinly disguised in pretty lyrics of Latin prose. The man seemed obsessed with fornication. To Skelton, women were either whores or goddesses. That I knew, for he idealized me in many flattering verses.

Such a man is not a suitable tutor for Harry, but what can I do about it? Nothing.

The answer was always the same. *Nothing.*

I gripped St. Mathilde's book to my breast. Once it had sustained those dearest to me. *Bear what you must,* I told myself, paraphrasing Mathilde's words; *forgive, and be comforted.*

❀

WHEN YULETIDE FINALLY ARRIVED, I WAS JOYOUS and all the palace celebrated with me, for Arthur was coming, and he was beloved in the land for his many works of charity and his kind, thoughtful nature, even in his tender years. The only one who didn't seem delighted was Harry. I couldn't help noticing the cold, hard-eyed look on his face when he regarded his brother. He was beginning to remind me a great deal of my mother: possessed of beauty and charm, but also of a temperamental and envious nature. Or was it his other grandmother, Margaret Beaufort, that he resembled; she who had to come first before all others, who would let naught stand in her way; not even conscience? I banished my black thought.

Once again, Arthur and I came into the presence chamber to find Harry on the throne, his friends flattened before him on all fours. I felt the blood drain from my face. Beside me Arthur paled.

"What do you here, brother?" he demanded.

Harry's frightened friends rose and backed away.

" 'Tis a game of pretense, Arthur, nothing more," replied Harry, making no effort to vacate the throne.

Skelton had done this. His flattery of Harry's accomplishments were sowing resentment in the boy and distorting his sense of place, raising the real possibility of future strife between the two brothers with its terrible consequences for the land. Feeling myself helpless and wishing to avoid confrontation, I had remained silent for four years and let Margaret Beaufort carry on as she wished. Now I realized I was the only one who could alter the course of future events. If I could find a way to reach Henry, he would put a stop to it. He would not want to hatch another Clarence. I decided to raise the matter with him as soon as Arthur left.

I found myself dwelling on my eldest son with even softer eyes than usual during the pageants and festivities that marked Yuletide. In this new year of 1501, he would turn fifteen and marry. His wedding was set for November.

Before Arthur left for Wales, Henry took us to the new palace where Sheen had stood. I dreaded going, for it was tied up in my mind with Perkin, and fire, and death. It had become evident that Perkin, desperate to kill either himself or Henry, had set the blaze that burnt down Sheen four years ago. My heart went out to Catherine Gordon, sitting on her black palfry, dressed in her widow's weeds, and I thought of fireweed, the strange, lovely flower that grew only on the scars of ruin and flame.

I tore my gaze from her and forced my eyes to the sight spread out before me. From the charred ashes of Sheen had risen the palace of Richmond that Henry had named for the earldom he had lost as a child.

" 'Tis like a second paradise," Kate said.

Indeed it was. Crowned by pinnacles and weathervanes of gilt and azure bearing the royal arms, the many-storied, multitowered palace of pink brick and stone glittered in the sunlight. The wide garden paths, though bare of flowers, were bordered with bushes and herbs laid in elaborate patterns. At the lower end of the garden stood butts for archery, courts for tennis, and houses for pleasure where we could play dice and chess on warm summer nights. Henry's chamber had running water, and my new chapel was furnished with golden crucifixes, the floors carpeted with heavy Oriental rugs. All the ceilings were emblazoned with Tudor roses and Beaufort portcullis in gold. In the Great Hall, I stood at the bay window that opened out onto what would, in summer, be fair and fragrant gardens with exotic fruit trees and rambling vines.

"My lord, this is the most beautiful palace I have ever seen," I marveled. "It must have cost a royal ransom."

Henry smiled. "It did. But Spain has the Alhambra, built of red clay, which is said to be one of the wonders of the world. We must not seem poor to the Spanish princess."

At the mention of Spain, my smile faltered.

❋

HENRY SAT AT THE TABLE GOING OVER HIS ACCOUNTS with his treasurer, his monkey beside him on a chair, perusing

Henry's new memorandum book. They made a comic scene, but my spirits were too heavy for a smile.

"Two shillings for a man who scared away crows around Sheen, is that not excessive?" Henry demanded. The monkey snickered.

His treasurer mumbled something, and Henry moved to another item.

"An entire pound for a woman who brought me cakes? 'Tis impossible I ate that many. She must either pay back the difference or bake us more cakes." He signed the page, and his monkey smacked his lips. "Aye, you shall have some of those she brings, Prince."

On this day, for some strange reason, the sound of the name felt to me like an old wound ripped open. I inhaled a sharp breath.

He looked up. "Dear lady, to what do I owe this pleasure?"

"My lord, there is a matter of some urgency I wish to discuss with you."

Henry's treasurer packed his books and withdrew, along with Henry's attendants. I approached and stood before him. "I fear for Arthur," I said.

Henry lifted his brow and looked at me uncertainly.

"Harry's behavior is beginning to remind me of my Uncle Clarence," I said.

"How can that be?"

"Jealousy drove Clarence to treason. He died trying to pluck the crown from my father's head."

"Harry is a mere child," Henry said dismissively. "How can you compare a ten-year-old with your Uncle Clarence?"

"My uncle was once ten years old."

I had his attention, and I lost no time going over Harry's behavior in detail.

"I see," Henry murmured thoughtfully when I was done.

A few weeks later, he raised the subject with me in the privacy of my chamber.

"I have given much thought to the matter we discussed," he said, his hands clasped behind his back as he gazed at me, "and have decided 'tis best Harry go to live in Derbyshire, far from the seat of government. I have purchased for him the castle of Codnore. 'Tis surrounded by extensive lands, manors, and the customary deer park. There, Harry shall enjoy a resplendent, but limited future. I am also considering entering him into the church once Arthur has a son and heir. He can be Archbishop of Canterbury. 'Tis a good life, and will curtail his political aspirations."

"What about Skelton? Shall he be dismissed?"

"My mother assures me there is no cause for alarm. He has done nothing to warrant such disgrace."

My face must have fallen, for Henry added, "All is well, Elizabeth. Do not fret."

But worry, I did, and soon I was given vindication—and also more to worry about. On the twenty-eighth of August, Skelton unfurled a short treatise he'd written on how a king should rule, and presented it not to Arthur, but to Harry. Handwritten, in black, crimson, and gold, it seemed strangely menacing.

"You dismissed my concerns, my lord, preferring to take your lady mother's advice. Here now is proof of all I have tried to warn you about. Harry can become king only in the event of Arthur's death—God forfend!" I crossed myself as sheer black fright swept through me. "Or by rebellion, as Clarence sought to do."

Henry's face turned dark. "Not only will Skelton be dismissed, but he shall be taken to the Tower. A stint there should clear his wits."

Though Skelton was replaced by a new tutor, I was tormented by the damage he might already have done. Arthur was in robust health. If he'd been ailing, Ferdinand and Isabella would never have given their blessing to the marriage. But Skelton believed Harry would inherit the throne. How could that be?

How?

Much as I loved Harry, I also feared him. Self-centered and demanding, he had shown streaks of cruelty, and unlike Arthur, he lacked empathy and had no feeling for the suffering of others. I woke up in the night, drenched in sweat. Had pupil and tutor set some evil into motion? Did Skelton know something? Had someone set something afoot to get rid of Arthur and place Harry on the throne? Was a ten-year-old child capable of such scheming? Or were these fears merely the product of my own imagination and a life's experience of the worst of humankind?

I didn't know. I forced my dreadful ramblings from my mind.

To speak them aloud would be to give them life. But I cursed Skelton. He had filled Harry's head with ideas that should never have been thought; spoken words that should never have been said.

⁕

"HARRY, WILL YOU TAKE A SEAT BESIDE ME HERE ON the settle?"

He came and flung himself down. I felt his rage seething within him.

"Do I surmise correctly that you are upset over the dismissal of your tutor, Skelton?"

He sat in stony silence, arms crossed, and did not look at me.

"Harry, you must understand something very clearly. For your own welfare, and for the well-being of this great land of ours, Arthur will be king. You shall not rule."

"Master Skelton said I will," he hissed.

"Harry, that could only be through some terrible event—" Again that black chill; I crossed myself. "How can you wish ill on your brother?"

He turned and looked at me then. "I don't know him. He's nothing to me. Master Skelton says I am more brilliant, and more suited to rule than he."

A cold shiver touched my spine. It was what Morton had told Buckingham, and Buckingham had revolted against Richard— after possibly murdering my brothers. This evil in Harry had to be nipped in the bud, or Blessed Mary, where would it end?

"But God did not find you worthy to rule, Harry. He sent you to us after Arthur. Clearly, God designed Arthur for the throne, not you."

Harry leapt to his feet. "Arthur, Arthur!" he mocked. "Grandmother says I must take off my cap in Arthur's presence, and keep it off until he deigns to tell me to put it back on! All I ever hear from you or my royal father is how perfect Arthur is! He's your favorite—yours and Father's. I count for nothing!"

I stared at him in astonishment. "Harry, we love you very much. But you must accept that Arthur will be king, and you will not. 'Tis not God's plan."

"Arthur shall have a throne in England, Margaret in Scotland, and Mary in France. What about me? I alone am without one! 'Tis not right. 'Tis not God's will. Skelton said so!"

The breath had gone out of me. My blood drained to my feet and I trembled like a leaf in an autumn storm. I quitted the room, forcing from my mind the image of my child as he raged, with his eyes protruding from his skull, his teeth tightly clenched, his small mouth stretched wide. Fury and hatred had made of him a fanged demon.

CHAPTER 28

Bright Star of Spain, 1501

CECILY KNELT BEFORE ME. "I AM HERE TO BEG FOR-giveness, my sister."

"I don't understand, Cecily."

"I have wronged you all my life. I was jealous."

"Jealous of what?"

"You had larger breasts than me."

We both laughed then, a hearty laugh filled with the angst of years, of memories shared, laden with joy and with sorrow. Abruptly, we fell silent and looked at one another. I put out my arms and she rose and fell into them. I heard a smothered sound and knew she wept. I smoothed her fair hair and kissed her brow.

"Hush, dear Cecily, no need for tears. You are married to your squire and happy now, aren't you?"

She wiped her tears with the back of her hand, sniffling as she smiled. "I'm so happy, Elizabeth. In sanctuary, all those years ago, I never thought to see the day come when Thomas and I would wed. 'Tis a dream."

"Thomas? Sanctuary?" I scarce believed what I heard.

"I met Thomas Kyme there. He was one of our guards."

"I . . . never knew."

"No one did; we were very careful. Those were dangerous days. Then King Richard wed me to Ralph Scrope, and hope seemed forever lost."

"But I thought Viscount Welles was your choice? You had your marriage to Scrope dissolved so you could marry him."

"O sister, you are so innocent! Does anyone have their choice of anything when 'that strong whore' is around?"

She said it lightly, expecting me to laugh, but I couldn't. I was swept with guilt. "Cecily, that is still on my conscience. If I hadn't mentioned it to you, you couldn't have told Margaret Beaufort about him, and the poor man wouldn't have been charged with treason and so heavily fined that he lost all his worldly goods."

She stared at me in bafflement. "But I didn't tell her!"

"How did she find out?"

"A neighbor turned him in. On his return, they asked him whether he'd seen you, and he said, aye, and would have talked more with you but that strong whore chased him off. Elizabeth, I swear, 'tis how it happened!"

Such a simple explanation had never occurred to me. I was suffused with shame for condemning Cecily without giving her the chance to explain. All my life I had avoided confrontation so much that I rarely voiced thoughts when they were unpleasant. This time my fault had cost us much. I embraced my sister. "O Cecily. I am glad you came, and glad we spoke of this, and I know the truth at long last. Can you forgive me?"

She gave me another hug in response. I lowered my voice to a whisper. "I thought you liked Henry's mother?"

"No," Cecily whispered back. "She liked me because I hated Richard for marrying me to Scrope, and I didn't see why he didn't make you wed Scrope instead. Welles lusted for me, and she arranged the whole thing with him."

I smiled wistfully, the days of sanctuary stirring in my heart. "I don't know how we didn't bump into one another."

"What do you mean?"

"I had a Thomas of my own. He was one of our guards, too. We used to meet by the stone bench by the pond. Henry almost executed him. I got him a pardon but his brother wasn't as fortu-nate—" I blinked to banish the vision that rose before me of Hum-phrey suffering a traitor's death.

"Who was he?"

"Best that it remain a secret, Cecily. For his sake. You under-stand?"

"What happened to him?" she asked, after a pause.

"He married someone else. He has a brood of children, so I hear tell."

Thomas had written me a note in the breviary; not much, but enough. He had thanked me for the gift of his life, and said all was well but that there were some things the heart could not let go. "He was a good man. I would have been happy with him." I turned my gaze to the window, where the outside world made tumult and wheeled past, oblivious of me.

"O sister, I'm so sorry—" She broke off and dabbed at her eye.

"No need, Cecily," I replied. "Fate determines life, and I must serve a penance."

"For what? What did you ever do that requires penance?"

"I loved my uncle."

Cecily took my hand. "He was a good man, Elizabeth. I have prayed for him."

I heaved a sigh. "Tell me, Cecily, what is it like being married to the one you love?" I asked.

"Every day is a blessing," she replied in a dreamy voice, "and a miracle."

AS WE PLAYED CARDS IN THE SOLAR AT RICHMOND, a messenger entered and fell to a knee before us.

"Sire, Your Grace, the princess of Spain arrived at Plymouth on the second of October," he said.

Henry smiled broadly. Not since Henry V conquered France and wed the daughter of the King of France had there been an English marriage of such grandeur. Not only was Arthur marry-ing the daughter of the most powerful monarch in Europe, but she was bringing with her as dowry wagons filled with an enormous collection of jewels, plate, tapestries, fine clothes, and beautifully carved beds.

"You shall have the honor of greeting the princess," Henry said, turning to Harry, "and accompanying her on her entry into London."

Harry beamed to be assigned such an important duty.

The next day, with an escort of nobles wrapped in thick capes against the pouring rain, Harry rode out the gates to meet Catherine of Aragon and escort her to Lambeth Palace. Arthur left his castle in the Welsh Marches to join them, and Henry and I departed for Westminster with the court. Soon my eldest son was riding up Fleet Street with his betrothed, to the wild cheers of the people. I heard the roaring of his name even at Westminster. "Arthur, Arthur!" they called. "Long live our beloved Prince Arthur!" Intermingled were shouts for Catherine: "Blessings on the Bright Star of Spain!" I ran to the window with Kate and Cecily to watch the procession approach. We all gasped at the same moment, our breath caught by the beauty of it all.

"It looks like some marvel from legend," I murmured in awe.

As far as the eye could see, gold chains glittered, jewels flashed, and the colorful silks and velvets of the English nobles shone in the sun, vying in splendor with the Moorish brocades of the Spanish dignitaries. In the center rode the princess herself, sidesaddle on a gorgeously caparisoned mule. I peered into the distance for my first glimpse of the girl who would be Arthur's wife. She had the aura of beauty, and though diminutive, made a striking figure with her red hair flowing loose beneath a broad brimmed hat tied at the chin with gold lace. Her Spanish ladies followed her on mules, their unbound tresses pouring down their backs, each paired with an English counterpart who wore a jeweled gable headdress and rode aside on a palfrey.

"Catherine is fair, and has a beautiful smile," Kate added.

"Indeed. And that must be her *duena* in the black."

"Is that Harry, on her right? He seems so small," Cecily noted.

"Don't tell him that. He considers himself a very large man," I smiled.

The procession clattered triumphantly across London Bridge,

which had been washed and hung with tapestries and carpets, the rotted heads taken down. Crowds pressed against the railings, cheering lustily. We went to the cobbled court and took our places to await the royal arrivals. As soon as Arthur caught sight of me, he leapt from his horse in one elegant, sweeping motion. I embraced my lanky son and gazed up at him through the tears of joy that always blurred my first sight of him.

"You grow ever more handsome, my dear one," I said with pride. Beneath a richly feathered black velvet cap, his dark chin-length hair framed a square face that had gained in maturity, and in his gray eyes was reflected the merry twinkle he reserved for me alone. I clasped him to my breast once again, unwilling to let him go. Soon he would be married at St. Paul's Cathedral and belong to someone else. Then I saw Harry watching us with his small truculent eyes.

Harry was always at his best on horseback where one saw neither his chunkiness nor his stocky build. Clad in a fur-lined coat with a heavy gold chain over his shoulders, his pink and white face filled with hauteur, his red-gold hair curling nearly down to his shoulders beneath a plumed cap, he cut a princely figure. He gave me a nod.

Henry moved forward in greeting. "Welcome, dear princess! We are heartily gladdened to have you here at last."

Arthur returned to Catherine's side. Placing his hands around her small waist, he helped her dismount. It seemed a moment taken from one of the glorious scenes of chivalry that flowed like murals in my mind: the handsome prince, the lovely princess uplifted in his arms, the gracious smiles exchanged between them as the prince looked up at her and she gazed down at him. Nor was the scene lost on those watching, for a loud cheer went up, and Catherine's *duena* took out a handkerchief and sobbed noisily.

We turned and entered the palace. Once the formalities were over, I embraced the sixteen-year-old girl and welcomed her in Latin, for I knew no Spanish, and she no English. As we sat together on the settle, I asked her many questions about Spain, hoping it would bring her comfort to talk about her home, and family.

"She seems a lovely girl, but she must be terribly lonely," I said to Kate and Cecily later that evening as we relaxed in my chamber after the gathering. "She is so far from home and everything familiar."

"I look at her and see what might have been my future," Kate murmured, "wed to the King of Castile, alone in a foreign land, learning strange customs. Poor child."

"I feel sorry for her, too," Cecily said. "Though she shall be a queen."

"Catherine of Aragon will accept her destiny, as we must all do," I said. "For royal princesses, there is no choice. 'Tis what God ordained for us."

Kate smiled at me. "But thanks to you, sister, I am one fortunate royal princess. For I reside here in England and am married to a man of my choice. 'Tis a good lot."

I squeezed her hand.

"And I," said Cecily, "who was once promised to the King of Scotland—and but for the grace of God, might be queen of the barbarous Scotsmen as we speak—am wed to a humble and most charming squire. 'Tis thanks to you, sister, that I am received again at court and have back some of the lands that were confiscated from me. I, too, am grateful for my lot."

"I wonder if Anne would say the same, were she here," Kate mused. "She was to wed Philip, Archduke of Austria, who has now taken mad Juana of Castile as wife. They say he is very handsome."

"Anne married for love, and I know she would have it no other way," said Cecily. "Why do you think she's not here with us now? 'Tis that she prefers her husband's company."

I smiled, but it was as if a sad wind sighed through my heart.

Kate said, "And Bridget is where she wishes to be."

Cecily took my hand and pressed it between her own. "Thank you, sister—thank you from us all for your gift to us of happiness."

❖

ON SUNDAY, NOVEMBER FOURTEENTH, 1501, I WATCHED the kneeling, white-satin-clad figures of Arthur and veiled Catherine at the altar of St. Paul's as they murmured the words that would bind them together until death. My babe had grown up, and I was losing him. Soon I would lose another child, for Maggie would assume the burden of wife in a foreign land, far from home and everything that was familiar and dear to her. Like this princess, Catherine of Aragon.

Perhaps life will treat them more gently, I thought. I could hope for that kindness. Yet I was gripped by a strange unease. *Are shadows lurking even now to take our joy from us?* The ghosts and horrors of the past always felt so close at times like these, and never closer than now, and for once I did not condemn Margaret Beaufort for sobbing loudly beside me. I shook my morbid thoughts from my mind.

The wedding banquet took place at the bishop's palace. I barely touched my food, tempted neither by tarts nor by castles of jelly. The evening seemed unreal; sounds came muffled to my ears and the scene unfolded before me dimly, as if I watched in a distant mirror. Catherine and her ladies were performing to a wild Spanish melody, whirling their skirts and clicking pieces of wood they held in their hands, and Harry had taken the floor to dance with Maggie, but why was he only in his hose and shirt? I looked at Henry. He was laughing. He said something about Harry being so excited that he had removed his jacket. Then Henry clapped. Why was he happy? Did he not realize that soon it would be time to give up yet another child? In December, the Scottish ambassadors would come to court to perform the proxy marriage of our Maggie to James IV of Scotland.

I pressed a hand to my temple; the vow she would take was hammering in my head: "I, Margaret, first begotten daughter of King Henry VII, having twelve years complete in age in the month of November last passed, contract marriage with the high and mighty prince James, King of Scotland . . . and thereto I plight him my troth."

The words would make her Queen of Scotland. I gripped the sidearm of my chair. *She cannot go yet—she will not go yet! She is too young! Twelve is too young—*

Twenty is too young, came the thought as I remembered my first night with Henry.

I made up my mind to confront him about her. If I did not speak up for my child, who would? Men did not know, could not imagine, the horror of the sex act forced on a woman without love. *Let her stay with me until she is fourteen,* I would plead. *There are too many dangers. What if she bears a child—it could kill her. She may be tall and comely, but she is still too young for the duties of a woman. Let me teach her more of the responsibilities of court before she leaves forever.*

If need be, I would fall to my knees before him.

I realized that the crowd had risen. They seemed drunk and were hooting and applauding. I turned to Arthur. He was leaving with Catherine. It was time to consummate the marriage.

I know not what else happened that night, for I was dizzy and nauseated, and my head pounded. But in the morning Kate told me that Arthur rang early for a drink and said, "I have this night been in the midst of Spain which is a hot region, and that journey has made me dry."

My son was a man. He would be king, and rule wisely with his beautiful queen. It was what I had always wished. So why did I weep?

Harry's voice came at my elbow as I stood in my chamber looking out the window. "Mother, why are you sad?"

I had not heard him come in, and I remembered the last time he had surprised me this way. I had been gazing at Richard's portrait, and I'd feared he would tell his father, but he had not, maybe because he hated his father more than he resented me. He stood before me now, his stout legs apart, his cherubic face gazing at me sorrowfully. I placed my arm around his shoulder.

" 'Twas a question I was just asking myself, Harry, and I know not the answer. Did you enjoy the wedding banquet last evening?"

His face lit. "I enjoyed it immensely, Mother!" he exclaimed with his usual exuberance. "And I like Catherine of Aragon so well, I would marry her myself."

I laughed.

"If something should happen to Arthur, may I wed her?"

My merriment vanished. I dropped my hand. "Why do you ask such a question?"

"People die. Edmund died."

"Edmund was only a year old. He died in infancy. Babes die in infancy. But Arthur is fifteen. Grown men are hardy and many enjoy long life, excepting war and execution. Look at Morton, and Rotherham. They lived to be eighty."

"Oh," said Harry, with a shrug.

He left the room, for it was evident to him that our conversation had come to a halt. Now I knew beyond all doubt that Harry wished Arthur dead. Misery engulfed me like a leaden weight. Swept with a need for movement and change of scene, I took my cloak and went out to the walled garden. I sat quietly on the cold, snowy bench. A few birds approached, but I had no crumbs to give them. Through my anguish and distress, I felt Arthur's arms enfold me in warmth.

"Mama," he said softly, as he had when he was a child. He bent over me from behind and hugged me, his cheek against mine.

"You have not lost me. When I return next year, who knows? I may bring you yet another to love, God willing."

I caught his hand and drew him before me. "You have always understood me, Arthur, even when you were but a boy." I heaved a long breath. "Forgive me, my sweet son. I am being foolish. Everything seems different now, yet nothing has really changed, has it?"

He took a seat beside me on the bench, and I laid my head against his shoulder. A little wind rustled through the yew.

"It seems to me that I have prepared myself for this moment since I first held you in my arms," I murmured. "It should be easy to let you go now. I've done it so many times before, after all." I smiled at him through my tears. "Yet it grows harder."

"I love you, Mother. You cannot know how much," Arthur said.

I kissed his cheek.

"When I was a boy, you seemed a goddess to me," he went on. "So beautiful, so serene, gentle and kind. A splendid queen in every way. Every time I read Malory, I would think of you. For me, you were Guinevere reborn, and I remember hoping I would find a queen just like you when I grew up."

"And now you have, Arthur. Catherine is a lovely girl and will make you happy."

For a long moment we sat together, savoring the winter scene and the song of the birds. "Before you came to me," I said in a low voice, dim with memory, "I was in darkness, and when you were born, my world filled with light. From that glorious moment, you banished the loneliness in my heart. Maybe 'tis for that your absence always pains me so."

The clock on the church tower struck the hour of Terce.

"Time passes so swiftly when you are with me." I sighed. "We should return to the others. They must be wondering where we are."

We rose, and I turned my blurred gaze full on his shining face. "Know that I am proud of you, Arthur. In you, I see my pledge to England redeemed in the most wondrous way. Go forth and fulfill your destiny, my beloved. And may the Blessed Mother have you in her keeping, always."

✿

WE CELEBRATED ARTHUR'S WEDDING WITH MANY feasts and disguisings and a lavish tournament in which Kate's husband, William Courtenay, proved his courage to the cheering crowds and won the prize of a ruby. Then, abruptly, the festivities ended.

It was drizzling the day Arthur left for Ludlow. I embraced my son for a long moment, more reluctant than ever to release him. Then Henry laid his hand on my sleeve. I forced a deep breath, and stepped back. Swept with desolation, I watched him ride away. *But I must not forget my blessings,* I thought, giving Maggie a kiss on her brow as I stood in the rain. She had been married before Twelfth Night according to plan, but Henry had listened to me. She would not go to Scotland until she was fourteen.

Nevertheless, the raw emptiness inside me could be mended only by prayer. I turned to my book of hours and my prie-dieu, I read Richard's book, *Tristan,* and gazed on his portrait when it was safe to do, and I received petitioners until I could no longer stand. All this gave me a solidity that kept sorrow at bay. Lucy Neville was always at my side, along with Kate, but that too would soon change. Lucy was betrothed to Sir Anthony Browne, and come May, she would leave for her own estates. I had contrived the match with her approval, for though Sir Anthony was twice her age, at thirty she was no longer young. Theirs would be a splendid match. He was kind, good, and rich. They would be happy together.

In April, the land shed its dull winter mantle, and my thoughts turned to Ludlow. *Perhaps, even now, Catherine is with child and we shall receive joyous news,* I thought. *How sweet to cradle Arthur's child in my arms. To know the little one shall be king after him, and Arthur's legacy shall be passed down through a succession of crowns, each king to rule England with wisdom and justice.*

It was just after dawn on the fifth of the month, and I had completed my prayers and was about to break fast with my ladies when a knock came at my door. Lucy Neville entered with a curtsy.

"My queen, the king desires your company in his chamber."

"At this hour?" I murmured, taken aback. Then I noticed the knight standing behind her, clad in Henry's colors. A warm glow flowed through me. "Is it news from Ludlow?" I asked, smiling broadly.

"I know not, Your Grace," he replied.

He seems glum to be the bearer of such glad tidings, I thought, and said no more to him. By the time I arrived at Henry's door, I knew from the somber expressions I had encountered along the way that something was amiss and my heart took up a rapid beating. I stepped into the room as the door shut behind me, and then looked at Henry and gasped. He was still in his morning robe, and his face, which had been an unreadable mask of iron control through all the troubles of his life, was distorted with grief. I did not, until this moment, believe he had the capacity to feel such a depth of emotion.

"What is it? What has happened?" I uttered through frozen lips.

He tried to speak, but there was only silence.

"What is it?" I repeated, moving forward.

"Arthur—" he broke off. "Arthur is dead."

"Dead?" I stared at him. "I don't understand."

"Our son is dead," Henry wailed.

" 'Tis not true. Arthur is well. I had a letter from him only last week."

He shook his head, and lowered himself into a chair. His shoulders heaving, he covered his face with a handkerchief, and sobbed. I listened to his weeping; I watched him wipe at his tears; and still I did not believe. It was as if I stood outside myself looking down at some macabre pageant.

" 'Tis not possible. There must be some mistake," I said.

Henry removed his handkerchief and looked at me with tear-stained, red-rimmed eyes. "No mistake," he mumbled. "His chamberlain came from Wales—arrived in the night—told my confessor—he brought me the news so early, I had not risen yet." He burst into another fit of sobbing.

My legs went numb. I rested my weight on the table and sank into a chair.

"He died suddenly on the second of April," said Henry. He threw his head back and a terrible moaning issued forth from his lips. It was the most wretched sound I had ever heard, and it unleashed in me a flood of pity for this man I had struggled all my life not to hate. He rose, looked at the window, stretched his arms to Heaven, and cried, "Why? Why—"

To my horror, his legs gave way beneath him and he fell to the floor with a dull thud. I ran to him, knelt down, gathered him into my arms. I rocked him back and forth, as I had done with Arthur when he was a child and had bruised himself.

"Hush, Henry, hush . . . If we receive good things at the hand of God, why should we not endure bad things?" I whispered. "You still have Harry. Your lady mother never had but one son, and that was you, and God in His grace ever preserved you, and has left you a fair prince in Harry . . ."

I spoke the words, but I didn't believe them. I knew that Henry believed, but it was only a bad dream, and someone would come and wake us up, or maybe it was a jest. A cruel jest. Richard's queen had let out the wail of a madwoman when she'd learned of Ned's death, and my mother had swooned into oblivion. I felt nothing. Therefore, it could not be true.

Henry calmed in my arms; his sobs eased. He pressed my hand in his own, and nodded. The gratitude on his face broke my heart. "We are still young, Henry," I said. "We can have more children."

I helped him to his feet and embraced him, but it seemed to

me that I held space in my arms. A vast empty space. He leaned on me, and I took him to his bed and laid him down. I watched him for a while, and when I heard his even breathing, I knew he rested. I pushed to my feet and made my way to my chamber. We had not slept together since the executions, and I knew not why I had invited him back to my bed, except that his sorrow had touched my heart.

As I walked, servants and courtiers bowed and retreated.

'Tis no jest. Arthur is gone. I see it in their eyes.

I turned into the hallway where I had walked so short a time ago holding Arthur's arm, gazing up at his handsome face. I closed my lids and dragged myself forward, one leaden step after another. I entered my antechamber and my ladies rose and murmured at me, but I heard not what they said, nor would I have answered if I had. Kate came to me; I felt her arms around me. I shook my head. I wanted to be alone. Papa had died in April. Richard's son, Ned, had died in April. Why did everybody die in April?

Could Arthur really be gone? Why had God demanded such brutal tribute? When Ned had died so suddenly at ten years of age, the people had called it divine retribution for the death of my brother Edward.

Was this divine retribution?

Henry's words echoed in my ears. " 'Tis either Edward or Arthur. One must die so the other can live." Now both were dead.

I gave a cry and grasped the bedpost.

Catherine of Aragon arrived in England on Richard's birthday!

Richard had loved his nephew Edward almost as much as his own Ned, and Edward had been executed on a false charge of treason to make way for Arthur's marriage to Catherine. *And Catherine had arrived on the second of October—Richard's birthday.* Now I remembered my frightening dream of Richard just before Edward's execution. *An omen? A warning? A threat?* I had not known at the time.

I couldn't stop Henry! I cried. I closed my eyes, tried to steady my dizzy head. *You know I couldn't! I had to accept everything. What choice did I have? I thought it was God's will. I tried to do my best. I tried to atone for the crimes Henry committed for his throne—*

The throne of your son Arthur, came a cruel inner voice.

"Arthur—" I cried aloud on one long sobbing wail, my heart tearing with agony and anguish. I couldn't breathe. My legs gave way beneath me. I let out a scream and fell to the floor in a heap. The door burst open. My ladies were all around me. I made out Catherine Gordon's face, tears in her eyes, standing aloof, behind them all. Had her husband truly been Dickon?

"Oh God—God—" I sobbed, my body heaving as if each breath I took was a blow. A priest arrived, tried to comfort me, but there were no words to banish the grief, to soothe the pain, to ease the sorrow.

I had failed to win Humphrey Stafford his life; to obtain Edward, Earl of Warwick, his pardon; to see my mother released from confinement. I had failed to help Warbeck, who might have been Dickon. But in all this I had been sustained by the knowledge that I was raising a noble king for England, one who would love his people as my father and Richard had loved them. But all my efforts were for naught, my dreams undone. I had failed at everything I had undertaken. My mother was right about me; I was useless. My aunt was right to hate me. All I had accomplished with my life was to secure the tyranny of a bastard over my father's good people. I thought I was doing my best; bearing all for England's sake; giving her a worthy king. And God took Arthur from me. This was God's judgment.

"Why?" I cried at the sky. "Why?"

I felt Henry's arms around me then, and I turned my gaze on him. Why was he here? Had he not done enough?

"Go!" I heard him say. "Go!" I cried.

There was a swish of skirts and the patter of running feet; the slam of a door, then silence. He lifted me into his arms and held me. "Hush, Elizabeth, hush . . . If we receive good things at the hand of God, why should we not endure bad things?" he said, repeating to me the words I had spoken to him. "My dear wife, we have endured much, and somehow we will survive this day. We are still young. We can have more children—" Then he dissolved into shattering sobs, and he clutched me, and I clutched back, and the blackness of my nightmares overtook me.

✳

I LAY BENEATH HEAVY COVERS OF DOWN AS VOICES
came and went, riding on the shadows. My father was talking, and
little Edward of Warwick was running, laughing after his hound. I
heard my terrier bark with joy. Johnnie of Gloucester said something, but I couldn't make out what it was. Oh, he wished a dance.
He was such a handsome boy, of course I would dance with him . . .
And there was Mother, huddled in a corner of the sanctuary, cheek
to cheek with little Dickon, speaking of secrets. Dickon vanished,
but Grandmother Jacquetta appeared. She was with Friar Bungey.
They turned away from me now and were whispering. Never
mind, Papa had come to join me, and he gazed at me the way he
always had, with adoration in his eyes. My golden, magnificent,
handsome father. "Papa," I murmured, smiling; "Papa, I love you."
He took my hand and kissed it. "You shall be queen," he replied.
He vanished, and Richard stood in his place. He inclined his head,
and held out his hand to me. Arthur joined us, and arm in arm
we three strolled through the crowded hall. Everyone surrounded
us with smiles; it was good to hear them talk of love and reunion.
Drifting in and out, the voices came and went; darkness lifted, light
broke. I opened my eyes.

A new dawn had risen.

CHAPTER 29

Elizabeth the Beloved, 1502

AFTER ARTHUR'S DEATH, REMEMBERING MY SISTER Mary, I waited for a sign from him. But there was nothing. No streak of blue light; only silence, and utter darkness. Queen Anne's words echoed in my mind: "Love is all there is, dear child. Ned has my love, and I keep his—here—"

Seated before my mirror, I laid my hand on my bosom, as she had done on hers, but there was naught there but a vast emptiness. *I have disappeared. I am a stranger; I walk, and eat, and am invisible.* A vision of Anne rose up before me. *Each time someone dies, he takes a piece of you with him,* she had said. *Until there is nothing left,* I added, laying down my mirror.

I dropped my head into my hands.

All the court waited to see if Catherine was with child. *As they had once waited for me to show with Richard's child.* But she was not. Kate sat with me in these days in quiet companionship. Once she asked how I felt.

"I know not how to answer that, Kate. Queen Anne said the ones we love are never gone, for we keep their love in our hearts, and they take ours with them to Heaven. But I cannot feel my heart anymore, Kate."

I continued with life as I always had: receiving petitioners, presiding over state banquets, darning and mending my gowns, and offering my prayers to Heaven. Yet nothing touched me. I was weary of life, weary of pretense, weary of yearning for what was lost.

Blessed Virgin, send me rest . . .

I did not attend Arthur's funeral, but I knew that his black-velvet-draped coffin was carried on a hearse drawn by six ebony horses to Worcester, where he was interred. They told me that all the torches of the city were lit in mournful greeting, and that the streets filled with tearful folk come to bid him silent farewell. After the prayers, the readings, and the sermons, the black horse that Arthur had loved so well was led into the chapel, and there was no man present who did not weep.

So I was told.

Henry gave me a month to mourn and came to my bed every night afterward, and every night he slept fitfully, disturbed by evil dreams. One time he bolted upright in bed in terror.

"I keep seeing their faces," he said.

I did not ask whose faces; there were so many now.

In June, I learned I was with child. Henry was elated. In that same month, Kate and I became sisters in grief, for her five-year-old son, Edward, died of a sudden illness.

"If my babe is a girl, I shall name her Katherine," I told Kate.

She attempted a smile and passed me a paper with a white satin ribbon attached. "Elizabeth, I found this tied to the rose bush by the bench where you sit."

I opened it, and bent my head to read:

> *In a glorious garden green*
> *I saw a comely queen*
> *among the flowers, once fair and fresh.*
> *She plucked a stem and held it in her hands.*
> *I thought I saw a lily-white rose,*
> *I thought it was a lily-white rose.*

And evermore she sang,
"This day dawns,
This gentle day dawns,
Another day dawns,
and when shall I go home to rest?"

I felt as if the rhyme maker had caught my soul. I reached out a hand to Kate, and she bent down and laid a kiss on my brow.

✿

AFTER ARTHUR'S DEATH, HENRY PLACED HARRY under guard. His movements were restricted, and he was as closely watched as I had been for the early years of my marriage. He was kept at his studies for long hours at a time, allowed to break only for prayer and the privy, and his every move was reported to Henry, who lectured him on what he had done that must not be repeated. Harry tried to escape his guards once by climbing over the garden wall. For an entire afternoon, no one could find him. Later, he was discovered hiding high up in a tree. Henry came himself to supervise Harry's retrieval. For Henry's dynasty hung by a thread now, as Richard's had once done.

"You have committed a serious offense that merits severe punishment," Henry told him.

"I'm not afraid of you!" Harry retorted.

A muscle quivered at Henry's jaw. "Bray—"

"Aye, sire?"

"Take Prince Harry to the Tower." Henry did not take his gaze from Harry's face. "Make sure he is shown the teeth-ripping claws, the bone-smashing wheel, and the cat paws that shred the skin, as well as the screws and presses. And the Iron Maiden that eviscerates a man alive." Harry listened, a look of excitement on his face.

After a pause, Henry said, "Then he is to be locked into an oubliette and denied food or water. He is not to return until he vows obedience."

Harry's expression changed to one of terror. "Father!" he cried as he was taken away.

Harry came back the next morning before luncheon, thoroughly cowed. I gazed at the garden bench. He sat languishing with a book open on his lap where once he had shot his arrows and engaged in wild revelry.

"Is there no other way, Henry?" I asked.

Henry joined me at the window. "We have already lost one son. We cannot lose Harry."

"Arthur was trained in kingship. But Harry has not learned to be a king. It does not bode well for the kingdom."

"Nevertheless, he must be carefully guarded. He is wild and might endanger himself otherwise." Henry paused. "Besides, away from us, our enemies could get to Henry as my—" he broke off abruptly, and reddened.

As my mother got to Richard's son.

Now I was certain, all doubt removed. I closed my eyes and saw Richard in the dream riding toward me. *This is Heaven's punishment on us. An eye for an eye.*

A son for a son.

❖

THE GOLDEN DAYS THAT HAD ONCE BRIMMED WITH joy and passed too swiftly now stretched out before me like an endless gray sea, bleak and empty. One afternoon, craving solitude, I left my ladies and went down to the walled garden below my chamber. The skies were dismal and it was drizzling, but I did not care. I sat down on the bench and drew my fur-lined cloak around me tightly. I had prayed for most of the night and read from Richard and Anne's Book of Ghostly Grace, and also Boethius. And I had taken out Richard's portrait from the coffer to gaze on his face. Now I needed to be alone with my thoughts, and with nature, for it was in nature that God's hand was most clearly seen.

Birds watched me from the barren trees as I withdrew a piece of bread from my cloak and scattered the crumbs out on the path. A sparrow found the courage to appear. Nervously, he drew near and took a peck, then another, one eye fixed on me. I made no movement, yet he flew away, leaving most of the bread untouched.

If only I had fled, I thought; *he could not have caught me; he could not have secured his hold on the throne.*

But then there would have been no Arthur. Would I have wished my eldest son never to have been born?

I could not wish that. Queen Anne's words came to me out of the past. *You have to find a way to live. You have to decide what you will stand for, fight for, die for.*

Arthur had been my way.

I banished my sorrowful thought and became aware of the murmur of voices on the wind. I turned and looked up at the palace. The tall windows of the solar stood open. I rose from the bench and drew near. I heard them clearly now.

"To survive in this world of enemies, you must see everyone as a rival," Henry was saying.

"Why not just kill them all, Father? Then you don't have to be concerned about any of them."

"No, Harry, the nobility has its uses."

"What use are they if they're always trying to steal your throne?"

"A wise king uses the nobility to raise himself high in the eyes of the people. The commons revere them for their ancient lineage. When they see them serve us at our banquets, and walk in our processions, and lead our armies, they esteem us even more. But you must keep your eye on the nobles, especially those of royal blood. Thin their ranks once in a while, for they will band together against you, if you give them a chance, Harry."

I groaned inwardly. Henry was growing ever more suspicious of those of my blood. My cousin William de la Pole, who had not fled England with his brothers, was in the Tower. Now Kate's husband, William Courtenay, who had discharged himself so valiantly in the tournament following Arthur's marriage, and who was innocent of any crime, had been sent to join him. Where would it end?

I dared not consider that. I did not have the strength any longer.

❖

I STOOD AT THE WINDOW AND GAZED DOWN AT HARRY, who sat on a bench, moping, as he often did these days.

"He's been utterly miserable since Henry brought him here," I said to Kate, who stood nearby. "He's lost his freedom, and he's too young to understand why." I was unable to suppress the sadness that

I felt for my boy, for well I understood what confinement meant. He was a prize in a jeweled cage, as I had been for many years.

Kate said nothing. She merely moved toward me at the window, and together we watched him. We had shared the loss of our sons within a few months of one another, and now there was William. I pressed her hand.

"Sweet sister, you cannot know how much it pains me that I am of so little help to you . . ." My voice trailed off. Henry's troubled mind, once it had seized on treachery, would not be soothed into submission, and I'd been unable to avert this cruelty. For him, life was a war he had to fight daily to keep what had come to him on a turn of Fortune's wheel. " 'Tis scant comfort, I know, but one day Harry will be king and we have spoken of William. He has promised me—"A glance at Kate told me she understood. As soon as Harry was king, he would release William.

Kate wiped a tear from the corner of her eye " 'Tis not your fault, Elizabeth. Though it breaks my heart to have William gone from my side, I am grateful for the five happy years we had. If it weren't for you, I would have been wed to someone not of my choosing. Anne feels the same way. We have spoken of it often— how much we owe you. Dear sister, you've always done so much for us, yet you've known little but sorrow yourself."

"Once, when I was a child in sanctuary," I said quietly, "and you were but a babe in arms, I was given a slice of cake for my birthday. I divided it into eight pieces, one for each of us. That meant no one received more than a few crumbs. But oh, how sweet those crumbs tasted. I still remember."

Kate turned her enormous fern-green eyes on me. "It takes a special kind of courage to bear what you have borne. Yet you've done it with grace and serenity. Did I ever tell you how much I admire you?"

Something stirred in my heart.

"I admire her, too," said a voice behind me. "But I know I never told her."

I turned. Cecily stood in the middle of the room, watching us with a smile on her lips. I put out my hand to her and she came to my side. "Are you leaving, Cecily?"

She nodded. "I've come to bid you farewell. I don't know why, but it saddens me to leave you."

" 'Tis a long way, the Isle of Wight," I murmured, seized with a sudden, inexplicable panic that I would never see her again. I swallowed hard on the rising fear. "Not yet—not yet. Stay a little longer, Cecily."

"I shall miss you, too, Elizabeth. I have thought often of our childhood together. If only we had realized how precious and fleeting that time was." She gave me a wistful look. "Do you remember the game we used to play on the Saracen carpet, you, me, and Mary?"

"Take me to the stars," I murmured. "I'd step on first, and speak those words, and you and Mary would follow me, and repeat them. We were always so disappointed that nothing happened."

Cecily grinned at me. "Then, when we realized we'd never get there this way, we had the brilliant idea of ordering the servants to bring the stars to us."

"Papa must have had a good laugh at that," I said.

"But the servants didn't find it amusing. They avoided us like the plague afterward, remember?"

Aye, I remember.

"Whatever made us think that standing on that silly Saracen rug and raising our right arms would take us to the stars?" Her voice was tender with memory.

I shook my head. "I know not. I only remember how happy I was." I looked down at Harry, sulking in the garden.

"He has a completely different childhood from ours, doesn't he?" Cecily murmured, following my gaze.

"He shall be king," I said sadly.

"They all say he's our father. But he's not, is he?"

I inhaled a deep breath. "On the outside, maybe."

"Who do you think he's really like?"

I shook my head, pretending I didn't know, but I was assailed by an overwhelming melancholy. *He's a Tudor,* I thought; *and Arthur was a Plantagenet.*

"I wonder what kind of king he'll make," Kate chimed in, and it seemed to me that her words were spoken on a sigh.

"A good one," I replied, with more hope than conviction.

Cecily slipped an arm around my waist. "Whatever kind of king he makes, surely you know you did your best, Elizabeth?"

Kate followed Cecily's example and slid a hand around my waist. I threaded mine around theirs and drew both my sisters close to me.

"You did your best." Kate repeated Cecily's words, and added, "For us. For everyone. For all England, Elizabeth."

"Your best," they echoed softly in unison.

I gave them each a kiss on the cheek, and we stood together before the great mullioned windows, arms linked around our waists, clad in our broad-sleeved black gowns of mourning, gazing down at Harry.

EPILOGUE

The Tower of London
In the early hours of February 11, 1503

THE WIND HOWLED AND WHIPPED ABOUT THE TOWER, and as sea birds screeched, voices came to me against the dark of night. Softly they spoke, as if they wished not to awaken me, a gentle soothing murmur on the shadows. They talked of the christening, always a splendid affair with canopies and candles, processions and song. Aye, it was best to have it done soon; the child, Katherine, was frail, and one never knew. The man's voice faded and a woman's rose, lifting the melancholy. But God be praised, the other children were well. Prince Harry was strong and sturdy, and naught could happen to him for he no longer attempted to escape his confinement, and they need not fear he would break his neck in the hunt, since he was no longer permitted such sport. He would live long, God willing.

Length of life is length of woe, I said, but they didn't hear me.

Silence came and went, broken by exchanged whispers. It was the servants, bless them.

"It shall be good to have the queen back again, won't it? 'Tisn't the same without her—the castle is glum, stern somehow. She always brings joy and has a pleasant word for everyone, a smile; a gift. So fair she is, even now, golden hair like an angel, that one."

"Elizabeth the Good," said another voice. " 'Tis no wonder the king likes to while away the evenings in her chamber."

"There shall be a christening . . . another celebration."

There came the sound of a log being thrown on the fire. I heard the flames licking and devouring the wood, and I thought of Sheen, and Dickon . . . Or was it Perkin?

"You shall be well soon, Elizabeth." My sister's voice.

Poor Kate, whatever got into Henry? Always so suspicious, so frightened. I had tried to allay his demons, but without success. Now William was in the Tower. But then, Sir Humphrey Stafford laughed and pointed to a hound, and I forgot about Kate and laughed with him. A friar appeared at Humphrey's shoulder. *Thomas, you've been gone a long time! I missed you so.* I lifted my lips, and he kissed me, then he gave me a breviary, but a child tugged at my skirts, and I had to let him go. It was Arthur, three years old, in his plumes. *Arthur,* I cried. But Arthur disappeared, and in his place stood Edward of Warwick, holding out a handful of soil to me. I wrapped my arms around him and smoothed his golden curls. *It's all right, Edward. Today is my birthday. We shall have marchpane—see, King Richard comes to join us. There he is—there in the mist, on his white horse, strumming his lute,*

> *For the time was May-time, and blossoms draped the earth,*
> *Wine, wine—and I will love thee to the death*
> *And out beyond into the dream to come.*

All at once his song ceased, and he was gone. It was quiet around me, and my body felt as heavy as marble. I could no longer move any part of it: not my hands, feet, or even my lids. There was no pain, but breathing was slow and difficult. Though I heard voices, I no longer recognized them; everything seemed faint, faraway, echoing as if in a dream. A flurry of sounds dimly penetrated my consciousness: footsteps, a medley of hushed voices, the rustle of fabric permeated by a stale odor. I held my breath. Someone leaned over and I heard them murmur, "My lady, 'tis the king."

A wild joy erupted in my breast, filling my cold body with the heat of sunshine and an ineffable, inexplicable lightness. My eyes opened, my head lifted, and a wide smile came to my lips; it seemed to me that I could even raise my arms for an embrace.

"*Richard!*" I cried.

AUTHOR'S NOTE

Devastated by Elizabeth's death, Henry VII shut himself away to grieve for his queen and threw her a lavish funeral at which Elizabeth's sister, Katherine, was chief mourner. Historians agree that Elizabeth exercised much influence over Henry VII for good, since, after she died, his character began to degenerate and his acts grew more violent, debased, and vile.[1] Katherine's husband, William Courtenay, remained imprisoned in the Tower until Henry VII's death and was freed by Henry VIII, but he was in poor health by then, and lived only nine months after his release. Katherine was much impoverished during her lifetime. Her son, Henry, was later executed by Henry VIII.

In order to keep from returning Catherine of Aragon's dowry, Henry VII offered to marry the young widow himself. Isabella of Spain was repulsed. She was anxious to have her daughter back, even if a betrothal with the second son could be arranged, for it was no longer honorable, she said, for her daughter to remain in England under such protection.[2] In retaliation, Henry reduced Catherine's allowance and left it unpaid often enough that the young princess was forced to beg for her sustenance and lived as a virtual pauper for some years.[3]

Henry VII died on April 21, 1509, most likely from consumption, after many failed attempts to secure for himself a rich royal bride, preferably one who was young and beautiful and had "sweet breath." To recover his health, he took to drinking the blood of sanguine young men.[4] Like his mother,

---

[1] Gairdner, p. 211.
[2] Ibid., p. 190.
[3] Bruce, p. 204.
[4] Wroe, pp. 506–507.

who lived only three months longer than her son, he met death in an abject emotional state, weeping and praying, and in horror of a horned devil diving into his throat to seize his soul. In his will he implored the Virgin that "the ghostly enemy nor none other evil or damnable esprit, have no power to invade me," a reference that Perkin Warbeck's biographer sees as carrying a final echo of his struggle with the pretender.[5] By the time of his death Henry VII was a reviled despot known for his "murders and tyrannies" and rapacious extortions.[6]

Virtually nothing has survived of Elizabeth, no letters or private thoughts; little that she said or did was recorded, though her vegetarianism was noted for posterity.[7] This is curious, since so much is extant about this period in all other respects. Francis Bacon says that Elizabeth Woodville thought her daughter "not advanced but depressed," meaning she considered Elizabeth not a true queen, but a puppet.[8] Despite this, the fact that Elizabeth was a gentle force for good and beloved by her people for her acts of charity and compassion cannot be disputed. In the words of her biographer, she "brought hope to those in despair, comfort to those in pain, and restraint to those in power."[9] That she managed to develop an affectionate relationship with one of the most unlovable of English kings is remarkable in itself.

Historians describe Elizabeth as an enigma, holding a separate, virtually unvisitable, and invisible court, emerging from the shadows only occasionally, and always with Margaret Beaufort at her side, usually dressed in a replica of her gown.[10] The Spanish ambassador, de Puebla, wrote to his sovereigns that the queen was kept in subjugation by her mother-in-law. Indeed, Margaret Beaufort emerges as one of the principal figures of this reign, and in contrast to Elizabeth, much is known about her, including her persecution of the widows of loyal servants, her ordinances, and her revered patronage as the benefactress of universities.[11] The contrast between these two women is striking, hence my conclusion that Elizabeth of York, a prize to the Lancastrian

---

[5] Ibid., p. 507.
[6] Words of Edmund de la Pole, Earl of Suffolk, himself executed by Henry VIII upon Henry VII's death, probably along with his brother, William.
[7] At a Christmas feast in the ninth year of Henry VII's reign, sixty dishes were served to the guests, but to Elizabeth of York none were "fish or flesh." Stowe, p. 415.
[8] Bacon and Levy, p. 84.
[9] Harvey, p. 202.
[10] Wroe, p. 458; Baldwin, p. 138.
[11] Jones and Underwood, pp. 106–108.

victor of Bosworth, was held in virtual captivity by Henry Tudor and his obsessive, domineering mother for most of her married life.

A great deal has been made of Margaret Beaufort's piety, but some historians have cast doubt on its sincerity.[12] They see her as a manipulative political creature, a woman who married her fourth husband with unseemly haste, before her third husband was even buried, in order to elevate her influence in the Yorkist court.[13] The splendid furnishings with which she surrounded herself denote someone more worldly than spiritual, unlike Elizabeth, who wore tin buckles on her shoes and gave most of her money away to those in need.[14] In 1503, Margaret Beaufort fought Henry for her manor of Woking, which he decided he wanted, and she finally recovered it a few weeks after his death, just before her own. According to many historians, she was a calculating, unprincipled plotter.[15] Sir William Cornwallis considered Richard III's clemency in allowing her to live a "weakness" in his rule that led to his fall.[16] Both Sir George Buck and Cornwallis see her as dangerous and a woman of pitiless ambition for her son. But Richard III, the last of the medieval kings and a protector of women, could not have done otherwise, given his character. With him at Bosworth Field died the Age of Chivalry, and it was left to the Tudors to impoverish, terrorize, and butcher women.

Bishop John Morton, friend, advisor, and fellow schemer of Margaret Beaufort and Henry VII, who received a cardinal's hat at the behest of his benefactors, was so hated during his lifetime that Henry VII felt obliged to pass a special act making it treason for anyone to contemplate his death. Morton has been called a plague; it was said that when he died, England was delivered of a pestilence.[17] His great claim to fame nearly six hundred years later, after service to three kings, is the argument he devised that extorts money from rich and poor alike, known as "Morton's Fork."

---

[12] John Britton's 200 pages of notes, drafts, and transcripts of letters between Margaret and her son, the king, as well as Britton's own research survive as Cambridge University Library Ms. 00.6.89. Like Sir George Buck, he sees her as a woman of shrewdness and guile, verging on trickery. Both Britton and Sir Horace Walpole ridicule the account of her vision of St. Nicholas by whom she had been guided in her choice of Edmund Tudor as husband.

[13] Jones and Underwood, p. 58.

[14] Ibid., p. 189.

[15] Ibid., p. 65.

[16] Ibid., p. 4.

[17] Woodhouse, p. vi. He cites as his source William Guthrie's *A General History of England from the Invasion of the Romans under Jul. Caesar to the Late Revolution in 1688.* (3 folio volumes). London: Browne, 1744; pub. 1744–1751.

Such then are the forces that molded the future Henry VIII. According to the biographer of his childhood, at seventeen he was no blank page. An angelic youth, "a divine prince," his ascension was hailed as the dawn of a new and glorious age. On his death thirty-seven years later, he left behind a horrific record of egotistical greed and brutality unrivaled by any other English monarch. Some point to syphilis as the cause of this incredible transformation, or to the blow to the head that caused him to lie unconscious for two hours. The most recent medical view is that the head injury did no lasting damage and that syphilis can be ruled out. During his life, Henry VIII showed no other sign of the disease, and had he been treated for syphilis, his ambassadors would have known, because this was a lengthy, drastic, and unpleasant process.[18] The medical consensus is that his condition was either a varicose ulcer or osteomyelitis.

On this basis, his childhood biographer concludes that there was no radical change in personality and that characteristics prominent in middle age were latent in his golden youth. Henry VIII was the product of heredity, which includes his Woodville and Beaufort grandmothers, and his father, who gave him his first lesson in political murder at age eight. The gentling influence of his mother was removed from his life when he was eleven years old. Environment, which might have lightened the burden of his genes, instead reinforced his sordid tendencies by the example of Cardinal Morton and the teachings of Henry VIII's vengeful tutor, the misogynist John Skelton. This is the basis for his characterization portrayed in this book.

My treatment of Elizabeth's feelings for her uncle is based on several clues. Queen Anne and Elizabeth of York did appear in the same gown on that last Christmas of Richard's life, giving rise to rumors of an illicit love affair that Richard was obliged to deny at the hospital of the Knights of St. John in Clerkenwell. Elizabeth could not have replicated the queen's gown without her permission; therefore, the copy must have been coordinated between them. According to Sir George Buck, Elizabeth wrote to John Howard, Duke of Norfolk, declaring her love for King Richard and her hope of becoming his wife. In Buck's words, the letter asks Norfolk "to be a mediator for her to the King, in behalf of the marriage propounded between them," who, as she wrote, was her "only joy and maker in this world," and that she was his in heart and thought, and in Buck's words, "withall insinuating that

---

[18] Bruce. p. 13.

the better part of February was past, and that she feared the Queen would never die." The letter has been lost, but I trust my portrayal of Elizabeth's motivation and the circumstances that surround its formulation are legitimate and based on probability.

More clues to Elizabeth's feelings for her uncle can be found in the books of King Richard's library. Among them is *Tristan,* which Elizabeth of York clearly read and treasured as a young woman at a time of crisis in her life when she was neither princess nor queen. An emotional involvement is suggested by her mysterious motto, *Sans Removyr,* "without changing" (never used by her again) inserted below Richard's ex libris.[19] A copy of *De consolatione philosophiae* by Boethius also carries her notations in the margins and is inscribed on the flyleaf with a fascinating combination of Richard's motto, *Loyaulte me Lie,* "Loyalty Binds Me," and Elizabeth of York's first name, both in her handwriting.

There can be no doubt that Henry VII was a cold husband.[20] The Spanish ambassador, de Puebla, wrote to his sovereigns that Elizabeth was "in need of a little love." Given her loneliness, it would be reasonable to assume that she remembered the shining impression of King Richard and looked back with yearning on a time when life had held out hope and a measure of happiness.

A final question remains: were the princes murdered, or did they survive?

Henry Tudor was as plagued by rumors that the boys were alive as Richard was by rumors that they were dead. In order to rewrite history and change Richard's reputation from hero to villain, the victor of Bosworth pursued the destruction of any documents unfavorable to his own version of events, including the Titulus Regius, the record of King Richard's Parliament that gave Richard's reasons for taking the throne and enacted legislation to protect the innocent. It is indeed fortunate for posterity that one obscure copy was missed. Documents that could exonerate Richard, such as Perkin Warbeck's letter of identity, or those proving Edward IV's bigamy, may have existed, but failed to survive. This is not surprising. The parties involved, including Perkin Warbeck, were imprisoned, and Warbeck was subjected to such torture in the summer of 1498 that the Spanish ambassador expected him not to live much longer.

---

[19] Livia Visser–Fuchs, "Where Did Elizabeth of York Find Consolation," *The Ricardian,* no. 122 (September 1993), pp. 469–473; Sutton and Visser–Fuchs, pp. 15, 221.
[20] Bacon and Levy, pp. 79–80; Gairdner, p. 182; Routh, pp. 57, 61–63.

As noted by one of King Richard's biographers, had he won Bosworth, his "usurpation," like that of Henry IV, would have been disregarded in the brilliancy that marked his kingly career. Furthermore, had it not been for King Edward IV's own shortcomings, Richard of Gloucester would never have found himself obliged to accept the throne and would have been commemorated by posterity as a prince of vigorous mind, sound judgment, and enlarged views, and as an able general, a dutiful subject, and a just and upright man.[21]

But history is written by the victors, and Henry VII perfected the art of propaganda with his use of misinformation.[22] Though the Tudors were anxious for history to believe that the princes were murdered and that Richard III committed the deed, there are some compelling pieces of evidence in favor of Richard's innocence. A fact often overlooked is that Richard had *three* little nephews who were legally barred from the throne. The Tudors would have us believe he murdered two of them, but not the third—Clarence's orphaned son, Edward, Earl of Warwick. Richard brought this child to live with him in his household, and as soon as Richard was slain, Henry Tudor imprisoned the boy, then eleven, in the Tower of London. Thirteen years later, he beheaded young Warwick on a pretext of treason, so that his son, Prince Arthur, could inherit a throne unchallenged by a rightful heir and marry Catherine of Aragon. Later, Queen Catherine would say that her marriage had been made in blood.

It was Henry Tudor, not Richard III, who had the most to gain from the deaths of all *three* little princes. The treatment of young Warwick alone speaks volumes about the difference in character between these two kings. In the actions of Elizabeth Woodville and her daughter, Elizabeth of York, can be found further evidence of Richard's innocence.

Elizabeth Woodville must have believed that Richard didn't murder her boys because she came out of sanctuary and wrote her son Dorset that all was well and to return to England. Eighteen months into Henry Tudor's reign, she suddenly incurred Tudor's disfavor and was locked away in an abbey, where she was held virtually incommunicado until her death. She must have lent her support to the rebellion, but was it because she'd learned that her

---

[21] Halsted, pp. 6–7, 385–386.
[22] It is interesting to contemplate what Churchill's and FDR's reputations would be today had Hitler won World War II.

son, Richard of York, was alive, or because she'd learned that Henry Tudor, or his mother, Margaret Beaufort, was responsible for the deaths of her boys? And why did Henry Tudor, who defiled Richard's body and his reputation so brutally, never formally accuse Richard of their murder? Was it because he knew Richard was innocent?[23]

As Henry VII's queen, Elizabeth of York won the hearts of her people with her charity and generosity, much as Anne Neville had done, and like Queen Anne, she was given the appellation "The Good." It is inconceivable that such a woman could have loved a man she knew had arranged the secret murder of her brothers, yet love him she did.

For some, the most convincing evidence that the princes died in Richard's reign is the fact that no one ever saw them after October 1483. However, in *Richard of England*, Diana Kleyn makes a persuasive case that Perkin Warbeck was indeed who he said he was. For those interested in pursuing the topic further, Audrey Williamson's *The Mystery of the Princes,* a Golden Dagger Award winner, also provides an intriguing and authoritative vindication of Richard III.

According to John Morton's biographer, the bishop "made the Tudor dynasty" and also made Sir Thomas More, to whom he gave the *History of King Richard the Third* that More claimed as his own work.[24] Here More–Morton states that Tyrrell confessed to the murder before his execution, but no one mentioned a confession before More did, and no record of one has survived. Yet More's account quickly became the accepted story of what had happened to Richard, Duke of York. It would seem, therefore, that Morton condemns himself by his account of the princes being buried at the foot of the stairs in the White Tower. Since Morton died in 1500, and Sir James Tyrrell, supposedly the confessed murderer of the princes, was not picked up until 1501, Morton's knowledge of the crime was premature and could have come only as a result of his own guilt.[25] The allusion to the bodies being moved later may have been intended to cover up his involvement.

---

[23] For an interesting discussion of this and other matters touched on above, see Baldwin, pp. 111–114.

[24] Woodhouse, p. vi.

[25] Tyrrell was beheaded in 1502. His confession, if it happened, was never made public, except in More's *History of the Reign of King Richard III*, which remained unfinished and was not published until fifteen years after his death. Archbishop Morton is given as the source of More's information.

If so, Morton seems to have been only partially successful in his efforts, because one of the princes may well have survived (see below). The skeletal remains that were found at the base of the stairs two hundred years later, put into an urn, and declared peremptorily to be those of the princes have never been validated. The forensic examination done in 1934 was flawed and did not even check for gender. More recent requests for DNA analysis have been denied, perhaps because the search for truth is complicated by its ramifications. If the results come back negative, or inconclusive, then one of the princes survived Richard's reign and Perkin may have been who he said he was. In that case, the notion that Henry VII may have executed the true King of England would cast a long shadow over the British monarchy. Perhaps for this reason, most British historians have always dismissed Warbeck as a false pretender.[26]

Another consideration in favor of Richard's innocence is the known record of the Tudors in removing those who stood in their way. Their pattern of elimination may have begun with King Richard's son and heir, nine-year-old Prince Edward of Wales, whose death threw the dynasty back into dispute, benefiting only one person—Henry Tudor. The child's death occurred exactly a year after King Edward IV's own on the previous Easter, an uncanny coincidence that suggests premeditation.[27] When taken together with the fact that the little prince died suddenly after eating, of a bellyache accompanied by great pain, it lends credence to the contemporary rumors of poison and may explain Richard's desperate attempt at Bosworth to engage Tudor personally. Given Margaret Beaufort's calculating nature, her plotting on behalf of her son, and her "pitiless ambition," Prince Edward's death may have come as a direct result of Henry Tudor's thirst for Richard's crown. This ghastly possibility no doubt occurred to Queen Anne, whose own death within a year further fractured Richard's fragile emotional health before Bosworth.

---

[26] Wroe never says who she thinks the pretender was, though her work builds a strong circumstantial case that he was indeed Richard of York. Her book, published in the United States as *The Perfect Prince*, was retitled *Perkin: A Story of Deception* for its publication in the United Kingdom. It should be noted the idea that Henry VII executed the pretender *because* he was Richard of York is entirely mine.

[27] Some authorities give the date Prince Edward died as April 9, the same date as King Edward's death. Whatever the truth of this, his death clearly fell on the first anniversary of King Edward's own at Easter, April 9, 1483, whether this happened to be April 9, 1484, or Easter, April 18, 1484.

Ultimately, in view of the actions and behavior of those most closely involved in the drama of the princes in the Tower, including Maximilian, Emperor of the Romans, and Margaret, Duchess of Burgundy, as well as statements made by Henry VII after Stoke, it seems likely that one of the princes survived King Richard's reign. In this case, the pretender may well have been who he claimed to be: Richard of England.

Lastly, Perkin Warbeck's name may provide another small clue to his identity. "Wesbecque" was a play on words by someone who knew Flemish as well as French: the Flemish *wezen*, "to be" or "to be real," and *weze*, the word for "orphan."[28] It is curious that the official narrative of this young man given under torture contains so many elements applicable to the life of the real prince, Richard, Duke of York. Here is a child whose name meant "real" and "orphan," of no known address or clear parentage, who moved all over Europe, always in the company of English people (to explain his fluency in the English language) and who lived for a time in Portugal, somehow managing to attach himself to the wife of a man whose name resembled one of Richard III's most loyal retainers, the Portuguese Jew Duarte Brandeo—Sir Edward Brampton. Even Edward the Fourth makes an appearance in Perkin's tale, acting as his godfather.[29] Both "princes" are linked by a common thread of wandering, jeopardy, and sorrow.

Catherine Gordon never returned to Scotland; she continued to live at court until Henry VII's death. She did not remarry during his lifetime, perhaps because Henry did not wish it. While he may have been repugnant to her for obvious reasons, she might have allowed him to show affection to her since her son's welfare and her own protection rested entirely on his goodwill. After his death, she married three more times and lived for a while in Wales. A rumor surfaced that her little son had been brought up there, and at least one family, the Perkins of Reynoldston, traced their descent to him. There is also the mysterious "Richard Plantagenet," otherwise known as the highly educated, reclusive bricklayer Richard of Eastwell, who read Latin and died in 1550. He might have been the child taken from his parents at St. Buryan. The account of his identity could be an amalgam of both the tale of Prince Richard's flight from England on the eve of Bosworth and the life of the pretender's own son, Richard. Certainly, his dates fit this explanation

[28] Wroe, p. 407.
[29] Bacon and Levy, pp. 152–153.

better than the more commonly held theory that he was a third bastard child of Richard III.

Catherine Gordon died in 1537 and was interred in Fyfield Church, where a monument was erected to her memory. After Perkin's execution, she wore black until her death.

SELECT BIBLIOGRAPHY

Alexander, Michael Van Cleave. *The First of the Tudors A Study of Henry VII and His Reign*. Totowa, N.J.: Rowman and Littlefield, 1980.

Bacon, Francis, and F. J. Levy. *The History of the Reign of King Henry the Seventh*. New York: Bobbs-Merrill, 1972.

Baldwin, David. *Elizabeth Woodville: Mother of the Princes in the Tower*. Stroud, England: Sutton, 2004.

Bruce, Mary Louise. *The Making of Henry VIII*. London: Collins, 1977.

Calendar of Letters, Despatches, and State Papers, Relating to the Negotiations between England and Spain Pt. 1. 1538–1542. Nendeln, Liechtenstein: Kraus, 1969.

Chrimes, S. B. *Henry VII*. Berkeley: University of California Press, 1972.

Commynes, Philippe de, and Sam Kinser. *The Memoirs of Philippe de Commynes*. Vol. 1. Columbia: University of South Carolina Press, 1969.

Commynes, Philippe de, and Sam Kinser. *The Memoirs of Philippe de Commynes*. Vol. 2. Columbia: University of South Carolina Press, 1973

Fields, Bertram. *Royal Blood: Richard III and the Mystery of the Princes*. New York: Regan Books, 1998.

Gairdner, James. *Henry the Seventh*. Boston: Elibron Classics, 2001. First published 1889 by Macmillan. http://www.elibron.com.

Halstead, Caroline. *Richard III as Duke of Gloucester and King of England* (2 vols.). London: Longman, Brown, Green, and Longmans, 1844.

Harvey, Nancy Lenz. *Elizabeth of York: The Mother of Henry VIII.* New York: Macmillan, 1973.

Jones, Michael K., and Malcolm G. Underwood. *The King's Mother: Lady Margaret Beaufort, Countess of Richmond and Derby.* Cambridge, England: Cambridge University Press, 1992.

Kendall, Paul Murray. *Richard the Third.* New York: Norton, 1956.

Kleyn, D. M. *Richard of England.* Oxford, England: Kensal Press, 1991.

Lockyer, Roger, and Andrew Thrush. *Henry VII: Seminar Studies in History.* London: Longman, 1997.

MacGibbon, David. *Elizabeth Woodville, 1437–1492: Her Life and Times.* London: Barker, 1938.

Nicolas, Nicholas Harris. *Privy Purse Expenses of Elizabeth of York, [and] Wardrobe Accounts of Edward the Fourth with a Memoir of Elizabeth of York and Notes.* London: Frederick Muller, 1972.

Pollard, A. F. *The Reign of Henry VII from Contemporary Sources.* New York: AMS Press, 1967.

Ross, Charles. *Edward IV.* Berkeley: University of California Press, 1974.

Routh, E. M. G. *Lady Margaret: A Memoir of Lady Margaret Beaufort, Countess of Richmond and Derby, Mother of Henry VII.* London: Oxford University Press, 1975.

Scarisbrick, J. J. *Henry VIII.* Berkeley: University of California Press, 1968.

Simons, Eric N. *Henry VII, the First Tudor King.* New York: Barnes & Noble, 1968.

Storey, R. L. *The Reign of Henry VII.* New York: Walker, 1968.

Stowe, John. *The Survey of London.* London: Dent, 1912.

Sutton, Anne F., and Livia Visser-Fuchs. *Richard III's Books Ideals and Reality in the Life and Library of a Medieval Prince.* Stroud, England: Sutton, 1997.

Temperley, Gladys. *Henry VII.* Westport, Conn.: Greenwood Press, 1971.

Weightman, Christine B. *Margaret of York, Duchess of Burgundy, 1446–1503.* New York: St. Martin's Press, 1989.

Williamson, Audrey. *The Mystery of the Princes: An Investigation into a Supposed Murder.* Stroud, England: Sutton, 1981.

Woodhouse, Reginald Illingworth. *The Life of John Morton, Archbishop of Canterbury.* London: Longmans, Green, 1895.

Wroe, Ann. *The Perfect Prince: The Mystery of Perkin Warbeck and His Quest for the Throne of England.* New York: Random House, 2003.

HISTORICAL FIGURES

MARGARET BEAUFORT: Shrewd, conniving, and supremely ambitious, she is a master of deceit who will commit any deed, no matter how vile, to give her son everything *she* wants . . .

KING EDWARD IV: Brave, golden, and wanton; courage wins him a crown, and love loses him a kingdom.

RICHARD III: Compassionate, noble, a champion of the people; his crown costs him everyone he has ever loved. Grieving and bereft, he has no heart to keep what Fate has bestowed.

ELIZABETH WOODVILLE: Edward's detested low-born queen, thought to be a sorceress. Manipulative and vindictive; her rapacious greed destroys the House of York and brings Henry Tudor to the throne.

HENRY TUDOR: He gambles everything on a single roll of the dice and wins a throne.

THE PRETENDER: Is he a "feigned boy" as Tudor claims, or the younger of the two princes in the Tower and the true king Richard of England?

ELIZABETH OF YORK: Daughter of a king, sister of a king, niece of a king; wed to a king and mother of a king, she embodies every virtue of womanhood and is beloved by her husband and by her people. But what of her own heart?